A Demon's Sacrifice

T'lar strode to the wild elf and caught him by the hair,
dragging him to the bowl-shaped depression.

The spider halted in its descent, twisting around
on its thread, just over T'lar's head. Watching.

T'lar held up Nafay's dagger and kissed the blade.
Then she yanked the wild elf's head back,
bending his body in an arc that exposed his throat.

He screamed—a wild wail that forced itself past the gag.
He fought T'lar with all her strength, trying to hurl
himself backward, to tear free and escape,
but her grip was relentless.

She touched her dagger to his throat. She pricked it,
making a puncture that barely broke the skin.

"Accept this sacrifice."

Dark Mother

FORGOTTEN REALMS®

The New York Times
Best-selling Author

LISA
SMEDMAN

THE
LADY PENITENT

Book I
Sacrifice of the Widow

Book II
Storm of the Dead

Book III
Ascendancy of the Last

FORGOTTEN REALMS®

LISA SMEDMAN

ASCENDANCY OF THE LAST

THE LADY PENITENT

BOOK III

WIZARDS OF THE COAST®

The Lady Penitent, Book III

ASCENDANCY OF THE LAST

©2008 Wizards of the Coast, Inc.

Cover art by Wes Benscoter

First Printing: June 2008

9 8 7 6 5 4 3 2 1

ISBN: 978-0-7869-4864-2
620-21735740-001-EN

U.S., CANADA,
ASIA, PACIFIC, & LATIN AMERICA
Wizards of the Coast, Inc.
P.O. Box 707
Renton, WA 98057-0707
+1-800-324-6496

EUROPEAN HEADQUARTERS
Hasbro UK Ltd
Caswell Way
Newport, Gwent NP9 0YH
GREAT BRITAIN
Save this address for your records.

Visit our web site at www.wizards.com

PRELUDE

The *sava* board hung in mid-air, a bridge across an endless divide.

On one side of this line lay the Demonweb Pits, a vast plain of tortured rock under a purplish-black sky. An enormous black spider with red eyes dominated this landscape: the goddess Lolth, in one of her eight aspects. Sticky white webs stretched from her body to points near and far within her realm. They zigzagged back and forth between the spires of black rock that twisted toward the sky, and filled the many jagged craters that pocked the ground. Tiny bulges pulsed through these hollow webs: creatures, mortal and otherwise, who had found their way into her realm, either through death or deliberate folly. Muffled screams and moans came from within, bleeding out into to the sulfurous air.

On the other side of the divide stood a forest: Eilistraee's realm. A wind carried a whisper of song through tall trees, rustling branches heavy with moonstones. Half of the fruit-like orbs retained their original coloration—milky white with glints of shifting blue. The rest had darkened to a shadow black that drank in the moonlight dappling the forest. All lent a sweet perfume to the air.

Under these branches stood the goddess herself, a tall, lithe figure with coal black skin and moon-pale hair that hung to her ankles. Once, she had walked proudly naked through her realm, but now she wore a loose black shirt and trousers that hid her feminine curves. A mask—black, but glinting with moonlight as her breath stirred it—hid her face from the eyes down.

Eilistraee's twin swords hung beside her hips, suspended by song and magic. As the goddess contemplated the *sava* board, she played with an assassin's dagger, absently twirling the blade by its strangle cord.

Spotting something, she stiffened. "What is this, Lolth? Another of your distractions?"

Lolth paused in her web spinning, tore her abdomen free of the sticky strands, and scurried closer. Faint wails poured from the severed strands of silk that fluttered in her wake. She lowered her head until her palps brushed the board. "I see nothing amiss."

Eilistraee flipped the dagger and caught it by the hilt. She pointed the weapon at the *sava* board. "There."

"Ah." Lolth's spider mouth smiled.

On the board stood hundreds of thousands of playing pieces. Slaves, Priestesses, Wizards, and Warriors stood alone or in clusters on lines that radiated from the players' respective Houses. At the spot Eilistraee pointed to—a spot uncomfortably near the heart of her House—the board had grown spongy. One of her Priestess pieces was slowly sinking into this spot. Already it was ankle-deep.

Lolth chuckled. "Looks like you're going to lose more than one piece."

Other purplish-red stains appeared on the board, all of them close to Eilistraee's House. They bulged. Figures rose from them: priest pieces that had not been in play before. All had the faces of drow, but with bodies like blobs of hardened wax.

Anger blazed red in Eilistraee's eyes. "Ghaunadaur," she growled. "And his fanatics." The swords at her hips thrummed their displeasure. She pointed her dagger accusingly at Lolth. "Leave was neither asked, nor given, for another to enter our game."

"Do not accuse me of cheating, daughter," Lolth replied. "The Ancient One heeds no Mistress. Ghaunadaur was old even before Ao's time. The god of slime comes and goes as he will. I neither command nor compel him."

"You drove him from the Abyss once before."

"And like a boil, he rises once more. Perhaps this time, you'll lance him for me?"

Eilistraee fumed. She had no doubt that Lolth was behind this. Even as she watched, several of her other pieces sank knee-deep in the spongy board. These spots of corruption, as dark as bruises on fruit, were spreading, joining together. If left unchecked, they would completely encircle Eilistraee's House, cutting off a large number of her pieces from the rest of the board.

Lolth must have maneuvered Ghaunadaur into choosing this moment to strike, but why? Eilistraee scanned the *sava* board, searching for the answer.

Then she saw it: the move Lolth must have hoped she wouldn't spot.

Eilistraee reached for her strongest Priestess piece, the one that held the curved sword. When she saw Lolth flinch, she knew she'd made the right choice. She moved the piece forward along a path that allowed it to spiral into the very heart of Lolth's House. The move wasn't an attack on Lolth's Mother piece, but it accomplished the next best thing. It blocked the Mother piece completely, preventing it from moving. Unless Lolth found a way to take the Priestess, her Mother piece would be held out of play.

Taking out the Priestess piece Eilistraee had just moved, however, didn't seem likely. It was in an unassailable position, protected on all sides.

Eilistraee leaned back, satisfied. "Your move."

Lolth's palps twitched. Her abdomen pulsed restlessly, and the webs of her realm quivered in response. She studied the board with her unblinking eyes. At last she rocked back on her eight legs, resting her bulbous abdomen on the ground.

"Perhaps luck will favor me," she said. She shifted into her drow aspect and reached for the dice. They were as they had been since Eilistraee had made her throw, earlier in the game: two octahedrons of translucent moonstone, each with a spider trapped deep within. Seven sides bore numbers; the eighth, a full-moon symbol representing the numeral one. One circle was the solid white of a full moon; the other dark, with only a new-moon sliver of white on one side.

"One throw per game," Lolth said. "I'll take it now."

"I thought you preferred to weave your own destiny."

"That I do, daughter," Lolth said in a silken voice. She rattled the dice in cupped hands.

Eilistraee waited, tense and silent. If Lolth threw double ones, Eilistraee would be forced to sacrifice one of her pieces. She knew which one Lolth would choose: the Priestess that threatened Lolth's Mother piece. Yet there was little cause to worry. The odds of both dice landing circle-uppermost were sixty-three to one. An unlikely throw. Except that Eilistraee herself had accomplished it earlier in the game, forcing Lolth to sacrifice her champion, Selvetarm. And now it was Lolth's turn to try.

Eilistraee nodded at the dice Lolth rattled between her slim black hands. "No tricks," she warned. "If I see any web sticking to those dice, I'll demand a re-roll."

Lolth arched a perfect white eyebrow. She wore the face of Danifae, her Chosen—the female she had consumed upon ending her Silence. Her features were beautiful: the lips seductive, the cheekbones high, the eyes a delicate hue. Yet her expression was as cold as winter ice.

"No webs," Lolth promised.

Then she threw.

The dice clattered onto the board between the pieces. One die rolled to a stop immediately, full moon symbol uppermost. The second came to rest against one of Lolth's Priestess pieces. The die lay edge-uppermost, balanced halfway between the eight and the one.

"The die is cocked," Eilistraee said. "The roll is—"

The spider inside it twitched.

The die toppled, landing moon-uppermost. The new moon. Slowly, its stain spread throughout the die, rendering it as black as the Spider Queen's heart.

"You cheat!" Eilistraee cried.

"Of course," Lolth said with a smile.

Eilistraee turned her face skyward. "Ao! I require a witness, Lord of All, and your judgment. Lolth has broken the rules, and must forfeit the game."

Ao's reply came not in words or gestures, but as a sudden knowing. The dice, he revealed, had always been loaded. Moonlight had tipped the balance, the first time. Lolth had arranged this—a form of cheating, it was true—but the first result had been in Eilistraee's favor. The second die roll would also stand.

Ao had spoken.

Eilistraee stared at the empty place on the *sava* board where the Spider Queen's champion had once stood. "You *wanted* Selvetarm to die. You arranged it."

Lolth gave a lazy shrug. "Of course. And now it's your turn to lose a piece of *my* choosing."

"No," Eilistraee whispered. A tear squeezed from eyes that had turned a dull yellow. It trickled down the goddess's face, and was absorbed by Vhaeraun's mask.

"Yes." Lolth answered. Smiling cruelly, she extended a web-laced hand to point at a Priestess piece. "That one. I demand her sacrifice. Now."

CHAPTER 1

The Month of Ches
The Year of the Cauldron (1378 DR)

T'lar slipped silently into the blood-warm river and clung to a gnarled tree root so the sluggish current wouldn't carry her away. The river slid smoothly over her skin without impediment; upon acceptance in the Velkyn Velve, she had shaved her body from scalp to ankle—there would be no incriminating flashes of white to give her away. Floating on her back, she pulled a tangle of dead creeper vines across her naked body to conceal herself. She stared up at the sky, awash with the light of thousands of stars, and listened to the rustling of the night's predators and the startled screeches of their prey. The World Above was a noisy place compared to the cool silence of the Underdark, but even over this restlessness she could hear the soft murmur of voices: the wild elf, and the female T'lar had been sent to kill.

She let go of the root. The current caught her. As she drifted toward the voices, concealed under the tangle of vines, she adjusted the grip of her fingers on her spike-spiders, two walnut-sized metal throwing balls filled with poison and studded with hollow metal needles. A prick from either would numb her hands. Used against someone who hadn't built up an immunity to their poison, they would render the entire body as rigid as petrified wood.

Through the veil of creeper vine, T'lar observed her target: a drow female standing on the river bank, turned sideways to the water, her attention focused on the strange-looking male who squatted at her feet. The female was about T'lar's size, but there the resemblance ended. The priestess had long, bone white hair, wound in a tight coil and bound by a black web-lace hair net at the back of her head. Black gloves embroidered in a white spiderweb design covered her hands and arms up to the elbow. She wore a thin silk robe, cinched at the waist by a belt from which hung a ceremonial dagger and whip. The whip's three snake heads twisted beside her hip, forked tongues tasting the air, alert for danger.

T'lar's target was a noble of House Mizz'rynturl. T'lar knew her slightly. She had once been of that House, and had even played with Nafay on occasion when both had been girls—games like Stalking Spider and Flay the Slave. But T'lar had given up all other allegiances the day she was shorn. From her second decade of life, she had served Lolth alone.

And Lolth had decreed that Nafay must die.

T'lar hadn't asked why—to have done so would have been insolence bordering on suicide. But she'd heard the whispers: that Nafay, who had only recently joined the Temple of the Black Mother, served Lolth only superficially. That her true devotions lay elsewhere—with Vhaeraun, it was rumored—though a female being accepted into the Masked Lord's faith was about as likely as the moon turning into a spider and scuttling away from the sky.

Still, Nafay had done something to incur Lolth's wrath. Something that had prompted the *valsharess* to set T'lar on the hunt. And what a long chase it had been. Guallidurth lay more than four hundred leagues from here, as the spider crawled. What had drawn Nafay to the World Above and prompted her to seek the company of such a strange-looking male?

The wild elf was heavily built—almost as muscled as a drow female. He had duskier skin than most surface elves. Yellow paint ringed his eyes, and his hair hung in tiny braids, each tipped with a tuft of downy white feathers. His only clothing was a baglike loincloth that accentuated his genitals. From its string ties hung a dart pouch. He squatted before the priestess, arms resting on his knees, holding a blowpipe, and spoke in a high-pitched, melodic voice that reminded T'lar of the chirping of a cave cricket.

The priestess answered him in the same language.

T'lar gave a silent mental command. Her earlobe tickled as the spider-shaped black opal on her earring stirred to life. She tilted her head slightly, encouraging the spider to crawl into her ear, and waited as it spun a web that thrummed like a second eardrum in time with the voices. Then she listened.

". . . lead me to it," the priestess said.

The male shook his head. "They will kill you. Strangers are not even permitted within the forest, let alone at the *yathzalahaun*."

The word had the cadence of High Drow. T'lar's spider-earring translated it as "temple of first learning."

"Yet I *am* here, within the Misty Vale."

"Yes."

The priestess leaned closer to him. "And you *will* lead me to the temple."

The male sighed. "Yes," he whispered. He gave her a tortured look of equal parts anguish and anticipation, as if she had promised him something—something he would pay dearly for.

T'lar drifted even with the spot where Nafay stood; in another moment or two, the current would carry her past. She exhaled and sank beneath the surface, letting the tangle of creeper vine drift on alone. She kicked, sending herself shoreward, then twisted so that her feet touched bottom. She burst out of the water hands-first, and in the same motion hurled the spike-spiders. One struck the male square in the forehead. He immediately stiffened and toppled sideways. The second sailed toward the priestess. Before it struck, one of Nafay's whip vipers reared. It snapped the spike-spider out of the air and swallowed it.

The whip viper thrashed wildly as the spike-spider jammed in its throat. The other two snake heads hissed in fury.

Nafay whirled. The holy disk hanging from her neck whipped around like a pendulum. She shouted a prayer and wove her hands together, glaring at T'lar through the tangle of her fingers.

T'lar felt the spell brush against her body. It pulled at her abdomen, bloating it unnaturally. It teased two strands of flesh from her left side, attempting to twist them, together with her left arm and leg, into thin insectoid legs. Her mind was yanked toward the priestess. Web-sticky fingers plucked at her thoughts, trying to weave them to Nafay's will.

T'lar fought back with all her will. With a jolt, her body returned to normal. She leaped from the water. In mid-leap she used the *dro'zress* within her to pass into invisibility. A mid-air tumble and a kick off a tree trunk placed her where the priestess wouldn't expect her. She jabbed stiffened fingers into the priestess's upper-left abdomen, into the vital spot over the blood-sac. Her other hand punched into Nafay's throat.

The priestess gagged and buckled at the knees, unable to breathe and bleeding within. She grasped her holy symbol and tried to flutter her fingers in a silent prayer, but T'lar spun and slammed a heel into Nafay's temple. The priestess collapsed, unconscious.

One of the whip's heads lashed out. T'lar leaped back. The snake's poison-filled fangs snapped at air. T'lar stepped carefully around the whip and crouched behind the priestess. She pressed hard against the neck, where the blood flowed, and choked off the pulse. Nafay's legs kicked once, and then her body relaxed. She was dead.

"Lolth tlu malla," T'lar whispered, giving the ritual thanks for a successful kill. *"Jal ultrinnan zhah xundus."*

Two of the whip's snake heads spat furiously at her. The third had stiffened; two of the snake-spider spines had pierced its scaly skin from within and were protruding out of its body. T'lar picked up the wild elf's blowpipe and used it to nudge the whip aside. Later, after she collected her gear, she would bag the whip and carry it back to Guallidurth as proof of her kill, together with Nafay's holy symbol. She slipped the pendant off the dead female and hung it around her own neck.

Then she turned her attention to the wild elf. His body remained stiff, but his hands trembled and his eyelids fluttered. He was stronger than T'lar had expected. The poison would relinquish its hold on him soon. T'lar knelt beside him and placed her hands on his throat, then hesitated. She knew she should kill him now. Finish the job. But curiosity gnawed at her. She yearned to know what had brought Nafay to this place, what was so valuable to the priestess up here on the surface. A temple, the wild elf had said.

Instead of tightening her grip, T'lar released the wild elf's throat. She wouldn't kill him—yet. She would force him to show her this temple first. She knew this might mean uncovering secrets the *valsharess* would prefer remained buried, but if that meant T'lar's death upon her return to Guallidurth, so be it. She would go to the altar willingly, certain in the knowledge she had served Lolth well.

She plucked the spike-spider from the wild elf's forehead. She removed the pouch from his string belt, sniffed the darts—they were poisoned—and set them aside. Then she drew Nafay's spider-pommel dagger and used it to cut strips from the priestess's silk robe. She used these to bind the wild elf's wrists behind his back, and to hobble his ankles. She wadded more silk into his mouth and tied this makeshift gag tightly in place. Then she waited. From time to time, she slapped him. When he at last flinched, she grabbed him by the hair.

"Blink twice if you understand me," she said. She spoke in High Drow; the earring only allowed her to understand the wild elf's language, not to speak it.

The wild elf glared. The whites of his eyes had a yellowish tinge, signifying a malaise deeper than just the poison, one that had been affecting his vitals for some time. She rolled him over, inspecting his body. She found what she'd been looking for on his left thigh and calf: a series of small, raised red lumps. Spider bites. She touched one of them, and found it felt hot. Without healing, he would be dead by the time the sun rose.

T'lar pointed at the priestess. "She promised to cure you, didn't she?" She touched the platinum disk that hung against her bare chest, fingers caressing the embossed spider, then pointed at the bites. "Would you like *me* to cure you?"

The wild elf stared at her. He couldn't speak while gagged, but T'lar caught the slight widening of his pupils. He understood her meaning, if not the words themselves. He believed she could cure him. He obviously hadn't dealt with the drow before now. He grunted something from behind the gag and jerked his head in a nod.

She yanked him to his feet. *"Yathzalahaun,"* she ordered, giving him a rough shove.

He stumbled away from the river, into the forest. She followed.

They walked for some time, the wild elf forced by his hobble to take short, shuffling steps. With his arms bound behind him, he fell frequently. T'lar yanked him back to his feet each time and forced him on. The moon rose, round and full, throwing the forest into stark patches of light and shadow. T'lar squinted against the glare and carefully noted the direction they traveled. She would need to find her way back, later, to the cleft near the river that led back to the Underdark.

Fortunately, this region of the World Above had many landmarks. They passed a number of mounded hills, each capped by a thick tangle of trees and vines, and chunks of weathered stone half-buried in the ground. T'lar clambered over a fallen obsidian column, carved in the shape of a person with four arms folded across their chest. Whether it was meant to represent male or female, T'lar couldn't tell; there were no obvious genitalia. Moonlight threw the glyph carved into its forehead into shadow. T'lar was no scholar—she couldn't read the glyph itself—but she recognized it as an archaic form of Espruar. She glanced around at the hills and realized they were the ruins of ancient structures. So perversely fertile was the World Above that soil and vegetation had completely hidden the tumbled buildings under a thick, loamy skin.

The wild elf halted before one of the hills and gestured by jerking his head in that direction. One of the trees sprouting from the hill had fallen, leaving a hole in the mound that revealed the masonry beneath. T'lar peered into the hole and saw a glint of metal: an adamantine door. Its hinges had torn free of the crumbling stone, allowing the door to fall inward. Now the metal formed a natural ramp into the darkness at the mound's hollow center.

The wild elf glanced back at her, obviously reluctant to venture into it. T'lar shook her head. She snapped a kick at the back of his legs, knocking him to his knees, and pointed. "Inside."

The wild elf glared at her, but complied. He wormed his way forward on his belly, into the hole. T'lar crouched and followed cautiously, Nafay's dagger in hand. She smelled damp earth, and spider musk. A cobweb brushed her face. But the attack she had anticipated didn't come. Though webs were everywhere, the inside of the ancient building did not contain a spider.

There was enough room inside to stand. T'lar looked around. The black marble floor had a bowl-shaped depression at its center. A tracery of white veins threaded through the marble: hair-thin lines reminiscent of a tangled web. The walls were carved, three of them in glyphs she couldn't read that ran in narrow rows from ceiling to floor. The fourth wall bore a mural topped by a glyph T'lar did recognize: Araushnee. Lolth's original name.

This was clearly an ancient temple.

T'lar fell to one knee and turned her head, exposing her neck. "Dark Mother of all drow, your servant offers herself."

This ritual performed, she rose and studied the mural. It depicted an enormous spider with a drow face superimposed upon its abdomen. Eight drow arms radiated from its body. Each ended in a hand with eight fingers. Lines extended from each hand, linking the central figure to four pairs of smaller spiders, each with a face on its abdomen. The faces of the first pair were masked, while the second pair had gaunt, almost skeletal features and hollow eyes. The third pair had faces like melted wax, sagging and distorted, while the fourth pair had mouths open and spider arms lifted, as if they were singing the larger spider's praises. The eight lesser spiders dangled from the central figure's finger-webs like newly hatched spiderlings twisting in the wind.

The imagery was like nothing T'lar had ever seen before. It felt old, archaic. Not quite right. Yet strangely compelling. And Lolth had woven a path for her to this place. Why?

Using Nafay's dagger, she pricked each of her fingers. She pressed her fingertips against the abdomen of the large spider, leaving small dots of blood. "Hear me, Dark Mother. Show me your will."

She heard a muffled voice behind her: the wild elf, trying to say something against his gag. She turned and saw a fist-sized spider descending from the ceiling on a thread of silk. The spider was night black, with a red hourglass on its abdomen. As it descended, purple faerie fire blossomed in a flickering halo around its body. The wild elf threw himself to the side, rolling away from it.

Lolth had made herself known.

T'lar strode to the wild elf and caught him by the hair, dragging him to the bowl-shaped depression. The spider halted in its descent, twisting around on its thread, just over T'lar's head. Watching. T'lar held up Nafay's dagger and kissed the blade. Then she yanked the wild elf's head back, bending his body in an arc that exposed his throat. He screamed—a wild wail that forced itself past the gag. He fought T'lar with all his strength, trying to hurl himself backward, to tear free and escape, but her grip was relentless.

She touched her dagger to his throat. She pricked it, making a puncture that barely broke the skin.

"Accept this sacrifice, Dark Mother," she intoned.

She jabbed again. A little deeper, this time. His muffled wail grew shriller. He fought with the frenzy of a trapped animal, but T'lar's grip remained as strong as adamantine. The wild elf twisted around and kicked her legs. She neatly sidestepped the thrashing limbs.

"Taste his fear."

Another thrust, a little deeper.

"Feast upon him."

Blood trickled down his throat. She stabbed a fourth time.

"Feast upon his blood."

Another thrust.

"Consume him."

She stabbed again.

"Rend his soul."

She thrust again. Deep enough, this time, to pierce the windpipe. His breathing grew rapid with panic. Blood bubbled in a froth from the wound.

"Take him!"

On her eighth and final thrust, the blade plunged to the hilt. She yanked it free, releasing a hot spray of blood. She jerked his head to the side, letting blood splash the mural. Then she forced the weakly squirming sacrifice down into the depression in the floor. The wild elf died then, and blood stopped pulsing from the wound. T'lar lifted him by the ankles and waited as he bled out. The bowl-shaped depression filled with blood. She cast the corpse aside and kissed the blood-slick dagger a second time, tasting his blood. Then she watched as the purple-limned spider resumed its descent.

It plunged into the bowl of blood. Faerie fire rippled upon the surface of the bright red pool, turning it the color of an old bruise. Then the blood drained away. The depression in the floor was as it had been before the sacrifice: empty and waiting.

T'lar heard the sound of stone grating on stone, coming from the direction of the mural. She whirled, dagger still in hand. Lolth's abdomen was sinking into the wall. Abruptly it fell away, crashing to the floor of whatever chamber lay beyond this one and sending up a cloud of stale dust. For several moments, there was silence. Then T'lar heard a scrabbling sound. She braced herself, preparing for whatever the goddess was about to hurl at her. Lolth was fond of testing her supplicants—and failure usually meant death.

A voice, as dry as ancient leather, creaked out of the opening a female voice, pitched too low for T'lar to make out most of the words. One came through clearly, however: the name of the goddess. Lolth.

"Spider Queen!" T'lar cried exultantly. "I am your willing servant."

Something moved in the space beyond the mural, something large and dark, forcing itself into the hole T'lar's sacrifice had opened. It squeezed through headfirst, then halted, its shoulders too broad to pass. A bestial face, more demon than drow, stared out at T'lar and snarled. Blood trickled out of the opening and puddled at the base of the wall. The opening suddenly widened, then contracted, forcing the demonic creature through. It landed on the ground, gasping.

The demon-drow was twice as large as T'lar was tall, and female, with eight spider legs protruding from her chest. Her hair was a matted tangle that looked like old spider silk. Under each of her eyes was a hairy bulge, from which a fang-tipped jaw curved, the points meeting above the mouth. The jaws gnashed as she lay on the floor, moaning.

T'lar was certain the demon-drow was Lolth's, though she'd never seen anything like her. "What are you?" she asked. "One of Lolth's handmaidens?"

The demon-drow looked up. "Lolth's *handmaiden?*" she croaked. The word wrenched itself from her mouth. Her wild cackle filled the hollow temple and sent a thrill down T'lar's spine. The laugh was chaos itself, uncontrolled and as dangerous as a rock fall.

Then the demon-drow began to sing.

The song was harsh, as if the creature's throat was tight and parched. Yet the notes filled the temple with magic that plucked at the spiderwebs and made them vibrate like the strings of a lyre. T'lar could feel it within her own body: a thrumming surge of power. The demon-drow had been withered and gaunt when she fell out of the hole in the wall, but she rose to her feet plumped and visibly stronger. When her song ended, she stood solid and strong. She stared down at T'lar.

"What month is it? What year?"

T'lar met the demon-drow's gaze unflinchingly. Lolth hated weakness, and so did the demons that served her. "The month of Ches, in the Year of the Cauldron—1378, by the reckoning of the World Above."

The demon-drow shook her head. "Five months." She stared down at her hands and arms, then abruptly clenched her fists. "Who are you?"

T'lar bowed. "T'lar Mizz'rynturl of the Velkyn Velve, assassin of the Temple of the Black Mother."

The demon-drow looked down at her, an expression of open amusement on her face. "Assassin?" she said. "Were you sent to kill me?"

"Indeed no! I serve Lolth."

"That's fortunate." The demon-drow's voice dropped to a harsh whisper, and she leaned closer, leering. "No mortal can kill me—though many have tried." She reared back and shouted, "The void itself has no effect on me!"

T'lar was starting to suspect that this was something much more powerful than a yochlol. Some new form of demon that Lolth herself had spawned. "By what name should I address you, Mistress?"

The demon-drow was silent for several moments. Her spider jaws gnashed. At last she answered, "The Lady Penitent."

It sounded like a title a powerful being might use. "Are you a demon lord?"

The Lady Penitent snapped out a laugh. Her eyes looked wild. "More than that. Much more." She waved a misshapen hand at the mural on the wall. "I even have my own temple."

T'lar nodded, her chest tight with excitement. Had she just played midwife to some ancient and long-forgotten deity? She kept her face expressionless, despite the surge of emotion that left her near giddy. The Spider Queen must have been watching when Nafay died. And again when T'lar offered up her sacrifice. Lolth was known for her caprice. It would not be unheard of for the goddess to reward a mere assassin with power that would make a priestess weep. The services of a demigod's avatar, for example.

"Your song," T'lar said. "I felt its power."

"Lolth's dark chorus? *Bae'qeshel?*"

T'lar hadn't heard the word before, but to admit that would be to show weakness. And deities spawned of chaos and blood despised the weak. She nodded and spoke boldly. "I want to learn it. Teach me."

The Lady Penitent cocked her head. For a moment, her expression seemed melancholic. Almost mortal. "You remind me of someone. A young female, heir to the throne of House Melarn. She asked the same thing, once."

"What happened to her?" T'lar asked.

The Lady Penitent bared jagged teeth. "She died."

T'lar refused to be cowed. "She was unworthy, then."

"Yes," the Lady Penitent said in a harsh whisper. "She was . . . weak." Her lips twisted into a grimace.

T'lar stood firm before the Lady Penitent. "In me, you will find strength. And determination. I journeyed all the way from Guallidurth to do my *valsharess*'s bidding."

"Guallidurth? The city with as many sects as an egg sac has hatchlings?"

T'lar felt a sliver of apprehension. The deity was challenging her—testing her faith. Fortunately, T'lar's commitment was strong. The Temple of the Black Mother was one of the youngest in the city. It had splintered away from the *Yorn'yathrins* a mere six decades ago and had yet to rise to prominence, but rise to prominence it would. Especially under the tutelage of a demigod's avatar.

"The priestesses of the Black Mother are fervent in their devotions," she assured the Lady Penitent. "They will serve you well."

The avatar lifted an eyebrow. *"Will* they?" A dark chuckle rose from her throat like a bubble of blood. "Guallidurth," she whispered, her eyes hungry.

T'lar nodded her head in a bow. "What is your pleasure, Lady Penitent? Shall I return to Guallidurth and announce your birth?"

The Lady Penitent smiled, a feral gleam in her eye. "Yes. Do that."

CHAPTER 2

The Month of Flamerule
The Year of the Lost Keep (1379 DR)

Leliana leaned on the railing of the bridge that spanned the Sargauth, watching as the three fisher-folk below hauled on the line that would bring in their net. Over the rush of the underground river, she heard voices from the Cavern of Song: the faithful, singing Eilistraee's praises. Though most of the voices were female, a few held a lower timbre. Even after three and a half years, it still seemed odd to hear male voices echoing through the caverns of the Promenade.

A shaft of moonlight sprang into being a short distance away, slanting down to the river. It was as if a window had opened in the rock overhead, allowing light to shine in from the World Above—light that overpowered the shimmer of *Faerzress* that permeated the cavern walls. The moonbeam was magical, a manifestation of Eilistraee's song—a reminder that the goddess was watching over her faithful in this, her holiest of shrines.

The moonbeam played briefly over the river, making the water's ripples sparkle. The fisherfolk tucked the line under their arms and made the sign of the goddess, touching forefinger to forefinger and thumb to thumb to form a full-moon circle. Only when the moonbeam disappeared did they resume hauling in the net. The line suddenly pulled taut, drops of water flicking from it. The three pulled harder on it, but the net didn't budge. It appeared to have snagged. Likely it had caught on the jumble of masonry on the river bottom: the remains of the original bridge.

One of the fisherfolk was a drow male; the second, a human female with skin so pale it seemed ghostly in the darkened cavern. The third was a muscular half-orc. He bared tusklike teeth in a grimace and pulled as hard as he could, but the net refused to come unstuck.

"Jub!" Leliana called down to him. "If you keep pulling like that, you'll tear the net."

The half-orc gave one last grunting pull—and sprawled backward on top of the other two fisherfolk as the tension left the line. A portion of the net rose from the river, dripping and filled with wriggling white blindfish. So did something else. Large and metal and rusted, it creaked as it moved. It looked like an enormous hook, thick as a heavy tree branch and tipped with a barbed point. The base of the hook, now bent, was attached to something deeper in the river that was too large and heavy to move.

Leliana belonged to the third of the temple's watches. Her patrol didn't begin until moonset. But she was a Protector, entrusted with one of the temple's legendary singing swords. Anything this unusual warranted her immediate inspection, on duty or off. She strode along the riverbank to the spot where the three lay worshipers stood.

She nodded at them and touched the ceremonial dagger that hung against her chest. Then she sang a prayer: one that began softly, but that rose steadily to a crescendo with the power of a waterfall. At its conclusion, she chopped a hand through the air like a sword blade slicing down. Forced apart by her magic, the river split in a **V**-shaped trough that extended almost to its center. The depression widened, forcing the water back on either side. The remainder of the river rushed on swifter than before, compensating in speed for the narrowed space.

The gap in the river revealed an enormous mass of rusted iron, large enough to fill a small room. It lay, tipped sideways, on the river-smoothed blocks of stone from the original bridge. It was the statue of an enormous scorpion, its legs twisted beneath it and one pincer claw splayed out to the side. Its barbed tail had snagged the net.

The human stared at it through dark-lensed goggles that allowed her to see in the Underdark. "What is it?" she asked. "A statue from the first bridge?"

Leliana shook her head. She'd been assigned to the Promenade little more than a year and a half ago, but she'd made it her business to learn all she could about the temple since then. In the earliest days of the Promenade, when the first bridge was in ruins and the river impassable, a scorpion-shaped construct had been sighted, on occasion, in the caverns that opened onto the eastern banks of the Sargauth. When the Protectors extended their patrols into the caverns to the southeast a few years ago, they'd expected to run into it, but the construct had seemingly disappeared. It had, they surmised, either wandered away into some deeper corner of Undermountain or been summoned home by its maker.

"It's a wizard's construct," Leliana answered. "Deadly when active, but this one looks frozen with rust."

The human and the drow male both took a nervous step back. Jub merely grunted. He clambered down into the trough in the magic-parted river and yanked on the net, trying to free it. Blindfish scattered from it and landed gasping on the slick rock. Jub put a foot on one of the construct's legs and boosted himself higher, trying to unhook the net from the barbed tail. Rust flaked away under his boots.

"Don't get so close to it, Jub!" the human called, stepping forward. "Be careful!"

Jub laughed. "It's not gonna come alive. Even if it does, there's a Protector here."

Leliana smiled. Three and a half years ago, at the time of the Selvetargtlin attack, Jub had been reduced to a few scattered body parts by a dracolich. The priestesses had recovered what remained, and resurrected him. He didn't fear anything any more. Not after he'd danced, briefly, with the goddess.

Jub climbed higher. Balanced with one foot on the scorpion's back and the other on the base of its tail, he wrenched at the net. The barbed tip bent with a loud creak. Then it snapped off, sending Jub tumbling backward in a tangle of net and wriggling blindfish. He scrambled to his feet and held up the net triumphantly. "There! All it took was a little muscle and—"

"Quiet!" Leliana barked.

Jub looked puzzled. "What—?"

"Listen! That crackling sound."

Jub cocked his head. He dropped the net and used his hands. *I don't hear anything.*

Leliana hesitated. Had she actually heard something, or was that just the rush of the river? Then a white-hot spark streaked out of the hollow stump where the tail barb had been. She smelled the sharp tang of lightning-burned air.

"Jub!" she shouted. "Get away from the construct! It's animating!"

She drew her sword and motioned the other two lay worshipers back. Then she leaped down into the hollow in the river. She motioned Jub behind her and braced herself, sword raised. Ready. The singing sword sharply pealed, eager for battle.

More sparks erupted from the tail. Leliana heard a scratching sound, like claws scrabbling against metal. It started inside the head of the construct, and worked its way down through the abdomen. Leliana began a hymn of protection, but before she could complete the verse, a smaller construct, this one made of gold and shaped like a crab, appeared at the broken end of the tail. It teetered a moment, like a plate on a blade's edge, then fell with a clang onto the riverbed. Leliana immediately changed her prayer to one that would disable the construct, but the crab was too quick for her. It scurried sideways and disappeared into the wall of suspended water.

"What was *that*?" Jub asked. "The scorpion's brain?"

"Good guess," Leliana said, impressed. For someone who was only half drow, Jub was pretty bright.

"There!" the drow male shouted. "It's climbing out of the river."

Leliana scrambled up the bank and looked where he was pointing. The gold crab was scuttling sideways across a cavern fronting onto the river—a cavern that opened onto a twisting maze of passages that held the ruins of a drow city.

Leliana ran for the bridge. "Stay there," she shouted over her shoulder. "Don't try to follow."

That last had been for Jub's benefit. The half-orc wasn't even armed, save for his fishing knife. If the construct was on its way back to its wizard master and Jub followed, he'd only get himself killed. Again.

"Right," he called back. "No favors. Got it."

Leliana didn't have time to wonder what he'd meant. She hurried into the cavern on the opposite side of the bridge, past its trio of columns, and on into the maze of twisting corridors. As she ran, she cast a sending. She tried to remember the name of the young Nightshadow who was patrolling that cavern. She could picture him clearly in her mind: he was as light-footed as a dancer, with straight-cut bangs above intense red eyes. A recent convert who worshiped the "Masked Lady" and wore a sword-shaped pendant in addition to his black mask.

Suddenly the name came to her. "Naxil!" she shouted.

Eilistraee's magic filled her. His mind touched hers. Alert. Questioning.

A construct is coming your way. A plate-sized gold crab. Halt it, but don't destroy it. Qilué will want to examine it.

His reply was tense, excited. *I see it!*

Leliana ran on, turning right, then left, then right again. She passed the first of the tunnels that led back to the Sargauth—back to the cavern the crab had scurried into after climbing out of the river. This first tunnel followed a laborious, winding path, but there was a shorter route just ahead. She turned into this second tunnel, and at last reached the cavern that overlooked the river. It was empty. She stood, panting, looking around for the Nightshadow.

Which way had he gone? Three different corridors led from this cavern to the maze of corridors beyond. She bent to inspect the floor, hoping the crab might have left a dribble of water that would show her which corridor it had entered.

Naxil emerged from the third tunnel, startling her. "Dark Lady," he panted. "My apologies. The construct escaped."

He met her eye unflinchingly as he delivered the bad news. For someone who'd left Eryndlyn behind only a year ago—who would still have the matron mothers and their ways fresh in his mind—Naxil was refreshingly bold.

"Where did you last see it? Show me."

Naxil spun and pointed. "This way."

He led her down a corridor that dead-ended, and pointed at the blank wall. "There."

Leliana examined the stone. It was utterly smooth, worn down by the oozes and slimes that had slithered through this area for centuries, prior to Qilué and her companions cleansing this place. There were no crevices into which the crab construct could have scuttled, no cracks in the floor or chimneys in the ceiling.

"Are you certain it didn't double back? Get past you?"

"I'm certain. It ran to this spot and . . . vanished."

"A portal," Leliana concluded.

Naxil nodded. "Must be."

Leliana sang a prayer and passed her free hand over the wall. She didn't expect her hymn to reveal anything: three and a half years ago, after the Selvetargtlin attack on the Promenade, these passageways had been carefully examined by priestesses more experienced in portal magic than she. The corridors had also been examined by mundane means: the Promenade's lay worshipers included several rogues who were adept at detecting hidden doors and passages. Even so, the construct had to have gone *somewhere*.

A flicker of *Faerzress* blossomed on the wall next to Naxil, momentarily washing his face with a faint blue glow. He was a handsome male—young enough to be Leliana's son, and in his physical prime. Later, when things were quieter, she just might take him. With his permission, of course, she reminded herself. Since her redemption, she'd played by Eilistraee's rules.

"Dark Lady?" Naxil asked. "Should I return to my post?"

"Not yet." Leliana sheathed her sword. She wanted to check the corridor one last time, to gather as much information as she could before reporting to the battle-mistress. "And call me Leliana."

She squatted to inspect the floor. As she ran her fingers across it she felt a slight tugging. It was almost as if the floor were a lodestone, exerting a pull upon the rings she wore. Yet neither ring should have been drawn to a lodestone. Her shield ring was platinum, and the one next to it—the ring that allowed her to levitate—was gold.

Just like the construct.

The pull suddenly intensified. Her hand jerked downward and touched the floor. She saw Naxil stagger sideways and felt her stomach lurch. A glow surrounded them: a golden circle in the floor, centered on the spot where Leliana crouched.

"Mother's blood," Leliana swore. She leaped to her feet and drew her sword.

They were no longer in the corridor. The portal had activated, sending them somewhere else: a roughly oval cavern about a hundred paces wide, with a ceiling so low Leliana could have reached up and touched it. A multitude of hair-thin crevices criss-crossed the floor, walls, and ceiling, giving them the appearance of old, cracked pottery. The stone glistened slightly in spots, as if wet: probably condensation; it felt hot and moist in here.

Leliana could see three exits, all of them natural tunnels. Two led off into darkness; from the third came a dull red glow. Warmth flowed out of it, stirring the air and filling the cavern with the smell of molten stone.

Defensive stance, Leliana signed with her free hand.

Naxil swiftly repositioned himself, his back to hers. He held his magical dagger by the point, ready for a throw. She heard him whisper a prayer of protection. Each scanned the area, their free hand held out where the other could see it in peripheral vision. Leliana's sword hummed softly, anticipating danger.

No threat spotted, Naxil signed.

No immediate threats, Leliana agreed.

Nor was there any sign of the construct. There were, however, half a dozen large jumbles of iron that might once have been other constructs, lying in rusting heaps on the floor.

Do you know this place? Naxil asked.

No.

The gold circle started to fade. Leliana squatted and touched her ring to the floor. Nothing happened. The golden glow disappeared. It looked as though they weren't getting out of here via the portal.

Fortunately, they had another way out: a prayer that would return them to the spot on the surface that Leliana had designated as her sanctuary. But she didn't want to invoke that magic yet. She wanted to learn more about where the portal had sent them.

She decided to send a brief message to the battle-mistress, before moving out. *Rylla,* she sent. *There's a new portal in a dead-end between Three Pillars and Dragon Throne Cavern. I accidentally activated it. Can you scry me?*

She waited. No reply came. The portal had either sent them to another plane—unlikely, this certainly *felt* like part of the Underdark—or this place was somehow warded to prevent magical communication.

Something dripped from the ceiling onto her shoulder. A moment later she felt dampness as it soaked through her chain mail, into the padded tunic she wore underneath—then a burning as it reached her skin. Acid! She heard Naxil suck air through clenched teeth. A drop must have struck him, as well.

She sprang away from the spot, and Naxil did likewise. They looked up. Acid-slicked strands of what looked like gray mucus were oozing from one of the cracks in the ceiling, directly over the spot where they'd just been standing. The strands twitched slightly, like worms, elongating even as Leliana watched.

Gray ooze, she signed. A quick glance around confirmed her fear: the stuff was weeping from several other spots in the ceiling. In some places, acid fell in a steady dribble. In others, it dripped. A drop of it landed on her hand, stinging it.

She pointed at one of the darkened tunnels. *Check it. See if it's safe.* Order given, she sprinted for the other dark tunnel and peered inside. The cracks in its floor, walls, and ceiling extended as far as she could see. Ooze seeped through the ceiling here too.

Naxil turned away from his tunnel. *No good. More ooze.*

Leliana hesitated. She glanced at the third exit. Was it wishful thinking, or was the floor in front of it slightly less slick? She flicked a hand: *That way.* If they didn't find a safe spot soon, she'd be forced to teleport them out of here.

She had to run nearly doubled over to avoid the strands of ooze hanging from the ceiling. Acid splattered her back, dribbled in between the links in her mail, and burned its way to her skin. Other drops struck the back of her head. Naxil slipped on the acid-slick floor, nearly falling. Leliana grabbed his arm and dragged him into the tunnel.

A few paces in, the acid dribbles stopped. Though the stone here was also cracked, the gray ooze didn't seem to like the dry heat. The farther up the tunnel they ran, the drier the floor got. At last Leliana called a halt. She gritted her teeth at the hot flares of pain in her back, shoulders, scalp, and hands. It was as if a dozen wasps were stinging her all at once. And those had just been *drips*. Once that ooze forced its way fully through the cracks in the cavern ceiling, there would be no going back.

Naxil's free hand strayed to his shoulder, fingers gingerly touching an acid burn in his leather armor. He winced.

"Have you been taught the healer's prayer?" Leliana asked softly.

Naxil nodded. "A lesser version of it."

"Use it."

Together they sang their prayers—softly, their voices mere whispers in the darkness. When they were done, Naxil sighed deeply and flexed his shoulder, stretching the healed skin. "What are the battle-mistress's orders?"

"Rylla didn't answer my sending. Looks like we're on our own."

Naxil glanced back the way they'd come. "I think I know where we are."

"Oh?"

"Does the name Trobriand mean anything to you?"

Leliana shook her head.

"He was an apprentice of Halaster—the wizard who used magic to carve out much of Undermountain."

"Him, I've heard of," Leliana said in a wry voice. Among the drow, Halaster was a name often followed by an oath. Centuries ago—long before Qilué had founded the Promenade—the "mad mage" and his followers had waged war upon the drow of Undermountain, slaughtering hundreds, if not thousands. Halaster had harassed the drow with his spells through the long centuries since. When the mad mage had died four years ago, Qilué had led the priestesses of the Promenade in a song of rejoicing.

"I've been thinking about the construct we followed here," Naxil continued. "Trobriand was known as the 'metal mage.' He was famous for his constructs. The portal may have deposited us in one of his sanctums. That would explain why the crab made for it."

"How do you know so much about ancient wizards?"

Naxil's eyes crinkled. "My father was a sorcerer. An alchemist. I was training as his apprentice, before I joined the Masked Lady's dance."

Leliana's eyebrows rose. Naxil was a boy of hidden talents. "Do you know any spells?"

"Only a couple of cantrips—and not terribly useful ones. I can inscribe objects with an indelible House glyph, and"—his fingers twitched, and his voice suddenly shifted to a point behind her—"I can shift sounds."

"Not bad," Leliana said. "So why did you give up wizardry?"

His expression flattened. "I got tired of the beatings."

A silent understanding passed between them. Leliana had been raised in Menzoberranzan, the daughter of a noble House. She too had learned early on that prestige and punishment walked hand in hand. Her back was clear now, but for years she'd worn the scars of her mother's lash. When she'd borne a daughter of her own, Leliana vowed to give her a better life.

She wrenched her mind back to the present. "Expensive, to build constructs out of gold," she commented.

"Practical," Naxil countered. "Gold resists acid—that's one of the ways you can distinguish it from the coarser metals. The only thing that will dissolve it is *aqua regia*. Trobriand obviously intended that the crab survive the oozes, once it had used the portal."

Leliana glanced up the tunnel, to the dull red glow. "Let's see what lies ahead," she decided. "I'll lead. You watch my back. Keep close, in case I need to sing us out of here."

They made their way down the tunnel. Here and there, Leliana could see a momentary flicker of the *Faerzress* that had spread far and wide when the Crones worked their fell magic with the voidstone. Its light was drowned out, however, by the red glow from up ahead.

The farther they went, the brighter the glow became. The air grew hotter and drier. Leliana breathed warily, alert for the first signs of lightheadedness. If there was lava ahead, as she suspected, the air in the tunnel could prove poisonous. She glanced back at Naxil and saw sweat beading his brow and trickling down his temples. His hair and clothes were damp, as were hers.

They came to a place where the passage bent sharply. Leliana motioned for Naxil to halt and peered around the corner. The tunnel beyond it was bisected by a deep crevice in the floor that glowed with an eye-searing red light. Heat made the air above the crevice shimmer. Leliana sniffed, and caught the whiff of sulfur she'd been expecting. Somewhere deep in that crack, lava flowed.

The gap was too wide to jump. She decided they'd risked enough for one day. Time to get out of here and report what they'd discovered.

"Touch my back," she whispered to Naxil. "We're leaving."

He did so, and she sang a hymn of return, but the sudden lurch of slipping sideways through the dimensions didn't come. The prayer should have conveyed them both to the Misty Forest shrine: her designated sanctuary. It didn't.

Naxil waited. His eyes held a silent question.

Leliana shook her head. "Trobriand must have warded his sanctum against teleportation. I'll try something else. Keep watch."

She stepped away from Naxil, sheathed her sword, and hummed a wordless prayer. With one hand touching her holy symbol, she turned slowly. *Which way?* she asked silently. *Which way is the Promenade?* She concentrated on its most prominent feature: the statue of Eilistraee that had been erected at the site of Qilué's victory over Ghaunadaur.

The magic took hold, halting her. Her extended hand jerked straight up.

"By all that dances," she exclaimed. "The Promenade is directly above us!"

Leliana nodded to herself. That explained how the tunnel ahead had cracked open deep enough to reach lava. Both it and the other, smaller cracks must have resulted from the powerful earthquake that had rocked Undermountain four years ago, a few months before the Selvetargtlin attack on the Promenade. If Eilistraee's statue was above this spot, the rubble-filled shaft leading to the Pit of Ghaunadaur would be somewhere nearby. It too would have been affected by the earthquake. The walls of the shaft must have cracked open wide enough for the gray ooze to slither out.

Leliana whispered her thanks to Eilistraee for setting her feet on this dance. She and Naxil had gathered important information this day, information the high priestess would want to hear. The oozes Qilué and her companions had driven from Undermountain and sealed in the Pit centuries ago were once again on the loose.

Leliana lowered her hand. The good news was that she and Naxil were still somewhere within Undermountain. Assuming this cavern system wasn't completely isolated—a dead end—they might yet be able find their way back to the Promenade. She prayed again. "Eilistraee," she whispered. "Show me the path. Lead me back to the Promenade."

She felt a sense of rightness coming from the direction they'd been headed, a sense of wrongness behind her. She led Naxil around the corner, closer to the lava-filled crack. "The way back lies on the other side of that gap. Can you climb past it?"

Naxil moved ahead to inspect the wall. He whispered a prayer that would protect him from the hot stone and jammed his fingers into a crack in the wall. He braced his foot on a slight ledge and eased himself up. The ledge immediately crumbled, and his fingers slipped out. He moved to a second spot and tried again, but with the same result. He turned and shook his head. "We can't climb past it. The stone isn't strong enough."

Leliana held up her hand and indicated her gold ring. "We'll use levitation magic to get across. I'll go first, then throw my ring to you."

He nodded.

Leliana sang a hymn that would shield her from the worst of the heat. She ran forward and activated the ring just before reaching the crevice. She drifted over the gap, supported by the ring's magic. Heat rose in waves, enveloping her body. She glanced down and saw glowing lava deep in the crevice. A puddle of something golden floated atop it. She thrust a hand against the ceiling, halting herself, and peered down through the shimmering heat waves. She'd been right. That *was* the construct.

Before she could push herself onward, a wave of dizziness swept over her. It was as if she'd just spun wildly in place. "But I didn't," she said aloud. "I was . . . the glow. Red lava gas flow dizzy down . . ." She drifted downward, away from the ceiling.

Naxil flicked a sign in silent speech. Leliana couldn't make sense of it.

"Leliana!" he shouted aloud. "Your sword!"

Leliana frowned. Why was the lip of the crevice rising up to hide Naxil, and why was he shouting about swords? There was nothing here to fight. She shook her head violently, trying to clear it. The sudden movement spun her in place, which only made her dizzier. "Up float dizzy I think I'm . . ."

The ring responded to her command, lifting her out of the crevice until her head and shoulders pressed against the ceiling. Despite her protective spell, the stone felt hot. She shoved herself away and drifted down again. No—that wasn't right, either! She tried to catch the lip of the crevice, but couldn't reach it. She caught a glimpse of gold on her finger. Oh yes, her ring. Levitate. Up. The words, however, came out all wrong: "Floating chimney down."

She descended.

"Down . . . no, up." She rose. Her head cracked the ceiling.

"Mistress!" Naxil shouted.

Naxil sounded . . . What was the word?

"Worried!" Leliana shouted, laughing with delight at having gotten the word correct.

It was hot bobbing around above the crevice. Really hot. Sweat trickled down her face. A tiny corner of her mind shouted that she should be doing something before her protective spell ran out. That thought was lost in the swirl of confusion that jumbled her thoughts like . . . like . . .

Naxil ran forward to the edge of the crevice and leaned over it, one hand extended. Did he want her to give him something? He made urgent gestures that reminded her of Jub pulling on his net.

"Hand over handover handoverhand . . ." Leliana sang. She knew she was babbling. Knew she should . . . sing a prayer or . . . something.

A bubble of glowing lava rose in the crevice. It oozed upward until it was no more than a pace below her boots.

Ooze.

The word was important.

Leliana gritted her teeth and fought the confusion that bubbled through her mind. She managed to coordinate her motions enough to thrust out a hand, and she felt Naxil grasp it. He pulled her up and out, tried and failed to force her feet to the floor, then gave up and fumbled at her hand. What was he doing—trying to steal her ring?

The lava reached the top of the crevice and started to flow out of it, onto the floor.

"We've got to hurry," he said in an urgent voice. "Go back the way we came. The lava's rising." He forced her hand around the hilt of her sword and yanked the weapon from its scabbard.

The sword pealed. The magical confusion fell away.

"That's not lava!" Leliana shouted, as realization dawned. "It's an ooze. Filled with molten fire and capable of enchantments." She negated the ring's magic and found her feet. She was furious with herself. If she'd been holding her singing sword when she crossed the crevice, this never would have happened.

"How do we fight it?" Naxil asked.

"Let me handle it. Keep behind me."

As Naxil danced back, the ooze cast an enchantment. Leliana felt it as a wave of exhaustion. Just as her eyes closed, the singing sword pealed loud and long, jolting her awake. She heard a sigh behind her, then a thump: Naxil, collapsing on the floor. She glanced back, praying he was still alive. There was no time to check, however.

The ooze surged out of the crevice in slow, rippling waves. It was enormous, twice as wide as Leliana was tall. It moved across the floor like molten iron, folding upon itself in wrinkles as it flowed forward. Its skin was a thick, clear membrane, cracked in places. Liquid fire dribbled from the cracks.

She lifted her sword. "You don't frighten me," she said aloud. The ooze was a mindless thing, and wouldn't understand, but saying it helped steady her.

The ooze bulged, forming an appendage.

Leliana chanted a prayer and released her sword. Borne by magic, it flew at the ooze and slashed at the expanding bulge. Magical steel met glowing fire and sliced neatly through it. The creature blazed like a bellows-driven fire as a portion of its "limb" fell away. Molten fire flowed from the wound, puddling on the cavern floor. Even protected by her spell, Leliana felt its heat as her chain mail warmed to an almost unbearable temperature. Sweat trickled down her body in rivulets, and into her eyes. Her singing sword glowed with heat; she was glad she wasn't holding it.

The creature flicked its severed appendage. Tiny drops of molten fire flew through the air, splattering Leliana. She gasped as they stung her arms and face. Like the acid burns, these she could heal with Eilistraee's blessing. Eventually. For now, she'd have to ignore the pain as best she could.

Then the ooze bulged in a second attack.

Leliana ducked just in time. Her sword parried, lopping off the second appendage—but not quickly enough. It slapped against Naxil's prone form, even as her sword severed it.

Naxil awoke, screaming.

Leliana swore. She pressed home the fight, menacing the ooze with her sword. As it drew back, she glanced anxiously at the screaming Naxil. What she saw made her shudder. Splatters of molten rock streaked his chest where the ooze had struck him, and were burning through his leather armor. Despite his magical protection, the molten rock had already charred deep ruts in the armor—and was burning down into his skin.

"Hang on, Naxil!" she cried. "Just a few moments more."

Leliana thrust at the ooze with her sword, worrying the creature and forcing it back to the crevice. Molten fire dribbled from each puncture.

Her *piwafwi* had been smoldering since the droplets of lava had struck it. Now the fabric ignited. Cursing, she slapped out the tiny flames. Then she smiled, as an idea struck her.

Keeping the ooze at a distance with her animated sword, she yanked off her smoldering *piwafwi*. She rushed the ooze, gritting out a prayer, and hurled the *piwafwi* onto it. As the garment landed on the ooze and burst into flame, she completed her spell.

"Eilistraee, aid me! Lend these flames the moon's chill light."

The flames dancing across the burning *piwafwi* turned from fire red to ice blue. The bitterly cold flames burned into the creature, punching a cold, dark hole in it. The ooze shrank back on itself and withdrew into the crevice.

The blue flames flickered out. The ooze rallied, rising again.

This time, Leliana shucked off her chain mail and cast it aside. She yanked her padded tunic over her head, hurled it onto the ooze, and repeated her prayer. Cracks radiated outward across the body of the ooze as the ice flames "burned" into it. The ooze tried to extend an appendage, but its skin cracked apart, and the limb fell to the floor. It shattered, with the chunks dulling like nearly extinguished coals.

One more time. That would finish it.

Naxil was no longer screaming.

Leliana yanked off her shirt and hurled it onto the ooze. "Eilistraee!" she shouted as her hand swept down for the third time. The flames burning the shirt turned from red to blue, and the ooze roared in anguish.

Then it exploded.

Chunks of cooling ooze flew off in all directions. One slammed into Leliana's shoulder, knocking her off her feet. Pain flared in her elbows as she struck the floor.

She rolled over as the smell of scorched hair filled her nostrils. And something more: burning flesh.

Naxil groaned. Low and deep.

She scrambled to his side. He lay face down. Leliana rolled him over, tore open his armor, and examined his chest. The burns there were so deep his flesh had been charred black; he'd need restorative magic to heal them. She tore his smoldering mask from his face and cast it aside. As she did this, she felt heat radiating from his face—it seemed to be flowing out of his nostrils and mouth. Something was happening to him. Something odd. Even those parts of his body that hadn't been directly struck by the creature were affected. Something pulsed under his skin, leaving tiny blisters that formed a tracery across his skin, like veins.

Those *were* his veins. They were glowing. Hot as fire.

Terrified, Leliana began a healing prayer. Before she could finish it, Naxil's veins erupted. Liquid fire oozed from the furrows, charring the surrounding flesh. More liquid fire oozed from his nostrils. A faint, sizzling noise filled the air: Naxil's eyes, cooking in their sockets.

"Eilistraee! Aid him!" Leliana cried, one hand on Naxil's forehead, the other extended to the place where the moon would be in the realms above.

Twined light and shadow swept down into the cavern, into Leliana, and on into Naxil. Elistraee's healing energy played about the body of the grievously wounded Nightshadow like a sparkle of ice in the moonlight, halting the burning within. As his body cooled, his veins lost their fiery glow. The trickles of liquid fire coming from his nostrils crusted over and fell away, and the burns in his body closed over. He was left, however, with terrible scars—and eyes that could no longer see. That was something Leliana couldn't repair here; it would have to wait until they got back to the temple.

"Thank . . . you," he gasped.

"Don't thank me," Leliana told him, wishing she could have intervened sooner—before he'd lost his eyes. "It's Eilistraee who saved your life." She touched his arm. "Can you stand?"

"I think so."

She helped him to his feet. He was remarkably steady, considering what he'd just been through. He moved with a certainty that suggested he'd been trained in blind fighting. He cocked his head, listening, as Leliana retrieved her singing sword. It lay next to the ooze's crusted remains. Even through the leather-wrapped hilt, the weapon felt hot. She noted the warp the creature's heat had left in the blade. It would no longer fit in her scabbard.

"What now?" Naxil asked.

"We press on," Leliana told him. She described for him what he couldn't see. "The ooze retreated back into the crevice before it died, and it's formed a natural bridge across the gap. As soon as it's cool enough, we can cross."

He nodded and touched his face. "My mask?"

"Burned."

His hand fell away. He turned his head, but she saw his stricken look just the same.

She took his hand and placed it on her shoulder. "We need to get moving," she said softly. "Get back to the Promenade and report what we've seen down here."

"The oozes," Naxil said grimly. "Ghaunadaur's minions. They're escaping from the Pit."

Leliana shuddered. "Let's pray the Ancient One isn't next."

CHAPTER 3

Cavatina made her way through the Hall of the Priestesses, a cavern filled with a soft blue-white light emanating from lichens on its ceiling and walls. Glowballs—off-white hemispheres that waxed and waned with the moon's cycles—studded the buildings. The combined illumination made the cavern as bright as a moonlit night in the World Above.

The buildings she passed—originally part of a Netherese outpost in the Underdark—had lain buried in rubble for seventeen centuries before Qilué and her companions excavated them and made them part of the Promenade. Constructed in terraced layers like a series of blocks stacked largest to smallest, the buildings were four stories high. Much of their original decoration had been smashed when the magic supporting the ceiling had dissipated at the time of Netheril's fall, but here and there Cavatina saw the grooves of what had once been a fluted column, or fragments of the friezes that had once adorned every wall.

Nearly two and a half decades of labor by Eilistraee's faithful had restored the buildings to a usable state, here and elsewhere in the Promenade. Now each bore the goddess's symbol above its front door: a silver long sword, set point-upright against the circle of a full moon haloed with streaks of white.

Priestesses and lay worshipers alike strode the streets, the former on their way to services in the Cavern of Song, the latter hurrying about their errands. Most of the priestesses were drow; only a handful were drawn from the elven races of the World Above. But the lay worshipers came from a multitude of races. Many had been rescued from the holds of slave ships, or from the flesh markets of Skullport. Each had turned, in gratitude, to the Dark Maiden's faith. The other priestesses saluted Cavatina, while the lay worshipers bowed low. Awed whispers followed in her wake.

Cavatina spotted a familiar face: Meryl, Qilué's halfling cook. The little female with the mop of tangled gray hair padded along on bare feet to the high priestess's house, a basket tucked under one arm. Cavatina altered course so their paths would cross.

Meryl's wrinkled face creased in a grin as she spotted the Darksong Knight. "Hello, Cavatina! It's been a while."

Cavatina arched an eyebrow. " 'Cavatina?' " she echoed. "Not, 'Most Esteemed Darksong Knight, Slayer of Selvetarm?' " she continued in a teasing voice.

Meryl laughed and waved a hand. "Yes, yes, that too. It's just hard to remember, sometimes. I still see, when I look at you, the babe Jetel danced with in her arms. Though"—she craned her neck, looking up—"you get taller and skinnier each time I see you. You're thin as a sword blade. You really should eat more."

Cavatina smiled. Though the halfling was a mere lay

worshiper, Meryl never—ever—used formal titles. She even addressed Lady Qilué by her first name.

"So what brings you to the Promenade?" Meryl continued. "Slain any demons lately? How are things in the Chondalwood? Are the elves still prevailing?"

Cavatina held up her hands, as if overwhelmed by the barrage of questions. Meryl seldom asked only one her tongue ran faster than her feet, more often than not. "Rylla's summons. Three yochlols. Good. And yes."

Meryl's head bobbed in a series of nods. She shifted her basket, and Cavatina heard metal clink inside it.

"Don't tell me you're stealing the silverware again," Cavatina teased. The jibe wouldn't sting Meryl, who prided herself on her stout-hearted loyalty. She'd been Qilué's cook for decades, and personally tasted every ingredient for poison before using it. A simple prayer of detection would have accomplished the same result, but Meryl insisted on putting her life on the line. If poison took her, she said, she'd go to Eilistraee's realm happy and content—and with a full stomach.

Meryl feigned shock. "Me!" she blurted indignantly. "I never, *ever,* would contemplate such a thing. Not in a hundred lifetimes. A thousand. Yes, it's true; that was the gleam of silver you saw." She cracked the lid of the basket, giving Cavatina a peek. "But I'm taking these vials *from* the Hall of Healing *to* the High House, as you could plainly have seen from the direction I was headed." With a flourish, she snapped the lid shut.

Now Cavatina was supposed to apologize. That was the way the game was played. But her brief glimpse inside the basket puzzled her. Those vials were used to hold one thing, only. "Is that holy water?"

Meryl nodded.

Cavatina should have cracked another joke—to ask, perhaps, if Meryl's kitchen was infested with undead mice—but her customary bluntness kicked in at last. "What does a cook need with holy water?"

"They're for Qilué. She told me to make sure there's an ample supply on hand when she gets back from her inspection tour of the shrines. She's used up all she had."

"Why doesn't she bless her own water?"

"I've no idea. But I'd recommend against asking her. Qilué's been awfully short-tempered lately. A tenday ago, she got angry with Horaldin. I could hear her yelling at him, even from the kitchen. She told him to follow her orders or else. And yesterday she shouted at me for scalding the soup." The halfling made a face. "I *never* scald my soup."

"That's not like her."

"No." Meryl shrugged. "She's got a lot on her mind, I suppose." The halfling crooked a finger, beckoning Cavatina closer. Her voice dropped to a husky whisper. "Yesterday, just before Qilué left, someone turned a blindfish into a golden crab. According to what I heard, the Protector who set out after it was eaten by a scorpion. It's all nonsense, of course—that statue was so rusted it couldn't possibly have swallowed anyone, and Leliana will show up eventually—but worrisome nonsense just the same."

"I see." It was no use asking Meryl to clarify this garbled tale; the halfling tended to jumble everything together, and was forever seasoning the resulting hash with a hefty dash of imagination. Rylla would clarify whatever Meryl was trying to tell her. She would also shed light, no doubt, on why the high priestess didn't bless her own water—if indeed Meryl had gotten that part right.

"I'd best be on my way," Cavatina said. "The battle-mistress is expecting me."

Meryl nodded. She shifted the basket into the crook of her arm. "Eilistraee's blessings," she said, touching thumbs and forefingers. "Dance in moonlight, and joyous song."

Cavatina touched her breastplate, her fingers resting lightly on its embossed moon-and-sword. "Joyous song." She watched as the cook entered a side door and disappeared into the high priestess's house, then sighed and shook her head.

She was just turning to go when the door opened again: Meryl, leaving, the basket still under her arm. Something about the way the halfling exited struck Cavatina as odd, though it took a moment to figure out what it was. Meryl had stepped outside, glanced around, and drawn back slightly, as if fearful. Cavatina glanced behind herself— whatever had startled Meryl must have been right behind her, judging by the timing of the reaction—yet Cavatina saw nothing amiss.

She walked to the cook. "What is it, Meryl? Is something wrong?"

Meryl didn't reply. Without so much as a glance in Cavatina's direction, she hurried away.

Cavatina followed. "Meryl?"

The halfling sped up.

"Meryl!" Cavatina shouted. "Wait! I just want to ask you something."

Meryl broke into a run.

Several paces behind, Cavatina ran after the halfling, her sense of unease strong. Meryl had been holding the basket a moment ago; now it had vanished. Meryl ran with a peculiar loping gait: a jiggly step-wobble-step.

Cavatina sang a prayer. She expected to uncover a spy: a denizen of Skullport or, at worst, one of Lolth's priestesses. What her spell revealed shocked her. The creature cloaking itself in Meryl's image was squat and hairless, with rubbery gray skin, beady red eyes above a drool-slack mouth, and arms so long the knuckles dragged on the ground.

A dretch—a demonic creature of the Abyss!

And it had come from Qilué's residence.

The dretch bolted into the corridor leading to the Hall of Healing. Cavatina drew her sword and sprinted in after it. "Stop that halfling!" she shouted. "That's not Meryl—it's a *demon!*" Her sword pealed out its own alarm.

Other priestesses took up the chase, sprinting into the tunnel behind Cavatina. One blew her hunting horn. The blare filled the corridor, drowning out the hymn that wafted down a side tunnel from the Cavern of Song.

"Encircle it!" Cavatina shouted over her shoulder. "Double back through the Cavern of Song, and upriver through the northern tunnel. Box it in!"

Priestesses and lay worshipers scrambled to obey. Cavatina ran on, singing a sending. As the battle-mistress's mind touched hers, Cavatina shouted a warning to Rylla. Not in words—she needed her breath for running—but with a mental shout. *A dretch disguised as Meryl is heading for the Empty Arches. It came from the High House. Search it for demons. See if Meryl lives.*

Rylla's reply came a heartbeat after her oath. *Wrath and blood! I'll send Protectors to the High House and meet you at the Hall of Empty Arches.*

Cavatina rounded a corner. There should have been a guard just ahead, to ensure unwanted visitors to the Hall of Empty Arches didn't wander into the priestesses' quarters. Yet there was no guard in sight.

She caught a whiff of something that smelled like rotten eggs and saw a cloud of yellow-tinged fog in the room beyond. The guard—an ordinary foot soldier, armed with mace and shield—came staggering out of it, retching. "Dark Lady," she gasped. "I couldn't stop . . ."

Whatever she'd been trying to say was lost as she doubled over and vomited. One hand flailed behind her. *That way,* she signed.

Cavatina shouted a song of dispelling that tore the noxious fog to shreds. She ran into the hall, alert for the slightest sound. She could see only a fraction of the room. Floor-to-ceiling stone partitions, lined up down the middle of the chamber like pews in a temple, blocked most of it from sight.

She heard the peal of an unsheathed singing sword from the far side of the room, followed by the battle-mistress's shout. "Cavatina! I'm in position! Northeast corner."

"Southwest corner!" Cavatina shouted back. Priestesses crowded behind her. At least one was a Protector, and Cavatina could hear the battle song of a singing sword harmonizing with her own weapon. It turned out to be Chizra. She greeted Cavatina with a terse nod.

Cavatina ordered Chizra and four other priestesses into the room. They formed up, weapons ready, then at her signal strode from one side of the room to the other, each moving between two partition walls. With their swords sweeping the air in front of them, they sang prayers that would strip the dretch of any concealments. When they reached the far side of the hall, they sang out in unison. "All clear!"

"Cavatina!" Rylla called from the far corner of the room. "Could the dretch have turned aside and entered the Cavern of Song?"

"No," Cavatina shouted back. "I sang a true seeing. It definitely came this way."

The gray-faced guard, at last in control of her stomach, nodded in rueful agreement.

Cavatina ordered the nearest priestess to stand guard, in case the dretch doubled back. Then she hurried to the far corner of the room. The battle-mistress stood at the room's second exit, a distant look in her pale gray eyes, her lips moving soundlessly. She was obviously listening—and replying—to a report from a searcher elsewhere in the temple.

Rylla was large, even for a female. Her broad shoulders and lighter skin were a legacy of her human father. She was an unusual choice for battle-mistress, but these were unusual times. Although she carried her sword, she was without belt or scabbard, and unarmored; she obviously hadn't had time to don her chainmail before responding to Cavatina's urgent sending.

Rylla nodded in agreement with whatever she'd just heard, then turned to Cavatina. "There's no sign of the dretch in the Hall of Healing. Nor in the Cavern of Song. It doesn't seem to have made it past this point. Another of the portals must have become active."

"The real question is how it got into the Promenade in the first place," Cavatina said. "How did it get past our wards?"

Rylla stared at Cavatina. "You're the expert in hunting demons. You tell me."

Cavatina had a bad feeling about this. The dretch's sudden appearance was all too reminiscent of the Selvetargtlin onslaught of three and a half years ago, and their trick of using ensorcelled gems to jump to the Promenade. She wondered if another attack were imminent.

She glanced at the closest partition wall. Like the others, it was carved in low relief with the likeness of two archways—decorative arches only, since the middle of each was solid stone. There were eight, in total. Each had once been a portal, but the magic that had sustained them had faltered centuries ago, when Netheril fell. Only one of the arches was still active, and then sporadically. Once it sputtered to life, it might remain open for the space of a heartbeat—or for more than a month. It led to the Hall of Empty Arches from a deeper level of Undermountain that was once part of a dwarven mithral mine predating even Netheril.

The occasional adventurer blundered through this portal, usually badly battered and in need of healing by the time it opened. Qilué had thus decreed that it not be sealed. Those who agreed to abide by the rules of song and sword were offered healing in the nearby hall. Those who didn't were either blindfolded and removed from the Promenade—or, if they proved hostile, were put to the sword.

Rylla motioned for Cavatina to follow, then sang a hymn. She walked slowly through the room, her free hand briefly passing across the front of each of the arches. "Dead. Nothing. Still dead . . ."

Cavatina followed, sword at the ready.

Rylla passed her hand across the face of the portal that

joined the ancient mine tunnel to the Hall of Empty Arches. She shook her head. "It's not active at the moment."

One arch remained to be checked: the one next to it. Rylla halted in front of this arch, holding her palm above it for several moments. Concentrating. Her eyebrows rose. "This one's active. In one direction only: away from here."

Cavatina leaned forward expectantly. Her sword hummed. A moment more, and the hunt would resume. "Where does it lead?"

"Nowhere. And—everywhere." Rylla lowered her hand. "My prayer revealed a maze of tunnels that were constantly shifting. Opening to infinity, then closing in again. I think it may lead to the Deep Caverns." She stared at the blank stone within the arch. "If the dretch went through here, it will be impossible to track."

"I can do it," Cavatina assured her. "The dretch must be captured and questioned. We need to learn who summoned it, and what they hoped to accomplish."

Rylla blocked her way. "Not so fast. It could take you a lifetime to track it down in there, and we need you here."

"I can find my way back from any—"

"You're staying here, in the Promenade. That's an order."

Cavatina was about to protest, but something about the look in Rylla's eyes halted her. The battle-mistress nodded at the arch. "The dretch didn't get in this way—that's a one-way portal." She turned. "How *else* might it have gotten into the Promenade?"

Cavatina fumed, but answered the question. "Dretches are weak. This one wouldn't have been able to breach the Promenade's defenses on its own. The dretch must have been summoned here—summoned by someone already inside the Promenade."

Rylla gave a tight nod. She'd already realized this much.

"Or perhaps it came here by means of a wish spell," Cavatina concluded, still thinking of the Selvetargtlin who had carried teleportation gems into the Promenade nearly four years ago.

Rylla's expression was grave. "I've ordered a full sweep of the temple, from the High House on down."

"Remind them to report any suspicious-looking gems."

"Already done."

"Have the Protectors located Meryl yet?"

"Yes, praise Eilistraee. She's unharmed."

Cavatina sheathed her sword. "Since you won't let me pursue the dretch, you might as well tell me why you summoned me to the Promenade. Did you have a premonition that a demon would show up here?"

"Yes, I did." Rylla's sending came a heartbeat later. *I need to talk to you about Lady Qilué. That's why I sent for you. Something's . . . wrong with her.*

Cavatina felt her eyes widen slightly. She opened her mouth to ask a question, and shut it again. She suddenly realized the dretch might be a symptom of a larger problem. It should have been impossible for it to enter the High House. Qilué's personal wards should have banished any creature of the Abyss back to the place it came from, the instant it tried to enter her residence—especially a minor demon like a dretch. If something was interfering with Qilué's ability to ward herself from a comparatively weak foe, Rylla had every right to be worried.

Cavatina nodded slightly, her eyes on the other priestesses. Rylla obviously hadn't shared her concerns with them. *Is something eclipsing Lady Qilué's magic? Is that why the dretch—?*

Later. In private.

Rylla turned to Chizra. "Guard this portal. Don't let anything—or anyone—near it. If we manage to flush another demon out of hiding, it may head this way. It may disguise itself, as the dretch did."

The Protector nodded grimly.

"Keep watch on each of the other portals as well," Rylla continued. "Even the inactive ones. We can't be certain of the status of any of them, any more. Give each guard a scroll that will enable her to seal the portal, if necessary."

Orders given, Rylla asked Cavatina to follow her. They made their way to the battle-mistress's residence, not pausing until they reached a sitting room furnished with three crescent-shaped benches that surrounded a scrying font. Tapestries on the walls showed ebon-skinned priestesses on the hunt, swords and horns in hand. Rylla's empty scabbard lay on a bench, next to her lute..

Cavatina spoke first. "What's wrong with Lady Qilué?"

Rylla turned—sharply—and raised a finger to her lips. *No names,* she signed.

The battle-mistress obviously didn't want Qilué eavesdropping on whatever it was she was about to say. Very well; Cavatina would play along. For now. "Battle-mistress, I report as summoned. You said you wanted my assistance in organizing the patrols of the Promenade. I'm happy to advise you on how the Protectors can best be—"

"That's enough," Rylla interrupted. "If she was listening, she'll have stopped by now." She sheathed her sword and continued to the scrying font. She stared into the alabaster bowl, moved her lips in a silent message, and passed a hand just above the surface of the water.

Cavatina struggled to hold her tongue. Her impulse was to tell Rylla she was being unnecessarily cautious. People spoke Qilué's name so frequently that it must have sounded like overlapping echoes to the high priestess. Listening in on everything that followed and trying to pick out the important nuggets from the endless drone of casual conversation would have been a full-time task. What's more, Cavatina had never known Qilué to answer by accident when her name was uttered. The high priestess only answered those who *intended* to call her.

Cavatina edged closer to the font and took a look. The scrying was focused on Qilué, who walked through a forest with half a dozen lesser priestesses in tow. Qilué stood head and shoulders above the rest, a majestic figure with her silver robes and ankle-length white hair. The sight of her filled Cavatina with reverential awe. Qilué had founded the Promenade, had lifted the worship of Eilistraee from an obscure sect to a force to be reckoned with. She'd made the faith what it was today. Every drow who had been raised from the Underdark over the past six centuries owed their redemption to her. Even though Cavatina had slain the demigod Selvetarm, she didn't rank nearly as high in the faith as Qilué.

Qilué was speaking to the lesser priestesses, but her words were too soft for Cavatina to make out. She held the Crescent Blade in her hand, and emphasized a remark by using it to point at something out of range of the scrying font.

There was a time, not so long ago, when the sight of the Crescent Blade in the high priestess's hands would have filled Cavatina with jealousy. Now it was just another weapon—albeit a powerful one, ensorcelled with magic that had enabled Cavatina to kill a demigod.

"What you have to say must be disconcerting, indeed, if you don't want . . . her to hear it."

Rylla passed a hand over the font, ending the scrying. She sat on one of the benches. "I've been speaking with one of the Seven Sisters," she began. "Laeral Silverhand. She paid me a visit recently, expressing concerns about . . . her sister."

Cavatina nodded. "Go on."

"Lady Silverhand pointed out something I'd noticed myself. A cut on the high priestess's wrist."

"Which wrist?"

"The right one." Rylla touched her own wrist. "Just here."

Cavatina shivered slightly, as if a chill breeze had just blown through the room. "That happened a year and a half ago. Just before our attack on the Acropolis of . . ." She faltered as the name that had been on the tip of her tongue an instant ago suddenly escaped her. "Of the death goddess," she said at last. "I was there when the high priestess cut herself. She was in the middle of an attunement, dancing with the Crescent Blade. She faltered in her dance."

"Not something she'd ordinarily do."

"No."

Rylla shifted the lute so that Cavatina had room to sit down. The fingers with the picks rested briefly on the neck of the instrument, as if yearning to pluck its strings. Then Rylla removed her finger-picks and set them aside. "Lady Silverhand mentioned something else. Something she noticed about the Crescent Blade. More specifically, about her sister's reluctance to let anyone else touch it. Each time Lady Silverhand asks to examine the sword, the high priestess refuses. She claims her bond with it will be broken if anyone else handles it."

"That explanation rings hollow," Cavatina said. "The only time you can't let go of an attuned weapon—be it magical or mundane—is during the actual attunement itself. The ensorcelments on the Crescent Blade are extremely powerful, but the same rules would apply."

"I suspected as much."

"You're overlooking one possible motivation," Cavatina continued. "Pride. The high priestess has decreed that she will be the one to kill Lolth, when that time comes. If she hands over the Crescent Blade to anyone else, especially long enough for a magical study to be made of it, she might miss her chance at glory."

There. It was said. Not so long ago, Cavatina might have spoken the words with bitterness, but the boil of anger and jealousy that had festered inside her for years had been lanced by her redemption. Now she spoke calmly and with detachment. Even so, she said a silent prayer of contrition, asking Eilistraee to forgive her for casting doubt on the high priestess's character.

Rylla met Cavatina's eyes. "We both know that's not the reason."

Cavatina nodded. "What, then?"

"You carried the Crescent Blade. Fought with it. Did it ever . . . communicate with you?"

"You're asking me if it's an intelligent weapon. The answer is yes. The Crescent Blade spoke to me."

"Did it ever say anything . . . odd?"

"What do you mean?"

"Did it ever urge you to do something rash? To take on opponents you couldn't or shouldn't fight?"

Cavatina laughed. "I *wanted* to kill Selvetarm, believe me." Then she shook her head. "On the other hand, the weapon did seem . . . proud. Boastful. It talked as if it had killed Selvetarm all on its own."

Rylla stared directly into Cavatina's eyes. "Did it *compel* you to kill Selvetarm?"

"No. It wasn't like that. Not at all."

"Did you feel *any* sort of compulsion while holding the Crescent Blade?"

"No. Well, yes, actually, but not until after I'd returned to the Promenade. When the high priestess commanded me to give the Crescent Blade to her, I didn't want to let go of it."

"But you gave it to her."

Cavatina bristled. It sounded like an accusation. "She ordered me to."

Rylla sighed. "I didn't call you here to try and find fault with you. I summoned you to the Promenade because I'm worried. I think the Crescent Blade may be the cause of our high priestess's recent . . . outbursts. Her orders have been rather abrupt lately, and she's been less than forthcoming about the rationale behind them."

"She *is* the high priestess," Cavatina countered. "Eilistraee's *Chosen*. As such, she's not bound to answer to anyone but the goddess for her decisions. She gives orders, and it is our duty to obey."

"*Are* they her orders?" Rylla asked.

Cavatina tensed. "Are you implying what I think you are?"

"The Crescent Blade never leaves her hand. Even when it's sheathed, her hand rests on its hilt."

"Are you telling me you think the Crescent Blade is *controlling* the high priestess?"

"I don't want to speculate. I want to *know*." Rylla rose to her feet and paced in a restless circle around the benches. "Describe for me the temple you recovered the Crescent Blade from—the one in the Demonweb Pits."

Cavatina did.

Rylla listened, interjecting a question here and there.

"Was the temple *truly* sacred ground?"

"My divinations revealed that it was."

"And the sword within it?"

Cavatina swallowed. Hard. Though she'd *felt* the Crescent Blade's holiness with a certainty as strong as song when she had first entered the temple, a seed of doubt had been planted the instant she read the inscription on the mended blade. Yet despite the broken inscription, the Crescent Blade hadn't failed *her*. It had severed Selvetarm's neck, exactly as it had been forged to do.

Of course, that was what Lolth had intended, all along. Halisstra had admitted as much. And it had been Halisstra who had led Cavatina to that temple. Halisstra the traitor. She'd pretended she was acting of her own volition—that she was seeking redemption—but she'd been the Spider Queen's foil, all along, little better than a web-snared fly.

"My divination revealed nothing amiss with the Crescent Blade," Cavatina answered at last.

Rylla waited. "But?" she prompted.

"But now I'm not so sure."

It was true. Until this moment, Cavatina had thought sacrificing Selvetarm was the extent of the Spider Queen's plot. But now she wondered if Lolth's schemes went even deeper than that. Soon after Cavatina had claimed the Crescent Blade, it had spoken to her.

You're not the one, it had said.

Had Lolth anticipated that Qilué would eventually claim the weapon for herself? Was the reforged Crescent Blade part of some trap that even now was springing shut? Was the weapon somehow goading Qilué toward a battle she would lose—a battle in which the Crescent Blade would fail her?

Until today, Cavatina's faith in Qilué's mastery of magic had been unshakeable. But now doubt crowded close.

Halisstra was the key to all of this. Cavatina was certain of it.

Cavatina's thoughts kept circling back to the last time she'd seen Halisstra. Where the fallen priestess was now was anyone's guess. After delivering Cavatina into the hands of the balor Wendonai, Halisstra had disappeared. She'd been spotted—briefly—by Kâras and Leliana during the battle atop the Acropolis. Then she'd vanished again.

Had she returned to Wendonai? If so, she'd have found nothing but a corpse. Wendonai had died on Cavatina's sword—albeit without the usual explosive aftermath. His body had remained intact after his death, as if its animating force had gone . . . somewhere else.

Suddenly, Cavatina realized where it might have gone. Into the Crescent Blade. *That* would explain how a dretch had wound up inside the High House. Wendonai could have summoned it—right under Qilué's nose—from within the Crescent Blade, just before the high priestess departed on her inspection tour.

It also explained the holy water Meryl had been carrying. Qilué herself must have suspected something was wrong with the weapon. She was trying to banish the demon—without, Cavatina suspected, much success.

Carefully, never once mentioning Qilué by name, Cavatina outlined her fears. She concluded with a recap of the conversation she'd had with the halfling, just before the dretch made its appearance.

Rylla's lips tightened. "What can we do?"

"If it's only the sword that's possessed, we can banish the demon back to the Abyss. If the possession has gone further . . ." Cavatina took a deep breath.

Rylla's eyes widened. "Eilistraee grant it's not as bad as that!"

"An exorcism is something best dealt with here, where Eilistraee's presence is strongest," Cavatina said. "But it will need sufficient preparation. How long will it be before the high priestess returns?"

"A tenday, at least."

Cavatina nodded. "All arrangements will have to be made in secret. If a demon has taken control of the high priestess, we won't want to tip our hand."

Rylla's face was gray with strain. "This shouldn't go beyond the walls of this room. It could cause a crisis of faith. One that could cost us dearly."

"Agreed," Cavatina said. She stared grimly at the font. "There's one thing I don't understand. Why would Eilistraee have permitted something evil to fall into the hands of her Chosen?"

"She wouldn't have," Rylla said firmly. "Unless . . ." She turned away—but not before Cavatina saw the pained look in her eyes.

"What? Say what you're thinking!"

"There are whispers. About what happened when the realms of Eilistraee and Vhaeraun were joined. If they're true, it might not have been Eilistraee who guided the Crescent Blade into the high priestess's hands."

Cavatina shivered. Her mouth felt as dry as chalk. To hear such blasphemy—and from the Promenade's battle-mistress! It was unthinkable.

Rylla gave a chuckle that sounded forced. "Those rumors are nonsense, of course. The Dark Maiden simply shifted the tempo of her dance. She had to, in order to bring the Night-shadows into the fold. Eilistraee still rules, by song and sword. Vhaeraun is dead."

"By song and sword," Cavatina echoed, touching the hilt of her weapon. The sword let out a low, soothing hum from deep within its scabbard.

It didn't help. Cavatina still felt as off balance as a dancer with one leg. If her guess was right—if the demon Wendonai now inhabited the Crescent Blade, and he in turn was corrupting Qilué—the Promenade was in grave danger. She held out her hands. "Sing with me."

Rylla clasped Cavatina's arms. Like partners in a frozen dance, they bowed their heads.

Together, they prayed.

Horaldin stopped in front of a door and glanced up and down the corridor. Though singing wafted from elsewhere in the Promenade, this corridor was empty for the moment. He opened the door, stepped through swiftly, and motioned for Cavatina to follow.

He shut the door behind them. This corridor was short, no more than a dozen paces long. It ended in a little-used door of solid black obsidian. The druid grasped the adamantine deadbolt at the side of the door and tugged, but the deadbolt didn't move. He nodded, as if he'd been expecting this.

Cavatina glanced over his shoulder. There was no lock visible. If the door was locked, it was held shut by magic.

Horaldin touched his fingertips to the door's glassy surface, closed his eyes, and whispered.

Cavatina tapped one foot impatiently. She'd sought out Horaldin, intending to get him to repeat, word for word, his argument with Qilué, in order to see if the high priestess had said anything telling. Instead of answering her questions directly, Horaldin had insisted on going somewhere "private" where they could talk. Now they were creeping about the Promenade like rogues with looted valuables in their pockets. Cavatina was starting to suspect it wasn't merely a quest for privacy that had caused Horaldin to lead her this way.

"Horaldin, please. Can't you just *tell* me what prompted your argument with—"

Horaldin's eyes sprang open. "Shh! Don't say her name! She'll hear you!"

Cavatina took a deep breath. "I wasn't about to do *that*. I was the one who reminded *you* not to speak her name aloud, remember?"

"I just hope she's not scrying us," Horaldin said.

That, Cavatina could agree with. Even though Qilué wouldn't return to the Promenade for several days, after her inspection tour of the outlying shrines was complete, it wouldn't hurt to be careful. No matter where Qilué went, she kept a scrying font close at hand.

The thought was even more disturbing when Cavatina admitted to herself that the high priestess was carrying around a sword that could contain a hidden demon.

Horaldin had closed his eyes again, and resumed his divination. Sweat beaded his temples. A wash of *Faerzress* played briefly on the wall beside him, giving an eerie bluish tint to his already sallow skin. The druid was a moon elf, and thus immune to the *Faerzress*, else his divination might have been interrupted. His wavy black hair hung in a root-like tangle to his waist, and his fingers were as slender as spider legs. Not a pleasant combination, when you came right down to it. But the druid was utterly loyal to the temple, despite his continued reverence for the Leaflord. As Horaldin so eloquently put it, Eilistraee was the fruit of Arvandor, and Rillifane the guardian of the tree from which she had fallen. Eilistraee planted seeds of hope in the Underdark, and by the Leaflord's decree, Horaldin's destiny was to help nurture them.

"The door's been magically sealed," he told Cavatina. "By . . . her."

"Why would she do that?"

"To prevent me from showing you what's on the other side of it."

Cavatina's skin prickled with anticipation. She rested a hand on her sword hilt. "Can you open the door?"

"Not by normal means. Only the most powerful spellcaster could undo her magic. But there is another way." Horaldin held his hands in front of him, pressing them together back to back. He whispered a moment, and forced his hands apart. A hole appeared in the middle of the door and gradually widened, as if the obsidian had become as soft as clay and invisible hands were parting it. When the gap was wide enough, Horaldin eased a leg through the hole, ducked, and stepped through the door.

Cavatina followed.

The room beyond was oddly shaped: square, but with one corner that had been cut off diagonally by a wall similar, in its zigzag shape, to a folding screen. In the center of the zigzag wall was another obsidian door—the room's second exit. This odd configuration gave the room eight "walls"—a significant number. The drow who had inhabited the caverns on the far side of the Sargauth nearly a thousand years ago had once maintained a temple to the Spider Queen here. The temple had been obliterated when Ghaunadaur's cultists summoned the Ancient One's minions to the city—an act that had been the city's downfall.

Centuries of visitations by oozes and slimes had worn down the altar and statue that once stood here. Qilué and her companions had finished the job, smashing what remained to dust and scouring the murals from the walls with holy water. Now all that remained was an empty room.

The former temple could have been a convenient shortcut from the western end of the bridge—located just a few paces beyond the second door—but the priestesses who patrolled the Promenade avoided this place. Cavatina could see why. Even though the room was bare and empty, being in it set her on edge. Now that she lingered in it, she realized the reason why:

in all of the Promenade, this was the one spot where silence ruled. Everywhere else, the hymn that constantly flowed out of the Cavern of Song could be heard, if only as a murmur. But in this tainted place, Cavatina couldn't even hear the rush of water from the nearby river.

"What is it you wanted to show me?" she asked.

Horaldin moved to the corner where the two longest walls met. "This." He pointed at a glyph that had been painted on the walls, straddling the corner. "The high priestess ordered me to paint it here."

"Ordered? Was that what your argument was about?"

Horaldin folded his arms across his chest and nodded.

Large as a shield, the glyph was one she didn't recognize. It looked a little like the protective enchantments elsewhere in the Promenade, but those were silvery red in color and dusted with powdered diamond and opal, while this one had been painted on the walls in shimmering streaks of powdered pearl, held in place by a clear glue that smelled faintly of honey.

"What is it?" she asked.

"An enchantment. Designed to attract those who worship Ghaunadaur. The high priestess said it was a trap that would lure any cultists who venture upriver from Skullport into a room where they might easily be slain."

Cavatina nodded. That seemed logical enough—and it had a precedent. Ten years ago, Ghaunadaur's cultists had laid siege to the Promenade for three long months. The attack had come from upriver, from the caverns to the northeast, closer to the Hall of Healing. The oozes the cultists commanded had been held at bay; not a single room or corridor of the temple had been overrun. Yet this likely wouldn't deter them from trying again. If they were preparing for another attack on the Promenade, it made sense to set a trap for any spies they might send. Those attempting to infiltrate the temple would likely make their approach via the river that connected the Promenade to the other parts of Undermountain.

But why place the enchantment here? It would make more sense to position it either at the northernmost cavern that opened onto the river, or the southernmost. Or both. Not midway between the two, close to vulnerable areas of the Promenade.

And why, having ordered the enchantment to be put in place, seal the room off so no one could reach it?

Cavatina walked to the second door and tested its deadbolt. Like the first, it was immoveable. Sealed by magic.

"You disagreed with the glyph's placement," Cavatina said.

Horaldin nodded. "That too."

Cavatina turned. "What else?"

"The high priestess ordered me to say nothing of what I'd inscribed here. To tell no one: neither the lay worshipers, nor the priestesses, nor the Protectors, nor even Battle-mistress Rylla."

"The very people who would *need* to be aware of something that might draw Ghaunadaur's cultists to this area, in order that they could be captured or eliminated."

"Exactly."

Cavatina frowned. "How did she explain the need for secrecy?"

"She didn't. It seemed to me she couldn't—and that this frustrated her. When I pressed her, it turned into an argument."

"Do you have any idea why she chose this spot?"

"Cast a divination. Search for magic."

Cavatina did. To her magically enhanced vision, the stone wall became as insubstantial as mist. Her body started to tingle. It felt as if something were trying to draw her into the wall—or rather, beyond the wall. Startled, she stepped back. "What is it? An illusory wall?"

"You can't inscribe a glyph on an illusion. The walls are real enough." He rapped his knuckles against the spot she'd just been viewing, hard enough to make a knocking sound.

"At least, to me they are. But there's a portal here—one that can only be used by drow."

"How did you figure that out?"

"Some time after the high priestess dismissed me—when I was certain she'd be gone—I returned and communed with the walls. They described a 'hole' that would take drow 'elsewhere.' That was clue enough."

Cavatina frowned. "I've patrolled every cavern, hallway, and chamber of the Promenade. Including this one. There wasn't a portal here before."

"No. The high priestess must have opened it."

"I wonder why."

Horaldin shook his head. "I have no idea. I was hoping you might know. And that you'd tell me . . ." He hesitated, a pained look in his eyes. "Tell me what it all *means*."

Cavatina hesitated, trying to decide how much she should say. Horaldin was worthy of her trust. He'd gone against the direct orders of the high priestess by showing her this. He deserved a partial answer, at least.

"Something's . . . clouding the high priestess's judgment. That's why the battle-mistress summoned me to the Promenade. We think . . ." She swallowed hard. Should she be saying this? The answer to that question was clearly no, but Cavatina was inclined to listen to her gut. She might be drow, but she'd been born and raised in the World Above. She hadn't been weaned on secrecy and subterfuge, but on blunt honesty.

"We think it may be demonic—and that powerful magic will be needed to remedy the situation. When the time comes to act, we may need your help."

Horaldin nodded. "I see. Thank you. It's the Crescent Blade, isn't it?"

Cavatina nodded. If it was obvious even to the druid, it wasn't going to stay a secret very long. "Say nothing of this. We don't want to start any rumors. It would—"

"Yes. I see that too." He glanced at the hole he'd made in the middle of the obsidian door. "We should be getting back, before anyone notices what we've done. I need to smooth the door over and hide any trace we've come this way."

"You go," Cavatina said. She nodded at the wall. "I need to see where this portal leads."

"Wouldn't you rather I wait for you?"

"No. Go to Rylla and tell her about this. Tell her where I've gone—and that I'll report back the moment I discover anything."

"If I seal the door, how will you escape this room?"

Cavatina smiled. "Eilistraee's blessings will see me safely home."

Horaldin nodded at last. "May she guide your steps," he intoned. He hurried across the room and squeezed through the hole in the door. Cavatina heard him repeat his spell, and the door sealed itself shut.

Cavatina prayed. "Eilistraee," she sang softly. "Is this the path you wish me to follow?"

A moment later, the goddess's reply came. Not in words, but in a gentle yet firm tug on Cavatina's hand—like a partner, inviting her to dance.

Cavatina drew her singing sword, took a deep breath, and stepped through the portal.

CHAPTER 4

Q'arlynd adjusted the hang of his *piwafwi* and gave himself a final inspection. Directing the palm-sized mirror in its orbit with one finger, he checked to make sure his shoulder-length hair was tucked into the clip at the back of his neck and that the hood of his *piwafwi* draped neatly over his shoulders.

The *piwafwi*, made from the blue-black fur of a displacer beast, shimmered slightly, hinting at the magic it contained. Atop it, hanging by a silver chain, was a pendant made from a clear crystal.

A flick of his hand brought the mirror up to eye level. He peered into it as he inserted an earring into his pierced lobe. Carved from the egg tooth of an unhatched spider, the earring was insurance against assassination attempts. Not that anyone was likely to try poisoning him in the middle of a formal meeting, but it never hurt to be prepared.

In the mirror, his forehead appeared unadorned. Yet the *selu'kiira* he'd wrested from Kraanfhaor's Door was there Its constant pressure was similar to the pressing of a cool thumb against his skin. As a precaution, he kept the lorestone invisible. None but a Melarn could utilize its magic—anyone else who tried to wear it would wind up a feeblewit—but there might always be someone foolish or desperate enough to try.

Much had changed in the seven years since the fall of Ched Nasad. He'd come a long way indeed from his days of grubbing in the ruins of that fallen city, little better than the slave of a rival House.

Q'arlynd was master of his own school of wizardry now—a school just one short step away from being sanctioned as Sshamath's eleventh official College. He'd truly made a new home for himself in this city of wizards. The only reminder of his former life was the House insignia he wore on his left wrist. Carved into the worn leather band's adamantine oval was House Melarn's symbol, a glyph shaped like a stick-figure person, arms bent and one leg raised.

The symbol of the dancing goddess, Eilistraee.

The goddess Q'arlynd had pledged himself to.

Inspection complete, he tucked the mirror into the breast pocket of his shirt. He slowly turned to go, savoring his surroundings. The private study was filled with expensive furniture, all of it studded with chips of *beljuril* that twinkled with green light. A scroll shelf stood against one wall, its diamond-shaped niches filled floor to ceiling with texts both arcane and mundane. On the opposite wall, darkfire flames danced like crackling shadows inside the hearth. The study was warm, filled with wealth—and entirely Q'arlynd's own. A level of luxury he hadn't experienced for years.

All thanks to the *kiira* on his forehead.

As he departed, he reset the door's lock with a whispered word. He doubted anyone would recognize the abjuration any time soon—the word was from the original language of the dark elves, a language much changed since the Descent. Like the other spells Q'arlynd had learned since "opening" Kraanfhaor's Door, the abjuration was not written in any spellbook. It was contained solely within the *kiira*, alongside the memories of those who had worn the lorestone before him.

As Q'arlynd strode down the corridor, students bowed. He gave each the briefest of nods. He'd deliberately delayed his departure, intending to teleport into the Stonestave just to prove that he could, despite the *Faerzress* that now surrounded the city.

Voices murmured inside one of the lecture halls. He glanced into it as he passed and what he saw made him halt abruptly. Zarifar, one of his five apprentices, was staring at a pentagram that had been painted on the floor with dribbled candle wax. His right forefinger jerked back and forth as he traced its outline in the air. With his head bowed, face obscured by a fuzz of tightly kinked white hair, the tall, thin drow seemed oblivious to his inattentive students. He made no move to discipline them as they chatted and chuckled amongst themselves, completely ignoring their would-be instructor.

A moment more, and the half a dozen students probably *would* have something to whisper at. Zarifar might be a brilliant geometer mage, but he was more likely to summon a monstrosity that would devour him than one that would obey him. Or recite the spell backward and send himself straight to the Abyss.

Using his master ring, Q'arlynd linked minds with his apprentice. As he'd expected, Zarifar's thoughts were deep in the pattern. He was imagining pentagrams within pentagrams while calculating the "golden ratio" of each in turn.

Zarifar! Where is Piri? He's supposed to be teaching this lesson.

Zarifar startled, as if someone had just poked the tip of a dagger into his back. Two of the students snickered. Their faces paled to gray as Q'arlynd strode into the room.

"Master Melarn," they gasped, each falling to one knee.

Q'arlynd ignored them—a worse punishment than reprimanding them, since it left them tensely anticipating what might come next. And when. *Where is Piri, Zarifar?*

"Oh. Yes." Zarifar blinked like a surface elf coming out of Reverie. "Down at the Cage, I think he said. He asked me to fill in for him until he got back."

Q'arlynd frowned. If Piri wanted spell components, he should have sent a student to fetch them. That he'd gone himself hinted that whatever he was purchasing was something others weren't meant to learn about. The timing of the trip to the Breeder's Guild was equally suspicious. Piri knew Q'arlynd was about to appear before the Conclave. There was no better moment for treachery.

Q'arlynd's jaw clenched. This wasn't Piri's first betrayal. Q'arlynd had already been forced, once before, to punish him as a result of his disloyalty. A *kiira* had later restored the apprentice to life, in order for the spell that had stripped the death goddess of her name to be cast. Q'arlynd had wanted to dispense with the apprentice afterward, but the ancestors inside the *kiira* had suggested an alternative. They'd promised to strip Piri of those memories that made him dangerous and disloyal, while leaving the bulk of his magical learning intact. Until this moment, Q'arlynd had believed they'd delivered on their promise. The mind-stripped Piri had been both compliant and, seemingly, trustworthy.

Now Q'arlynd wasn't so sure.

"This lesson is over," he announced, waving a hand above the floor. The pentagram disappeared in a puff of smoke, leaving the smell of melted candle wax behind. "Go."

The students scurried from the room.

Q'arlynd closed his eyes and activated his master ring a second time. Piri came instantly into view; the apprentice hadn't bothered to remove his ring. He'd probably assumed Q'arlynd would be much too busy to scry him. Piri stood next to a narrow column of stone: one of the posts in the shimmering walls of force that caged the deepspawn the Breeder's Guild tended. His face and hands glinted with an oily, greenish tinge: the quasit demon, stretched skin-thin, that he'd bonded with, years ago. His hair stood up in stiff spikes, white and hard as bone. He held a wand in one hand, and stood back to back with another of Q'arlynd's apprentices: Eldrinn, son of Master Seldszar, the master who would be nominating Q'arlynd's school for admission to the Conclave in just a few moments' time. Eldrinn also held a wand in his hand.

"Mother's blood," Q'arlynd swore. "They're *dueling.*"

Little wonder his apprentices had chosen this moment for their duel. Q'arlynd had expressly forbidden mage duels in an effort to preserve the fragile harmony within his school. More often than not, duels led to serious injury. Sometimes death.

The injury or death of a student or teacher was something most masters took in their stride. They encouraged backstabbing and betrayal among their apprentices, believing that it flensed the meat from the bone, allowing only the best to survive. Q'arlynd held a different view. Any student accepted into his school was warned that any debilitating attack or suspicious death would be traced to its root. And then that student would be expelled.

The same rules applied to the five apprentices who served as the school's teachers.

Q'arlynd glanced at the water clock in the corner of the lecture hall. He was supposed to be appearing before the Conclave just a few moments from now. He tapped his foot impatiently, inclined to leave bad enough alone—until he noticed the femur that lay on the ground between the two apprentices as a dividing line.

This was no mere grudge match. It was a duel to the death.

Eldrinn had a determined look on his face, but his tight grip on the wand betrayed his tension. He was a mere boy, a half-drow with ash gray skin. He wore his usual spider-silk shirt and ornately embroidered *piwafwi,* but his waist-length hair was unbound. He'd either been tricked or goaded into leaving behind the contingency clip that could save him from whatever Piri's wand hurled at him.

The timing was too coincidental. The absence of seconds and a *jabbuk duello* to oversee the duel was equally telling. Someone must have manipulated Piri or Eldrinn into this. Someone powerful enough to have ensured that Master Seldszar wouldn't divine, ahead of time, that his son was about to enter into a potentially fatal duel.

If Eldrinn died, however—no, *when* Eldrinn died—Seldszar would learn of it immediately. Whoever had maneuvered the two apprentices into this would certainly see to that. Once alerted to his son's death, it would take the master diviner less time to learn the circumstances than it took most males to draw breath. Then Q'arlynd's school would suffer the consequences. Contrary to all that was natural, Seldszar actually cared for his son. He'd blame Q'arlynd for the boy's death—and would point accusingly to Q'arlynd's stubborn insistence on keeping the demon-skinned Piri at his school.

Seldszar would likely revoke his nomination.

Q'arlynd told himself not to panic. Eldrinn was a less experienced wizard than Piri, but he might just get a lucky shot in with his wand after the pair raised defenses.

The water clock dripped. Q'arlynd was due before the Conclave this very moment. He'd have to leave his apprentices to their duel and hope that Eldrinn won.

Just as he was about to end his scrying, however, Piri sneaked a glance down at his belt. Q'arlynd couldn't see anything on the belt but an empty wand scabbard, but he'd learned long ago not to trust his eyes alone. He yanked the master ring off his finger and held it just behind the gem on his pendant, peering through both at the same time. The images he was seeing shrank, now filling the center of the ring, rather than looming large within Q'arlynd's mind. He couldn't make out details, but fortunately the object revealed by the gem's magic was large: a thin iron hoop hanging from Piri's belt. Q'arlynd recognized it at once as half of a ring gate.

The gem also revealed a quasit demon, cloaked by invisibility, that hovered in the air near the spot Eldrinn would wind up in after marching ten paces. Its wings fluttering, a malicious smile on its green-skinned face, the quasit held the second ring gate in one warty hand.

It was instantly clear to Q'arlynd what Piri planned. The demon-skinned apprentice was going to use the ring gates to attack Eldrinn from behind.

"Ten paces," Piri said over his shoulder. "Then turn, cast a single spell, and fire. Agreed?"

Eldrinn nodded. "Agreed."

Q'arlynd gritted his teeth as he pushed the master ring back into place on his finger. Piri had left out one word from the ritual agreement. It should have been "Cast a single *defensive* spell." Eldrinn had just agreed to a change in the rules that would cost him the initiative. Q'arlynd had to do something, and quickly. But what? Sshamath's laws dictated that no outside party could influence the outcome of a duel; those who interfered in a lethal duel could be put to death themselves. But perhaps Q'arlynd could get away with merely *delaying* the duel.

Piri's foot lifted slightly. "Ten—"

With a thought, Q'arlynd activated his ring. Both apprentices froze in place, each with his right foot slightly lifted from the floor.

The water clock dripped. Now Q'arlynd was late.

He teleported.

He'd planned to make a formal entrance, but there was no time for that now. Instead he teleported directly to the heart of the Stonestave, to a spot just inside the great double doors of the Conclave's meeting chamber. Unfortunately, someone was coming through the doors. The edge of a drift-disc crashed into Q'arlynd's back, sending him staggering. He caught himself on the railing that enclosed the speaker's sphere and saw to his dismay that several of the Conclave were frowning at him. Without apologizing for his tardiness or awkward entrance—any excuse he might give would be exploited as a weakness—he bowed to the speaker's sphere: a ball of quicksilver suspended by magic at the center of the circular hall.

He snuck a glance at the driftdisc as he rose. On it was a female he didn't recognize. She was bald and well muscled—not seated cross-legged on the driftdisc as was normal, but crouched on it like a spider waiting to spring. She wore a black, short-sleeved, skin-tight tunic that hugged her torso and thighs, and ended at her knees. Not a single weapon or magical item was visible on her. Even so she exuded an aura of danger.

One of the masters must have invited her to the Conclave. She would never have gotten past its guards and wards otherwise. Q'arlynd wondered what her business here could possibly be. He hoped it could wait until after the vote.

Master Seldszar waved a hand at Q'arlynd. "Masters of the Conclave, I present Q'arlynd Melarn." The Master of Divination beckoned Q'arlynd to stand next to his podium. Q'arlynd strode smoothly to that spot. Seldszar smiled benevolently at Q'arlynd through the crystals orbiting his head, but at the same time his nostrils flared slightly: a reprimand for Q'arlynd's tardiness. In this hall, where all displays of emotion were tightly constrained, it spoke louder than a shout. Aloud, Seldszar said, "As you all know, the reason we have convened is to discuss the promotion of an eleventh school to the rank of College, and the addition of another master to our conclave. As I gave notice in my sending, it now pleases me to nominate Master Q'arlynd's School of Ancient Arcana for elevation to College."

"I second the nomination," Master Urlryn said from across the room.

So far, so good. The Master of the College of Conjuration and Summoning had made good on his promise, and he had good reason to. In return for second-speaking Q'arlynd's nomination, the awarenesses inside the *kiira* on Q'arlynd's forehead would assist Urlryn with an ongoing problem: the *Faerzress* that surrounded the city. It hampered divination and prevented mages from teleporting in and out of the city—something that had caused no end of embarrassment to Urlryn's school.

Urlryn might have the appearance of a slothful indulger, with his heavy jowls and soft, corpulent frame, but the mind behind those heavy-lidded eyes was as sharp as a dagger. He knew which side of the *sava* board to play if he wanted to restore his College to its former standing.

As the female on the driftdisc moved to the podium occupied by Master Guldor, Q'arlynd quickly scried his two apprentices. Piri and Eldrinn were just as he'd left them, frozen back to back. He was thankful that the Cage occupied an infrequently visited corner of Sshamath. With luck, the Conclave's debate would be brief, the vote would carry, and Q'arlynd would be able to teleport away before anyone noticed what he'd done to the duelists. With even more luck, he might talk his apprentices out of killing each other.

As the driftdisc sighed to a stop beside the Master of the College of Mages, Guldor touched the gold ball that hovered in the air in front of him. The speaker's sphere assumed the likeness of his face: a chin as pointed as his ears, and eyes that matched the slant of eyebrows that extended to meet the hair at his temples.

"I too have a school I wish to nominate this day," Guldor said, his voice seeming to come from the animated quicksilver head.

Q'arlynd swore silently. Seldszar had warned him to expect opposition from the College of Mages, but not this. Things *weren't* going to go as quickly as Q'arlynd had hoped. Not if the Conclave had two nominations to consider.

"I present to the Conclave T'lar Mizz'rynturl," Guldor continued. "I nominate her School of *Bae'qeshel* Magic for elevation to College."

Q'arlynd's breath caught in his throat. Years of practice at stifling his reactions allowed him to hide any further reaction. The *bae'qeshel* tradition was extremely rare, with only a handful of practitioners. His sister Halisstra had been one of them.

He took another look at the female on the driftdisc. Had Halisstra known her? The more he looked at T'lar Mizz'rynturl, however, the more he doubted it. Had someone so distinctive visited Ched Nasad, Q'arlynd would have remembered her.

"What's this School of *Bae'qestel* Magic?" Master Antatlab asked, mispronouncing the name. His deep bass rumble reverberated through the floor, up into the soles of Q'arlynd's boots. Even without the benefit of the speaker's sphere's augmentation, it had that effect. The face of the Master of Elemental Magic was as square as a granite block, and just as deeply pitted. "I've never heard of such a school before!"

"Nor have I," said the much quieter voice of Master Seldszar.

"You should pay more attention to cavern clack," another of the masters said. "This past month, the mage halls have been buzzing with rumors that a new school had been founded. Everyone was trying to guess what it might specialize in."

The speaker's sphere shifted back to Master Guldor's sharp-angled face. "The School of *Bae'qeshel* Magic is based on an ancient bardic tradition."

"Bardic magic!" Master Antatlab exploded, pounding his fist on the golden ball in front of his podium. The quicksilver face quivered as if an earthquake were surging through it. "This is a conclave of mages, not minstrels!"

"Our constitution only prohibits *clerical* magic," Master Guldor countered. "It is silent when it comes to the bards' arts. And why? Because the mages who founded the Conclave recognized that bardic magic is a brother to sorcery. Both arts draw their power from the same source: the practitioner's own heart and will."

Q'arlynd cleared his throat softly in an attempt to get Master Seldszar's attention. According to the rules of the Conclave, Q'arlynd was forbidden to speak unless directed to. If only he *could* speak, he could end this, right now, by pointing out the one thing the masters didn't realize. While it was true that *bae'qeshel* was a bardic tradition, it was one that could only be practiced by someone who had taken a particular goddess as her patron deity.

Lolth.

On the surface, Guldor's nomination of T'lar Mizz'rynturl's school looked like nothing more than a means of countering Seldszar's play for an allied eleventh master on the Conclave. Yet Q'arlynd knew it had to have deeper roots than that. Guldor Zauviir shared a House name with the priestess who headed up what remained of Lolth's temple in Sshamath. And there were rumors the ties were knotted even tighter than that. *Streea'Valsharess* Zauviir smoldered like a coal under the heels of the wizards who had ground out her rule in Sshamath. T'lar Mizz'rynturl's "school" was likely the high priestess's attempt to burn the Conclave from within.

If Q'arlynd could only catch Master Seldszar's attention, T'lar's "school" would have as much hope of being accepted into the Conclave as a boy did of becoming matron mother of a noble House. A few quick flicks of Q'arlynd's fingers would do the trick.

Q'arlynd cleared his throat a second time.

Seldszar still didn't acknowledge him.

Another of the masters was speaking. "Guldor does have a point." The speaker's sphere bore a female face now—that of Master Felyndiira, a breathtaking beauty with long-lashed eyes and luxurious hair that swept back from a peak on her forehead. What the Master of Illusion and Phantasm really looked like was anyone's guess. "Bards *are* very similar to sorcerers."

Ah, so Felyndiira was allied with Guldor. Seldszar had wondered if she might be. There were rumors she worshiped the Spider Queen in secret.

Antatlab threw up his hands, not even bothering to touch his golden ball. "So are shadow mages, and you fought their admission to the Conclave dagger and nail!"

Felyndiira rolled her eyes. "The School of Shadow Magic was merely a cloak for Vhaeraun's clerics. Everyone knew it—everyone but *you.*"

Q'arlynd cast a cantrip that plucked at Seldszar's embroidered sleeve, but the Master of Divination paid it no heed. Seldszar reached for the golden ball in front of his podium. As he touched it, the quicksilver face widened, and its eyes darted back and forth in time with Seldszar's own. Even at this critical juncture, his attention was at least partially on his scrying crystals. "This Conclave was convened to consider the nomination of the School of Ancient Arcana, a nomination that has already been second-spoken," he said with a nod at Master Urlryn. "Since no second has spoken for the so-called 'school' Guldor has nominated, I suggest we focus on the task at hand and not be distracted by frivolous—"

"I second the nomination of the School of *Bae'qeshel* Magic." The sphere's features shifted, adopting the face of the only other female among the ten masters. Shurdriira Helviiryn, Master of the College of Alteration stared at Seldszar and arched an eyebrow, as if daring him to protest her second.

The speaker's sphere shifted to a gaunt male face with hungry eyes. "The nomination has been second-spoken," it said in a paper-thin whisper that filled the chamber—the voice of Tsabrak, Master of the College of Necromancy. The vampire drow's real face was little more than a shadow, lost in the hood of his bone white robe. "Two nominations stand. Let the debate begin."

One by one, the masters stated their arguments and counter-arguments. Warily, they fenced back and forth. Q'arlynd could imagine the unspoken calculations that must be whirling through their heads. Support one nomination? Both? What was to be gained—and lost—by building or breaking alliances? Was it better to speak first, or hold back until others declared themselves?

With this second, more complicated nomination to consider, the debate might go on for a full cycle. Or more.

Q'arlynd snuck another look at his apprentices. They were still frozen in place next to the shimmering wall of force. Behind it, one of the tentacled deepspawn the Breeder's Guild raised stared hungrily out at the two duelists.

Then Q'arlynd noticed something that chilled his gut like ice water. A crack had just appeared in the wall of force, next to the duelists. A crack that was widening.

There could be only one explanation for the rupture in what was otherwise a carefully tended wall. Someone must have spotted the two frozen duelists and decided to weaken Q'arlynd's school by ensuring the "accidental" deaths of two of its apprentices.

Q'arlynd couldn't wait for the debate to end. The second nomination had to be made null and void. Now.

He gripped the railing in front of him and took a deep breath. The moment there was a gap in the debate, he spoke. "I realize none but a master is permitted to speak, but there's something you must hear!" he said in a loud, clear voice. *"Bae'qeshel* magic is—"

Suddenly, Q'arlynd couldn't move. A sphere of glass, surrounded by solid stone, enclosed him.

A magical imprisonment! The favorite tactic, it was rumored, of Master Masoj—who supposedly was in full support of Q'arlynd's nomination. Q'arlynd hadn't felt the Master of Abjuration touch him—hadn't felt anyone touch him, for that matter. Yet the spell had been cast anyway.

Q'arlynd was trapped like a fly in amber. He couldn't cast spells, couldn't escape. He might never see Sshamath again, let alone realize his dream of being elevated to the Conclave.

He realized he'd been both hasty and stupid. Arrogant enough to think the Conclave would listen to him, that the masters wouldn't punish him for breaking protocol. Of all the things Q'arlynd had ever done, this had been among the most foolish.

He might be trapped, but there was one course of action open to him: thanks to his master ring, he could still scry. He refocused his attention on his apprentices. He might as well twist the dagger in deeper by watching Eldrinn die.

Via the scrying, he watched as Piri and Eldrinn unfroze. Neither noticed the crack spreading through the wall of force. Each glanced suspiciously at the other, then down at the ring on his finger. No feeblewits, they. Not like their master. They had figured out what had just happened, and what to do about it. With jerky motions, fighting the compulsions Q'arlynd had built into their rings, both Piri and Eldrinn tugged them from their fingers. They shouldn't have been able to do that. In ordinary circumstances, Q'arlynd would have wondered what magic was used to counter the rings' hold on their minds. But this was hardly the time to ponder such trivial betrayals.

No! Q'arlynd silently raged. It's not me you have to be worried about. It's—

The scrying ended.

Time passed.

Had Q'arlynd's heart been beating, he might have measured time by it.

Suddenly, he was back inside the Stonestave's central chamber, facing the Conclave once more. He immediately dropped to one knee and turned his head, exposing his throat. "My profound apologies, masters. I bow to your . . ."

He noticed something: a golden ball, hovering in the air just ahead of him. He glanced up and saw all ten masters staring at him. Nine of them had golden balls hovering in the air in front of them; Master Seldszar did not. He'd temporarily forfeited his right to a voice on the Conclave, so Q'arlynd might say his piece.

The speaker's sphere bore Master Tsabrak's visage. The vampire drow's voice whispered out of it. "Rise, Q'arlynd. Finish what you started to say earlier."

Q'arlynd rose to his feet and nodded his thanks to Seldszar. Q'arlynd was certain he'd pay for this later—pay dearly— but he was glad to have been given a second chance. He turned to face the female he was about to accuse. She stared back at him from her perch on the driftdisc—a flat, level stare that held a promise of retribution for whatever he was about to say.

Q'arlynd couldn't worry about that now. Nor could he let himself be distracted by speculating how much time had passed while he'd been imprisoned, and whether one or both of his apprentices were dead. He would keep this short and to the point. He touched the golden ball.

"*Bae'qeshel* is a bardic tradition, it's true," he told the Conclave, his eyes still locked on those of the female on the driftdisc, returning her challenge. "But it is only practiced by members of a particular faith—by those who worship Lolth."

T'lar didn't flinch. Didn't even blink. Someone else in the room must have, though. Q'arlynd heard more than one sharp intake of breath.

Guldor was the first to touch his golden ball. "How can you make such accusations? You know nothing of *bae'qeshel* magic!"

"My sister was a *bae'qeshel* bard."

Guldor was good: his face didn't even flush. "You lie."

"A simple divination will prove that I do not," Q'arlynd said quietly. He waited a moment or two—long enough for any of the masters who had a spell that would detect falsehoods to cast it. "My sister, Halisstra Melarn, was a *bae'qeshel* bard. She was also a devotee of Lolth. You cannot be the first, without the second. Something you were no doubt privy to, Guldor Zauviir."

The sphere assumed Master Shurdriira's face. "I withdraw my second."

For several moments, there was silence in the chamber. Then Master Tsabrak spoke. "T'lar Mizz'rynturl, leave us."

Never once taking her eyes off Q'arlynd, T'lar moved back. Instead of the anger Q'arlynd expected, T'lar looked as if she were appraising him—sizing him up. The doors to the chamber opened silently, and the driftdisc slid out, whisking her away.

Guldor's face was purple with barely suppressed rage, but he rallied quickly. "Q'arlynd Melarn," he said in a soft voice. "Do *you* worship the Spider Queen?"

Q'arlynd answered warily, aware that whatever divinations the masters might have cast earlier would still be detecting falsehoods. "I was raised to follow Lolth—as are all drow. But I never formally pledged myself to her."

Guldor smiled. "Because you worship Eilistraee?"

Q'arlynd's eyes narrowed slightly before he could prevent it. He was on dangerous ground, here. Eilistraee's worship was not forbidden in Sshamath—the Conclave officially permitted all faiths—but her worship was still a quick way to make enemies, among those masters who had, secretly, taken the Spider Queen as their patron deity.

One thing was in his favor, however. Guldor had to be guessing. If not, he would have phrased that last as a statement, rather than a question.

"Only females are welcomed into Eilistraee's circle," Q'arlynd answered. He arched an eyebrow. "Surely you don't mistake me for one?"

"Males can become lay worshipers."

Q'arlynd waved a hand dismissively—the hand that *didn't* bear Eilistraee's crescent-shaped scar. He turned away from Guldor. "He's grasping at spider silk," he told the other masters, feigning a lighthearted tone he didn't feel. "Appropriate, considering the company he keeps."

Someone chuckled.

Out of the corner of his eye, Q'arlynd watched Guldor. The master's lips were pressed tightly together. Guldor would have anticipated that his nomination of T'lar Mizz'rynturl might fail, but he hadn't expected to be mocked. Q'arlynd had just made a lasting enemy of the master of a very powerful College.

The face on the sphere grew fatter, more jowly. "Now that only one nomination remains to be considered," Master Urlryn said, "Why don't you tell us, Q'arlynd, why the School of Ancient Arcana should be named a College."

That was better. Things were back on track. And Eldrinn couldn't have been dead yet—if he had been, Master Seldszar wouldn't have looked so unperturbed. Though gods only knew what was happening, down at the Cage.

"The reason is simple," Q'arlynd began. He followed the speech he'd rehearsed with Seldszar earlier, down to the last syllable. "Accept my school as Sshamath's eleventh College, and your city will reap the rewards. To the city itself, my College can provide powerful magic: spells that have been forgotten since the time of the Descent, spells that have been revealed to me by . . . this."

He pointed to his forehead with a flourish, and dropped the invisibility that had been hiding the lorestone. A corresponding bulge appeared on the forehead of the face on the speaker's sphere. "Only a few of you will have seen its like before," he told the masters. "It's a *selu'kiira* of ancient Miyeritar."

Eyes widened. The masters must have noted the lorestone's deep color.

Q'arlynd held up a cautioning finger. "Lest any of you think of claiming it, I offer this warning. The lorestone will only share its secrets with a descendant of House Melarn—and I am the last surviving member of that noble House. Everyone else, from its matron mother to the lowest boy, lies buried in the rubble of Ched Nasad. Anyone else who attempts to wear House Melarn's lorestone will wind up feebleminded."

Heads nodded slightly at that. All remembered the state Eldrinn had been in, when Q'arlynd had returned the boy to the city two and a half years ago. The connection was obvious.

His speech concluded, Q'arlynd fell silent. There was a further incentive for certain masters, but it couldn't be spoken aloud. Master Seldszar had spent the last year carefully tracing the lineage of each of the current masters of Sshamath's Colleges. Two other masters, besides Seldszar, could trace their lineage back to ancient Miyeritar. Like him, each might be able to claim a *kiira* from Kraanfhaor's Door, so long as he was shown how—something that wouldn't happen until the College of Ancient Arcana became a reality. Neither of the two masters would know for certain whether anyone else had been promised a *selu'kiira*. Each would do whatever he could to influence the rest of the Conclave, in order to claim his reward.

"A pretty promise," Master Shurdriira said. She tipped her head. "But how do we know you will share this magic?"

Q'arlynd smiled. "I have already." He watched as that sunk in—as the masters glanced covertly at one another, wondering who had already benefited. Then he added, "Do you dare run the risk of being the only one without access to my spells?"

Master Seldszar flicked his fingers: *My ball.*

Q'arlynd inclined his head, then nudged the gold ball to Seldszar. The Master of Divination touched it, and the speaker's sphere assumed his likeness. "I suggest we end this debate and put the nomination to a vote."

"Agreed," Urlryn said.

"Agreed," Tsabrak echoed.

One by one—with the exception of Guldor, who remained sullenly silent—the other masters gave their assent.

Tsabrak spoke. "Q'arlynd Melarn, leave us."

Q'arlynd bowed. Even before he'd finished rising, he teleported away.

He appeared straddling the femur that was the dividing line, his hands raised and ready to cast a spell. Piri lay on the ground a few paces away, either unconscious or dead, his wand beside him. Eldrinn was in even more dire straights.

The deepspawn had already squeezed three of its six tentacles through the gap in the wall of force. One was wrapped around the boy's chest, and held him dangling above the ground. Though Eldrinn still held his wand, he was either too frightened or too badly hurt to use it. His eyes widened as he spotted Q'arlynd, and his mouth worked, but no words came out. Judging by his purple face, there wasn't any air left in his lungs.

Q'arlynd conjured lightning. He aimed for the base of the tentacle that held Eldrinn, but the monster was unaccountably fast. It yanked that tentacle—and Eldrinn with it—back behind what remained of the wall of force. The magical barrier absorbed the eye-searing bolt.

"Mother's blood," Q'arlynd swore. This monster was a fast one.

Suddenly he recalled what his masters at the Conservatory had taught him about these creatures, so many years ago: deepspawn were capable of listening in on thoughts. For someone who could cast spells to shield his mind, this wasn't a problem. But Q'arlynd had trained as a battle mage. He had dozens of lethal spells at his fingertips, still more that would shield his body. But none that would hide the contents of his mind.

The deepspawn retreated fully behind the wall of force. It waved a tentacle at Q'arlynd, taunting him. The other two tentacles continued to cling tightly to Eldrinn and to something invisible: Piri's quasit. Even as Q'arlynd watched, Eldrinn stopped struggling, and slumped. His wand fell from his fingers and clattered to the ground.

Q'arlynd had to think of something, and quickly. If he didn't, the deepspawn would kill Eldrinn—assuming it hadn't already done so. And now that the monster had withdrawn behind the walls of its cage, Q'arlynd would only be able to target it through the hole. He edged to the side, trying to get into position to do that, but the deepspawn read his mind and moved away.

Come out from behind the wall, coward, he thought at it. *Let's see if you can catch a lightning bolt in your tentacles.*

Q'arlynd moved to the spot where his other apprentice lay, bent down, and touched his fingers to Piri's throat. Blood pulsed beneath the skin. Piri, at least, was still alive. As Q'arlynd straightened, his foot nudged something that scraped across the ground. Something metal. He looked down, but didn't see anything there.

Then he realized what it must be: Piri's ring gate!

Q'arlynd hurled himself at the ground. As he did so, the tentacle holding the quasit flicked forward, trying to toss the demon away. This time, Q'arlynd was faster. Before the deepspawn could release the quasit, Q'arlynd landed, chest down, on the spot where the ring gate lay. As he made contact with it, he shouted an incantation. The mirror in his shirt pocket shattered, fueling his spell. Energy rushed out of it, as fast as light. It erupted out of the second ring gate, into the deepspawn. Intense silver light played over the tentacled monster, altering the very substance of its body. When the light vanished, so too did the creature's natural coloration. A heartbeat before, the deepspawn had been a living, breathing thing. Now it was transformed into clear, solid glass.

Its body, no longer suspended by magic, crashed to the ground. Tentacles shattered.

Q'arlynd stood and brushed himself off. Tinkling bits of mirror fell from the ruin of his shirt pocket. "Bet you didn't expect that one," he said dryly. Then he hurried forward. He stepped carefully through the rent in the wall of force and felt its powerful energies lift the hair on his arms and scalp. When he was underneath the transformed deepspawn, he reached up and grabbed the tentacle that held Eldrinn, and wrenched on it. As it snapped, the boy tumbled to the ground. Eldrinn groaned, low and deep—a sound that was music to Q'arlynd's ears. The boy was still alive!

Q'arlynd scooped up Eldrinn's wand. It was of a type he didn't recognize: solid white, with an inscription in Espruar, the script of the surface elves, spiraling around it. Q'arlynd didn't have time to solve the puzzle the wand presented, however. In a few moments his spell would lapse, and the deepspawn would revert back to flesh. Even missing its tentacles, it would be a formidable foe.

He touched Eldrinn and teleported away.

They materialized within the private hospice of the College of Divination. Q'arlynd barked out an abbreviated explanation to the startled attendant. Instead of springing to his cabinet of potions, however, the elderly apothecary shifted Eldrinn's sleeve, revealing a vial that was tied to the boy's forearm. "Why didn't you use this?" He yanked out the vial and uncorked it. "It's just as potent as anything I have here."

"It is?"

"I ought to know. It's one of my best."

Q'arlynd shook his head at yet another mystery he didn't have time to solve. Eldrinn had obviously been given the potion by the apothecary, but how had the boy expected to consume it in the middle of a duel?

"Is there more of that?" Q'arlynd asked.

The apothecary nodded at his cabinet as he parted Eldrinn's lips and dribbled the potion into the boy's mouth. "In there. Why?"

"Get it ready," Q'arlynd said. "There's another of my apprentices who might need it, once I've finished with him." Then he teleported away.

He returned to the Cage in time to see a member of the Breeder's Guild rushing to the spot where the wall of force had been breached. The fellow skidded to a halt, reached into a pouch at his hip, and held up a pinch of something. Crushed gemstone dusted his dark fingers. He hurled the dust at the breach in the wall and chanted an incantation—but abruptly halted when he noticed the transformed deepspawn, its clear glass body all but invisible behind the shimmering wall.

"Hey! What did you do to our breeding stock?"

"A transmutation," Q'arlynd shouted back. "I suggest you complete your spell. The transmutation's only temporary."

The guild member hesitated, as if wanting to challenge Q'arlynd further, but decided against it. He waved his hands and chanted, hurriedly completing his repair.

Q'arlynd picked up Piri's wand, touched his apprentice, and teleported away. This time, the destination was his private study. He'd have to placate the Breeder's Guild—they'd demand compensation for the damage to their deepspawn— but that could wait. He patted down Piri's pockets, looking for the ring the apprentice had removed earlier. He found it—the compulsion built into the rings was too strong for his apprentices to rid themselves of the rings entirely—and slipped the ring into his own pocket. As he waited for Piri to recover, he examined the apprentice's wand. It was made of ebony, inlaid with chips of red agate: a fire wand. A wise choice for a duel, given Piri's demon skin. If the wand's blast had been deflected back at Piri, the fire would have sloughed off his body like water off a slate roof.

Eventually, Piri groaned and rolled onto his back. His eyes opened, then widened as he took in his surroundings—and the fact that Q'arlynd was pointing Eldrinn's wand at him. Suddenly, they blazed red as forge-heated steel. Twin beams of red streaked out of Piri's eyes at Q'arlynd—only to bounce off the magical protection Q'arlynd already had in place. The heat beams ricocheted off the master's magical shield and scored deep burn marks on the ceiling instead.

Q'arlynd stared down the length of slim white wood at his apprentice. "I don't know what this wand does," he told Piri. "But I'm curious to find out. How about you?"

Piri shook his head. Though his green-tinged face seemed devoid of expression, his wide eyes gave him away. He was afraid of the wand in Q'arlynd's hand. Deathly afraid.

Q'arlynd dug Piri's ring out of his pocket and held it where the apprentice could see it. "Let's have a talk. Mind to mind. I want to know why you and Eldrinn were dueling. Let me look into your thoughts, then maybe I won't use this wand on you."

"No!" Piri blurted. But at the same time, his fingers twitched. *Do it.*

Q'arlynd forced the ring onto Piri's finger, then shoved his way into the apprentice's mind. What he found there made him nod. Piri's thoughts weren't the only ones fluttering through the apprentice's brain. Q'arlynd detected a second presence in there, one that spoke in a high, tittering voice.

The quasit demon Piri had bonded with hadn't been content to remain inside the skin the apprentice now wore. It was also whispering around inside Piri's skull. Piri was either listening to it—or being controlled by it. Thanks to the ring, Q'arlynd could read its thoughts.

The quasit had goaded Piri into seducing Alexa, the only female among Q'arlynd's five apprentices. The demon had also ensured that Eldrinn, her consort, learned of the tryst. Despite his anger, Eldrinn wasn't stupid enough to have challenged Piri; it had been the other way around. In the end, Eldrinn had been forced to accept the challenge. To have done anything else would have meant forever being subservient to the other apprentice.

The demon's motivation in all this was simple—and simple-minded. Power shared between four apprentices was better than power shared between five. It had hoped to eliminate Q'arlynd's apprentices, one by one, and thus claw its way to the top.

Even now, Piri was struggling against the demon's influence—and failing. He'd rallied enough to agree to wear the ring, but was suffering for it now, as the quasit flayed his mind from within.

And why not? The quasit had nothing to lose. Not now. Q'arlynd knew, by reading its thoughts, which wand Eldrinn had selected for the duel. A wand of banishment, created by a moon elf cleric. A wand capable of sending the quasit back to the Abyss.

Eldrinn had been clever. Flensed of the demon skin, Piri would suffer greatly. Perhaps even die. But there was healing magic that would enable him to live—the magic within the vial Eldrinn had carried. Eldrinn had gambled that he'd be quick enough, and lucky enough, to preserve Piri's life after killing his real foe in the duel: the demon.

From the floor, the apprentice glared up at Q'arlynd with demon red eyes. His lip twitched in a snarl. "I'll have my revenge," the quasit said aloud, forcing Piri's voice into a high, brittle twang.

"I don't think so," Q'arlynd said. He took a deep breath. He didn't want to do this, but he had to. Even if it killed Piri.

Q'arlynd retreated from Piri's mind and activated the wand.

Piri screamed—his own voice, this time—as the demon skin wrenched itself from his body. Blood seeped from Piri's body as fat, muscles, and ligaments were suddenly exposed. Q'arlynd leaned forward to teleport Piri to the apothecary, but before he could touch him the apprentice's body disappeared. Q'arlynd's fingers brushed blood-soaked carpet instead of weeping flesh.

Q'arlynd started. Had the quasit yanked Piri into the Abyss after it?

He attempted to scry his apprentice, but when he tried to call a vision through the ring, none came. Where was Piri? Even if the apprentice were dead, Q'arlynd should have been able to scry him—unless the ring had been removed from Piri's finger.

Q'arlynd closed his eyes and sent his awareness into the lorestone. *Ancestors,* he asked. *Is there any other way I might find him?* A chorus of voices answered from within the *kiira*. None held out any hope.

Perhaps he could ask Master Seldszar to attempt a scrying. But then he discarded the notion. Even if he tele-ported to the Conclave's chamber this instant and somehow managed to convey what he needed without mentioning the duel and raising Seldszar's ire, it would probably already be too late.

Piri would, most likely, already be dead.

Q'arlynd stared at the blood-soaked carpet a moment longer, then sighed. There had been no way to predict what had just happened, he told himself. He'd done everything he could to save his apprentice. The guilt he felt was a sign of weakness.

Something a master of a College couldn't afford.

Not weakness, a female voice whispered from the lorestone. *Compassion.* Q'arlynd gave a mental shove, forcing his ancestor away. Sometimes the lorestone felt a little too close for comfort. Especially after what he'd just seen in Piri's mind.

He walked to the cabinet, opened a drawer, and placed Eldrinn's wand inside it. As he closed the drawer, a voice whispered into his ear. "Congratulations, Master Q'arlynd. The College of Ancient Arcana is officially recognized."

It was Seldszar, communicating by magic. The diviner's voice sounded clearly in the room. He was no doubt scrying on Q'arlynd and casting the spell through a font. This, despite the study's magical protections. It had to be a deliberate intrusion, designed to remind Q'arlynd who the more powerful mage was.

"My thanks," Q'arlynd answered. Steeling himself, he prepared to tell Seldszar about the duel. "Your son—"

"Yes. The duel," the voice answered. "I just learned of it. I'll take my pound of flesh from you later, for permitting Eldrinn to indulge in such foolishness. But just now, there's work to be done. Urlryn demands a solution to the problem of the *Faerzress.*" He paused. "As do I."

Q'arlynd bowed. "You'll have your solution," he promised. It was the truth—or at least, true enough to have passed any other divination Seldszar might have just cast. The memories of Q'arlynd's ancestors, stored all these centuries within the *kiira,* did indeed hold the key to severing the bond that high magic had wrought between the drow and *Faerzress*. His ancestors not only knew what spells had been cast, but how to undo them.

The only thing they didn't know was precisely where those spells had to be cast, in order for the bond to be undone. Nor had Seldszar's divinations been able to solve the problem. But with luck—and the aid of a shipment that was on its way to Q'arlynd, even now, from distant Silverymoon—they would uncover that missing puzzle piece.

Q'arlynd hoped he was right. If he failed to deliver, Seldszar wasn't going to be happy with him.

CHAPTER 5

Cavatina gaped at the strange landscape the portal had transported her to. It was as if she'd stepped into the heart of a huge mound of rubble. All around her, jagged pieces of gray stone crowded close on every side—except that the "stone" was blurred and indistinct, and had no substance. When she swept her sword in front of her, the blade passed right through the stones, and when she took a step forward she slid through the rubble like a ghost.

Was she a ghost? She didn't think so. Whatever this place was, it didn't look a thing like the Fugue Plane. Nor could she hear Eilistraee's welcoming song.

A curtain of bright silver shimmered behind her. It was about the size of a door and folded in a **V** that corresponded to the corner of the room she'd just stepped from. She touched it, and felt a crackling energy that slowed her fingers until it felt as if they were pressing on solid stone. The same thing occurred when she reached around the edge of the curtain and touched it from the other side. It appeared the portal only worked in one direction: from the Promenade to . . . here.

She glanced at her feet, and saw that she "stood" inside a chunk of stone. She felt a flat surface under the soles of her boots—one that remained constant even when she lifted a foot and placed it on the edge of a rock. She couldn't feel the sharp edge of the stone, but she could step up "onto" it. And though she sensed which way "down" was, she couldn't *feel* it. When she leaned forward, it felt as if she still stood upright. Leaning backward produced the same result. Before she could stop herself, she was perpendicular to the silver curtain, which now hung above her head. Even so, she still felt a flat, solid surface beneath her feet. Dizzy and disoriented, she scrambled "upright" again.

What *was* this place?

She breathed—rapidly, due to her exertions. At least she was still alive. Her body felt solid enough. She slapped a hand against her breastplate and heard the thud it made—though the sound came to her ears an instant later than it should have. She could also hear the low hum of her singing sword. Her movements, however, seemed slow to her eyes. Every motion took twice as long as it should have. Yet she felt no impediment. Though she stood entombed in hundreds of chunks of broken stone, it wasn't these that slowed her down. When she stuck her fingers into a gap between the stones and wriggled them, they moved just as slowly as they did within the middle of a block of stone.

Short of dying and becoming a ghost—something she was certain hadn't happened—she knew of only one way to move through objects: by being rendered ethereal. She was loath to leave the portal, but standing next to it and staring wasn't going to tell her where she was—or how to get back to the Promenade. Still, it was her only landmark. She decided to keep the portal at her back, to move in a straight line away from it. She'd go as far as she could without losing sight of the V-shaped silver curtain, then repeat the process in a different direction if the first search proved fruitless.

She walked away cautiously, sword at the ready. It was difficult not to flinch as she moved through what appeared to be a wall of jagged rubble. Each time her head seemed about to strike a rock, she half-turned away. Eventually, she adjusted to the odd sensation of passing through objects that only looked solid—objects she couldn't touch or feel.

At about the thirty-pace mark, the portal behind her all but vanished. All she could see of it was the faintest shimmer of silver amid a gray blur of jumbled stone. About the same distance ahead of her, slightly lower than the spot where she "stood," she saw a dark purple shape. She couldn't make it out entirely—like everything else in this place, it looked as though it lay behind a pane of frosted clearstone—but it had the general shape of a broken column. A piece of masonry that might have once been the column's capitol lay nearby.

She glanced behind her. If she kept going, she might never find her way back to the portal. Then she realized how useless it was to her. She might as well leave it behind. The ruined column, on the other hand, might offer a clue as to where she was.

As she moved closer, she saw that the column had been carved from mottled purple stone. Other smashed pieces of column lay nearby, resting on a slab of the same purple rock that must once have been their foundation.

This was the ruin of an ancient building. One that appeared to have been smashed to pieces by a rockfall.

Carefully, she noted the shape and orientation of the broken column. She moved from it to the next closest chunk of the building, and then to the next. She'd expected the smashed building to be rectangular or circular, but the foundation slab had an irregular shape, with bulges around its circumference. The placement of the columns, judging by what remained of their bases, had been equally random. Even the columns looked odd. They weren't smooth cylinders, but tapered and bulged along their length, as if the masons hadn't been able to decide which thickness to make them. She tried to touch one, but her hand passed through it.

Some of the columns had inscriptions on them: lines of text chiseled here and there like random graffiti. Cavatina peered closely at these but couldn't read them. No matter how hard she stared, the writing wouldn't come into focus. It blurred just enough to render it indecipherable. She tried to trace a line of it with her finger, but couldn't feel the outline. She might as well have been touching a wisp of shifting smoke.

During her investigation, her body had drifted upward. She was high enough to see that the foundation of the building was carved with an enormous symbol. It took a moment to puzzle it out, as the lines were interrupted where the slab had shattered, and partially obscured by the fallen columns. But eventually she realized it was a triangle with a **Y**-shape superimposed on it.

She shivered. That ancient symbol hadn't been used in millennia. It had long since been replaced by the more common eye-within-double-circle. Yet Cavatina, like all of the Promenade's priestesses, had been taught to recognize it.

The symbol of Ghaunadaur.

Cavatina knew, now, where the portal had delivered her: to a spot far below the Promenade. This was the temple that had lain in ruins for nearly six centuries, ever since Qilué and her childhood companions had defeated the Ancient One's avatar. They'd driven it from the caverns that became the Promenade, consigning it to a deep shaft that had then been filled in with rubble and sealed with magic.

A shaft that led to the god's domain.

"By all that dances!" she whispered. "I'm in the Pit!"

A moment later, a burst of bright purple light pulsed from the **Y**-shaped symbol, banishing shadows from the cracks in the broken stones covering the slab. With it came a sensation: It was as if something wet and slippery had just fouled Cavatina's skin.

"Eilistraee, protect me!" she sang. "Shield me from the Ancient One!"

Eilistraee's moonlight shone out from Cavatina's pores, evaporating the slime, turning it to flakes of shadow that exploded from her body. The purple light was waning now, but even so, Cavatina backed away. Her sword pealed out a warning as something momentarily blocked the fading glow. Blinking away the spots from her eyes, Cavatina saw a tarry black blob atop the foundation slab. The ooze was faster than Cavatina. Before she could withdraw farther, it squeezed upward through cracks in the rubble and brushed against her weapon. She yanked her sword back—in what felt like slow motion—and was relieved to see that the blade was still whole. Though the ooze had "touched" it, the acid had failed to dissolve the metal.

Ignoring her, the ooze continued upward through the gaps in the rubble.

Realizing it was escaping, Cavatina sang a prayer that called down Eilistraee's wrath. Shadow-streaked moonlight punched down in a shaft all around her, throwing the tarry black ooze into sharp relief. The light should have reduced the ooze to a smoldering puddle. But the creature slithered on as before, as though it hadn't even noticed the attack.

Cavatina laboriously followed. She readied a second spell, but by the time it was ready, the ooze had flowed beyond the limits of her vision. Normally she would have been able to run twice as fast as an ooze could slither. But with her body rendered ethereal, Cavatina moved with an agonizing lassitude. Her voice was slow and deep, her hymns dirgelike. The heartbeat that pounded in her ears had a lethargic cadence.

Eilistraee's purpose in guiding her to this place was now clear. That burst of purple light had been a planar breach. A temporary one, brief as a flicker, but it had lasted long enough for one of Ghaunadaur's minions to squeeze through, into the Prime Material Plane.

Cavatina could guess, now, why Wendonai had tricked Qilué into inscribing a symbol that would draw Ghaunadaur's drow worshipers to this spot. Through their prayers, the planar breach could be wrenched wide open—something that would allow Ghaunadaur's avatar to pass through it.

Qilué must have known that a planar breach existed here. On all of Toril, it was the most likely of places for one to occur. What could Wendonai possibly have said to convince her that ushering Ghaunadaur's worshipers to this spot would pose no danger?

She tried to imagine the arguments he might have posed. Perhaps he'd convinced Qilué that Ghaunadaur's avatar would be no match for her. She'd defeated it once before, after all. Or perhaps he'd told her that the slime god itself would come through the breach—that armed with the Crescent Blade she stood a chance of killing Ghaunadaur.

That argument, of course, was as thin as rotted cloth. The Crescent Blade's blessings specifically enabled it to kill by decapitation, and Ghaunadaur was a shapeless mass without a neck or a head. But perhaps Qilué was so deeply in the demon's thrall that she wouldn't think of this.

Whatever the demon might be whispering in the high priestess's ear was a puzzle Cavatina couldn't solve just now. What she could do, however, was inspect the seals on the Pit to ensure that whatever oozes slipped through the flickering breach weren't a threat to the Promenade.

Chasing after the black ooze had left Cavatina with no clear sense of which way was up Fortunately, there was a way to figure this out. She chose a direction at random and moved until the rubble ended. Beyond it was a wall of stone that had been fused to a glassy sheen by the outpouring of silver fire Qilué had used to drive Ghaunadaur's avatar down the Pit. Turning her body so that this wall became "down," she walked along it.

After what seemed an eternity, her head bumped against what felt like a solid surface: the magical barrier that capped the Pit. It shone with a bright silver glow, blocking her way. The Promenade, she was thankful to see, was still safe from an incursion from below—by material and ethereal creatures alike.

She sang the hymn that would allow a priestess to enter the Promenade, and felt the barrier above her soften just enough to let her pass. She pushed her way up through it, into the cavern above.

Everything looked exactly as it should have. The floor was the usual smooth, raked field of stone chips, and the statue of Eilistraee was intact. Made up of tiny chips of stone, it stood on tiptoe with arms extended overhead, forefingers and thumbs touching. It moved, almost imperceptibly, in a dance that kept time with the passage of the moon through the skies of the World Above.

A Protector stood guard at the bottom of the secret staircase that wound down to this cavern. Slowly, Cavatina moved toward her, and the female's face gradually came into focus. It was Zindira, one of the priestesses who had accompanied Cavatina on the expedition to the Acropolis of the death goddess, more than a year ago. Cavatina waved a hand in front of Zindira's face, but the other priestess showed no sign of realizing she was there.

"Zindira!" Cavatina shouted, this time passing her hand back and forth through the Protector's body. "There's a planar breach at the bottom of the Pit!"

Zindira shivered. She drew her sword and glanced around.

"Yes!" Cavatina cried. "I'm here. Can you hear me, Zindira?"

A moment later Zindira shrugged and resumed her sentry's pose. She did, however, continue to grip her softly humming sword. As Cavatina shouted again, the volume of the hum rose slightly. Zindira glanced at the weapon.

Struck by sudden inspiration, Cavatina switched from shouting to singing. The sword hummed in time, harmonizing with her melody. By spacing out her words, she could make the sword's song wax and wane. She sang a battle hymn—a strident call to action. Though the song was drastically slowed, and without words, Zindira listened carefully to it. She glanced back up the staircase as if debating whether to leave her post, then seemed to change her mind and sang a quiet evocation. "Rylla, it's Zindira. Something strange is happening at the Mound. My sword is singing a warning."

Cavatina breathed a sigh of relief. Her warning had been received, if not completely understood. It was the best she could do for now.

Rylla hurried down the stairs a few moments later. Cavatina resumed her song. The battle-mistress listened to the sword, then nodded. She glanced around, then strode over to the Mound and inspected it.

"Yes!" Cavatina breathed. "That's exactly what I wanted you to do." When Rylla sang a trueseeing and stared intently at the statue, Cavatina tried to move to a spot where the battle-mistress could see her, but she was too slow. Rylla's survey of the room just missed her.

"I see nothing amiss," the battle-mistress told Zindira. "Resume your post. Be watchful. After that scare with the dretch, we can't take chances."

Zindira saluted the battle-mistress and moved back into position at the bottom of the staircase. Rylla departed up the stairs.

Cavatina clenched her jaw in frustration. Unless she could find a way to render herself material once more, she'd never be able to warn the others about what was happening below. She briefly considered following Rylla—trying to make her understand—then decided that she probably wouldn't have much luck.

She could, however, find out where that ooze had gone.

With her sword balanced on her shoulder, she climbed down through the rubble.

This time, she scrutinized the walls of the shaft more carefully. The stone was smooth for most of its length; the cracks were in the lowest section of the Pit, far below the level of the Promenade. Here, she found numerous places where an ooze or a slime might escape.

She entered the cracked wall and saw a shimmering wall of emerald green light a short distance ahead. At first, she thought it was just a passing ripple of *Faerzress,* then she realized it was holding steady. Another portal? With rising excitement she moved to it—only to bump into a barrier that felt as solid as stone. It appeared to be a magical ward, capable of keeping ethereal creatures at bay.

The green glow extended far above and below her, and for some distance on either side. Like the stone, it had numerous cracks, wide enough to admit an ooze, but too narrow for Cavatina to pass through. She forced herself against the barrier, hoping it would give way, but it didn't.

She pressed her eye to one of the cracks and peered inside. She saw a natural stone cavern with cracks in its walls, floor, and ceiling. The black ooze was inside the cave, slithering toward a score of other creatures: slugs, oozes, and slimes of varying hues. They sat, quivering, at the center of the room, as if waiting for something.

Several tunnels led away from the cavern. Cavatina spotted movement inside one of these: a figure walking toward the main cavern with smooth, flowing steps. It turned out to be a naked drow—an exquisitely beautiful male with eyes of a shade Cavatina had never seen before: pale green, like a newly budded leaf. The odd-looking drow moved without hesitation to the oozes, slimes, and slugs. He halted, his arms raised. As Cavatina watched, horrified, the creatures swarmed him, flowing over the drow in layers like quivering blankets. When they parted again, the drow was gone. Not even a smear remained.

"Self-sacrifice," Cavatina whispered. Had the drow been drugged? Compelled by an enchantment to offer himself to the creatures? Or had he been one of Ghaunadaur's followers, going willingly into the maws of the slime god's minions? She'd heard the fanatics sometimes did that. She shook her head in disgust.

Cavatina decided to see where the drow had come from. She made her way around the edge of the cavern to the tunnel he'd just come through. The magical barrier surrounded that tunnel, too. Like the cavern, the tunnel had numerous cracks in it—cracks that extended to the magical barrier. She worked her way around the tunnel, looking for a gap large enough to pass through. There wasn't one. She expanded her search. The magical barrier, she learned, enclosed an enormous space—an area that might be almost as large as the Promenade itself.

By pressing herself against the shimmering green glow here and there and peering through cracks, Cavatina could see what lay inside the rest of the space. Most of the areas she peered into were natural caverns like the first, but a few were proper rooms, cut from the native stone. One of these held an enormous iron scorpion that turned restlessly, its stinger tail scraping the ceiling of the too-small room.

"A scalander?" Cavatina mused aloud. Was this the one Meryl had babbled about? It had been down here a long time, judging by the accumulated grit on its body and the numerous gouges its stinger had scraped in the ceiling.

Cavatina continued to explore the limits of the magical boundary. Tunnels led away from the central caverns, each surrounded by a tube-like extension of the magical barrier. All dead-ended after a short distance except one: a tunnel that led past what looked like a recent lava flow. Just beyond this point, a staircase slanted upward. It was enclosed by the glowing green barrier too.

Cavatina climbed through the stone beside the staircase, and found herself in an abandoned mine tunnel with a ceiling level with her chest. That told her she was in one of the oldest sections of Undermountain, far below the Promenade: the ancient mithral mine excavated twenty-six centuries ago by the dwarves of Melairbode. Bluish light rippled through the wall and disappeared. Even this deep, there were traces of *Faerzress*.

The portal that led back to the Hall of Empty Arches lay somewhere within these mine tunnels—though Cavatina doubted it would be much help. Even if she did manage to find it, she doubted it would transport her while she was in ethereal form.

The magical barrier extended only as far as the top of the stairs, which ended in a simple, open arch, just high enough for a dwarf. Inside the arch, the magical barrier was a different color. Instead of green, it glowed with a golden light that shaded to green at its edges. On the other side of this barrier, at the top of the staircase, sat an enormous gray ooze. It pressed itself up against the barrier that filled the arch, attempting—and failing—to force its way out.

Cautiously, Cavatina touched the golden barrier. It blocked her, just as the green glow had. She glanced up and down the mining tunnel, wondering which way to go next. She spotted scuffs in the dust on the floor—someone had crawled away from the staircase—and decided to follow them. She walked along, in solid stone from the waist down but with her head and shoulders inside the tunnel, trusting to Eilistraee to guide her steps.

A short time later, she spotted a second dwarf-sized arch, this one plugged with stone, just like those in the Hall of Empty Arches. Two drow sat next to it, their backs against the wall. Cavatina moved closer, trying to see who they were. She didn't recognize the male, who turned out to have a horribly scarred face and ruined eyes, but she recognized Leliana at once. The Protector was naked from the waist up. Her chain mail tunic and a warped and blackened sword lay on the floor next to her.

Another puzzle piece from Meryl's garbled story dropped into place. *This* was where Leliana had disappeared to. Whatever she'd been doing, she must have hoped to return through that portal to the Hall of Empty Arches—only to find that it wasn't active.

Leliana looked strained and exhausted. As Cavatina watched, she made the sign of Eilistraee's moon and prayed. "Aid me, Lady, in my dance. I've done battle in your name; the moonlight within me has waned. Turn your face to me, and fill me with your light that I might return safely to my place of sanctuary."

Cavatina touched her on the shoulder. "Leliana? Can you hear me?"

Leliana paid her no heed. The male, however, turned his head. One hand groped blindly for Leliana and bumped against her arm. His fingers moved swiftly. *Lady. I sense something. A creature draws near.*

Cavatina blinked in surprise. "Can *you* hear me?" she asked. If he could, perhaps she could use him to alert the battle-mistress to the planar breach. But the male didn't respond to Cavatina's touch on his shoulder. *There!* he signed, pointing with his other hand.

Not at Cavatina, but at something behind her.

She turned.

"What is it?" Leliana whispered to the male. "I can't see anything."

Cavatina could, however. An ooze was flowing out of the wall, not half a dozen paces behind her. It quivered a moment, bulging first this way, then that. Then it moved toward the spot where Leliana and the male sat. Part of its body remained inside the wall; it was moving through solid stone!

It was ethereal. Just like Cavatina.

She'd heard of such creatures. Able to shift between physical and ethereal form at will, they were deadly opponents. Unless Leliana and her companion moved away from this spot—quickly—the ooze would engulf them. It would slither over them, resume its material form, and consume them, unless Cavatina stopped it.

She smiled. The ooze might just be her passage out of here.

She stepped into its path, sang a hymn that would shield her from its acid, and kneeled, her sword tucked tight against her body. She cringed as the creature touched her shoulder, dribbling acid onto her, but she held fast. The ooze recoiled, then suddenly bulged forward, engulfing her.

And squeezed.

The pain was excruciating. Pressure drove the air from Cavatina's lungs. Tendrils of ooze forced their way into her ears, pressing against her eardrums until they rang in agony. Still more tendrils slid into her nostrils, plugging them.

Eilistraee, she silently cried. Strengthen me. Lend your might to my sword arm.

She thrust her weapon away from her, driving it into the ooze. Then she twisted in a kneeling pirouette, wrenching her weapon around with her. The singing sword pealed in muffled joy as its blade bisected the ooze from within.

The ooze shrank away in alarm. Cavatina followed, staying within its flesh, and felt a sudden lurch as the creature entered the material plane. At the last moment, she remembered to duck. Even so, her head scraped the ceiling of the mine tunnel.

She'd done it! Passed back into the Prime Material Plane in the belly of the ooze.

Now she needed to carve her way out of it, before it squeezed the life out of her.

Through a gelatinous blanket of flesh, she saw Leliana rise to her knees and grasp her sword, an alarmed look on her face. "Another ooze!" the Protector shouted—her voice muffled to Cavatina's ears. Then Leliana sang. Her hymn smashed into the ooze, sending shudders through it. Yet the creature continued to squeeze Cavatina, undeterred by the magical assault.

Cavatina had no air left in her lungs. The ooze forced its way down into her throat. Gagging, she hacked at the thinnest section of its body—the side opposite the spot where Leliana and the male crouched. Cavatina's knees scrabbled on the acid-slick floor. Had it not been for her spell, her clothing and armor would have dissolved by now, and her flesh with them. Behind her, she could hear the male's muffled shouting.

The ooze squeezed harder. Spots of bright light crackled in Cavatina's vision. She felt a rib crack. She thrust again with the sword and felt its point break through the outer skin of the ooze, into the air beyond.

Suddenly, the ooze was gone, vanished back into the Ethereal Plane.

Cavatina sucked in a shuddering breath, exhaled through her nostrils, and blew out the sludge the ooze had left behind. She sang her thanks to the goddess—but couldn't hear anything. Movement behind her caught her eye: Leliana scrambling to her in utter silence, sword in hand, an astonished look on her face. The Protector halted at the edge of the acid slick the ooze had left behind and shouted something—but her words were lost in the magical silence. She switched to silent speech instead.

Where did you come from? Where did the ooze go?

The second question was the important one. *It's ethereal,* Cavatina signed back. *Be careful. It might materialize again.*

Behind Leliana, the male touched his fingers to the floor. He waved, hoping to catch their attention, then signed. *Keep still. When the spell wears off, it will be able to feel us moving.*

Cavatina glanced at Leliana. *He cast the silence?*

Leliana nodded. *He's a Nightshadow.*

Smart. But where's his mask?

Later.

The Nightshadow, his ruined eyes staring sightlessly, maintained his vigil, his fingers lightly touching the floor. The three waited—long enough for the acid that was everywhere to dry to a crust. Cavatina would have to renew her protection when she eventually washed it off. But that was the least of her worries. What mattered now was whether the ethereal ooze rematerialized.

It didn't.

Cavatina realized she could hear herself breathing.

"That was close," Leliana whispered.

The Nightshadow cocked his head. Nodded. *Too close,* he signed.

Cavatina was impressed. The male's senses were sharp. "I think we're safe now," she said, speaking aloud for his benefit. "If the ooze were going to attack again, it would be on us already. Oozes aren't intelligent enough to lie in wait." She crawled to the arch. Leliana followed.

"Where *did* you come from, Lady Cavatina?" Leliana repeated. "Did you find the portal?"

Cavatina was surprised. "You knew about it, too? How did you get into the room?"

"What room?"

Cavatina realized they must be talking about different portals. "Why don't you start by telling me how *you* got here, Leliana. In detail."

Leliana told a strange story of following a wizard's construct into a cavern that wept gray ooze. "It must have escaped from the Pit," she concluded. "It—"

"Yes. There's a planar breach."

"How did you know?"

"I saw it," Cavatina said grimly. "Finish your report."

Leliana bowed her head in acknowledgement of the order. She continued her report. It seemed that she and the male, whose name was Naxil, had done battle with a molten ooze—the one that had disfigured him. They'd journeyed to this spot along the route Cavatina had explored, past the now-solidified lava and up the staircase.

"How did you get around the barrier at the top of the stairs?" Cavatina asked.

Leliana held up her hand and nodded at the ring on her finger. "The same way I activated the portal. By touching gold to it—on purpose, this time."

That explained the golden glow. Cavatina took a closer look at the ring. It looked like an ordinary band of gold. "Is it magic?"

"Its ensorcelments have nothing to do with it. I think that anything gold will activate the portals." Leliana's smile faded. She slapped her ringed hand against the blocked archway. "Except for this one."

Cavatina nodded. Her thoughts were on the archway at the top of the stairs, and the ooze pressing against it. "Let's just pray that the oozes haven't fed on anyone wearing gold jewelry," she said, thinking of the sacrifice she'd seen earlier. "Or the ones that *aren't* ethereal will escape too."

"I hadn't thought of that," Leliana said. Then she shook her head. "But oozes are mindless things. They don't have enough intelligence to open the barrier on purpose, and the odds of any gold they carry inside them coming into contact with the barrier by random chance are small."

The Nightshadow flicked a hand. *Something's happening.*

"What is it?" Cavatina hissed. "The ethereal ooze?"

The Nightshadow shook his head. He slid his fingers along the intricate carving that formed the frame of the arch. "The stone feels warm," he whispered back. "I think the portal may be activating."

"Finally!" Leliana exclaimed. "Go on through, Naxil."

The Nightshadow started to move toward the arch. Cavatina caught his shoulder. "One moment, Naxil."

He halted. "Lady?"

"Once we're back in the Promenade, say nothing of the planar breach until I've had a chance to report it to the battle-mistress. We don't want to start a panic." The real reason, of course, was that she didn't want it known she'd seen the planar breach first-hand. If word of that reached Qilué's ears, the high priestess would realize that Horaldin had not only recognized her portal for what it was, but had led Cavatina to it.

Naxil bobbed his head. "Of course, Dark Lady."

"Off you go, then," Cavatina said.

"Wait for me on the other side, Naxil," Leliana added. "I'll guide you to the Hall of Healing."

"Someone else can take him there," Cavatina said. "Battle-mistress Rylla will want to hear your observations, as well."

"But it will only take a moment to—"

Cavatina held up a warning finger. "You're coming with me. That's an order, Protector."

The Nightshadow crouched by the arch, waiting.

Leliana's cheeks darkened, but she made no further protest. "Go on through, Naxil," she said gently. "I'll catch up to you once I've made my report."

He nodded, crawled forward into seemingly solid stone, and disappeared.

As soon as he had gone, Leliana wheeled on Cavatina. "There's something you're not telling me. What is it?"

Cavatina sighed. Suddenly, she felt utterly exhausted. "Rylla will explain."

"What about Lady Qilué? She'll want to hear our report too. Has she been called back to the Promenade?"

Cavatina hid her wince at the use of the high priestess's name. She resisted the urge to glance around. Was Qilué now listening in on their conversation? Was Wendonai? "She'll be contacted, if Rylla deems it necessary."

" 'Necessary?' " Leliana repeated, her voice incredulous. "Of course it's necessary that Qilué—"

"Lady Leliana," Cavatina said sternly. "This portal may only remain active for a short time, and we don't want to be trapped down here. Step through it, please. Promptly."

Visibly fuming, Leliana at last stepped into the portal. As the Protector disappeared, Cavatina briefly closed her eyes. If Qilué *had* been corrupted by a demon, the Promenade was in danger from two fronts: from without and within.

What was it that Qilué had said, when she'd ordered the attack on the Acropolis of the death goddess? The memory of that conversation returned like a chilling premonition. "Cut off the head, and the temple will fall."

"Eilistraee protect us," Cavatina whispered. "Grant that it not be so."

She squared her shoulders and walked through the "stone" that filled the arch. A heartbeat later, she emerged on the other side, within the Hall of Empty Arches. Leliana and Naxil stood there, together with Rylla, who must have been called to the hall the moment the portal reactivated.

Qilué was just behind them.

Cavatina exchanged glances with Rylla as they followed Qilué back to the Hall of the Priestesses. Leliana was with them, but Naxil had been led away to the Hall of Healing. Just as well—that was one less person who might let something slip in Qilué's presence. Cavatina noticed Rylla toying with a strand of hair. The battle-mistress was keeping her hand close to her holy symbol.

Qilué walked at the front of the group, looking imperious in her silver robe. She never once looked back at her priestesses, expecting them to follow her without question or pause, as they always had done. The scabbard at her hip was empty, and Qilué held the Crescent Blade in her hand. Its blade rested lightly on her shoulder, just below her ear. Cavatina wondered if the sword were whispering to the high priestess, even now.

"Praise Eilistraee you've *returned,* Lady Qilué," Cavatina said. Her fingers moved in a silent question at her side, where only Rylla would see them. *When?*

Just now, Rylla replied.

Cavatina silently groaned. The high priestess must have heard Leliana speak her name—and the snatch of conversation that had followed. Out loud, Cavatina continued, "We found a portal in one of the tunnels south of the river. It leads to caverns below the level of the old mine. We sighted oozes down there. I'm worried the Pit may have developed a breach."

Leliana shot Cavatina a quick look, obviously noting Cavatina's use of the words "may have." Fortunately, the Protector was well behind Qilué, and the high priestess didn't notice.

"Troubling news," Qilué answered in a flat voice, without even breaking her stride. The high priestess's shoulders had tensed, Cavatina noted, at the word "portal," then relaxed again at the mention of it being south of the river—a location that was nowhere near the ancient temple.

Detection? Cavatina signed to Rylla.

No evil seen. You try.

Leliana had dropped back slightly, forcing Cavatina and Rylla to shift awkwardly to hide their silent conversation. The Protector obviously realized something serious was in the offing—even if she had no idea, yet, what it was. She watched them out of the corner of her eye.

Cavatina was forced to sign with Leliana watching. *Report dretch,* she suggested.

Rylla moved up beside Qilué. "Lady Qilué, there was an intrusion you should know about. A dretch was spotted . . ."

As Rylla sketched out the events that had followed the dretch's discovery, Cavatina dropped back another pace and sang under her breath—softly, so Qilué wouldn't hear her. Her prayer took hold, causing the holy symbol that hung against her chest to softly vibrate. She scanned the Crescent Blade, looking for the bruised purple aura that accompanied evil. To her surprise, the sword was clean.

Had she been wrong about Wendonai being inside the Crescent Blade?

Rylla glanced back briefly. Cavatina flicked a quick message at her. *Nothing.*

Illusion?

Doubtful. Cavatina had never heard of a balor capable of conjuring illusions.

Banished? Rylla signed without looking back.

An excellent question—one that Cavatina didn't know the answer to.

"The oozes concern me more than one lone dretch does," Qilué told her battle-mistress. "They're the real threat to the Promenade. Are the seals on the Pit intact?"

"Yes, Lady," Rylla answered. "I checked them myself, earlier today."

Cavatina, still well back, whispered a second prayer. The silver aura that accompanied holiness sprang into view around the high priestess. But it was fainter than it should have been: a dull gleam, rather than a sheen so bright it caused the eyes to ache. The silver glow was faintest near the hand that gripped the Crescent Blade—the hand whose wrist was marked with a small, still-visible scar.

The Crescent Blade itself was devoid of an aura. For an item forged from moon metal and consecrated to Eilistraee, that was telling indeed.

Wendonai must have been inside it, Cavatina decided, even if he wasn't there now. Perhaps, having done Lolth's bidding by persuading Qilué to open a portal to the Pit, he'd departed. The Spider Queen could very well have restored his corpse to life, allowing him to return to the Abyss.

All well and good, but it left a gaping hole. With Wendonai departed, there was nothing to prevent Qilué's priestesses from pointing out to the high priestess what she'd been tricked into doing—and then reversing it. Lolth might be insane, but she was cunning. She wouldn't have overlooked this flaw in her plans.

The more likely possibility—vastly more terrifying—was that Wendonai had departed the Crescent Blade for a living host: Qilué.

Cavatina shifted her song a second time, and saw what she'd missed before: a faint purple glow, just above the scar. *That* was where Wendonai must be hiding.

She fought to hide the revulsion she felt. The situation was more grave than she'd dreamed. Was Qilué's mind still her own? Was this a *demon* Cavatina was talking to?

No. Some part of Qilué remained. A significant part. Or her aura wouldn't have shone silver at all.

Cavatina prayed that Wendonai wasn't listening in on her thoughts. If he'd heard what had just passed through her mind—or was listening to whatever Rylla was currently thinking—he'd counter whatever they tried next. She prayed that redemption was an armor he couldn't penetrate.

There was still time to arrange an exorcism—as long as nothing happened to tip their hand. No rash moves, she decided. Nothing that would force the demon to react before they were ready. She'd play along, make her report, and slip away as quickly as she could to make the necessary preparations.

Cavatina directed a sending at Leliana—a carefully worded one that wouldn't send the Protector into a panic. *This may be an imposter, not Qilué. I need to question her without alerting her. On my signal, sing a truth psalm. Do nothing more.*

Leliana's lips tightened. She nodded.

They approached the High House. Rylla reached for the door, but Qilué blocked her. "Thank you for your report, battle-mistress. Please return to the Mound, and re-inspect the seals on the Pit."

"Surely someone else can tend to that, Lady." Rylla nodded in the direction of Cavatina and Leliana. "It's important that I hear what these two have to."

"Do it," Qilué said in a terse voice. "Now. A *thorough* check, this time, or I will hold you personally responsible for whatever follows. As will Eilistraee."

Exorcism, Cavatina spelled while the high priestess's back was turned. *Prepare.*

Rylla stiffened. Hopefully, the high priestess would think this a reaction to the insult she'd just handed her battle-mistress. Rylla bowed stiffly and hurried away.

Qilué watched her leave, then pulled the door open and motioned for Cavatina and Leliana to enter. Cavatina tensed. Was the demon taking them somewhere out of the public eye, somewhere it could attack?

Qilué directed them to the room at the very heart of the High House: the chamber that housed her private altar. A holy place, filled with Eilistraee's blessings. Was the demon trying to prove something? That Eilistraee's relics were of no consequence?

As Leliana paused before the door, she caught Cavatina's eye and lifted one eyebrow slightly. Cavatina decided the time was not yet ripe. She would play this move out, and see what followed. "After you, Protector," she said.

Qilué closed the heavy stone door behind them.

The circular room, shot through with hair-thin threads of moonlight, had walls painted with a mural of a forest. When the stone door was closed, the illusion was complete. Moss, sustained by magic, carpeted the floor, filling the shrine with a woodland smell. A pedestal plated in gold, its top even with Cavatina's eyes, stood at the center of the room. Perched atop it was a rust red, deeply pitted rock the size of a loaf of bread: a fragment of the boulder that had parted from the moon and streaked through the sky on the night Ghaunadaur's avatar had been defeated.

Qilué raised the Crescent Blade above her head and began to dance around the altar. As the high priestess passed behind the pillar, Cavatina caught Leliana's eye and nodded before beginning her own dance. Leliana lifted her blackened singing sword and joined in, her lips moving in a whispered song. She spun her blade in a tight circle above her head—a gesture that looked as though it were part of her dance, but was actually part of her spellcasting.

In the same instant that Leliana unleashed her truth-compelling prayer, Qilué quickened her dance and spun behind Cavatina, out of the spell's path. Cavatina felt the tingle of magic and realized, to her horror, that Qilué had maneuvered her into the path of the magic.

Qilué wheeled on her. "How did you know the Pit has a breach?" she demanded.

"I—" Cavatina tried to lie, but couldn't. Words tumbled out of her mouth—not the carefully worded "report" she'd been rehearsing, but the truth about what had transpired. Horaldin showing her the portal; Cavatina slipping through it and becoming ethereal; seeing the planar breach, the ooze flowing out of it, the self-sacrifice of the green-eyed drow . . .

Qilué cut her off at that point with a curt, "That's enough."

Cavatina hid her relief. The high priestess hadn't thought to ask *why* Horaldin had shown Cavatina the portal. Yet.

Leliana had listened, sword in hand. Now she glanced uncertainly back and forth between Cavatina and the high priestess—as though she'd like to silently ask what to do next, but didn't dare. Her singing sword let out a low, worried hum.

"Sheathe that," Qilué ordered.

"Why would you have me do that, Lady Qilué?"

"Because it's annoying."

Leliana shifted the weapon slightly. "It no longer fits in its scabbard, Lady Qilué."

"Then find another way to silence it!" Qilué barked. "Lay it down."

Leliana obediently placed her sword on the floor, ending its song.

Cavatina smiled to herself as she realized why Leliana had asked the question. Qilué's blunt answer seemed to indicate the truth spell had taken hold of her, as well, despite her attempt to shield herself from it by stepping behind Cavatina. Before Qilué could gather her wits, Cavatina spat out a question of her own. "Why did you open a portal to the Pit, Lady Qilué?"

Qilué scowled—an expression as foreign to her face as a look of mercy would have been on the cruel visage of the Spider Queen. Then, as abruptly as it came, the scowl disappeared. Cavatina could see, how Horaldin had known there was something wrong with the high priestess. Everything about Qilué's posture, tone, and expression was subtly wrong. Even Qilué's color was off. Her skin looked clammy, like that of someone who ought to be confined to a sick bed. She even smelled bad—as if it had been some time since she'd bathed.

"Fortunately for you, Cavatina, my preparations are incomplete."

Cavatina's heart fell. Qilué wasn't answering her question! Was the demon capable of resisting Leliana's magical compulsion? Or was the answer simpler: that it was Wendonai who had opened the portal—if so, the demon wouldn't have been compelled to answer a question directed at Qilué. Cavatina's hands dampened with sweat. She resisted the urge to clench her sword tighter; Qilué might spot the slight movement and attack.

Cavatina tried another question. "What preparations?"

"A symbol. Had you blundered upon that ruined temple once it was visible, that would have been the end of you. You would have wandered the Ethereal Plane forever, gibbering and broken."

"I *did* see a symbol—the mark of the Ancient One. Is that the one you mean?"

"Of course not," Qilué snapped. "I'm talking about the symbol I inscribed on *top* of it."

Cavatina cautiously nodded. If there had been another symbol atop Ghaunadaur's, she'd failed to detect it. "What symbol is that?"

"One that provokes insanity." Qilué smirked: another expression she never used. "The idea came from Ghaunadaur's own scriptures." She spoke quickly, as if she couldn't get the words out fast enough. Maybe Leliana's prayer *was* affecting her. "Millennia ago, the Ancient One rendered mindless the oozes and slimes that were his original worshipers. I'm going to do the same to the drow who worship him. They're incapable of redemption, so we're going to destroy them instead. *That's* why I opened the portal in the abandoned temple. Our spies will lure his clerics into it with a feint the fanatics can't help but follow. Especially once I open the door for them."

"You're going to allow Ghaunadaur's fanatics to enter the *Promenade?*" Cavatina gasped.

Qilué missed the point. "They won't realize we've 'allowed' it. Each group will think it's mounting a sneak attack. They'll never realize that others have preceded them, since the ones who have gone before won't be in any condition to warn them, once the trap is sprung. They'll all walk into it one by one, as meek as rothé."

Cavatina was absolutely certain that this was Wendonai speaking. Qilué would never have slain drow outright—even those who worshiped so vile a god—without first offering a chance at redemption. Nor would she have allowed the Promenade's defenses to be compromised.

"When are these 'sneak attacks' to begin?"

Qilué smiled. "My plan is already in motion."

Leliana broke in. "But Lady Qilué, if the symbol is not yet visible—"

Qilué whirled around. "I know what I'm doing! Your opinion is not wanted, Protector."

Leliana stood, her mouth open. Her fingers spread slightly, and her posture shifted. In another moment she'd lunge for her singing sword. Behind Qilué, Cavatina frantically shook her head. *Not yet! Play along!* she signed.

Leliana bowed. "Lady, my apologies for speaking out of turn."

"The plan has its merits," Cavatina said, trying to draw the high priestess's attention back to her. "But the Protectors will need to be notified."

"Of course," Qilué said without turning around. She pointed at Leliana. "They just have been. A little sooner than I would have liked. There may be spies among us."

"Not among the Protectors," Leliana assured her.

"Not among the priestesses, you mean. There are Night-shadows whose loyalties I'm less certain of."

She at last turned to Cavatina. "You can see why I've been so short-tempered, of late. It's a big gamble I'm taking—but one that, if all goes well, will prove as rewarding as our assault on the Acropolis."

Cavatina nodded, trying not to betray the tension she felt. "I don't like it," she said. "It's too risky." Then she shrugged, as if in resignation. "But I bow to your greater wisdom, Lady Qilué."

"As do I, Lady," Leliana echoed.

For a moment, no one spoke. Then Qilué nodded. Cavatina relaxed—a little. Hopefully, Wendonai was arrogant enough to think he'd fooled them.

A knock sounded on the door. As Qilué crossed the room to answer it, Leliana caught Cavatina's eye. Her hand flicked a word: *What—?*

Ask to leave.

"Lady," Leliana said. "May I check on Naxil?"

"Not yet," Qilué said without turning around. "There's more we need to discuss."

"Agreed," Cavatina interrupted. "And the battle-mistress should hear it. Leliana, go find Rylla. Ask her to join us."

"No!" Qilué snapped. Her hand was on the door. "Remain where you are, Leliana. I've already sent for the battle-mistress."

Cavatina's heart sank. She could think of only one reason for Qilué to keep the Protector here: Wendonai *hadn't* been fooled. And it was worse than that. As Qilué turned back to the door, Cavatina caught a glint of something: silver fire, kindling deep within the high priestess's eyes. Was Wendonai about to unleash it? Could he? If so, their lives would be measured in heartbeats unless Cavatina did something, and quickly.

Eilistraee, she silently prayed. Dancing Lady, aid me.

She caught Leliana's eye and glanced down at the other female's singing sword. One finger flicked. *On my signal.*

Leliana moved her feet slightly, getting ready to dive for her sword. With luck, the Protector would survive long enough for Cavatina to take Wendonai down and stop him—by killing Qilué, if necessary.

Cavatina prayed that it wouldn't be.

Qilué opened the door, revealing Meryl. The halfling held up a tray on which stood a single goblet. Or . . . was it Meryl? For all Cavatina knew, this might be another dretch in disguise.

Cavatina raised her hand slightly, about to give the signal to attack. Before her fingers could move, a voice sang into her ear. *Wait.*

Eilistraee? Cavatina wondered. Or the demon, mimicking her voice?

Watch, the voice urged. As before, the word sang out in a duet, blending male and female timbres.

Eilistraee. Cavatina felt certain of it.

Meryl glanced into the shrine, at the two priestesses—then yelped and stepped back quickly as Qilué snatched the goblet, spilling part of the clear liquid it held, and shut the door in the halfling's face.

Cavatina held her hand still. Leliana would be wondering why she hadn't signaled yet. Logically, now was the time to move, while the "imposter's" back was still turned.

Goblet in hand, Qilué turned.

Leliana waited, her body tense.

Suddenly, Cavatina understood what the goddess wanted her to do. As Qilué drank from the goblet, Cavatina whispered a hymn of detection. She finished it as Qilué lowered the empty goblet. Cavatina saw the high priestess's aura brighten, returning to its usual gleaming silver—except for a faint dimple that was the scar on her wrist. She realized that it must have been holy water the high priestess had just drunk—and that it had done its work.

Cavatina shifted her whispered song. As she'd suspected, there was a dark purple aura surrounding the Crescent Blade. Wendonai was back inside it. Yet even as Cavatina watched, a thread of purple found its way back to the scar on Qilué's wrist, and taint began to flow back into her.

So soon? Surely holy water would have a more lingering effect than that.

Unless it had been tainted by a dretch.

That *hadn't* been Meryl. The halfling would have reacted to Cavatina in some way, giving an inappropriate wave, or saying hello. This "Meryl" had simply given Cavatina a flat, unrecognizing stare.

Cavatina needed to act—and quickly! This might be her only chance to banish Wendonai while he was still vulnerable, before he fully re-entered the high priestess. Yet she'd had no time to prepare. Wendonai was a balor—the most powerful demon of all. Cavatina would need something more than just her sword or holy symbol to . . .

Wait a moment! Her eyes fell on the sacred stone atop the pillar. Wendonai had been overly clever in bringing Cavatina and Leliana to the shrine. He'd placed the perfect tool for an exorcism within Cavatina's reach.

Cavatina's fingers flashed. *Now!*

Leliana swept up her sword and lunged, her weapon pealing its attack—a feint Qilué met with a slash of the Crescent Blade. Their weapons met with a loud crash. Cavatina leaped for the sacred stone. She scooped it from the top of the pillar and hurled it, aiming at the sword in Qilué's hand. "Begone, Wendonai!" she sang. "Return to—"

Silver fire filled the air with a flash of heat. Cavatina heard a crack—the sacred stone had struck the wall. A welter of fragments pattered onto the floor. Blinded by the aftereffects of the bright flash, she leaped forward, trying to locate Qilué by feel.

A strident note wailed past her ear once, twice: Leliana's sword blade.

Cavatina ducked. "Leliana! Hold!"

The sword's singing halted.

Blinking against the streaks that obscured her vision, Cavatina fumbled for the door. Her hand encountered an utterly smooth surface: magic-fused stone—hot enough to scorch her fingertips. She yanked her hand back and sang a hymn, one that should have sent her into the corridor beyond. But Eilistraee didn't answer.

As the room swam into focus, she understood why. The stone door had been fused shut by Qilué's silver fire. On top of that, the entire chamber was glowing. Bright green light sparkled from within the floor, ceiling, and walls: a magical barrier, just like the one Cavatina had seen when she'd been ethereal.

Qilué had disappeared, and they were trapped.

Cavatina turned to Leliana. "The demon's escaped!"

"That was a demon? A *demon* took Qilué's form?"

"Worse than that," Cavatina answered grimly. "That *is* Qilué, but only partially. A balor is sharing her body."

"Eilistraee save us," Leliana whispered, her face paling to gray. Her singing sword let out a mournful peal. She looked around. "Why didn't it kill us?"

It was a good question. But Cavatina didn't have time to speculate. With an urgent whisper, she tried sending a warning to Rylla.

No answer came.

Cavatina tried contacting Horaldin—the druid knew spells that would soften stone, and would soon have them out of here—but he also failed to answer.

Cavatina glanced around the shrine that had become their prison, furious at herself for having become trapped here. The battle-mistress needed her. Rylla was adept at exorcism and a skillful swordswoman, but she would be facing the Crescent Blade, backed up by Qilué's silver fire.

Cavatina bowed her head and prayed. Eilistraee, surely, could still hear her. "Grant Rylla the strength she needs to do battle in your name, Dark Maiden. Shield her, and strengthen her sword arm."

"By song and sword," Leliana whispered.

Cavatina hoped it wasn't already too late for their prayers.

CHAPTER 6

Kâras yanked the reins of his riding lizard to stop it from snapping at the tail of the mount in front. All around him, the twenty-six other priests who would ride out to the Gathering did the same. Their lizards, cramped together in the portico, were restless and aggressive as they waited for the drawbridge to fall.

A novice in oversized purple robes hurried into the portico, carrying a lacquered black tray. On it was a whiplike tentacle rod and the ring that controlled it. With eyes downcast, the boy halted next to Kâras and lifted the tray.

Kâras caught the eye of the priest on the mount next to him and feigned a greedy smile. "Mine?"

The priest—a greasy-haired, hollow-cheeked drow named Molvayas—smiled, revealing brown, stained teeth. "Yours. To replace the one you lost."

The brownish red tentacles of the priest's rod were coiled over one shoulder and around his chest; their suckers puckered the fabric of his tabard. They sucked and released the purple-encircled eye embroidered on the front of the tunic as if nursing from it. His shield bore the same symbol.

Kâras could feel the other priests watching him out of the corners of their eyes. This was a test. He reached for the ring: a band of black obsidian, set with an equally dark stone. The bitterly cold ring stuck to his sweat-damp fingers. He jammed it onto his left thumb and tore his fingers away. Cold shot through his thumb to the bone, turning the meat of his thumb a dull gray. With a thought, he adjusted its color back to black.

He held up his thumb and flexed it—a motion that would draw the others' scrutiny away from his other hand as it surreptitiously brushed against the belt that cinched in his tabard: a belt that was actually his disguised holy symbol. Masked Lady, he silently prayed. Lend me strength.

Feeling returned to his thumb.

He grabbed the rod's leather-bound handgrip. Finger-thick, rubbery tentacles uncoiled and animated as he lifted the rod from the tray. When he held it at arm's length, the tentacles brushed back and forth against the slate floor, leaving streaks of frost in their wake. He flicked the rod, and a shiver ran through the tentacles. They snapped briefly to attention, then relaxed again and suckered the floor with faint wet pops.

"A fine weapon," he said. "My thanks to House Philiom."

"Gather well," Molvayas said.

Kâras flicked the weapon a second time as he waited, and a third, pretending to admire the balance of its long metal shaft and the suppleness of its three black tentacles. At last he had to coil the weapon around his body, lest the others become suspicious. He suppressed his shudder at the touch of its tentacles against his skin.

Without warning, thuds sounded as the House boys on either side of the drawbridge slammed sledge hammers to release the pegs that held its counterweights. Chains rattled, and the drawbridge fell with a tremendous *boom*. En masse, the riding lizards surged forward, their riders urging them onward with hisses. The novice who'd handed Kâras the rod gasped as a lizard knocked him down. He screamed as scrabbling claws shredded his tabard and back into a bloody fringe. The screaming fell behind as Kâras's riding lizard surged onto the drawbridge with the rest.

The sour smell of green slime rose to Kâras's nostrils as his mount crossed the moat. Soon it was replaced by the fetid stench of the manure in House Philiom's mushroom fields. The riders poured out of the black spire that was House Philiom's keep, their riding lizards' clawed feet sending up a splattering of mud that fouled the hems of their robes. Startled slaves rose from their mushroom picking to watch the mounts pass.

Kâras wheeled his lizard past the slave hovels, blinking away smoke from the smudge fires the slaves used to keep midges at bay. Soon the hovels fell behind. The riders emerged onto the wide expanse of silt that covered the floor of the low-ceilinged cavern. As their lizards scuttled forward in a blur of legs and claws, the priests gibbered the name of their god, spittle flying from their lips.

"Ghaunadaur who lurks, Ghaunadaur who sees, Ghaunadaur who devours."

Kâras mouthed the refrain without giving voice to it. The harsh chirps and hisses of the lizards and the wet slap of clawed feet through mud masked his silence.

He marveled at the contrast. In other cities, merely speaking the Ancient One's name aloud resulted in immediate retribution. Here in Llurth Dreir, it was a different story. Lolth's temples had been scoured clean when an avatar of the Ancient One had risen from Llurthogl, consumed Lolth's faithful, and descended again. Over the centuries since, there had been frequent "spawnings"—eruptions of oozes, slimes, and slugs—ensuring that Lolth's clergy didn't return. At the moment, thankfully, the lake was still and quiet. Its scum-covered surface lay undisturbed, apart from the occasional bubble of foul-smelling gas.

Kâras unwound the tentacles from his body and let them trail behind him as he rode. He wheeled his mount with the others as they turned to the black spire of rock that was House Abbylan's keep. Slave hovels fringed the base of it. As the riders drew near the outermost of these shanties, figures scattered like spiders from a torn egg sac. Goblins, kobolds, and orcs—even a handful of pale-skinned humans—flailed through the mud in a panic. Beyond them, House Abbylan's soldiers poured oil through slits in the keep, to prevent the attackers' lizards from scaling its walls.

The priests rode the slaves down, lashing out with their whiplike rods. Slaves collapsed as the tentacles struck them, magic turning muscle to jelly, or loosing a spray of slime that blinded and maimed. Some of the slaves stood dazed and staring, their wits sucked out by the lashing rods. Others leaped, screaming, from tentacles that left bands of fire across their flesh.

Kâras lashed out with his rod, the unfamiliar weapon awkward in his grip. By mere chance, he struck a kobold with a tentacle The tiny reptilian squeaked in agony as its bones and cartilage turned as cold as ice, sending it into a stiff-limbed tumble.

Molvayas chanted a gurgling prayer. Rubbery black tentacles, as tall as saplings, sprang from the mud in a long line that extended back to House Philiom's keep. Like slaves picking mushrooms, they plucked the fallen from the mud and passed them back, tentacle to tentacle, toward the keep.

The Gathering had begun.

A gong sounded from the top of the nearby keep. Low and shuddering, it boomed once, twice, thrice. House Abbylan's drawbridge crashed down, sending up a spray of mud. Lizard-mounted riders—garbed in identical tabards, but with green robes instead of purple—raced from the keep.

"Consume them!" Molvayas cried.

Riders slammed spike-spurs into their mounts, sending them leaping at the enemy. Spells flew thick and fast between the slave hovels as the rival groups battled. A roiling wave of conjured slime smashed one of the huts flat and broke against the mount of one of House Philiom's priests. The lizard convulsed, thrashing its tail in agony, but the priest went down laughing, his arms waving above his head as he sang his god's name. A heartbeat later, a dark purple boil burst up through the slime, assumed the vague outline of a drow, and staggered on quivering legs toward the nearest enemy. It wrapped its "arms" around that rider's mount. As the lizard collapsed, its body dissolving, another of House Philiom's priests launched a spell that imploded the rider's head.

Kâras spurred his mount between two of the slave hovels, seeking refuge. As soon as he reached a point where the others couldn't see him, he reined his mount to a halt. He threw down his tentacle rod and whispered a prayer to the Masked Lady, healing his frost-burned thumb.

A hiss made him look up. He wasn't the only one back there; Molvayas had followed him. The fanatic had heard Kâras's prayer. He bared his stained teeth in a furious grimace. "Imposter!" he howled. His arm jerked up, flicking his tentacle rod back—ready to strike.

Kâras shot a poisoned bolt from his wrist-bow, but Molvayas whipped up his shield and gurgled a one-word prayer. The metal shield turned into a shimmering disk made up of droplets, which caused the bolt to dissolve instantly when it struck. .

Molyvas smiled and flicked his whip.

"Masked Lady, cloak me!" Kâras cried as the tentacles flicked toward him. A sphere of darkness leavened with sparkles of moonlight sprang into being around him. The tentacles smacked into it and glanced aside—all but one, which brushed Kâras's left knee, instantly deadening it. His leg muscles felt as though they'd turned to mush. He'd been leaning in that direction, and his left foot slipped out of the stirrup. He toppled sideways to the muddy ground, the weakened leg collapsing beneath him, his right foot still tangled in its stirrup, which had twisted up and over the saddle. The lizard, struck in the tail by a tentacle, twisted around to bite at its weakened, useless tail, dragging Kâras behind it.

Molvayas flicked the tentacles back, readying for a second strike. Kâras twisted to face his opponent. He spat out foul-tasting mud, pointed, and chanted a prayer. It should have immobilized Molvayas, but the Ghaunadaurian priest somehow shrugged it off. His arm whipped forward, and the tentacles lashed out a second time.

Kâras at last yanked his foot out of the stirrup. He tried to roll behind his mount, but wasn't quick enough. Tentacles struck his shoulders and the back of his neck. His arms immediately numbed and fell limp at his sides. His head flopped forward on a loose-boned neck. Gasping, desperately trying to blink the mud from his eyes, he mumbled a prayer through numbed lips. "Masst Laybee, dribe him frum me . . ."

A foot squelched in the mud next to his ear. Kâras twisted around and saw Molvayas looming over him. The tentacles of his rod were coiled around his waist; the handle hung like a sheath at his side. As he chanted, a green tinge appeared around his hands. Slime trickled down to his wrist, then fell, hissing, into the mud next to Kâras's ear. In the distance, Kâras heard the sounds of battle, and the squelch of his mount limping away.

"See him," Molvayas chanted. "Devour him. Destroy him."

Kâras steeled himself. He was ready. A moment more, and he would go to his god—and find out, at long last, if it really was the Lady of the Dance who wore the mask, or if the Shadow Lord wore *her*.

Molvayas bent down, his slimed fingers splayed. But before he could touch Kâras, a cord appeared around his neck and yanked him backward. A bolt of darkfire erupted out of his chest, burning a smoking hole through the eye embroidered on his tabard.

Yet still the priest didn't go down. He clawed at the strangle cord around his neck, choked out a word, and his neck softened to the consistency of jelly. The strangle cord slipped through it and was gone. His neck solid again, Molvayas twisted furiously to meet his opponent, his hands raised to cast a spell.

Kâras seized his chance. He flailed with his good leg, snapping it against the back of Molvayas's knee. The priest staggered and toppled sideways, forced to check his fall with his hands. They slid into the foul-smelling mud. Snarling, he reached for his rod. But before the tentacles could uncoil from his body, a second bolt of darkfire caught him square in the mouth and exploded out of the back of his head, carrying bits of brain and skull with it. Molvayas fell over backward with a strangled cry. The rod's tentacles suckled at his smoking remains for a moment, then fell still.

A green-robed drow with distinctive pink eyes stepped over the corpse and kneeled beside Kâras. His mud-splattered tabard bore Ghaunadaur's unblinking eye, but the prayer he whispered as he touched Kâras's weakened arms, neck and leg was to another god entirely. "Masked Lord," he intoned, "heal him."

Sensation and strength returned. With a shudder, Kâras sat up. "My thanks, Valdar. That was close."

Valdar helped Kâras to his feet. "Not much of a 'truce between Houses,' is it?"

Kâras shook his head in agreement. "The fanatics' vows don't seem to count for much, when it's time for a Gathering. Let's just hope it doesn't turn into full-scale war."

"Have you heard anything yet? Has she been in touch?"

" 'Soon,' was what she said, the last time we spoke." Kâras wiped mud from his face with a sleeve. "I pray she's telling the truth. A tenday-plus-two is long enough. This is worse than Maerimydra."

A kobold burst out of a nearby hovel, skidded to a stop as he spotted the two drow, and tried to duck back through the door. Valdar whirled and threw; his knife buried itself in the slave's throat. A snap of his fingers brought the knife back to his hand, even as the kobold fell.

"May the Masked Lord grant that prayer," he said as he wiped the blood from his blade with a white silk handkerchief. He tucked the weapon back into its wrist-sheath. "I'm certainly ready for her call. My bunch is slurping out of the palm of my hand. Ripe for Gathering, you might say."

Kâras shook his head. Valdar actually seemed to be *enjoying* this mission.

They paused to listen. The shouts and cries of battle continued. Over them came a distant gonging: the call for House Philiom's priests to return to their keep. The larders were once again full, and the Gathering was at an end.

"Time for me to go," Kâras said.

"Me too." With a wink, Valdar vanished. One moment he stood next to Kâras; the next, he had teleported away, as silently as he'd come.

Kâras picked up his tentacle rod. He glanced around. His own lizard had curled against the wall of a hut to chew off what remained of its tail. But Molvayas's mount was whole. Kâras ran over to it and sprang into the saddle. He drove his spurs into its flanks and hissed. The lizard scuttled away, climbing up and over the nearest hovel. As it descended the opposite wall, he heard shouts of triumph: the priests of House Abbylan had discovered Molvayas's corpse.

Kâras rode away from the hovels, onto the field that separated the two keeps. The House Philiom priests were just ahead, forming up their mounts. This done, they rode hard for their keep, following the line of bubbling black pools left behind by the tentacles' return to the earth. Some of the priests were wounded and clung to their saddles. One sagged, then tumbled backward across his lizard's tail. His body dragged for a moment, but then his foot slipped from the stirrup, and he fell away. The other riders ignored him and continued to ride.

Kâras rode with them. The priests of House Abbylan followed for a time, hurling spells at the retreating group, but soon gave up the chase. Eventually the priests of House Philiom reached their own, now empty fields. The slaves, rightfully fearing they might be gathered along with the slaves of House Abbylan, would have fled when the line of tentacles sprouted from the earth. Kâras rode past the hovels, to the keep, and over its drawbridge. When the last of House Philiom's priests was inside, House boys sprang to the capstans and cranked the drawbridge shut.

Kâras dismounted. The surviving priests glanced around, taking stock. They'd lost five of their number, including Molvayas.

"Where's Molvayas?" asked Shi'drin. He was their second-in-command, a stunted drow with a pustule-crusted face. "Did anyone see him fall?"

"I did," Kâras answered. "One of House Abbylan's priests killed him." He flicked his rod, sending a shiver through its three black tentacles. "I dealt with him in turn." He didn't bother explaining why he was mounted on Molvayas's lizard. Those who followed Ghaunadaur's creed took what they needed, scorning those who were too weak to keep it.

Shi'drin nodded. He touched the eye on his tabard. "Ash to ash; mud to mud," he intoned. "May the Ancient One consume what remains."

The other priests—all but one, who had collapsed after dismounting and was being eaten by his lizard, bringing the total lost to six—touched their tabards. Kâras did the same, doing his best to ignore the wet rip of flesh and the gulps of the lizard as it bolted down the dead priest. He wanted desperately to escape to the solitude of the room he'd been assigned after he arrived on House Philiom's doorstep, claiming to be from Skullport. He wanted to cleanse his body of mud, shroud himself in magical darkness and silence, block out the shrill screams that echoed constantly down the keep's foul-smelling corridors, and pray. Pray for the strength to continue this blasphemous charade and see his mission through.

In each of the keeps of Llurth Drier, other Nightshadows were, no doubt, thinking the same. Their counterparts were stationed in distant Eryndlyn, and in Shadowport, and in the surface cities of Waterdeep, Bezantur, Calimport, and Westgate—everywhere Ghaunadaur's foul cult festered.

Kâras wondered if the Nightshadows he and Valdar had chosen for this mission still lived. It had been a knife's-edge thing, this day, for Kâras himself. By the Masked Lady's grace, Valdar had been there to step in, but it would only be a matter of time before one of the Nightshadows was caught and revealed them all.

A boy took the reins of Kâras's lizard. He climbed down from it and walked across the portico, edging his way through the crowd, to the exit. Before he reached it, a hand fell on his shoulder.

"You will be rewarded," Shi'drin said in a low voice, his eyes gleaming. Then, louder, to all the priests, "Come! We will feed the altar this very cycle in celebration of our Gathering." He pointed at the nearest House boy. "You! Spawn! Tell the boys to prepare the sacrifices."

Kâras choked down his apprehension. He could tell by the look in Shi'drin's eye that the priest realized he was somehow responsible for Molvayas's death. Now one of two things would follow. Reward, for ensuring Shi'drin's promotion to Molvayas's former role as the keep's Eater of Filth. Or retribution.

Both might very well take the same form: sacrifice, on Ghaunadaur's altar.

Yet Kâras could do nothing—not with a score of gleeful priests sweeping him along in their midst. Stinking of blood and sweat, babbling their joy at a successful Gathering, they hurried down the corridor to the shrine at the heart of the keep. Had Shi'drin not singled Kâras out, he might have slipped away, perhaps even feigned collapse and been left behind. But the new Eater strode just behind Kâras, prodding him forward.

They burst through a curtain of damp, rotted black silk into a room with walls, ceiling, and floor polished to the slickness of glass. A dozen columns of the same mottled purple stone, each carved with a rune, ringed an irregularly shaped dais that rose in two tiers. Atop the dais stood a lump of porous black stone: the altar itself. A gong hung above the dais, its bronze deeply pitted by the acid that condensed on it, trickled down its sides, and dripped onto the altar.

A purplish mist drifted through the chamber. As he passed through a patch of it, Kâras touched his disguised holy symbol and silently prayed for strength. The mist left a stinging film on his skin and clung to him like lingering dread. Just setting foot in the shrine took all of Kâras's courage. The air was so foul he felt as if he were wading through liquid sewage. The closer he got to the altar, the worse it got. He was an intruder here, a person from another faith. At any moment he'd be exposed, consumed.

Then they'd be on him, like carrion crawlers on a corpse.

He shook his head furiously. If he didn't get a hold of himself, he'd soon collapse in a gibbering heap on the floor. With a shaking hand, he gripped his disguised holy symbol. *Masked Lady*, he silently prayed, swallowing down his bile. *See me through this. Help me to do your work. Shadow my doubts and cloak my fears.*

The priests halted in a loose-knit group before the altar. Shi'drin stepped to the front, turned, and raised his hands. His fingernails were filthy, the sleeves of his robe soaked with slime and blood. He caught Kâras's eye. For one terrible moment, Kâras thought Shi'drin might ask *him* to perform the sacrifice. Then Shi'drin closed his eyes.

"Ghauandaur, your faithful servant calls," Shi'drin intoned. "In your name, I feast." Then he transformed. His fingers melted into his hands, his arms trickled toward his body like melting candle wax, and his head turned into a blackened puddle on his shoulders. Soon all of him, including his robe and tabard, had turned to ooze. The black blob he'd become bulged against the lowest step of the dais, and flowed up to the altar.

The other priests formed two lines, stretching from the doorway to the dais. Kâras, by careful maneuvering, placed himself as far from the altar as he could get, beside the chamber's only exit. He pretended to follow along as the priests muttered their devotions and swayed back and forth. He moved his lips in time with the rest, mumbling what he hoped would pass as a prayer.

Fortunately, Ghaunadaur's faithful had no set liturgy. Like the god they worshiped, their rituals were amorphous and ill-defined. Each priest praised the Ancient One in his own fashion. If any of the others noticed that Kâras was uttering nonsense, it wouldn't matter. He just prayed that the Ancient One itself wasn't listening.

A few moments later, the first of the sacrifices staggered into the altar room: an orc, her eyes glazed, a dribble of the drug she'd been forced to drink drooling from her mouth. Even from a distance, Kâras could smell its licorice-sweet scent. The tempo of the priests' mutterings increased, found a rhythm. "Onward. Oblivion. Onward."

With each word, the captured slave took a step forward, stumbling as if shoved by invisible hands between the two rows of priests. Compelled by their magic, the orc made her way, one halting step at a time, to the dais. At last she bumped her shins against it, fell forward, and cracked her head on the stone. She rose, her snout bloody. She levered herself up onto the first layer of the dais. Then the second. Then onto the altar stone itself.

The priests fell silent. With a wet, slurping sound, the black ooze that was Shi'drin slithered onto the altar. As it engulfed the orc, the glaze fell from her eyes. Her cry of anguish was cut short as her flesh sizzled. The stench of burned hair filled the room. For a heartbeat or two she struggled, then fell still. A pitted bone poked momentarily out of the black ooze, then got slurped back inside.

Now a second slave stumbled into the room, this one a male half-orc. Like the first sacrificial victim, he stank of the drug he'd been forced to consume. The priests began their chant anew, compelling him forward.

Sickened, Kâras played along. "Onward. Oblivion. Onward."

One by one, eleven more captured slaves marched to the dais, climbed to the altar, and were consumed. Feeling faint, Kâras wondered if the sacrifices were ever going to end. He vomited in his throat, and harshly swallowed the bile down again.

As the thirteenth captive was being dissolved, a sound like stone being slammed by a sledge rent the air. Instantly, the priests fell silent. Heads turned. Kâras peered down his line and saw that a Y-shaped crack had opened in the altar stone and the altar had split into three pieces. Judging by the reactions of the priests, it was an auspicious omen. They seemed tense, anticipatory.

Kâras didn't like the thought of that.

A greenish sludge oozed out of the cracks and puddled on the upper level of the dais. It dribbled onto the lower level, then onto the floor. Kâras watched it, his every muscle tense. When it reached his boot, he shifted his foot slightly. Its stench made his stomach lurch. But he couldn't very well flee, not with the others watching. He stood his ground, sweating, as the sticky green ooze flowed past his boots. He prayed it wouldn't dissolve the leather, burn through to his feet, and reveal him as a spy.

It didn't.

No more victims staggered through the curtain; the sacrifice seemed to be at an end. Yet the priests continued to sway and chant Ghaunadaur's name. Kâras glanced at the curtain, wondering if he could slip away without anyone noticing. He decided not to risk it. Meanwhile, the green stuff kept oozing from the altar like blood from a wound. It was obviously a manifestation of Ghaunadaur. But what did it mean?

A moment later, one of the novices burst into the chamber. He threw himself onto the floor and wormed his way to the altar through the sludge, fouling his robes. "Masters!" he cried, his voice shrill with excitement. "The lake is in turmoil! It's turned a bright purple. A spawning has begun!"

The black blob on the altar flowed upward, assumed the shape of a drow, and morphed back into Shi'drin. The Eater's eyes grew wild with anticipation. "It is come!" he cried. "The Great Devouring is at hand!"

"They have come!" the other priests chanted. "His servants have come!" As one, they turned and rushed from the room.

As the other priests jostled each other in an apparent frenzy to be devoured by whatever was rising out of the lake, Kâras hung back. He felt dizzy with fear. Llurthogl was spawning? Why now? Had Ghaunadaur sensed an enemy among his fanatics? Kâras glanced nervously at the green ooze that fouled his boots, wondering if it was about to consume him.

Soon, Kâras and the prostrated novice were the only ones left in the shrine.

"Go!" Kâras shouted, his voice tight with strain. "Make your preparations!"

The novice heaved himself to his feet and ran from the room.

Kâras wiped nervous sweat from his brow. Every instinct screamed at him to flee Llurth Dreir and never look back. There was an easy exit close at hand: the columns ringing the altar, with their teleportation runes. He reached into his pocket and found the lump of amber that had, at its heart, a crescent-shaped spark of moonlight. Touching the amber to any of the runes would alter its destination, linking it with one of the three columns in the Promenade that had, centuries ago, been ensorcelled by Ghaunadaur's cultists.

He struggled to make his decision. Should he abandon everything he and Valdar had worked so hard to set in place these past few tendays, or stay here and try to brazen it out? He had, until now, been able to fool the Ghaunadaurian priesthood—even in the heart of the Ancient One's shrine, even during a sacrifice. But during a *spawning?* The oozes and slimes boiling up out of the lake were mindless creatures that couldn't tell the difference between friend and foe, but that was of little comfort. It only meant that his disguise wouldn't save him, if one of them decided to consume him.

Kâras swore. Until a few moments ago, it had all been going so well. All he'd needed to do was continue the facade, and wait for Qilué's signal. That would be his cue to reveal his "discovery"—a portal that had, "by the grace of Ghaunadaur," opened between one of the columns in their shrine and the Promenade. In a carefully choreographed dance, each of the other spies would do the same. One by one, at precisely timed intervals, they would usher their fanatics straight into the trap the high priestess had prepared. Qilué, meanwhile, would ensure the Protectors and other faithful kept well back, out of sight but ready to deal with the fanatics, should they stray from the designated path.

Qilué had explained that the Masked Lady herself had approved this plan. Valdar, when first told of it, had seen the Masked *Lord's* hand in it at once. Inviting Eilistraee's most resolute enemies into the heart of the Promenade, he told Kâras, was something the goddess would never contemplate. Eilistraee was a goddess who fought with song and sword, not shadows and subterfuge. This plan was *Vhaeraun's* doing.

Kâras had been convinced. He'd persuaded the high priestess to let him select the Nightshadows who would carry out "Eilistraee's" divine will, and ensured that Valdar was among them. When Qilué's call came, the hand-picked few would lead their Ghaunadaurians into the Promenade not in small, easily contained groups, but all at once—*away* from the trap. The temple would be overwhelmed, and the priestesses swept aside—while the Nightshadows sat out the battle in safety, downriver in Skullport. Later, when it was all over, they would re-assume their disguises and steer the fanatics into the trap Qilué had prepared, cleansing the temple a second time.

Once the Promenade was theirs, converts would be drawn from across Faerûn to a reinvigorated faith. And those of Eilistraee's priestesses who managed to survive would reap the bitter fruit of their misplaced trust. The females would be the ones given a choice, this time around: to don Vhaeraun's mask, and worship in silence and shadow, or to die by Vhaeraun's sword.

That had been the plan-within-a-plan. And it had been a good one, needing only subterfuge and determination to see it through—until oozes and slimes had come boiling up out of the lake. Surely Vhaeraun didn't intend to fill the Promenade with such filth! It would take an army to scour the temple clean, after that.

Masked . . . Lord, Kâras silently prayed, the honorific feeling out of place after nearly four years of praying to the Masked Lady. *Your servant seeks counsel. Is it your will we continue?*

No answer came.

Kâras stood, sweating. The future of his faith hung upon what happened next. Upon what he *decided* next.

As he hesitated near the doorway, listening to the shouts of excitement echoing through the keep, a voice sang into his mind. Qilué's voice! Clear as a tolling bell, the high priestess called to her spies. *It is time to begin the dance. Are you ready?*

The timing of the message couldn't be mere coincidence. The Masked Lord *had* to know what was happening, down here in Llurth Dreir. He obviously had confidence in Kâras— confidence enough to allow Qilué to set everything in motion, spawning or no.

Kâras squared his shoulders. The Masked Lord was depending upon him.

I stand ready, Lady Qilué, he thought back. *Expect the first group in moments.*

Begin, then. And may Eilistraee guide your steps. Her voice faded from his mind.

Kâras pulled the lump of amber from his pocket and walked to the nearest column, his feet slipping in the green sludge coating the floor. He had to force his body to move in that direction; the closer he got to the altar, the more difficult it became. He could feel the Ancient One's presence, terrible and grim, evil beyond words. Forcing himself against it bent him almost double.

He lifted the amber to the column and waited. Ready.

He heard shouts, drawing nearer: Shi'drin's voice, urging the others back to the altar room. Overlaying them was a sound that sent shivers down his spine—the sound of oozes sliding over stone.

Kâras pressed the amber to the column. A hole opened. "Quickly, brethren!" he cried. "Come and see! One of the columns has opened. It will lead us to the Pit of Ghaunadaur!"

Qilué strode through the Cavern of Song, past the faithful who gave voice to Eilistraee's eternal hymn. Those in her way took a quick step back as she passed, giving her room to pass by. One faltered in her hymn. Qilué strode on, not bothering to admonish her.

Qilué fumed. How had this happened? She'd been so careful! Yet somehow, Cavatina had figured out that a demon was inside the Crescent Blade—not only that, but which one. She should have expected that, from the Darksong Knight. She'd been foolish to think she could keep Wendonai hidden, especially from the one who had "killed" him.

She wished she could tell her priestesses that her strange behavior was just a charade, but she couldn't—not without also telling Wendonai, since he could see and hear everything within range of the Crescent Blade, including her otherwise silent mental communications. Fortunately, by Mystra's grace, he wasn't privy to her thoughts.

Qilué! Wendonai bellowed. He'd learned, early on, that calling her name forced her to pay attention to him. *The Darksong Knight knows. You should have slain her.*

I make the decisions, demon. Not you.

Poor decisions. She'll tell the others—if she hasn't already.

No point in killing her, then, is there?

They'll banish me—destroy the Crescent Blade.

Qilué almost wished someone *would* banish Wendonai. The cut on her wrist burned. The Crescent Blade felt heavy in her hand. She longed to have someone relieve her of this burden, yet she had to see this dance through to the end. The fate of hundreds of thousands of souls hung in the balance.

You might as well have killed those two priestesses, the demon continued. *Sealed inside the shrine, they'll die of thirst—a slow, lingering death, rather than a quick one.* He paused, and she could imagine his sly grin. *How very dhaerrow of you—something your ancestors would have appreciated.*

Qilué made no comment. The two priestesses wouldn't starve. Eilistraee would answer their prayers for sustenance.

What mattered was to contain the problem before it spread. Horaldin had been easy enough to silence, but Rylla would be more difficult. The battle-mistress either knew about Wendonai or suspected, judging by the way she'd been acting. It was unlikely she'd told anyone yet—she would have realized this would start a panic. More likely, she'd be preparing a banishment spell of her own.

If she succeeded, it would ruin everything.

Where *was* Rylla? Qilué had to find her. She realized that she should have kept the battle-mistress near her, instead of sending her away. She should have trusted her instincts.

Are you sure you didn't already bear my taint? Wendonai asked mockingly, continuing their previous conversation. *You certainly think like an Ilythiiri.*

Watch your tongue, demon, or I'll banish you myself.

And destroy the weapon that will kill Lolth? Without my essence sustaining it, the Crescent Blade will crumble to dust.

Be silent! She grasped her sheath and tried to shove the Crescent Blade into it, but felt the familiar resistance, like two lodestones pushing each other apart. She struggled against it, but the sword proved stronger. It sprang out of the sheath.

"Abyss take me!" Qilué swore—an oath she hadn't used since her childhood.

The demon chuckled. *Perhaps it will.*

Qilué stalked on through the cavern. She could have sheathed the sword if she'd tried harder, but she needed Wendonai to think he was in control—and that she feared the weapon would fall apart, were he not within it. That wouldn't happen, of course. Eilistraee's blessings would sustain it, just as they always had.

Her statue was just ahead, tucked into an alcove in the Cavern of Song. Carved from black marble, it showed a youthful Qilué with singing sword held high, exulting in the defeat of Ghaunadaur's avatar. The statue looked heavy and immovable—a false impression. In fact, it concealed the winding staircase that led down to the sealed Pit.

Qilué strode up to the halfling Protector who guarded it and stared down at her. "Is Battle-mistress Rylla below?"

Brindell shook her head.

"Has she passed this way recently?"

"No, Lady. Not since I took up station here."

"Where *is* she?" Silver fire crackled through Qilué's hair as her irritation flared.

Brindell took a step back. "Lady Qilué. What's wrong? Is the Promenade under attack?"

"What are you talking about?" Qilué spat. She'd never realized, until just this moment, how ridiculous the halfling looked, with her ink-stained face and mop of copper-colored hair.

Brindell pointed a pudgy finger at the Crescent Blade. "There's blood on your sword, Lady Qilué."

"There is?" Qilué lifted the weapon. A thin line of red trickled down the blade. The cut on her wrist must have been bleeding; the bracer that served as sheath for her silver dagger must have rubbed it open again. "It's nothing. Just a scratch." She glared down at Brindell. "Hold your post. Contact me—immediately—if you see Rylla."

Brindell gulped. "Yes, Lady."

Qilué strode away. She realized she'd been sharp with Brindell, but it was all part of the act. And it was drawing Wendonai in. She could feel it.

In recent months, she'd stepped up the tempo. Sometimes she "forgot," until it was almost too late, to drink the holy water that held Wendonai at bay. This gave the balor the illusion he was gradually wearing down her defenses, one cloven-hoofed step at a time. Two steps forward, one back. One step forward, two back. All part of the dance that would lead him exactly where she wanted him.

A dangerous gamble—one that might cost her the Promenade. But a necessary one, if the *dhaerrow* were to be led back into the light.

The Crescent Blade would be the key.

Ironically, Wendonai had given her the idea, when he'd derided her crusade as "futile." For each drow redeemed and brought up into Eilistraee's light, he'd gloated, a dozen were born with his taint. For every step Qilué led the drow forward, Wendonai yanked them twelve steps back.

The balor's taint ran constant and deep in the drow, in every one with even a drop of Ilythiiri blood in their veins. The only way they could be led out of this dark pall was through redemption—and redemption was something that took courage and strength. The very taint they needed to struggle against and overcome was what seduced most drow into choosing a less morally challenging, more "rewarding" path. They wound up, like flies, caught in Lolth's vast web. Even if they somehow managed to escape or avoid this, more often than not it was only through seeking out alliances with other, even more loathsome deities, like Ghaunadaur.

Qilué had experienced this taint, herself. After her failure to attune the Crescent Blade and drive the evil from it, the cut on her wrist had allowed the demon to slowly worm its way into her. She had been on the verge of purging his taint—a simple matter of releasing Mystra's silver fire within her body, rather than without—when she'd realized something. If she could somehow draw *all* of Wendonai's taint into herself she would, in the process, remove it from every drow on Toril. Then she could burn herself clean in one blinding flash of silver fire. She could set the drow free to choose a better path—to be led into Eilistraee's dance.

Qilué herself would likely be consumed in the process, her very soul reduced to ash by the incineration of so much evil, so much guilt, so much hatred. But the Crescent Blade would remain. Someone else—Cavatina, most likely—would carry on Eilistraee's work. Be named high priestess in Qilué's stead, take up the Crescent Blade, and kill Lolth.

Qilué sighed. She had the lancet she needed for the blooding that was to come: the Crescent Blade. She even knew the one place, on all of Toril, where it could be done; Eilistraee had revealed its location to her. But she wasn't quite ready, yet, to set her plan in motion. There always seemed to be something else that needed doing first. Q'arlynd, for example, was on the verge of attempting his casting, and would soon require her assistance. And within the Promenade itself, there were a dozen other things to tend to.

Like finding Rylla, and silencing her.

Perhaps, Qilué decided, she could flush the battle-mistress out. An "attack" by Ghaunadaur's cultists should do just that.

She sang the word that would make her symbol visible. A second song dispelled the locks she'd placed on the doors of the chamber that held the glyph-inscribed portal. Then she sent out a silent message to her spies. *It is time to begin the dance. Are you ready?*

Their answers came like a spatter of rain, the words overlapping each other. Some of the Nightshadows sounded eager, others tense. Two didn't answer at all. Perhaps they were dead. She prayed their souls had found their way to the

Masked Lady's domain. Kâras assured her he would be able to bring his group through Qilué smiled. That should bring Rylla running.

Begin, then, she replied. *And may Eilistraee guide your steps.*

That done, Qilué turned down the corridor that would take her to the river—the corridor that wound past the Moonspring Portal. The Protector guarding the magical pool saluted as she passed.

"Have you seen Rylla?" Qilué asked.

"No, Lady."

She's lying.

Qilué whirled. "Liar! She used the portal, didn't she?"

The Protector's face paled to gray. Her mouth opened, but no words came out.

Qilué felt the blood drain from her own face. She hadn't meant to say that aloud. "My apologies, priestess. I was answering a sending from someone else."

It wasn't much of an excuse, but it seemed to satisfy the Protector, who nodded and stiffly resumed her post.

Qilué kneeled and sang a scrying, passing her hand over the pool. She smiled as it revealed Rylla. Qilué's smile vanished abruptly as she recognized the chamber Rylla was standing in. The battle-mistress hadn't used the Moonspring Portal, after all. She was still within the Promenade—in the last place Qilué had expected to find her: the chamber that contained the trap for Ghauandaur's cultists!

Even as Qilué watched, the battle-mistress dispelled the symbol Horaldin had inscribed. Now she began a prayer—one that would seal the portal Qilué had so painstakingly created!

"No!" Qilué cried. She couldn't let that happen. Not now, with the first wave of Ghaunadaur's minions about to come through.

She sang a hymn that instantly conveyed her to the chamber along a beam of moonlight. Her boots slipped as she landed; the floor was ankle-deep in water. Rylla whirled, her prayer interrupted. "Qilué!" *Is it you?* she sent.

It would have been a clever ploy—had Wendonai not been able to listen in on Qilué's private conversations.

She thinks I'm controlling you.

You're not.

Not yet.

Be silent! Qilué shook her head. Rylla. She needed to concentrate on the battle-mistress. "Of course it's me. What are you doing?" Rylla hadn't tried to banish Wendonai yet. Perhaps she *didn't* know.

"Making sure everything's sealed up tight—as you ordered. There's a portal in this room that shouldn't be here." She began her prayer anew.

"Stop that!" Qilué cried. She sang a note into the shout that fused Rylla's fingers together, preventing her from completing the gesture that would seal the portal. "I created that portal. It leads to a trap. One that's about to be sprung. Go and find Horaldin—I need him to recast his enchantment! Now!"

Rylla turned. She was terrified—Qilué could smell the other female's fear—and her voice quavered. "Horaldin's dead."

She's lying. Trying to confuse you.

"What?" Qilué rubbed her wrist. "No, he's not. I just spoke to him." In fact, she'd just placed a geas on him: one that would compel him not to communicate with anyone—not by speech, nor spell, nor written word—until she gave him leave. She'd sealed the geas by drawing a line across his throat. The instant he tried to speak, he'd be wracked by a fit of violent coughing.

Coughing blood.

Qilué blinked, startled. Where had *that* thought come from?

"You cut his throat," Rylla said. "Decapitated him." She glanced, pointedly, at the Crescent Blade.

Qilué's eyes were drawn to the sword. To the blood on it.

She's trying to trick you. That's your blood. Your cut is leaking again.

Qilué lifted her arm.

Rylla tensed, her fused fingers gripping her holy symbol.

Qilué yanked her bracer up. She stared at the cut on her wrist. No—not a cut. A scar. Old and gray.

It wasn't her blood on the blade.

You had to do it. You had no choice. He would have ruined everything!

"He would have ruined everything," Qilué whispered. Her head was pounding. She felt a slight pressure against her calves and realized the water in the room was rising. Was the river overflowing? She glanced over her shoulder. No, the door behind her was shut. The water inside the chamber was expanding. And swiftly. As it topped her boots and spilled inside them, she felt sensation return to her feet. She hadn't realized, until this moment, that they'd been numb, nearly dead. They'd felt heavy, lumpish, hard . . .

The water rose to Qilué's knees. Her legs tingled.

Rylla moved closer, her feet swishing in the water. The battle-mistress's eyes locked on Qilué's. "Fight it," she whispered. "Pray. Drive Wendonai out." She sang out a word that filled the air with moonlight and lunged forward, slamming into Qilué, who toppled backward into the water.

She's trying to drown you! Wendonai howled.

Qilué nearly laughed at such an obvious lie. The water tasted pure and sweet on her lips. Rylla's song, pealing out from above, landed like sparkling drops of rain upon the water's surface. Qilué felt the battle-mistress's hands around her wrist and realized Rylla was trying to force the Crescent Blade down, into the water.

Into the healing, holy water.

No! Wendonai shouted. *That will destroy it! You'll never kill Lolth!*

His hand—Qilué's hand—punched up. The sword hilt slammed into Rylla's nose, knocking her backward and ripping her hands away from Qilué's wrist. Qilué felt her body leap up and shout a word that instantly burned the water from her skin. A familiar, heavy deadness returned and her thoughts slowed. It felt as if each were forcing its way through thick, stinking mud. From the waist down, however, her body was still within the holy water—and still her own. She threw herself to her knees, and suddenly the water was level with her mouth. She gulped it down, and felt its holiness force the demon out of her. Back into the Crescent Blade.

Drink your fill, Wendonai gloated from the sword, which she held just above the surface. *I've built up a resistance to it. I'll be back inside you the moment you surface.*

Another lie? Qilué suspected so, but she couldn't be certain of anything. Not any more. How long had the demon been warping her perceptions? What other crimes against her faith had he used her to commit? She ducked lower, submerging her head, but holding the Crescent Blade above the surface.

Inside the holy water, she was safe. She tried to decide what to do. One swift tug, and the Crescent Blade would be underwater with her. That would banish Wendonai. But it would also banish her one chance to eradicate his taint from the drow.

Yet she could see that this idea had been a seed planted by Wendonai. The irony was that it *was* possible. There was indeed a prayer that Qilué could use to draw all of Wendonai's taint inside her. And once his taint was within her, Mystra's silver fire would indeed destroy it. But the flaw in this plan—the flaw Wendonai had blinded her to, until now—was that with so much of his taint inside her, Qilué would lose control. Permanently. The demon would rule her body, as completely as Lolth ruled the Demonweb Pits. Any silver fire she did manage to summon would be twisted to an evil purpose.

Qilué stared at her battle-mistress through the water. Rylla floated nearby, face down, blood drooling from her broken nose. No longer breathing. Later, once she'd decided what to do next, Qilué would revive her. For the moment, she was just thankful Wendonai hadn't been able to swing the Crescent Blade. If it had severed Rylla's neck, her soul would have been destroyed.

Just as Horaldin's had been.

Qilué prayed that the Crescent Blade hadn't completely severed the druid's neck, that his soul had survived to join Rillifane under the great oak.

Qilué! Wendonai bellowed. *I know you can hear me. What will you do now? Banish me, and abandon any hope of saving your race?*

What indeed? Mystra's silver fire flickered in and out of Qilué's nostrils. Though her head was submerged in water, her long tresses spreading like seaweed across the surface above, she felt no need to breathe. She had all the time in the world to consider the question—unless, of course, someone opened one of the doors to this chamber, letting the holy water spill out.

Her spies, for example. The first group of Ghaunadaur's cultists would be arriving in the Promenade any moment, and heading this way.

She flicked a hand, resetting the locks.

She briefly considered telling the Nightshadows to abandon the plan, destroy their ambers, and flee Ghaunadaur's temples—then decided against it. Too much effort had been spent in putting them in place.

She considered her options. Had she inscribed an insanity symbol on the ruined temple—or was this another of Wendonai's tricks? She decided that it really didn't matter. If a symbol was in place, and the fanatics could be coerced into entering the portal, they would be turned into raving madmen who wouldn't even remember what a temple to their god looked like, let alone what to do with it. And if the symbol *didn't* exist, the fanatics would gain no benefit from a visit to the bottom of the Pit. If they somehow found their way back from the Ethereal Plane, they wouldn't have learned anything new about the Promenade. The planar breach had existed for centuries, sputtering on like a guttering candle, ever since Ghaunadaur had been driven through it.

Even if the worst happened—if the fanatics, despite being ethereal, found a way to open the breach enough for an avatar to come through, it wouldn't matter. The seals at the top of the Pit would ensure that the Ancient One's avatar didn't escape.

As she sat, thinking, the water surrounding her began to vibrate: the result of an alarm, close by, its clamor shrill enough to pass through stone. The timing was too close to be a coincidence. Kâras must have brought his group through.

Confirmation came as three different priestesses shouted Qilué's name at once, urgently reporting they'd spotted fanatics approaching the Promenade, from the far side of the bridge. That they were going to engage them until reinforcements arrived.

Qilué gave a mental command in reply, ordering them to allow the fanatics to cross the bridge, and *not* to engage them, but instead to set up defensive positions at least fifty paces back from the western side of the bridge. She wondered if they would heed her—how many of her priestesses, besides Cavatina, Leliana, and Rylla, now knew about Wendonai, and would be suspicious of her commands.

Kâras, she sent, *where are you?*

Far side of the bridge.

There's bad news. The portal is still in place, but the enchantment glyph has been dispelled. You're going to have to talk your fanatics into entering the trap—but not quite yet. The doors of the room are still sealed. I need a few moments more before I can unlock them. You'll have to stall, once you're across the bridge. Can you manage that?

I'll try.

Qilué nodded. It was all she could ask of anyone. She sent a mental command to the rest of her spies. *Nightshadows—*

the plan is postponed. Remain in position, and do not bring the cultists through until I contact you.

She broke contact, not bothering to wait for their acknowledgements. It was time to do something she should have done, long ago: destroy the Crescent Blade.

She started to draw the sword under the water, ignoring Wendonai's screams of protest, his wild promises, his shouts that he wouldn't die, that he'd have his vengeance—that even if he couldn't personally revenge himself, then Lolth certainly would, since her powers were equal to—

Qilué abruptly halted, the blade only halfway submerged.

There *was* a way to purge Wendonai's taint from the drow, she realized. *She* didn't have to be the one who called down silver fire—it could be directed into her body from without. Any of her sisters could provide the lethal blast that would incinerate the demon's taint.

Assuming, of course, one of them could be persuaded to do it.

Laeral, she decided. She'd already guessed something was wrong with the Crescent Blade and would take less convincing.

Qilué steeled herself. Was she really ready to bid farewell to the Promenade, her Protectors, her priestesses—everything she had worked for centuries to build? She had to. It would be the salvation of the drow. All of the drow. The dawn of a glorious new day. Out of the darkness, and into the light.

Qilué, however, wouldn't survive to see it.

Tears blended with the water. *Eilistraee,* she silently sang. *Is this your will?*

The answer came not in words, but in a sign. A beam of braided moonlight and shadow lanced down into the water, directly in front of Qilué. She had only to touch it to be transported to the place she had just thought of—the place where the deed would be done.

Qilué nodded. Very well then.

Myroune, she sang.

Use of the truename would ensure that Wendonai wouldn't know whom she was contacting. It would also ensure a prompt reply.

Her sister answered at once. Wasting no time, Qilué told Laeral where to meet her and what needed to be done—in carefully couched language that used references only Laeral would understand. All the while, she could feel Wendonai's seething anger as the sword vibrated in her hand.

Laeral agreed to do as she asked, but with great reluctance. *Do you truly wish this, Sister?*

Eilistraee wishes it, Qilué replied. *For the sake of the drow, it must be done.*

I will meet you there. Laeral's voice faded from her mind.

Now there was one last thing that needed to be done.

Qilué touched the mind of her Darksong Knight. *Cavatina,* she sent. *Your suspicions were correct: Wendonai corrupted me. I am removing myself from the Promenade. I may not return. If I do not, you are to lead the ritual that will choose the next high priestess. You must also assist Q'arlynd with the casting he is preparing. May Eilistraee bless you, and guide your steps. Take up her sword and sing.*

That said, Qilué unlocked the doors to the room with a flick of her hand. Then she reached out of the water to grasp the moonbeam, and teleported away.

CHAPTER 7

T'lar watched from above as Guldor strode into his private sanctum and closed the door behind him. The wizard pulled a pinch of glittering dust from a pocket and flicked it at the door while muttering a spell. He tested the handle and nodded.

T'lar, perched like a spider on a ceiling beam above, tensed as he began a second incantation, this one directed at the center of the room. She held her dagger by its point. If the wizard lifted his head even slightly, she'd embed it between his eyes.

Guldor's second spell, however, had no visible effect. Nor did he glance in T'lar's direction. He unfastened his cloak and flung it to the side. The garment halted in midair and was neatly folded by an invisible conjured servitor. Guldor, meanwhile, flopped face down onto a divan and gestured at his boots. They tugged off, revealing narrow feet. Dimples appeared in the grayish soles as the servitor massaged them. Guldor, however, remained stiff and unrelaxed. It looked as though the tension of the recent Conclave meeting had not yet dissipated.

As the invisible servitor continued to massage the wizard, T'lar spotted movement within a full-length mirror that was mounted in an ornate gold frame on the wall. The reflection of the room wavered and was replaced. It was as if a door had opened onto another chamber. A figure stepped into view within the mirror: that of *Streea'Valsharess* Zauviir, high priestess of Lolth. Imperious in her spider-silk robes and silver web-crown, the priestess stared into the wizard's private sanctum.

Guldor glanced up at the mirror. He didn't look pleased to see his aunt.

The high priestess scowled out of the mirror. "I heard what happened today."

"Bad news travels quickly."

"How could you have overlooked the fact that his sister was a *bae'qeshel* singer? I thought you were more thorough than that!"

"*You* were the one who wanted to move quickly," Guldor snapped back. "I was the one who advised patience."

"Patience!" the high priestess spat. "Don't you lecture me on patience. We've been waiting *years* to secure a second position on the Conclave, only to miss our chance! If we'd moved even a cycle sooner, this newly minted master wouldn't have been there."

"You were the one who chose this cycle, not me. What's more, you promised a distraction that would prevent him from appearing before the Conclave—a promise you failed to keep!"

"My decisions were based on information you provided! You said the other masters would be looking for a way to counter Seldszar's latest alliances. That was *your* recommendation, boy!"

"You'd do well to remember, Priestess, that this 'boy' is

one of those who rule this city," Guldor retorted, "while you merely sit in the shadows and spin."

"Pah!" The priestess tossed her head, causing the tiny obsidian spiders hanging from her crown to tinkle. "Your lack of diligence has made our position even worse than it was. This new 'master' is one of Eilistraee's."

"Perhaps." Guldor made a wry face. "Or perhaps not. My accusation was a spear thrust in the dark. We'll have to delve deeper before we can be certain."

"Perhaps it's time someone a little more certain headed up your College."

Guldor's head jerked up. "Is that a threat?"

T'lar listened as the pair continued to argue. The politics of this city mattered little to her. She merely carried out the Lady Penitent's commands.

When *Streea'Valsharess* Zauviir had invited the Temple of the Black Mother to invest a shrine in Sshamath, T'lar had expected the Lady Penitent to reject the offer out of hand. The priestesses of Sshamath were weak; they'd been responsible for one of Lolth's greatest defeats. The Lady Penitent, however, had decided to accept. T'lar remembered her words: "Where better to spin my web, than in the void where Lolth's was torn asunder?" And so T'lar had been sent north.

Streea'Valsharess Zauviir had promised great things, describing Sshamath as an egg sac seething with discontent and ready to burst. She'd promised to deliver the entire city into the Lady Penitent's hands. She'd lied—T'lar could see that. The Conclave held this city in an adamantine grip. Instead of fighting the masters, the high priestess hoped to join them.

Weakness. The very thing the Lady Penitent most despised.

Streea'Valsharess Zauviir would have to be eliminated—sooner, rather than later.

The image in the mirror faded. Guldor at last relaxed. When he closed his eyes, T'lar hummed a melody that shifted her appearance to match what she'd just seen in the mirror, then sprang off the beam. She drew upon her *dro'zress* an instant before she landed, halting her downward momentum, and landed soundlessly on the floor behind the wizard. She jabbed stiffened fingers into pressure points on Guldor's back, sending him into a spasm. Guldor gasped in pain. His eyes sprang open, and he saw T'lar's reflection in the mirror. "How—?"

Before he could complete the question, she grabbed his hair, yanked his head back, and sliced his throat.

Blood soaked the cushions of the divan and ran in streams onto the floor. T'lar caught some of the warm liquid in a cupped hand and raised it to her lips. "Strength," she whispered. Then she drank. Behind her, the invisible servitor mindlessly continued the task it had been set: massaging its dead master's feet.

T'lar pointed her bloody dagger at the mirror. You're next, she silently vowed. But before she dealt with the high priestess, there was something T'lar wanted to know. Like an itch, her curiosity had to be scratched.

She sang the hymn the Lady Penitent had taught her. She exhaled, and felt her body fold inward on itself and become gaseous. With a thought, she sent herself wafting toward the door Guldor had oh-so-carefully sealed with his magic. She slipped through the crack underneath it and was gone.

Q'arlynd sat on a low, round pillow, his legs crossed, deep in Reverie. He felt the heat from the darkfire hearth on his skin, smelled the remnants of his rothé-and-sporeball stew, and could still taste the last sip of wine he'd taken before settling into his trance. His eyes were open, but his mind was far away.

His thoughts wandered back several decades, to his days as a student in Ched Nasad's Conservatory. He thought of Ilmra, one of the females who had made the rare decision to become a mage, rather than a priestess. She'd been a fine-looking female, one he'd fantasized about more than once during their time together as novices. He'd imagined himself victoriously battling Ched Nasad's enemies beside her, then "surrendering" to a struggle of a very different sort.

During their days at the Conservatory, one of the first things the novices had been taught was a cantrip that revealed magical auras. Q'arlynd had mastered it readily enough. The gesture was a simple flicking of the fingers that mimicked an eye opening, and the trigger was a single word: *faerjal.* Yet Ilmra had miscast the spell when a magical item was brought out for her to examine, and had failed to identify the item correctly. She'd been strapped as a result—hard enough to fracture a finger. Later that cycle, when her turn came to list the colors of the auras around the items laid out on the table, she'd faltered a second time. Q'arlynd had tried to help her by signing the answers.

Instead of taking his help, she'd pointed out what he was doing to their instructor—even though this meant admitting her own failure. She'd watched, smiling, as he'd been lashed, then submitted to a lashing herself. Later, after Q'arlynd had been sent to his room to meditate on the folly and futility of trying to aid another, she'd slipped into his chamber and taken him. Even now, decades later, he vividly remembered her fingers digging painfully into the hot red welts that criss-crossed his shoulders as she mounted him.

It had been one of the sweetest experiences of his young life.

His forehead warmed: the *kiira,* absorbing the memory. An image formed in his mind: one of the ancestors who'd worn the lorestone millennia ago. She had white hair, yet her skin was a faded brown, rather than black. *You tried to help Ilmra, out of compassion. You followed Eilistraee's dance, even then.*

Q'arlynd laughed out loud. "Hardly. I did it because I wanted her to take me. And it worked—just, not the way I'd expected." He lingered in the memory. He wondered if Ilmra had survived the fall of the city. Probably not.

The *kiira* cooled slightly—a sign of his ancestors' displeasure. Q'arlynd gave a mental shrug. They'd asked him to include memories he thought were instructive. The one he'd just placed in the lorestone was doubly so. It taught the magic-detection cantrip, and at the same time, served as a reminder that all reward came at a price.

He heard a crackling sound: the darkfire flames, flickering. A breeze down the chimney must have disturbed them. He was so deep in Reverie that he paid the noise no heed at first. He was reliving a night in the World Above, when he'd used a spell to spy on Eilistraee's priestesses as they danced with swords in hand around the goddess's sacred stone in the Misty Forest. It had been windy that night, with snow blowing through the trees. Yet the priestesses had danced naked.

He smiled, savoring the memory. He'd watched, half-hoping they'd catch him in his transgression. It had been a long time since a female had taken him . . .

The darkfire settled down again as the breeze ended. The flames resumed their steady flickering—not that his body needed warming anymore. Remembering the priestesses' dance was—

All at once, he remembered he was in Sshamath. No breezes blew here—except magical ones.

"Luth—"

Something stung the back of his neck. It felt like several needles pressing into his skin at once. Whatever had just pricked him fell to the floor with a thud. As his flesh deadened, he realized whatever had just struck him had been poisoned. His jaw locked, his neck stiffened. He couldn't complete his abjuration. Nor could he turn his head to see his assailant. Then his magical earring drew the venom up his neck, into his left ear, and into itself. All that remained was a bitter taste in his mouth—which told him what the poison was. Made from the excretions of a carrion crawler, it was designed to paralyze, rather than kill.

He sensed movement behind him. His assailant, coming closer. Q'arlynd feigned paralysis. He slowly shifted his left thumb to the fur-wrapped needle of glass that pierced his shirt cuff. As his thumb touched the spell component, he whispered a word under his breath. His finger bones tingled as lightning crackled to life inside his hand. A flick of his fingers would release it.

His assailant stepped into view. He recognized her at once: T'lar Mizz'rynturl, the *bae'qeshel* bard whose "school" Guldor had tried to nominate. She moved in utter silence; even when she squatted next to him, her clothing didn't rustle. She held a dagger with a spider pommel. Ready for use, but not threatening him with it yet. She stared, pointedly, at his groin. "Thinking of me, were you?" She laughed.

Q'arlynd felt thankful he was already aroused. T'lar was disturbingly close, and the menace she exuded was a powerful aphrodisiac. Yet he wasn't foolish enough to give in to it completely. He held the lightning within his hand, trusting to surprise to give him the edge when the time came to cast his spell. For the moment, he wanted to know what she was up to. Had she come to steal something? He kept utterly still, not even moving his eyes. Soon, however, he'd need to give in to the urge to blink.

You play a dangerous game, Grandson, whispered his ancestors from inside the *kiira.*

T'lar hummed softly. Q'arlynd felt magic brush his mind, as light as a cobweb. Her spell proved no more durable. It tore to pieces the instant it met the *kiira.* She didn't seem to realize this, however. Perhaps under the impression her spell had succeeded, she leaned in close and asked a question that was clearly designed to stir up his thoughts.

It wasn't the one he'd expected.

"Why was your sister killed?" she whispered, her breath hot against his ear. "What did she do to anger the Lady Penitent?"

His concentration slipped. A spark crackled from his fingertips. T'lar leaped away from him—so quickly Q'arlynd didn't even see her move. One moment she was squatting next to him; the next, she stood halfway across the room, her dagger poised. Her arm whipped forward, and the dagger flashed through the air. Q'arlynd twisted aside and hurled a lightning bolt at her. She dodged, faster than his eye could follow. The lightning struck the shelf behind her, exploding it apart and setting several scrolls on fire. Q'arlynd frantically searched for his assailant, and felt a sharp pain in his side as he moved. He touched his shirt, and his hand came away bloody. Unlike her, he hadn't dodged quickly enough.

He saw a flash of motion out of the corner of his eye: her kick. Her foot slammed into his face. Spitting blood, he went down. He landed on his back, bent across his cushion like a sacrifice on an altar stone. She hurled herself on top of him, straddling his stomach, hooking her legs around his, and twining her fingers in his so he couldn't gesture. Her legs squeezed. He gasped as the wound on his side pulled open and tried to buck her off, but she was too strong. Swift as a striking spider, she transferred both of his hands to one of hers. Her free hand scooped up her dagger, and she jammed the hilt into his mouth like a bit. He tasted metal and sweat-impregnated leather, and the legs of the spider-shaped pommel dug sharply into his cheek. She forced his head back, pushing so hard he thought his neck would snap. Involuntary tears sprung to his eyes. He tried not to gag.

"I could kill you," she told him. "Quicker than a blink." The dagger jerked for emphasis. He gurgled from the pain, tasting the blood that slid down his throat from his split lips. "But first, I offer you the opportunity to do penance."

The arousal he'd felt a moment ago was gone. Fear had replaced it, along with confusion. He tried to talk, but all that came out was, "Whuh—whuh—?"

"You're Eilistraee's," she hissed. "Forswear her, and live. Embrace the Lady Penitent. Embrace Lolth."

Q'arlynd felt sweat break out on his forehead. Not so long ago, it would have been easy to renounce Eilistraee. That was no longer possible. His ancestors whispered fiercely at him from within the lorestone. *Fight her,* they urged. *Die proudly, with Eilistraee's song on your lips!* Q'arlynd found himself swept up in their strident chorus, unable to speak the words T'lar had ordered him to. Nor did he want to, he suddenly realized. He took comfort in the fact that it was Eilistraee, rather than Lolth, who would claim his soul after death. He finally understood what Leliana had tried to explain to him, back when they'd first met: that to have tried, even if failure was the result, was more worthy than to surrender and survive. He remembered her words still: "To Eilistraee, struggle is honored equally with success."

Of course, to *pretend* to surrender wouldn't hurt.

"Will you do penance?" T'lar asked. She stared at him intently, her lithe body silhouetted by the light of the burning scroll shelf.

Q'arlynd managed the slightest of nods.

She removed her dagger from his mouth and reversed it. The point pricked his neck. He didn't dare swallow, lest it's the razor-sharp steel slice open the bulge in his throat.

T'lar smiled. "Pledge yourself to Lolth, then, and be redeemed. Refuse, and I'll open your throat. You'll be dead before your magic can save you."

Q'arlynd opened his bloody lips, drew breath, and prepared to speak the only spell that might save him. It required no gestures, no components. Just a single word.

Whether it would work given that Sshamath was surrounded by *Faerzress*, was an open question. He decided to aim for somewhere close at hand.

"Da'bauth!" he spat.

Magic wrenched him sideways through space. He landed hard on his back in the hallway outside his study, cracking his head on the floor. He shook off the pain and sprang to his feet. With a wave, he unlocked the door. Wrenching it open, he hurled a spell into the room. Yellowish green vapor poured from his palm, filling his study with a deadly, swirling cloud. He slammed the door shut and locked it again.

He waited, using the beats of his pounding heart to mark the time. After twice the amount of time required, he cast a protective spell on himself and opened the door. His study was a shambles. Burning scrolls littered the floor. Everything was dusted with the residue of the poisonous fog he'd conjured. He scanned the room for footprints, but saw none. Nor did he see T'lar, even when he peered through his gem.

She had vanished as mysteriously as she'd arrived.

He stood, holding the wound in his side, wondering if she would be back. He doubted she'd make the same mistake twice: the next time they met, she'd kill him, rather than trying to convert him.

The more he thought about it, the odder the encounter seemed. "Redemption" was something Eilistraee offered. Lolth's priestesses never gave those who had strayed from the web a second chance. Blasphemy was always cause for retribution—the only variation was whether the blasphemer's death was swift or lingering.

And just who was the Lady Penitent? Was that another of the new titles Lolth had assumed since ending her Silence?

As he stood, pondering the mystery, he heard footsteps approaching along the hallway. He whirled, and lightning crackled from his fingertips. He stopped short of casting it when he saw Alexa gaping at him. He still held his trueseeing gem and raised it to his eyes to confirm that this was, indeed, his apprentice, before he allowed the lightning to dissipate.

"Master—you're wounded! Permit me to assist you." She rushed forward, lifting a gold chain from around her neck. Q'arlynd twisted away. "It's just a scratch," he said harshly, anger rising in him as he realized how close he—a master of his own College—had just come to getting killed. "No need for that."

He waved the healing periapt away. The blood red gem was carved with a stylized spider: symbol of the faith that had created it. Q'arlynd didn't want anything of Lolth's touching him, ever again. "I'll use a healing potion, instead."

Alexa bowed her head. "As you wish, Master Q'arlynd." Though straight-cut bangs shaded her eyes, Q'arlynd could see her gaze slide sideways, to take in his ruined study, as she replaced the periapt around her neck.

She lingered, when she should have taken the hint and left.

"What is it, apprentice?" Q'arlynd snapped.

"The gorgondy wine has arrived."

That, at least, was good news.

Alexa waited, a gleam in her eyes. There was something else she wanted to tell him.

"And?" Q'arlynd prompted.

"Master Guldor's dead. *Streea'Valsharess* Zauviir killed him."

Q'arlynd cracked a smile. More good news.

"She slit his throat," Alexa continued. "They sent for a diviner, and he saw the whole thing. She did it with a ceremonial dagger. It was a sacrifice to Lolth."

Q'arlynd's eyes narrowed as he remembered T'lar's dagger. "Did she offer him a chance to repent, first?"

Alexa looked puzzled.

"Never mind." Q'arlynd waved a hand—and winced. "Tell the slaves to fetch me some clean clothes. Something formal. I've got an important meeting to attend."

Q'arlynd nodded to the three seated masters and set the decanter on the low table, next to the goblet that already stood there. The decanter's cut-glass contours sparkled, reflecting the glimmer of the blue-white faerie fire that danced across the ceiling of Master Seldszar's scrying room. The wine the decanter held was a rich ruby red. Even with the crystal stopper in place, Q'arlynd could smell its heady bouquet. The fragrance tugged at his mind, causing his thoughts to wander to . . .

He shook his head and stepped back from the ankle-high table. "Gorgondy wine," he announced.

Master Urlryn leaned forward on his cushion to examine the decanter. The golden goblet hanging against his chest swung forward slightly on its mithral chain. He caught it before it could strike the decanter. "I wonder . . .—If my goblet samples a little, might I be able to alter the vessel's enchantment so that it produces *gorgondy* wine upon command?"

Master Seldszar interrupted the study of the spheres orbiting his head just long enough to give Urlryn a cautionary look. "There's only one draught. We'll need it. All of it."

Urlryn settled back on his cushion, which flattened under his weight. A smile briefly played across his face, causing his jowls to twitch. "A pity. Gorgondy is worth its weight in mithral."

As the two masters bantered, Q'arlynd circled to the only available cushion. He stepped cautiously to avoid bumping Urlryn's phantasmal guard dog with his foot. He knew where it sat: a sheen of drool marked the pale green chrysolite tiles on the floor. He seated himself across the table from the third master and placed his hands flat against his bent knees, where the others could easily see his fingers. Masters only trusted each other so far. Keeping one's hands visible and unmoving was a sign of good faith.

The master on the opposite side of the table—Master Masoj—was as lean and wiry as Urlryn was corpulent. Masoj kept the front half of his scalp shaved. The bone white hair capping the back of his head hung in a single braid that touched the floor behind his cushion. Glittering dust covered his face, neck, and hands—and, presumably, the rest of his body under his clothes and boots—a protective abjuration capable of deflecting even the most powerful spells. Q'arlynd imagined it must feel gritty and uncomfortable, especially in the armpits and groin. But perhaps the Master of Abjuration had a spell that would negate that.

Q'arlynd noted—without looking directly at Masoj's forehead—that it was smooth, without indentation. He wondered if Masoj was one of the two who'd been promised the chance to claim a *kiira*. Seldszar was playing his pieces close to his chest on that one. Even Q'arlynd didn't know which two masters, besides Seldszar, were descended from Miyeritari stock.

Seldszar sat with his arms folded. Even though they hid the largest of the eyes embroidered on his *piwafwi,* the other eyes all seemed to stare vigilantly in every direction at once. Seldszar's own eyes—a strange, pale yellow—remained fixed on the crystal spheres orbiting his head. Clear eyelids swept across his eyes every few heartbeats.

Though Seldszar never removed his gaze from his crystals, Q'arlynd felt the master's attention shift to him. "Master Q'arlynd," Seldszar said. "Thank you for joining us."

Q'arlynd sat straighter. Master. He loved the sound of the word. He inclined his head in acknowledgement of Seldszar's formal greeting.

Masoj shifted slightly, his bony knees creaking. "Let's get to the point, shall we? My vote wasn't enough. You require something else from me before I can claim my prize. What?"

Ah, Q'arlynd thought. The Master of Abjuration *had* been promised a *kiira*. Whether Masoj's bloodline was pure enough for him to claim it, however, remained to be seen.

"Yes, young Master Q'arlynd," Urlryn said. His voice dropped just enough on the title to imply scorn, without openly stating it. An act, for Masoj's benefit. Urlryn didn't want the Master of Abjuration to know how much hope he'd balanced on the knife's edge of this meeting. Urlryn's College had been greatly weakened by the augmented *Faerzress*— though not nearly as severely as the College of Divination. He nodded across the table at Seldszar. "Tell us what our combined centuries of study couldn't. How is the *Faerzress* to be unmade?"

"It isn't," Q'arlynd answered bluntly. "Sshamath's *Faerzress* will remain long after we four are dust. What we will do, instead, is remove ourselves from it. Sever the link between drow and *Faerzress.*"

"*All* drow?" Urlryn asked—another scripted question.

Q'arlynd shook his head. He repeated what his ancestors had told him. "Not all. Those who worship the Spider Queen will derive no benefit from our casting."

He waited. This was the moment of revelation. Seldszar had been able to learn much about Masoj, but not his faith. If the Master of Abjuration worshiped Lolth, these careful negotiations would be for naught.

" 'Our' casting?" Masoj asked, lifting an eyebrow.

Q'arlynd touched the lorestone on his forehead. "I'll be present, though not actively participating. The ancestors of House Melarn will be on hand to provide advice, should you three have any questions."

We stand ready, they whispered.

Masoj nodded, but his attention was on the other two masters. "What spell am I to provide?"

Q'arlynd hid a sigh of relief. Masoj *wasn't* a spider kisser. "The casting is complex, requiring several participants," he explained. "The Colleges of Masters Seldszar and Urlryn will provide mages to cast the simpler abjurations: those that break enchantments and remove curses. I have also secured a promise of assistance from a priestess capable of evoking a miracle."

Masoj's eyebrow rose a little farther. He didn't ask which deity the priestess honored—that was easy enough for him to guess, thanks to Guldor's accusations at the Conclave. Q'arlynd wondered how Masoj would react when he actually met Qilué.

"What we need from you," Q'arlynd continued, "is your expertise in reversing magical imprisonments."

"Where is the abjuration to be cast?" Masoj asked.

"We don't know yet."

Masoj's nostrils flared slightly.

"But we will in a moment," Seldszar interjected. He nodded at the decanter. "A vision will reveal it presently. That's why I invited each of you here. One of us may recognize something the others do not."

That wasn't quite true, Q'arlynd reflected. Masoj wasn't nearly as well versed in ancient lore as the other two masters, and he wouldn't be that useful. Letting him observe the vision first hand, however, would give the impression that the others had nothing to hide.

Masoj folded his arms. "And if I refuse to participate?"

Seldszar lifted his hands, fingers poised. "Then you'll never learn what it feels like to pluck at the strands of the Weave, and play it like a harp." He mimed playing an instrument, and lifted an eyebrow. The *selu'kiira* on his forehead turned visible.

Q'arlynd, watching Masoj, resisted the urge to smile when the other wizard's pupils dilated. Seldszar was not only a master wizard, but a master manipulator. Masoj was reading between the lines, just as Seldszar had hoped. He obviously believed Seldszar had already dabbled in high magic. Judging by the way Masoj's eyes slid sideways to Urlryn, he must have been wondering if the Master of Conjuration and Summoning also had a *kiira*. Ironically, Masoj didn't once look at Q'arlynd—the only one of the four who actually *had* worked an *arselu'tel'quess* spell—not just once, but twice.

"Well now." Masoj's lips settled in a forced smile. "That should give those web-shrouded bitches pause, should they start thinking about taking out another of the Conclave." One hand flipped upward, its fingers curled: the sign for a dead spider.

Q'arlynd joined the other masters in polite laughter.

"That's settled, then." Master Seldszar leaned forward and removed the decanter's stopper. He poured some of the contents into the goblet. He flicked a finger, and one of his crystals left its orbit. It drifted above the center of the table and hung there, spinning slowly in place. He drank down the wine and set the empty goblet back on the table. His pupils narrowed to pinpricks.

"Where was the spell cast that turned the dark elves into drow?" he intoned, staring intently at the crystal.

Urlryn, Masoj, and Q'arlynd leaned forward expectantly. In a moment, the gnomish "vision wine" would do its work. Seldszar would tear aside the hazy screen the city's *Faerzress* had imposed on his divinations and pinpoint the spot where the spell that would set the drow free must be cast.

Slowly, an image filled the crystal. At first, it was too small to make out. But as Q'arlynd stared at the crystal and concentrated, the vision filled his mind, obliterating the room in which he sat. It was as if he were a bird, looking down upon a clearing in a forest. Tiny figures—surface elves, but too distant to make out their individual features—moved back and forth across the clearing, entering and exiting a round building whose domed roof reflected flashes of sunlight. The dome, he saw as the image drew closer, was constructed of thousands of leaf-shaped shards of pale green glass that had been fitted together like a puzzle. They were held together not by strips of lead, but by the interwoven branches of trees whose trunks buttressed the building's sides.

An awed female voice whispered from inside the lorestone: *One of his temples.*

Q'arlynd's heart quickened. He didn't need to ask which god the temple honored. The ancestor who had spoken had lived at a time when the Seldarine were still worshiped by the dark elves, and had paid homage to this one, in particular. Q'arlynd knew, without needing to ask, which god she was referring to: Corellon Larethian, First of the Seldarine.

Creator and protector of the elves, she added in a hushed, reverent voice.

The god who condemned us, another voice said harshly—a male voice, this time. Q'arlynd recognized it as belonging to one of his post-Descent ancestors.

Q'arlynd had drifted away from the vision while speaking to the ancestors; he saw it anew as a gauzy curtain, overlaying the room. The other three masters stared at the crystal in silence, their eyes squinted against the World Above's harsh glare. All three wore slight frowns. They obviously didn't recognize the building.

"It's a temple to Corellon Larethian," Q'arlynd told them. "In the forest of . . ."

He waited for his ancestor to supply the name, but there was only silence.

I never worshiped at that temple, the female said. *I have no idea where it is situated.*

Nor do I, the male added.

Like echoes rippling through a cavern, other voices followed: *Neither do I. Nor do I. Nor I . . .*

Q'arlynd felt his cheeks grow warm. He turned slightly to Seldszar. He hated to pressure the more senior master. Yet he had no choice.

Seldszar, however, didn't acknowledge Q'arlynd's cue. His eyes remained locked on the temple. "If it's Corellon's, that would explain the oak trees," he observed.

Thirteen of them, the female voice said. *One for each branch that supports the Creator.*

Three fewer, after the Fall, the male added. *They withered, without Corellon's grace.*

At first, Q'arlynd couldn't understand what they were talking about. Then he remembered what he'd been taught during his short tenure at Eilistraee's shrine in the Misty Forest. Corellon Larethian had, indeed, once ruled thirteen lesser Seldarine. Two betrayed him—Lolth and her son Vhaeraun—and a third allowed herself to be banished from Arvandor, together with her mother and brother, so the drow might one day find redemption: Eilistraee.

That number grew to eleven, during the time I trod the Underdark, the male voice said. *The Black Archer's priests slew several of our House.*

Q'arlynd's ancestor supplied the name of the god who had found favor in Corellon's court: Shevarash the Black Archer, the once-mortal surface elf who had vowed never to rest, smile, or laugh, until the last drow was slain. A slaughter

Corellon condoned—despite the fact that its victims included Eilistraee's drow faithful, even though they had rejected the wanton cruelty of their race.

Q'arlynd snorted. So much for the surface elves' high ideals.

He realized the other masters were staring at him. They too had withdrawn from the vision. The crystal that had provided the vision left its spot above the table and resumed its orbit around Seldszar's head.

Q'arlynd cleared his throat. He repeated what his ancestors had just told him. "You'll have noted there were thirteen oak trees supporting the dome," he told the other masters. "A significant number. The vision showed us a temple that was built at a time when Lolth, Vhaeraun, and Eilistraee were still counted among the Seldarine."

"But that was thirty *millennia* ago—before the first Crown War!" Urlryn blurted.

"Indeed." Seldszar wet his dry lips. "The vision tasted of dust."

"Surely the temple no longer stands," Urlryn continued.

Masoj waved a bony hand. "As long as the abjuration is cast in the same spot, it won't matter if the temple's fallen."

"You miss my point," Urlryn said. "Without knowing what the spot currently looks like, we can't teleport to it. Even the most experienced teleportation mage couldn't find it." He nodded in Q'arlynd's direction.

Q'arlynd inclined his head, proud that the other master was acknowledging his expertise in that field.

Masoj stared pointedly at Seldszar, "Do *you* know where the temple stood? Does your lorestone?"

Seldszar sat quietly a moment, communing with his *kiira*. "No," he said at last. He stared pointedly at Q'arlynd's *kiira*.

"My ancestors . . ." Q'arlynd swallowed nervously. "They, ah, didn't recognize the forest."

It would be somewhere in Aryvandaar, the female voice said. *Or Keltormir.*

"But it's somewhere in the lands that were once home to ancient Aryvandaar, or Keltormir," he repeated aloud. A memory sprang into his mind. He stared, through the eyes of one of his long-dead ancestors, at a map spread on a table. Kingdoms were labeled, in a flowing hand: Aryvandaar, Illefarn, Miyeritar, Shantel Othreier, Keltormir, Thearnytaar, Eiellûr, Syòpiir, Orishaar, and Ilythiir. He knew where Miyeritar was—today that portion of the World Above was known as the High Moor. Aryvandaar, he saw, lay just north of it, while Keltormir was well to the south of that.

Q'arlynd described what he'd just seen.

"That's hardly very helpful," Masoj said.

"At least it's better than 'somewhere on the surface,'" Urlryn countered. "That's the best most drow can do, when it comes to ancient geography."

Q'arlynd stroked his chin, thinking hard, as Masoj and Urlryn traded glares. Something niggled at him. At last he worked out what it was. "There's something that's bothering me," he told them. "Sages date the Descent to just over eleven thousand years ago. Yet Master Seldszar's vision showed us a temple that had to have been built at least *thirty* thousand years ago. That's a difference of nineteen thousand years."

Urlryn shrugged. "A mythal could have sustained the temple for that long."

"That's indeed possible," Q'arlynd agreed. "But if the temple was still standing at the time of the Descent, why didn't my ancestors recognize it? Some of them are dark elves—one of them worshiped Corellon Larethian." He paused. "I think she didn't recognize the temple because it was gone before her time. Smothered by the forest, perhaps. But the site must have remained holy, at least until the time of the Descent. I think that's why the high mages whose magic invoked the Descent chose the spot: because no one, save them, knew where it was."

Seldszar tapped his fingers together in a patter of applause. "Well done, my boy, well done." He nodded at the others. "You see why I chose to nominate him to the Conclave?"

"We're *still* no further ahead," Masoj protested. "We already knew the casting was done at one of Corellon Larethian's temples."

No, we didn't, Q'arlynd thought. But he held his tongue.

Seldszar tapped the empty decanter. "The question we should be asking ourselves," he told the others, "is why the gorgondy wine gave an image that didn't precisely answer the question I posed. 'Where was the spell cast that turned the dark elves into drow?' was how I phrased it. The vision should have showed us what the area looks like now, not thousands of years ago."

Urlryn frowned. "Are you suggesting the high mages stepped back in time?"

"It's possible," Seldszar said. "Gorgondy wine is a gnomish vintage, made using water drawn from a series of magical pools whose waters provide glimpses of the past. The pools are also rumored to have other enchantments. Their ripples, for example, are said to spontaneously form teleportation circles to the place being viewed—though it's unclear whether the traveler arrives there in the present day, or slips into the past."

Q'arlynd nodded. He already knew that much. Years ago, when listening in on Flinderspeld's thoughts, his former slave had briefly thought about the pools. The svirfneblin had been pondering the very question Seldszar just posed—whether he could use the so-called Fountains of Memory to slip back to a time before Blingdenstone fell, and warn its residents of the impending attack. Flinderspeld had decided they couldn't, for one, very obvious, reason.

"The pools *couldn't* send a traveler into the past," Q'arlynd said aloud. "If they did, the svirfneblin would have used them already, to do just that, and a number of the calamities that befell their race would never have happened. The fall of

Blingdenstone, for example. If the pools do hold teleportation magic, they must be a gateway to the *present*."

"Past or present—it doesn't matter," Urlryn said. He rocked his bulk forward on his cushion, not bothering to hide his excitement. "We can still use the pools to reach the spot where the temple stood. As long as they take us to the right spot, the magic can be undone!"

"Precisely!" Seldszar agreed. "There is, however, one problem." He glanced at the empty goblet. "Only the deep gnomes know where the pools lie—and they're not telling."

"Easily remedied," Masoj said with a chuckle. He nodded at the decanter. "Detain the svirfneblin who sold you the wine. Slice the information out of him one finger at a time. Give him five chances to talk—ten, if he's stubborn."

Q'arlynd felt the *kiira* grow cool against his forehead. He heard his ancestors' whispered disapproval. He interrupted. "No need for that, Master Masoj. A svirfneblin who owes me a favor knows the location of these pools. I'll have the answer, soon enough."

Urlryn snorted skeptically, and Masoj made a sour face. Seldszar, however, looked thoughtful. After a moment of staring at the crystals orbiting his head, he slowly nodded. "Do it. Ask him."

Q'arlynd hadn't mentioned the svirfneblin's gender. Seldszar might have guessed it, of course. He'd have had an even chance of being right. Yet Q'arlynd doubted the diviner ever guessed—about anything.

Seldszar must have foreseen success.

Funny, how Eilistraee's dance worked, Q'arlynd mused. After all these years, he would finally learn what had become of his former slave, Flinderspeld.

Halisstra walked around the throne, her fingers caressing its smooth black marble. The throne was carved in the shape of a spider, resting on its back. The head formed a foot stool; the cephalothorax, the seat; and the bulging abdomen, the backrest. Four legs served to support the chair, while the other four splayed out from either side of the seat and curved toward the ceiling. Between these stretched steel-thread webs festooned with tiny red spiders. Halisstra plucked a strand of web with the tip of her claw. The steel thread vibrated, shedding spiders like drops of blood and filling the audience chamber with a shrill note. The sound sent a visible shiver through the priestess who crawled behind Halisstra, never once lifting her glance from the flagstone floor.

"Beautiful," Halisstra said. She closed her eyes to savor the way the note—chill as a draft from the grave—made the hair on her arms rise. Then she leaned down and curled her fingers in the priestess's long white tresses. She yanked the smaller female into the air and whispered in her ear. "I am pleased with its song. You will be rewarded."

The priestess, clad in a bodice-hugging black robe that would have vanished against her skin in the darkened room but for its hair-thin tracery of white lines, winced at the pain of being held aloft by her hair. "Your pleasure is my reward, Lady Penitent."

Halisstra leaned closer, until the jaws protruding from her cheeks brushed the priestess's neck. "And your pain is my pleasure." She bit, just deep enough to puncture the skin. Then she opened her fingers and let the priestess drop. The priestess fell to her hands and knees, and grunted as the poison took hold, rendering her body rigid.

Halisstra settled herself on the throne. The marble felt cool against her bare skin. She sang a breeze into existence and used it to set the webs vibrating. A thousand shrill notes encircled the throne, like the hum of fast-spinning blades.

"Send in the first petitioner," she ordered.

Unseen hands pushed a female out of the magical darkness that clouded the arched doorway: a priestess of Eilistraee.

She staggered into the room. Her eyes had been seared blind, and her fingers broken. Her dark skin was welted from the beating administered by Halisstra's worshipers, and her lips were swollen and bloody. Yet even as she faltered to a halt, she drew herself erect with a remarkable inner strength.

Halisstra despised her.

"Kneel," she shouted. She wove magic into the word, turning it into a compulsion the priestess could not help but obey. The priestess fell to her knees as if smashed with a hammer. One broken hand lifted to her chest—to the spot where her holy symbol used to hang—then jerked away as it brushed against the obsidian spider that now hung from the silver chain. Her head, however, remained erect. "Eilish . . . tray . . . hee . . ."

"Blasphemy!" Halisstra shrieked. "Do not utter that foul name in the presence of the Lady Penitent, or it will go harshly for you!"

The priestess made a gurgling noise. She laughed! Halisstra sprang from her throne. "You . . . *dare!*" she hissed. She towered over the priestess, her spider jaws clacking in fury. The eight legs protruding from her chest arched open, ready to grab. Her jaws fairly ached with the desire to bite and rend.

The priestess spat.

Halisstra snarled and swept the priestess up to her mouth—then realized this was what Eilistraee's bitch wanted. A quick, clean death: to be delivered into the arms of her goddess. "I'm not going to give it to you," Halisstra muttered. She tossed the priestess aside, spun on her heel, and settled herself on the throne. She idly stroked the head of the female who still knelt, paralyzed, beside the throne, properly subservient. The webs continued to shrill.

She had an idea. "You *will* be redeemed," she told Eilistraee's priestess with a smile. "I give you a choice: the song or the spider."

The priestess shook her head. "Nuh."

Halisstra shrugged. "Very well then. I'll choose for you." She tapped her claw-tipped fingers against the arm of her throne, pretending to consider. In fact, she'd been lying when she'd offered the priestess a choice: the spider's venom was reserved for those truly worthy of it. "I think you'll choose ... the song." She turned to the webs beside her and began to play.

Magic jerked the priestess to her feet. Tugged by the compulsion Halisstra's *bae'qeshel* music wove, she staggered in a circle around the throne. Halisstra plucked faster, and the dancer's tempo increased. The priestess spun in a ragged pirouette, her arms flailing and broken fingers raised above her head as she circled the throne. Halisstra gave a gleeful peal of laughter and played on. And on. The priestess staggered and fell, but immediately rose to her knees and continued her dance. Her knees left bloody smears on the flagstones.

Halisstra watched, gloating. In a moment or two, it would be over. The priestess would crack and repent. She would shed Eilistraee's faith and cast the tattered skin aside. Embrace the pain, the sorrow, the self-loathing. Sacrifice herself to a force greater than herself. She would become a penitent, redeemed through sweat, blood, and suffering.

Halisstra would break her.

The priestess suddenly lunged at the throne. Halisstra reared back in alarm, but it wasn't an attack. The priestess flopped forward, bringing her neck down atop the web. Steel threads sliced into her neck. Hot, sticky blood sprayed as she fell limp across the arm of the throne like a loose heavy cloak, her head lolling on a near-severed neck

The web strings fell silent.

Halisstra hissed her fury. She yanked the priestess off the web, snapping a strand of it, and stared into the slack-jawed face. "You *smile?*" she screamed. "You fool! You will never, *never* be redeemed!" She hurled the body across the room.

The kneeling priestess twitched; her paralysis was starting to wear off. Halisstra leaped off the throne and grabbed her minion, intending to tear her apart for her insolence—she hadn't been given *permission* to move, Abyss take her—but a whisper of song distracted her. It was coming from the webs on the throne. Halisstra cocked her head, listening. The voice belonged to T'lar, the assassin who'd been the first to accept penitence and redemption.

Lady Penitent, the webs sang. *News from Sshamath.*

Halisstra dropped the priestess and climbed back onto her throne. *Sing on,* she ordered. It had better be good news, she thought. She wasn't in the mood for more insolence.

Streea'Valsharess Zauviir is dead. The temple is ours.

Halisstra barked out a delighted laugh.

There is something else you should know. There is a wizard in Sshamath who opposes us.

"Hardly news," Halisstra laughed. "All of Sshamath's wizards are hostile."

This one will bear watching. His name is Q'arlynd Melarn.

Halisstra's breath caught. Her brother Q'arlynd, alive? "Impossible! He died in the collapse of Ched Nasad!"

The webs fell silent for a moment. Halisstra frowned. "T'lar? Are you still there?"

I do not believe the one who calls himself Q'arlynd Melarn to be an imposter, Lady Penitent, T'lar sang back. *He told the Conclave he had a sister who was a* bae'qeshel *bard—a sister who died. He said her name was Halisstra Melarn.*

"Halisstra!" Halisstra howled. She broke into shrill laughter. "She's Halisstra no more. She's—" Suddenly realizing what she was saying, she snapped her mouth shut. Her spider legs drummed against her chest; She forced them still with an effort. "Describe this wizard," she ordered.

T'lar did.

The description fit. It *was* Q'arlynd. Halisstra shook her head, wondering how he'd managed to escape the golem. Not to mention getting crushed by the stones of a falling city.

There is one thing more, Lady Penitent. Q'arlynd Melarn has taken Eilistraee as his patron.

Halisstra's eyebrows rose. "He has? How *dare* he!"

He refuses to repent.

Halisstra's lips curled in a sneer.

Lady? T'lar's voice asked. *What is your will?*

Halisstra clenched her fists; her claws dug into flesh. "If he is Eilistraee's," she said slowly, "he must die. Kill him."

It will be my pleasure.

And his pain, Halisstra thought grimly. She laughed at her own joke.

The webs in her throne vibrated, shaking off the last drops of the dead priestess's blood.

CHAPTER 8

Cavatina startled at Qilué's message. "A new high priestess?"

Leliana's head lifted sharply. She'd been in Reverie, her sword across her knees and her head bowed. "What's happened? Has Eilistraee spoken to you?"

"Not Eilistraee—Qilué." Cavatina repeated the sending she'd just received.

"*Was* it Qilué?" Leliana looked nervously around. "Or another of the demon's tricks?"

"I've no idea." Cavatina rubbed her forehead. Was it just her, or had the world grown heavier, of late? "I'm not certain about anything anymore."

Leliana said nothing.

Cavatina realized the other priestess had been looking for strength, for leadership—for the Slayer of Selvetarm to come up with a way out of here.

Cavatina wished she could help. Yet there seemed little she could do. She squinted against the green glow that filled the chamber. The magical barrier resembled an overbright *Faerzress*; she supposed it might very well be. It was difficult to see through it, to the cavern's stone walls. If Cavatina had been a wizard or a druid, she might have bored a hole through that stone with magic, or transmuted the stone to mud. Then she and Leliana could have dug their way out with their bare hands, just like a—

Cavatina gasped. That was it! *They* couldn't dig through solid stone, but there were creatures that could. She thought back to those Kâras had listed when they'd planned their assault on the Acropolis. A purple worm would be too dangerous—it might swallow Leliana and Cavatina whole. An umber hulk was too volatile to control. Rather than dig, it would do its best to claw them to pieces. Delvers, however, were generally docile creatures. And—she smiled as her eye fell on the gilded pedestal—they were drawn to metal. Especially gold.

None were creatures that prayers would ordinarily summon, but with Eilistraee's blessing—with a miracle—it might be possible. Cavatina squared her shoulders. There was only one way to find out if it *were* possible.

She outlined her plan to Leliana. The other priestess nodded. "Do you really think it will work?"

"Eilistraee grant that it does."

They dragged the pedestal across the chamber and leaned it against the fused door. At Cavatina's nod, each lifted her holy symbol and walked in a slowly widening spiral, singing her prayer. Cavatina reached out with her mind to the celestial realm. Her mind's eye ranged over a host of creatures—lesser animals, elevated to celestial status, their bodies glinting with the metallic sheen that was the aura of all that was pure and good. None of them were the creature she sought.

"Eilistraee," she sang. Her voice harmonized with Leliana's, their music in time with their shared footsteps. "Hear our prayer. Send us a willing servant, in our time of great need. Send us the creature we seek."

A sharp, acidic odor filled the room. The priestesses leaped back, their nostrils flaring, as a creature materialized in a burst of silver gold light. A delver!

Its fat, pear-shaped body nearly filled the chamber. Yellowish spittle drooled from its gaping mouth. Its two clublike arms were tipped with blunt black claws. Its head twisted back and forth as its single, glossy black eye swept the room. Then it surged at the pedestal, heaving itself up on its arms, the rest of its body following on a rippling under-belly. As it moved, it left an acid-singed patch of dead black moss in its wake.

A thick stench filled the air. Cavatina's eyes teared, and her nose felt congested. On the far side of the room, Leliana wiped her eyes with the back of her sleeve. Her expression, however, was exultant. The delver was doing its work. The gold-plated pedestal disappeared into its maw with a grinding noise, as did a chunk of the door. One bite at a time, the delver chewed at the stone. Rock dust filled the air, and the floor trembled. A head-sized hole appeared in the door, revealing the corridor beyond. As the delver gouged deeper, the hole widened. Chunks of brittle rock fell to the floor like scattered crumbs, hissing and bubbling from caustic spittle.

Suddenly the delver disappeared. The prayer that had sustained it had waned. Eilistraee's magic could hold a celestial on this plane only for so long.

Cavatina strode forward. They'd done it! She crouched, ready to squeeze through the hole as soon as the rock stopped frothing. She heard a muffled peal: the alarms. She turned to Leliana. "Ghaunadaur's fanatics must be inside the Promenade already."

Leliana listened. "Sounds like they've come well past the spot where Qilué planted her trap." She shook her head. "So much for them walking into it 'meekly as rothé.'"

Cavatina squeezed through the hole. Leliana followed. Together, they raced through the High House.

As they hurried down a corridor, Cavatina noticed the door to Qilué's scrying room was open. She glanced inside and saw Meryl, standing beside a broken scrying font. The halfling was reaching for an object that lay on the wet floor: a metal cylinder as long as the halfling's arm, with a knob at either end. Qilué's blast scepter.

Was it Meryl—or a dretch?

Cavatina leaped into the room. Her sword flashed between Meryl's fingers and the floor, preventing the halfling—or dretch—from picking up the scepter. Meryl jumped back, her eyes as wide as dinner plates. Her mouth worked to form words, but none came out. She pointed at the scepter. "I couldn't . . . the font . . . the demon . . ."

Cavatina glanced at where Meryl was looking. Bare, sickly-pale feet protruded from behind an overturned table: a dretch, lying prone and unmoving. A vial, its silver tarnished, lay on the floor nearby.

"My mother's name," Cavatina demanded, her sword point against the halfling's chest. "What is it?"

Puzzlement crowded out Meryl's fear. "Why . . . it's Jetel. Jetel Xarann."

Cavatina lifted her sword. This *was* Meryl. She walked around the overturned table and ensured the dretch was dead.

Leliana, who had run past, returned to the doorway. "What's wrong?"

Cavatina waved her away. "It's under control. Go. Find Rylla. She'll need your help."

Leliana nodded curtly and raced away.

Cavatina knelt beside the halfling. She noted the tears spilling down Meryl's cheeks, and the bloody scratches on the little female's arms and hands. Cavatina patted her shoulder. "Good work, Meryl. You fought well."

The halfling sniffed. She picked up the blast scepter and held it out to Cavatina. "I couldn't figure out how to work it.

I had to use it like a club." Her lips trembled. "That thing . . . scared me so. I wasn't brave. Not like you."

"Yes you were. There aren't many who can stand up to a demon's magical fear." Cavatina gently took the blast scepter from Meryl. "Stay here. Lock the door. Don't answer unless you're sure it's a priestess."

"But how will I—?"

"Get whoever knocks to sing a stanza of the Evensong."

Meryl drew herself up and wiped away her tears. "Don't worry about me. I'll be fine. Go. You're needed elsewhere."

Cavatina saluted the halfling with her sword, and hurried away down the corridors, to the residence's main entrance. As she drew closer to the open double doors, she heard shouting over the ring of the alarms. From the distance came a dull *whumph* that sounded like an explosion.

She sang a protective hymn and stepped outside. Just ahead, a priestess herded a gaggle of lay worshipers away from the direction the explosion had come from. A half-elf and a drow staggered after them, carrying a body on a drift disc that no longer worked. Cavatina couldn't tell if the victim was male or female, as much of the body had dissolved. A Protector charged by in the opposite direction, singing sword pealing.

She heard what sounded like a battle raging to the south, in the direction of the Stronghall. She hurried to the corridor that linked the cavern with that one. As she drew closer, she saw a figure running down the corridor. The floor behind him was covered in glittering sparks. These surged forward like a moving ankle-high carpet, contained within a gelatinous mass.

An ooze—within the Promenade! How had it penetrated so deep into the temple? The Protectors should have thrown up a songwall to contain it.

The running figure wore a purple robe with a leering black eye on the front of his tabard—Ghaunadaur's symbol. His anxious expression and frightened glances over one shoulder suggested he wasn't in control of the ooze. As it threatened to overtake him, he halted and raised his tentacle rod. He whipped it forward, lashing at the ooze with its tentacles. In that same instant, the monster bulged and squirted out a line of ember-like motes. Tentacles met glitterfire in a thundering explosion. Waves of heat and cold exploded out of the corridor.

Qilué's scepter grew warm as it absorbed the heat. But it proved no protection against the cold. Cavatina drew in a lungful of icy air, and shivered. She marveled at what she'd just seen: Ghaunadaur's faithful, fighting each other?

Before the fanatic could turn, she sang a hymn that rendered him rigid. He toppled. She ran to where he lay, intending to drag him out of harm's way and question him at sword point. The glittering ooze was faster however. It was about to engulf her fallen foe.

She raised the scepter. "Eilistraee!" she cried. "Smite this abomination with your song!"

A peal sounded from the scepter—louder, even, than the clanging alarms. Sound waves shimmered through the air, expanding into a cone that slammed into the ooze. The glittering monster was blown back like a yanked carpet folding upon itself. The ooze surged forward again, but Cavatina blasted it a second time, and a third. As the third soundburst struck, the ooze exploded, splattering golden sparks onto the wall. These glowed for a moment, then faded. A few smears of mucous-like goo, dotted with black soot, were all that remained of the ooze.

The fanatic groaned. His robe smoldered in spots, and was damp with melted frost in other places. As he flopped over, Cavatina recognized him. Kâras, in disguise! He must have been among the spies Qilué sent out.

She dispelled her hymn and extended a hand. "What's going on, Kâras?"

The Nightshadow rose shakily to his feet. "I just came from Llurth Dreir," he shouted back over the clangor of alarms. "Qilué's orders: I brought Ghaunadaur's fanatics through a portal. I was to lead them into a trap, but oozes followed us."

He yanked a black ring off his thumb and flung it aside, then kicked the rod after it. The rod rolled away, its limp tentacles flopping. He spoke a word, and his robe and tabard transformed into a close-fitting black shirt and trousers; his sash shimmered and became a mask. Tying it into place around his face seemed to calm him. All traces of the frustration he'd shown a moment ago disappeared.

Cavatina shook her head in exasperation. "Couldn't you tell something was *wrong* with Qilué?" She had to shout to be heard over the clanging alarms. "With this 'plan' of hers? It didn't occur to you to question the logic of leading our enemies into the heart of the Promenade?"

Kâras met her eyes. "She's the high priestess. Through her, the Masked Lady commands—and I obey."

"Did the fanatics enter the trap?"

He hesitated. "I'm not sure. I didn't see what happened. The ooze chased me this way." He eased back a step, expecting a reprimand. Yet this wasn't his fault. He'd only done as Qilué had ordered.

Four priestesses ran past, toward the fighting. As soon as they spotted Cavatina, their fearful expressions vanished. They shouted that fanatics, backed up by oozes, had invaded the Stronghall. Cavatina waved them on, saying she'd lend her sword to the battle in just a moment. Kâras turned to follow the priestesses, but Cavatina caught his arm.

"Kâras," she said urgently, "Qilué was tricked. Her 'trap' is actually a portal—one that renders you ethereal. It leads to the bottom of the Pit. To a planar breach. That breach was intermittent when I saw it, but if the fanatics reach it, and open it fully, Ghaunadaur's avatar will be able to pass through."

Kâras's voice came out as a croak. "I don't understand. Why would the Masked Lor—Masked Lady permit—"

"I don't have time to explain. What's important is that we prevent the fanatics from getting to that portal. We'll make for the ruined temple by different routes: I'll go south, through the Stronghall, and you circle around through the Cavern of Song. Eilistraee willing, at least one of us will reach the portal in time."

Kâras stood, unmoving. His mask wavered slightly; he must have been praying.

"Let's *move!*"

He swallowed, then bobbed his head in a nod.

She watched long enough to make sure he was headed in the right direction, then sprinted down the corridor to the Stronghall. As she reached it, she saw a battle that could use her assistance. A priestess and three lay worshipers were fighting a jellylike mass of roiling shadow. Cavatina blasted it with the scepter as she ran by. Her attack drove it back, giving Eilistraee's faithful the moment's reprieve they needed to regroup. As she ran on, she heard them cheer her name behind her.

Everywhere she looked, the faithful desperately fought tentacle-wielding fanatics and a host of Ghaunadaur's minions. Cavatina spotted an ooze that looked like an enormous puddle of blood, glowing with searing heat; another like congealed fog, chill as a wind from the grave. A third resembled a roiling cloud of snowflakes. Yet another flickered with a purple light that twisted into glowing symbols, deep within itself. The latter ooze spat out a snake from one puckered orifice, a centipede from another. Both animals glowed with a fiendish light that marked them as creatures summoned from the Abyss. Cavatina slashed at centipede and snake, killing both, and blasted the ooze itself with the scepter. The half-dozen lay worshipers who'd been retreating from the monster cried a prayer of thanksgiving.

She had run almost the length of the Stronghall; the corridor leading to the ruined temple was just a short distance ahead. She pounded around the corner of a building, only to find the street blocked by a bone white ooze that had overwhelmed a Protector. The priestess lay, screaming, as the mass flowed onto the lower half of her body.

Cavatina's eyes widened. It was Tash'kla—the Protector who had fought so valiantly beside her during the expedition to the Acropolis.

She raised the scepter, but realized that its sound blast didn't discriminate between friend and foe. She sang a moonbeam into existence instead, and hurled it at the creature. The ooze shuddered as twined moonlight and shadow bored through it, carving a wound that bled sour-smelling clay. The ooze pulled back from the fallen Protector.

It took Tash'kla's bones with it, reducing her legs to empty, bloody sacks of muscle and skin. Cavatina watched, horrified, as the ooze splintered the bones and squeezed the marrow out.

Furious, she attacked the ooze with the scepter. It took more than one blast to kill the thing. When the ooze at last exploded from the sonic attack, a bone splinter whizzed past Cavatina's ear. She didn't flinch. She moved to Tash'kla, kneeled, and touched her throat.

No blood-pulse. Tash'kla was dead.

Fortunately, the ooze hadn't consumed her utterly. Enough remained that Tash'kla might be resurrected—assuming anyone from the Promenade survived to revive her. In this cavern alone, there were so many oozes that Cavatina was starting to have doubts about how the battle would go.

She wiped a splatter of ooze from her forehead with a shaking hand. Was this how it had been for Qilué, when she and her companions battled Ghaunadaur's avatar? Cavatina's sword was slippery with foul-smelling slime, and its song was a dirge. She tightened her grip on the weapon, grimly wondering where the high priestess was. Trapped within her own body by the demon—forced to watch as her cherished temple fell?

No, Cavatina thought angrily. It wouldn't come to that. Eilistraee wouldn't permit it.

She ran down the street, and at last reached the corridor she'd been making for. It turned out to be choked with the bodies of the fallen. Most were unrecognizable, reduced by acid to weeping mounds of reddish flesh, or blackened by searing heat to unrecognizable lumps. She gagged at the sour smell of spilled entrails and charred flesh and pressed on, slipping and sliding on the fouled stone.

Just ahead, the tunnel widened into a cavern that overlooked the river before turning sharply right. This gave her two options: she could follow the tunnel, or the river. She ran to the edge of the cavern and peered out, toward the bridge that spanned the river.

What she saw sent a shiver through her.

Ooze after ooze, differentiated from each other only by color, flowed across the bridge to the main part of the Promenade. At first Cavatina thought they were coming from the caverns on the far side of the river, but as she watched, a bulge formed on one of the three stone columns that supported the ceiling at the far side of the bridge: another ooze. As it plopped to the ground, quivering, another slime bulged out of the column. It was as if the stone wept slimy tears.

That column must be the portal Kâras had led the fanatics through. She wondered how the Nightshadow fared—if he were any closer to the ruined temple than she was. No wonder he'd been so shaken; unleashing this horror on the Promenade would have driven anyone to tears.

The voice of Erelda, Rylla's second in command, sounded in Cavatina's mind. *Protectors! Fall back on the Cavern of Song. The oozes are converging upon it!*

Cavatina's heart pounded as she realized the implications. Oozes were near-mindless things, driven by basic instincts like hunger—or the need to draw closer to their god. She could think of only one reason for them to converge upon the Cavern of Song: to reach the Pit. Had the fanatics already succeeded in wrenching open the planar breach?

The seals, Cavatina sent back. *Are they still intact?*

Erelda's response came a moment later. *The Mound is untouched. The seals are in place.*

Cavatina sighed in relief. *There's a planar breach at the bottom of the Pit,* she warned Erelda. *If the seals are destroyed . . .*

They won't be. By sword or song, we'll do whatever it takes to prevent that.

Cavatina heard a sound behind her: another ooze, headed her way. She debated which way to go. The tunnel she'd been following was the most direct route to the ruined temple, yet its narrowness would make it easy for the oozes to block her way.

She decided to swim, instead.

She sheathed her sword—she needed at least one hand free to swim—and dived into the water, the scepter held out in front of her. The shock of hitting cold water made her sputter as she surfaced, but a quick prayer blunted the worst of the cold. As the current moved her to the bridge, she sang a hymn that rendered her invisible. It wouldn't fool the oozes—they'd sense her footfalls the moment she climbed from the water. But it would conceal her from any fanatics who might be nearby.

As if on cue, a drow tumbled out of the portal column. Even from this distance, Cavatina could see the eye symbol on the front of his tabard. As he stood, another of Ghaunadaur's fanatics emerged from the portal. Then a third, and a fourth. They stood in a group as the first one pointed downriver—away from Cavatina, and away from the ruined temple.

The bridge loomed, cutting off her view. Cavatina swam to the wall on the far side of the river from the fanatics. Above her was a cavern mouth. At the back of that cavern, down a short corridor, was a door leading to the ruined temple. If she could drive the oozes back, using the blast scepter, she might reach it.

She climbed.

Halfway up, she glanced over her shoulder to see where the fanatics had gone. She couldn't spot them. She'd have to be wary, in case they'd crossed to this side of the bridge.

As soon as she reached the ledge, she used the blast scepter to drive the oozes back from the cavern, then heaved herself up onto its acid-slick floor. Additional blasts from the scepter kept the oozes at bay. They retreated to the left and right, revealing the corridor that led to the ruined temple.

Cavatina sprinted into it. The oozes closed ranks behind her, blocking the way back to the river. She blasted them over her shoulder with the scepter, forcing them back.

The door to the ruined temple was closed. Cavatina pushed on it, praying it wasn't locked. When she at last forced it open, a rush of liquid flowed out. She leaped back, worried it might be more acid. The force of the liquid inside the room pushed the door shut. She glanced down. Her boots were still intact, and her feet didn't sting. The liquid probably *wasn't* acid.

An ooze slid into the corridor behind her. She turned to blast it with the scepter.

Nothing happened. She'd used it once too often, draining it of its magic.

She slammed her shoulder into the door, opening it again. She braced it as a rush of water flowed out. Something carried by the flow bumped against her knees: a body.

"By all that dances," Cavatina cried. "Rylla!"

She dragged the battle-mistress's body into the room with her, and let what remained of the water push the door shut. As she threw the deadbolt, she heard the wet slap of the ooze striking the door. She dropped the depleted blast scepter down in the ankle-deep water and bent to examine the battle-mistress. Rylla's nose looked broken. Water dribbled from her open mouth as Cavatina lifted her. Rylla appeared to have drowned.

Had her death been the fanatics' doing, or Qilué's?

Cavatina lay Rylla down again and drew her sword. The weapon hummed softly, ready for battle. She looked around. The compulsion glyph Horaldin had inscribed on the wall was gone—had the portal been sealed, too? She sloshed to that corner of the room and sang a detection.

The wall turned as thin as mist. The portal was still active.

Had Qilué passed through it?

Cavatina glanced at the chamber's second exit and saw a dull brown ooze squeezing its way through the cracks between the door and its frame. Kâras wasn't likely to show up, and she doubted he'd get past it if he did. The other ooze, meanwhile, was squeezing its way around the door she'd bolted shut.

There was only one way out now.

Into the portal.

Cavatina didn't want to leave Rylla behind. If her body was consumed by an ooze, the battle-mistress might never be resurrected. She grabbed Rylla with her free hand, dragged her body to the portal, and stepped through it.

She emerged from the **V**-shaped curtain of shimmering silver into a jumble of misty-looking stone. She released Rylla—the battle-mistress's body could remain where it was, for now—and moved cautiously to the ruined temple, sword in hand. She expected to see Ghaunadaur's fanatics clustered around it, offering sacrifices. But as the foundation slab and its shattered columns hove into view, she saw no one. Had she reached it before the fanatics?

She must have: the symbol wasn't glowing. The planar breach was inactive; the necessary sacrifices had not yet been made.

Nor was there any sign of Qilué.

Cavatina hesitated. What now?

Stand guard, she decided. Stay here and cut down any fanatics who made it through the portal. They would be rendered ethereal, just as she was. She could kill them. As she moved to the ruined temple, looking for the best place to make her stand, its tumbled stones came into sharper focus. A glimmer of silver caught her eye. Another portal? No, it looked more like a . . .

Symbol.

For a time briefer than a blink, Cavatina experienced a moment of terrible clarity. Qilué hadn't lied: she *had* inscribed a symbol over Ghaunadaur's: a powerful, potent symbol scribed in mercury and diamond dust.

A symbol of insanity.

Cavatina's mind crumpled. She saw . . . She felt . . . That screaming! Make it stop! She dropped her sword and clapped her hands over her eyes. A bright purple glow penetrated the cracks between her fingers. The symbol! No, the *symbol*. Bright—it hurt her ears. Her skin felt wet. Slime. Foul taste. She spat it out. Upside down? Why was it above . . . ? The purple glow should have waned, but didn't. The dancer's name would save . . . Cavatina opened her mouth, but confusion came out of her ears. A presence moved past her now. Green. Slimy.

Evil.

Purple smoke. The smoke stared at her. *At* her. An eye smiled.

My sacrifice.

"No!" Cavatina shrieked. She spun, tumbled, flailed. Clawed away, rolled, swam through rubble. Rock bubbles. She couldn't . . . her sword gone . . .

She had . . .

Failed.

Leliana ran out the door of the High House and caught the arm of the nearest priestess. "Where's the battle-mistress? Have you seen Rylla?"

The priestess shook her head. "No! Erelda's taken command."

"What about the high priestess?"

"Qilué?" Another head shake. "Haven't seen her either."

Leliana stopped a lay worshiper who ran by, and a Nightshadow. Their answers were the same. Behind her, Cavatina left the High House and ran south, to the Stronghall. Everyone seemed to be headed there. From that direction, she heard sounds of battle.

Asking questions was futile. No one knew anything—except that the Promenade was under attack from the south by Ghaunadaur's fanatics: the demon's plan, put in motion. It was the second attack, the one from *within,* Leliana dreaded. Where *was* Qilué?

A lay worshiper ran by—with, of all things, a lute strung across her back.

"Hold it!" Leliana cried. "You there. Is that lute Rylla's?"

The novice halted and glanced over her shoulder at the instrument as if seeing it for the first time. "I—I don't know. I must have slung it over my shoulder when I helped carry the body to the Hall of Healing."

Leliana stiffened. "Whose body? Rylla's? Is she dead?"

"Whoever it was, she was wounded. Bad." She swallowed hard, then shuddered. "Her face. . . ."

Leliana touched her holy symbol. If it was Rylla, and the battle-mistress could be healed, perhaps she might know where the high priestess was.

She sprinted down a corridor in the direction of the Hall of Healing. As she neared the Hall of Empty Arches, she passed Chizra, leading six lesser priestesses in the opposite direction. A seventh priestess remained on guard within the hall, a bundle of prayer scrolls tucked under one arm. She looked unhappy at being left behind. Leliana saluted her and ran on, following the corridor to the enormous hall that had been reclaimed in Eilistraee's name.

The Hall of Healing was choked with people. Lay worshipers bustled in with the wounded on makeshift stretchers. Priestesses moved from one injured person to the next. The revived rushed out again to rejoin the fight. At the far end of the room stood a golden statue of a pair of scales, balanced on a warhammer: a reminder of life's delicate balance, and the forces that could tip a soul toward death. Leliana looked for Rylla but didn't see her.

She questioned the head healer, who assured her the battle-mistress had *not* been among those they'd treated.

"Is she among the dead?"

"No time to check," the healer curtly replied. She bent over a burned male, a holy symbol in her hand. "Too busy." She touched his injuries, and prayed.

"Leliana!"

She whirled. Naxil! His face was a mottled gray—his flesh healed, but still discolored. His eyes were bright above his makeshift mask. He clasped her arms, and she returned his light squeeze.

"Have you seen the battle-mistress?" she asked him. "Or the high priestess?"

"Aren't they in the Stronghall directing the battle? That's where the oozes and slimes are coming from: out of the river. There's a *lot* of them, but by the Masked Lady's grace, we'll push them back again."

"Oozes and slimes?" she gasped. "But I thought it was supposed to be *fanatics* who came through the . . ."

She caught sight of a lay worshiper who had just entered the Hall of Healing. He peered about as if looking for someone. The front of his shirt was soaked with blood, yet he waved away the healers' offers of assistance. He was strikingly handsome. But that wasn't what had drawn Leliana's attention—it was the extremely rare color of his eyes: leaf green.

He had to be the male Cavatina had described—the one who'd sacrificed himself. The fanatics must have raised him from the dead. But how, if his body had been consumed? And what was he doing *here*, in the Hall of Healing?

She spotted a ring on his finger. A *gold* ring. That told her how he'd gotten into this part of the temple. He'd used the ring to pass through the magical barrier in the level she and Naxil had discovered below, then come through the portal to the Hall of Empty Arches. Leliana wondered if the priestess she'd seen there, just a moment ago, was still alive.

The fanatic completed his circuit of the hall and turned, heading back for the door.

Leliana jabbed Naxil's stomach with a finger. *Green eyes,* she signed between them. *Enemy in disguise. You stall; I'll sing a truth song and question. Go.*

Naxil bowed, hiding the drawing of a dagger. He moved away, concealing the weapon under his *piwafwi.*

As Naxil made his way to the disguised fanatic, Leliana flicked her sword in a circle—a *small* circle, near her boot; she didn't want to draw attention to her prayer. Naxil greeted the fanatic, but instead of engaging him in conversation as planned, Naxil turned and walked to the exit. Did he mean to draw the fanatic into the corridor, where it would be more difficult for him to escape?

Leliana strode to the side of the fanatic and matched his pace. As she walked, she shifted her sword so it was pointing at his feet, and loosed the magic she'd just sung into being. "I need help carrying the wounded," she told him. "Where are you headed?"

Leaf-green eyes met hers. A puddle of warmth filled her. The urge to smile at him overwhelmed her.

"To the Pit. I'm needed there." His eyes glistened. "Won't you show me the way?"

Anxious to please him, Leliana nodded. As she did, her sword sang a warning. It sliced through his enchantment, dousing the warmth inside her like a slap of ice water.

Powerful magic. If it hadn't been for her singing sword. . . .

The fanatic tensed. He'd realized she knew what he was. Leliana leaped back and swung. Steel flashed toward his neck.

The fanatic jumped aside—but not quickly enough. Her sword took off an outflung hand. She expected a spray of blood. Green slime oozed out instead. Before he could rally, she thrust at his vitals. Her blade plunged into soft, quivering flesh that offered no resistance. She reversed direction and yanked the sword back, but the fanatic's body—now a bright green and only vaguely drow-shaped—bulged outward, engulfing her weapon. The bulge solidified, and the mass twisted, tearing the weapon from her hands.

"A ghaunadan!" she shouted as she danced back from him. She'd heard of these creatures, but never seen one. Most oozes were mindless things, but ghaunadans were intelligent beings—budded fragments of the Ancient One itself. Fragments that could temporarily assume drow form.

Shouts of alarm filled the Hall of Healing. Priestesses leaped to their feet, singing. The ghaunadan slapped one of them; she toppled, body rigid. Then a barrage of spells struck it at once. The ghaunadan reeled as moonblades sliced it, holy words slammed into it, and magical wounds sprang open in its quivering flesh. Within moments it had been reduced to a smoking pile of green-smeared clothing and a pair of boots that lay on the floor, suppurating ooze.

Leliana stared down at them, glad the ghaunadan was dead. Unfortunately, there wasn't any corpse left to question.

"He came through the portal in the Hall of Empty Arches," she warned the others. "We need to seal it, before more ghaunadans come through!"

Someone handed her singing sword back to her. Leliana took it and ran for the room's only door. She glanced up and down the corridor, looking for Naxil. The battle with the ghaunadan had taken only a moment, yet Naxil was nowhere in sight. Where had the ghaunadan's magical compulsion sent him? North, to the Hall of Empty Arches, or south, toward safety?

"Naxil!" she shouted. Her voice was lost amid the hubbub as half a dozen priestesses crowded through the door. Leliana ordered one of them to hang back and chant a magical songwall to prevent enemies from reaching the Hall of Healing. She told the rest to follow her.

As they ran to the Hall of Empty Arches, Erelda's voice sang into Leliana's mind. *Protectors! Fall back on the Cavern of Song. The oozes are converging upon it!*

Converging? Leliana swore. Did that mean that oozes were

headed to the Cavern of Song from the south, *and* from the north—from the Hall of Empty Arches?

The answer came as she rounded a bend in the corridor. The way ahead was blocked by a horrific creature: a waist-high, gray-brown lump covered in eyes and mouths that bulged from its body and were subsumed again. From these emanated a ghastly chorus of nonsensical words that tumbled over one another like pebbles in a gurgling brook.

Leliana shouted at the priestesses to halt, but the two up ahead didn't heed her. They walked on toward the monster, shouting nonsense. Leliana heard an overlapping babble of female voices behind her, and flung out her arms to hold back the other priestesses. As she did so, the creature attacked the two priestesses up ahead. It spat a stream of acid at one and bulged forward to wrap a limb around the other. The first priestess's gibbering turned to screams as her skin burned away; the second grew grayish-pale as the ooze's mouths bit hard and began to suck blood.

"Eilistraee!" Leliana cried, "Shield me!"

Her singing sword pealed out a steadying note that blocked the worst of the creature's magical effect. Even so, Leliana teetered at the edge of madness. Screaming her fury at the monster, she dodged around the priestess who had been felled by acid and hacked at the limb coiled around the other priestess. As the blade sliced through it, another limb bulged out to grab her; she sliced that one off too.

The creature spat acid. The stream struck the magical shield she'd just sung into being and deflected to the side. Again she slashed at the monster, but as her sword descended, her right foot sank into something soft, throwing her off balance. She glanced down. The stone floor was quivering, like quicksand. As her left foot also plunged downward, she staggered and fell. She threw out a hand to halt herself, but her arm sunk into the floor, up to the elbow.

The creature rested lightly upon the vibrating floor, as if floating gently atop it.

That gave Leliana an idea. Instead of trying to rise, she dived into the quicksand. With her eyes tightly closed, she waited for the monster to pass her. When the quivering above her subsided, she twisted and found a solid surface with her feet. She shoved hard, and shot out of the quicksand behind the monster. Her sword flashed down in a deadly arc. Eyeballs exploded and teeth shattered as her sword sliced through the monster, cutting it in two.

The quicksand began to congeal. Before it could trap her, Leliana scrambled out.

The priestesses she'd led here all lay on the floor moaning, their skin burned by acid and covered in bloody bites. Leliana ached to heal them, yet there was no time. Not if the Promenade was to be saved. As she ran on to the Hall of Empty Arches, flakes of hardening stone fell from her body like dried mud.

At last she reached the hall. As she entered it, she heard a slurping sound: an ooze, departing, by the sound of it, through the exit on the far side of the chamber. She squinted against the bright sparkle of *Faerzress* that filled the room. She ran along the wall, her feet slipping on the slime that fouled the floor. She peered down each of the spaces between the partitions in turn.

"Naxil!" she shouted. "Are you here?"

Up ahead, she spotted a misshapen lump of flesh, in front of the portal that led here from the abandoned mine tunnels. Her throat caught—until she realized, by the partially dissolved chunks of chain mail armor the body had been wearing, that this wasn't Naxil. It must have been the priestess Chizra had left behind. Soggy fragments of curled paper lay next to the body: the scrolls the priestess had held. They were rapidly turning to mush as the acid dissolved them. One scroll, however, had landed just beyond the spray of acid that glistened on the walls and floor.

Breathing in shallow gulps—the smell was nauseating—Leliana ran to the spot where it lay. A mottled purple eyestalk bulged out of the arch as she passed. She twisted aside to avoid it and scooped up the scroll, hoping it was one she could use. She whirled, shaking it open one-handed. She didn't dare let go of the singing sword, as it was the only thing that would cut through another sound-based attack.

To her infinite relief, the scroll held a portal-sealing spell. She began to sing the hymn inscribed on it.

A second eyestalk bulged out of the portal, followed by the head of the creature: a purple slug the size of a horse, its mottled flesh studded with twisted chunks of rusted metal. One of these scraped against the side of the arch with a sound like a sword being dragged across a whetstone. Its rump slid through just as Leliana finished the hymn. A ripple of magical energy filled the archway, sealing the portal behind the monster.

Leliana dropped the scroll—now blank—and lifted her sword. She braced herself as the slug slid toward her. She'd take off the eyestalks first.

The slug halted. A loud humming filled the air. The acid-pitted remains of the dead priestess's chain mail vest flew at the monster. So did the clasp on Leliana's borrowed *piwafwi*. She felt a yank on her sword, and though she clung to it with all her strength, it flew from her hands. Last to go was her holy symbol. The mithral chain around her neck snapped and flew at the slug, the miniature sword trailing after it. All stuck to the creature's slimy body—except the silver holy symbol, which by Eilistraee's infinite grace dangled from its chain, refusing to adhere.

The slug reared up, exposing a puckered mouth. It yawned open, revealing rows of needle-pointed teeth.

Leliana was in no mood to be eaten. She leaped forward, grabbed her holy symbol, and yanked it free.

Behind her, she heard suspicious sounds. She glanced back, and saw an ooze that looked like a boiling puddle of blood, blocking her way out. She was trapped! The ooze wasn't moving toward her—yet. But it was expanding, rising like blood-leavened bread.

With her singing sword, she might have fought her way out—but it was stuck fast to the slug. There was one song that could get her out of here, but with *Faerzress* crackling through the hall, it probably wouldn't work.

The metal-studded slug slithered closer. Behind her, she felt the ooze's steadily growing heat on her back. Already, it felt as hot as the Abyss.

She glanced at the archway next to her, remembering what Rylla had told Qilué earlier. The dretch had escaped through a portal in the Hall of Empty Arches. This portal! Was it still active? Rylla had said that it opened onto infinity. Maybe—just maybe—if Leliana sang her hymn of return as she passed through it, she could control where she wound up.

With Eilistraee's blessing, it just might work.

She turned, poised to leap into the arch. As she began the hymn, the slug attacked. Shards of metal exploded from its body in a whirling storm. Several punched into her, tearing ragged gouges in her flesh . . .

She leaped—and passed through the portal, still singing. Moonlight blazed around her . . .

She fell, face first, onto a clump of ferns in a moonlit forest.

For several moments, all she could do was lie there. Slowly, with blood-slick hands, she forced herself up. It took a moment before she stopped trembling. She was bleeding from more than a dozen lacerations, yet she didn't care. The pale white fog hugging the ground was a sign she'd arrived at her destination: the Misty Forest shrine.

"Praise Eilistraee," she gasped. "It worked!" If she ever saw Q'arlynd again, it would be something to brag about. He wasn't the only one capable of "impossible" teleports.

She stood and sang a hymn to close her wounds. She was pleased with her night's work. She'd sealed the portal that led to the Promenade from below, preventing any more of Ghaunadaur's foul minions from oozing through it. That should buy the temple's defenders some time.

Now she needed to get back to the Promenade and continue the fight. Fortunately, the moon was above the horizon. She could use the sacred shrine and return through the Moonspring Portal.

She walked through the woods to the sacred pool. As she approached it, she heard singing. Peering through the trees, she spotted a dozen or so priestesses. They jabbed the air with their holy daggers, their voices rising and falling in an urgent harmony. Leliana heard wet, popping noises, and saw that the surface of the sacred pool was rippling.

The priestess directing the song was a younger version of Leliana: lean and graceful, but with yellow-shaded instead of ice white hair—her daughter. Rowaan's eyes widened as Leliana entered the clearing. She ran forward and clasped Leliana's arms. "Have you come from the Promenade? What's *happening* there?"

"It's under attack. By Ghaunadaur's fanatics—and a host of oozes. We have to get there, and quickly. Join the battle."

Rowaan's face paled in the moonlight. She gestured at the pool, a stricken expression on her face. "We can't reach it. The portal's blocked."

Leliana moved closer. She saw, to her horror, that the pool was dappled with tiny oozes, each shaped like a pan-fried egg with a blood red center. The priestesses' magic had destroyed scores of them already, but for each one their magic ruptured, two more bubbled to the surface.

Leliana clenched her empty fists—a reminder that her singing sword was gone. The sacred sword had been one of those carried into battle by Qilué's companions, centuries ago, during their victory over Ghauandaur's avatar. Now, it was lost.

Short of a miracle, the Promenade would be lost too.

Rowaan guessed her mother's thoughts. "The Promenade won't fall," she said determinedly. "Eilistraee won't allow it." She turned back to the pool, and to the hopeless task of trying to clear the blood-slimed water.

Leliana nodded, without conviction. She wanted to cling to hope, but couldn't. Rowaan was denying the patently obvious. The oozes had reached the Moonspring Portal and were passing *through* it—something that would only have been possible if one of Eilistraee's faithful had sung a hymn to open it. Leliana could guess whose deed that had been. Someone who was using her magic for ill, now that a demon rode her.

Qilué.

Leliana looked up at the sky. The moon would set soon. When it did, the portal in the Moonspring would close. Until the next moonrise, the Misty Forest would be secure from attack from the Promenade.

That should have offered a shred of hope.

It didn't.

Not at all.

CHAPTER 9

Kâras ran into the Cavern of Song. Two priestesses still sang the sacred hymn, their swords pointed at the ceiling, toward the spot where the moon passed through the night skies of the World Above. Their voices, however, were lost in the general commotion.

The cavern was filled with people. Priestesses and soldiers ran south and east to the battle, while lay worshipers, too young or weak to fight, struggled in the opposite direction, to shelter in their living quarters in the Hall of the Faithful. The Protector Erelda, fully armored in chain mail and breastplate, stood next to the statue of Qilué, shouting orders. The statue had been moved aside to reveal a staircase that spiraled deep below. Another Protector disappeared down it, sword pealing.

The ruined temple lay due south of here. The quickest route to it would be the one Cavatina had suggested: take the corridor past the Moonspring Portal, and strike south. Kâras didn't go that way, however. He knew it would be impassable—too many of Ghaunadaur's minions would block his path. His had been the first group of fanatics to come through the portal in the column south of the river. Scores of oozes, slugs, and slimes would have poured through since then.

He had no idea how many of the other Nightshadows had made it through the column-portal. Kâras himself had been forced north, away from the river. He'd only managed to extricate himself from his fanatics after they entered the Stronghall. When he finally *had* managed to slip away from them, a fiery ooze had driven him farther north still. And then he'd run into Cavatina and learned about the planar breach.

Was *nothing* going to go as he'd hoped this night?

He elbowed his way through the crowd, to a narrow tunnel that snaked southeast from the Cavern of Song. One of the priestesses shouted at him to stop, that this corridor had been evacuated and was about to be sealed, but he ignored her. He entered it, leaving the commotion behind. He followed its twists and turns, squinting against the occasional glare of flickering *Faerzress*, trying to remember—and avoid—the side tunnels that branched off into dead-end caverns.

There! He recognized the cavern up ahead. He was going the right way. A short distance beyond the cavern, he came to a spot where the corridor branched: one arm veered north, then east, to the ruined temple; the other bore south, then turned west to Skullport. He halted at the juncture, faced with a difficult decision. Skullport, and safety? Or make for the ruined temple and try to prevent the fanatics from releasing Ghaunadaur's avatar?

He kept going over what Cavatina had told him. "Qilué was tricked," she'd said. By the Masked Lord, he'd assumed. But why would Vhaeraun want the fanatics to release Ghaunadaur's avatar? That made no sense. Capturing the

Promenade from within would have been an enormous coup for the Masked Lord, one that would rekindle the faith. If the temple fell to Ghaunadaur's avatar, the Nightshadows might never reclaim it. The wealth of its Stronghall, the Promenade's strategic position within the Underdark, its prestige—all would be lost.

Perhaps—loath as Kâras was to think this—it was Vhaeraun who had been tricked. Or rather, outmaneuvered by Ghaunadaur. The Ancient One must have learned of the Masked Lord's plans, and taken advantage of them. And Kâras had been the one who had set this in motion.

He stood, racked by indecision. Should he try to undo what had been done? He was ill prepared for a prolonged battle against multiple foes. He had his dagger, a few magical trinkets, and his prayers. Cavatina, slayer of Selvetarm, was much better suited to make a stand in front of the portal and prevent the fanatics from passing through it. Yet what if the Darksong Knight didn't even reach the ruined temple? She might have slain a demigod, but that didn't ensure she would always be triumphant. It had been a near thing for her, atop the Acropolis. She'd only survived that battle with his help.

"Masked Lord," Kâras prayed. "Is it your will the breach be opened? Have you—" He hesitated, then forced himself to say it. "Have you allied yourself with the Ancient One?"

This time, the god answered. Not in words, but in the distant peal of a hunting horn. That alone wouldn't have convinced Kâras; it might have been one of the priestesses, signaling the others. But as the horn sounded, a rectangle of darkness with two eyeholes appeared in the air a short distance away, within the tunnel leading to the ruined temple. The bottom of this "mask" fluttered, as if the mouth behind it were lending its breath to the hunting horn's peal. Dots of angry red blazed where the eyes would have been.

That decided it. Kâras wouldn't run. He'd fight.

Just as he turned in that direction, a fanatic ran out of the tunnel Kâras had been making for. Kâras whipped up his dagger—but checked his throw as he recognized pink eyes.

"Valdas!" he cried. "You made it through!"

Valdas halted at the spot where the three tunnels converged. He was still disguised in the green robes and eye-embossed tabard of House Abbylan. His face was bare. He nodded at the other tunnels behind Kâras. "Can we reach Skullport through that?"

"Yes, but—"

"Good. Let's get going. The tunnel behind me is choked with oozes."

Kâras heard the wet slap of an ooze on stone, from somewhere behind Valdar. Would it be possible to get by it and reach the ruined temple? He pointed in the direction Valdar had just come. "We need to go back and stop the fanatics from entering Qilué's trap, or they'll summon Ghaunadaur's avatar to the Promenade."

"They will?" Valdar's pink eyes glittered. He laughed. "That's perfect! It will take care of whatever priestesses the oozes and slimes miss."

"But we'll lose the temple," Kâras protested. "We need it as a base to rebuild our faith."

"We don't need it. From here, we move on—and keep moving. Infiltrate Ghaunadaur's temple in Skullport, and persuade the fanatics *there* to summon an avatar. Scour that city clean. Then we'll do the same in Eryndlyn. After that, we'll lure Ghaunadaur through one of the portals of Sschindylryn, and then—"

"But . . ." Kâras felt his face grow cold, under his mask. "Our target is the matriarchies and their temples. Ghaunadaur's avatar will devour everyone—male and female alike. Who's going to be left to convert if—"

Valdar leaned closer. Kâras could smell the sweat that clung to his dark skin. "I want to kill those spider-kissing bitches. Make them pay. Any male who didn't have the guts to tie on the mask before now deserves to die with them."

"I see," Kâras said. And he did. Valdar was insane. He didn't want to build—only destroy. It didn't matter to Valdar that he'd entered into what amounted to an unholy alliance with Ghaunadaur's fanatics. Nor did he care what ultimately became of the drow. Whatever had happened in that crystal-lined cavern on the night that Eilistraee's and Vhaeraun's realms joined had twisted Valdar, made him blind to the consequences of his actions. He'd yanked the mask up over Kâras's eyes as well. Until now.

The wet hiss of something slithering on stone drew nearer. A chill seeped out of the tunnel behind Valdar.

"You're right," Kâras lied. "We'd better get moving." He pointed at the right-hand corridor. "That's the way to Skullport."

Valdar turned to the tunnel. "Lead the—"

Kâras lunged—but Valdar leaped aside. Kâras's dagger struck nothing but air.

"So that's how it is," Valdar said in a soft, lethal voice. He drew his own dagger—a black-bladed weapon that Kâras didn't remember him having before. "Let's finish it, then—that little dance we began three years ago."

Kâras shifted his weight, as if readying for a lunge.

Valdar's other arm whipped up. The wide sleeve of his robe fell back, and his wristbow twanged. Kâras shouted a holy word and flicked his hand. The bolt glanced off the invisible shield the Masked Lord had just bestowed and shattered on the wall behind him.

Valdar lunged. Kâras met it with a lunge of his own that drew blood from the other male's hand. Their blades clashed, bright steel sliding past black metal. Valdar flicked a hand at Kâras and spat a word, but Kâras twisted aside. Whatever spell Valdar had been trying to catch him with missed its mark.

Kâras feinted and hurled a prayer back at Valdar. It should have left Valdar shaken and open to attack, yet it had no visible effect. Was that their mutual deity, preventing them from harming one another with their prayers? Or was Valdar's will simply too strong to be overcome by Kâras's spell?

They rushed each other. A blade whispered past Kâras's ear, nicking it. The point of his own dagger snagged Valdar's robe. They danced apart.

As they circled, Kâras saw movement in the tunnel behind Valdar: a patch of roiling darkness, momentarily backlit by a temporary ripple of *Faerzress*. It looked like an enormous blob of shadow, smooth and bulging. Kâras's pulse quickened as it flowed into the room. Shadow and ooze, together? Was its presence a sign that he'd guessed wrong? Perhaps the Masked Lord had indeed aligned himself with Ghaunadaur. Killing Valdar might have been the wrong choice.

"Ooze!" Kâras shouted. "Behind you."

Valdar laughed. His fingers flicked. A flicker of light danced at the edge of Kâras's peripheral vision: a forceblade, forged from moonlight and shadow. It streaked toward Kâras—only to slam into his magical shield and explode in a halo of moonlight. Yet in the instant that Kâras's attention was diverted, Valdar's other hand whipped forward. Kâras felt a blow like a dull punch, then an ache. He looked down: Valdar's black blade had buried itself hilt-deep in Kâras's gut.

Valdar started to gloat,—only to grunt in pain as the shadow-ooze engulfed his legs, knocking him prone. His face paled to gray, and his eyes widened. He struggled in vain to free himself as the shadow-ooze flowed slowly up his body. "It . . . You weren't . . ."

"Bluffing?" Kâras edged back, one hand pressed to the blood-slippery shirt where Valdar's dagger had punched home. He knew better than to draw the blade out. It would only do more damage. "No."

He stepped back again, keeping out of range of the bulging shadow-ooze. He sang a prayer to the Masked Lord that should have squeezed the dagger from his gut and stitched the puncture shut.

Nothing happened.

"No use," Valdar gasped. "It's a life stealer."

Worried now, Kâras tried to yank the dagger free. It didn't

budge. A cold centered in his midriff, and he felt his life spiral down into the blade.

Valdar lay on the floor, the ooze covering all but his shoulders and head. The magic sustaining his disguise bled away, revealing his mask. He tried once more to crawl—painfully, slowly—as the ooze sucked him fully into itself.

"You were wrong," Kâras told the vanished Valdar. His voice quavered—and not just from the drain of the magical blade. Yet he kept speaking, if only to convince himself. Blackness crowded the edges of his vision. It wouldn't be long now before he'd go to the Masked Lord's embrace. He gestured weakly at the ooze. "This wasn't . . . what the Masked Lord . . . wanted."

The last of Kâras's life-force drained away, conveyed by the magical blade to the great Void. He collapsed. His mask fluttered as his last breath left his lungs. Then it settled against his face. *Masked Lord,* he prayed as he died. *Draw me into your eternal Night.*

His awareness shifted. He stood on a vast gray plain, neither in light nor in shadow. Beside him was another awareness: Valdar. Oddly, Kâras bore the other Nightshadow no ill will.

A voice called to them: a voice that was neither male nor female, but both. A moment later, it became a pool of utter silence. Then song, then silence. Opposites, twined together, yet somehow harmonious.

Side by side, the awarenesses that were Kâras and Valdar drifted to the place where the song-silence was coming from. It caught them like leaves and swirled them up toward itself. They drifted in front of an enormous face. Moonlight bathed the face's upper half in shining radiance; the lower half was shadowed in utter blackness. A glint of blue danced across eyes the color of moonstones.

Masked Lord, Kâras asked. *Is it you?*

A feminine laugh rustled the mask.

Masked . . . Lady? he ventured.

The chuckle deepened, became male.

Hands moved to the blackness that was the deity's mask. Fingers gripped its edges. Kâras tensed, and felt the eager anticipation of the awareness that was Valdar.

The mask lifted.

Kâras wept.

So did Valdar—and as he did, Kâras saw into the other Nightshadow's heart.

The emotions that had prompted their tears were as different as moonlight from shadow.

"Seal those corridors!" Erelda shouted.

She pointed with her sword. Priestesses scrambled to the tunnels leading north, east, and south from the Cavern of Song, raised their holy symbols, and sang. Shimmering barriers, bright as moonlight but steeled with black shadow, sprang into being and sealed the tunnels. These would offer a temporary reprieve. Eilistraee's faithful could pass through, but the barriers would hold the fanatics and their minions at bay.

For a time.

Erelda ran a hand through her sweat-damp hair. The Stronghall had fallen. The Hall of the Priestesses would likely be next The handful of priestesses and lay worshipers staggering back from that cavern were badly wounded, and most had lost both swords and shields. According to the sending she'd just received, a few priestesses held out in the Hall of Healing, but it had been cut off by a flow of oozes from both the north and the south. The healers were on their own now.

The winding maze of tunnels to the south of the Cavern of Song was rapidly filling with oozes. What had that Nightshadow been *thinking,* when he ignored the Protector's warning and hurried into them? With oozes choking the Sargauth, she had to assume that the handful of Protectors who'd been patrolling the opposite side of the river were lost. The lay worshipers, meanwhile, crowded fearfully into the Hall of the Faithful. If oozes came bubbling up out of the breach Cavatina had reported and broke through the seals to reach the Cavern of Song, at least the lay worshipers would be out of harm's way.

For the moment, the Cavern of Song was secure. That was a starting point. But they needed to retake the rest of the Promenade, or they'd be trapped here. The Moonspring Portal was on the other side of the shimmering barriers Erelda had just ordered into place. That would be their first objective. They'd fight their way to it, and clear it of the oozes that fouled it. Then reinforcements from the shrines could get through.

"Lady Qilué," she called. "Where are you? The Promenade needs your sword and silver fire. Please answer!"

Nothing. Where *was* the high priestess? For that matter, where was Rylla? No one had seen either of them since the battle began. If things didn't turn around soon, they were going to lose the temple; she could feel it. The shrines would survive, but without the Promenade it would be a gutted faith. Anger flared. *Eilistraee! You can't allow this to happen!*

Outwardly, however, Erelda was steel. She directed the last of the wounded to the Hall of the Faithful, and ordered its two northernmost entrances magically sealed with a plug of stone. If the oozes did break through from the north, her Protectors, priestesses, and foot soldiers could fall back through the Cavern of Song without having to defend these entrances. This done, she redeployed her forces, assigning two novices to keep the holy song going at all times, to ensure that Eilistraee's shimmering moonfire still danced through the cavern. She strode from one defender to the next, offering encouragement to her depleted forces.

This was a test, she told herself. A test of her faith. She needed to *believe* they would triumph. Just as Qilué had let belief sustain her, centuries ago. The Promenade's defenders would rally and drive Ghaunadaur's minions back.

A scream came from the corridor leading to the Moonspring Portal. Erelda turned in time to see a novice and a soldier stagger through the magical barrier. Their arms were melting into slime, their fingers dripping away. A priestess rushed forward to aid them. But before she reached them, they collapsed, screaming, into a bubbling mass of ooze.

The magical barrier wavered as a multicolored sheen that glistened like a soap bubble spread across it. The stone on either side of the tunnel rippled, as if viewed through a heat shimmer. So did the floor and the ceiling. Just behind the barrier, something enormous bubbled forward. A portion of it bulged against the barrier and popped, breaking a hole.

"Defenders!" Erelda shouted, her sword pealing in her hand as she pointed with it. "A breach. An ooze is—"

The floor in front of the tunnel rippled. The walls slumped. The defenders closest to that entrance shouted as their feet sank into mud, slowing their charge. The ooze bulged through the songwall, rupturing it, and a swirling, stinking fog roiled into the room. Priestesses collapsed, choking, as it engulfed them.

A Protector ran forward on a prayer-wrought moonbridge, her singing sword pealing a challenge. She hurled a bolt of twined moonlight and shadow at the monstrous ooze. It bored through the creature, popping several of its bulging membranes. But then a wave of energy rippled from the ooze and rushed back along the moonbridge in a wave of chaotic color. The Protector tried to leap from the bridge, but the energy reached her before she could spring. She disappeared. For a heartbeat, a rent remained in the place where she had just stood. A cacophony of sounds, colors, and smells poured out of it, flickering between sensations faster than the eye could blink. Then the rent sealed shut.

"By all that's holy," Erelda whispered. "Where did it just send her?"

The ooze was fully inside the Cavern of Song now. It looked like a collection of multicolored, inflated sacs, glued together with shimmering slime. These popped as the prayers the priestesses hurled ruptured them, then reformed. Triumphant shouts came from behind the creature. The instant it was fully inside the cavern, half a dozen fanatics came howling in after it, their tentacle whips flailing. A Protector cut one of them down even as he leaped into the cavern, her singing sword pealing victoriously, but the fanatic beside him shouted a prayer. Green slime flowed from his fingers and turned into a wave that smashed into the Protector, knocking her down. When it subsided, she was gone.

The ooze, meanwhile, pushed its shimmering wave of chaotic energy ahead of it. One of the novices maintaining the sacred psalm was engulfed by the energy and vanished, screaming. The other, a pale-skinned moon elf, quavered on. The few lay worshipers remaining in the cavern either fled, screaming, or raised their arms in desperate prayer.

"Defenders!" Erelda cried. "To me!" She sang a blessing, and a ripple of shadow-dappled moonlight pooled around her, bathing the defenders closest to her in its pure, cleansing light. The blessing would anchor them, and prevent the bubbling ooze from tossing any more of them into whatever hostile realms it had hurled the others.

One of the defenders couldn't reach Erelda in time, and went down under a fanatic's lash. The priestess next to Erelda retaliated with a holy song that crumpled the fanatic where he stood. Erelda herself fended off an attack by a ghaunadan who transformed himself into a walking purple ooze when she tried to cut him in two. She finished him with a prayer that flung him into a wall, splattering him to pieces.

A ragged cheer went up from the priestesses around her, and she realized her foe had been the last of the fanatics. Yet the bubbling ooze remained. Thankfully, it was smaller, reduced in size by the priestess's attacks. "Praise Eilistraee," Erelda gasped. "We *will* hold the temple."

She realized she could hear herself speak. For the first time in decades, the sacred song had faltered. "The Evensong!"

she shouted. The priestesses next to her took up the hymn. With her sword raised, Erelda stepped forward to finish off the ooze.

The world flip-flopped. Up became down. Erelda tumbled, flailing, to the ceiling, together with the handful of defenders who had been standing next to her. She slammed into stone, and saw stars. She scrambled upright—the floor of the cavern reeled dizzily over her head—and realized the ooze had some-how distorted the natural laws of reality. She hurled a bolt of moonlight and shadow "up" at the ooze, but it didn't stop the thing. The ooze slithered over the statue of Qilué, fouling it. Then it disappeared down the staircase leading to the top of the Pit.

Erelda and the others fell. Erelda's wrist snapped as she landed, and pain flared. She rose, cradling the arm against her chest, and sang a hymn of healing. Without looking to see how the others fared, she clambered over the slime-fouled statue and ran to the staircase, shaking feeling back into her hand.

She ran down the spiral stairs two steps at a time, one hand on the inside wall to steady herself, the other tightly gripping her sword. She slipped, scrambled, sometimes tumbled down the steps, which glistened with the multicolored slime left by the creature as it squeezed its way down the narrow stair-case. Always the monster was just around the bend. Just out of sight.

Gasping, Erelda at last reached the bottom of the staircase. She slipped on the final steps and tumbled into a cavern. Its floor was a bumpy field of broken stone: the fragments of the walls Qilué had collapsed to fill the Pit. The Protector who'd been stationed at the top of the Mound was gone. The ooze was just ahead, bubbling toward the statue of Eilistraee. The statue, made up of tiny chips of magic-suspended stone, was no longer moving. It would have halted its dance when the sacred song faltered. That it hadn't resumed its slow pirouette was a grim sign. Hadn't *anyone* survived above?

Erelda leaped, her sword flashing. It sliced through the ooze, severing one glistening sac after another. The ooze deflated—but as it did, a rush of multicolored energy rippled outward from it and struck the statue. Half of the stone chips instantly disappeared, and the rest were transmuted to mud that fell like dirty rain onto the spot where it had stood.

Erelda gasped. Her throat tightened. The seal on the Pit—gone!

The rubble where the statue had stood glowed with a purple light. Tendrils of violet mist seeped out through cracks between the stones. A feeling like ice slid into Erelda's gut as she realized what this meant. The breach at the bottom of the Pit had opened!

The rubble quivered. Something was rising upward through the Pit.

"Eilistraee!" she cried. She leaped over the deflated ooze and hurled herself, face down, atop the Mound. She couldn't fuse the rubble—only Lady Qilué could do that with her silver fire—but she *could* sing into being a blessing that would hold back whatever was rising out of the Pit, for a time. "At this time of darkness, I call down your light. Make holy this—"

Her song slowed to a dirgelike moan as the purple mist filled her lungs. The cavern was thick with the stuff; she could no longer see the walls. A tentacle erupted out of the rubble next to her, as thick as her arm and glistening with slime. It knocked her tumbling. She turned—slowly, slowly—and saw the eye at the end of the tentacle open gummily, releasing beams of bright orange light that lanced through the purple smoke. One of these struck her sword, which vibrated as if it had just clanged against an opponent's blade. Its song shrilled to a panic-filled wail, and the steel glowed red with heat.

Erelda grabbed the sword and struggled—slowly, slowly—to her feet, clinging grimly to her weapon. The leather wrapping the hilt smoked, and the tip of the blade grew white hot. Molten metal trickled down it, like wax from a candle, and dripped onto Erelda's hand. She screamed and dropped the weapon. It fell silent.

Determined not to fail her goddess, she resumed her hymn.

A second tentacle emerged from the portal, beside the first. A second eye opened. Erelda's mind raced at a speed her body couldn't keep up with. *Eilistraee aid me,* she pleaded. *It's Ghaunadaur's avatar! It's escaping from the Pit!*

She kept singing. Slowly. The hymn was almost complete. One final word . . .

A ray of orange light struck her in the forehead, filling her with a panic that exploded through her body like shards of ice. Her song turned into a scream. Then she crumpled in despair.

She'd failed. The Promenade was lost.

Laeral stood in the jungle, clad in a silk nightgown that offered scant protection against the night. She would have dressed, had there been time, but Qilué had demanded her *immediate* assistance. The urgent message had awoken Laeral from a sound sleep. She'd pulled on her slippers, swept up her magical necklace from her bedside table, fastened her wand belt around her waist, and cast a quick contingency that would blink her out of harm's way should the Crescent Blade be turned on her. Then she'd teleported here, to the spot Qilué had so precisely described.

This place was evil. Laeral could feel it. Even though it was night, the air was sticky and hot. A faint sound grated at the edge of her hearing: a distant, wailing cry like the sound of women mourning. The trees here were black and twisted, their heavy branches devoid of leaves. A choking tangle of dead vines snaked between fallen masonry, the smell of their wilted flowers reminiscent of corpses ripening in the sun. The ground was uneven, with blocks of stone barely visible under a thick blanket of rotting, bug-infested loam. Laeral could sense a jungle cat observing her from the darkness, its eyes glinting. Though it was hungry, and she probably appeared easy prey, it didn't approach. It slunk away into the jungle, its tail lashing.

What *was* this place? Laeral reached deep into herself and used a pinch of her own life-force to channel power to her spell. She rested her fingers on a block of masonry, and posed the question again—this time, with a whispered incantation. She tapped the fingers of her free hand to her closed eyelids. *Show me,* she commanded.

As she opened her eyes, a vision sprang into place around her. She stood not in a jungle-hemmed ruin, but in an audience chamber with towering walls. Sunlight shone through stained-glass windows, painting everything it illuminated blood red. An elf with dark brown skin and thinning gray hair sat on the throne; wearing thread-of-gold robes and a silver crown. His hands moved in a complicated series of gestures, his twisting fingers teasing wisps of dark smoke out of eight guttering yellow candles. These had been set at the points of a complex eight-sided star that was painted on the floor in what looked like fresh blood. As Laeral watched, breathless, the streams of smoke twined together and thickened, taking on the shape of a monstrous demon with bat wings, horns, and cloven feet. A sword with a flame-shaped blade was strapped to the demon's back, and crackled to life, its flames matching the red blaze of his eyes. Soot, snorted from his nostrils, drifted onto the floor near his feet.

Who summons me? the demon growled.

Geirildin, Coronal of House Sethomiir. The wizard leaned forward on his throne. His hair, now bone white, was shot through with glints of red from the windows above. His eyes glittered. *Kneel before your master.*

The demon's lip curled, yet he did as he was commanded. As he dropped to his knees, one cloven foot kicked over a candle. Its flame guttered and went out. The wizard-coronal tensed, and his hand tightened around a spider-shaped amulet that hung from his neck. The demon drew its foot back inside the eight-sided star, and the wizard relaxed again.

Your name, demon, he demanded.

The demon stared him in the eye and bared his jagged teeth in a feral smile.

Wendonai.

These are dark times, the wizard told the demon. *Our enemies press us on every side. You will help us turn the tide, Wendonai. The brutal conquests of Aryvandaar must be halted, or we Ilythiiri shall all be slaughtered.*

It will be my pleasure, Geirildin, the demon answered.

The vision ended. The jungle and ruins returned.

Laeral shivered as she realized what her vision had just revealed. *This* was where it had happened, nearly thirteen millennia ago—the event that had precipitated the descent of the dark elves of Ilythiir into madness and shadow. Qilué had spoken to Laeral of this before. She'd related enough of the early history of these dark elf ancestors of the drow for Laeral to understand what she'd just seen. According to everything her sister had read, the Ilythiiri had been a greedy people, bent on conquest and determined to achieve victory at any cost. Their noble Houses had embraced the corruption of the Abyss, in order to win the wars they'd waged with neighboring elven kingdoms. Yet Qilué questioned whether they had truly been as ruthless as the histories painted them—or whether they had instead been desperate victims. The vision seemed to hint at the latter. Whatever the coronal's motivation might have been, the summoning Laeral had just witnessed had been his people's downfall. Wendonai was the balor demon who had corrupted Qilué's ancestors—the demon who now lurked inside the reforged Crescent Blade.

The demon whose taint Qilué was about to draw into herself.

And this was the spot where she was going to do it.

One detail of the vision had been especially unsettling. Laeral knew only a little about summoning—the very idea of deliberately unleashing a demon upon the world sickened her—but she could tell that something had gone amiss with the casting she'd just seen in her vision. The demon had displayed a great deal of control: first knocking over the candle—which the wizard had noticed—and then drawing his foot back in such a way as to scuff the lines painted on the floor.

Which the wizard *hadn't* noticed.

Was there something Qilué had also missed? The plan she'd so cryptically outlined to Laeral seemed sound, on the surface. Qilué would draw in the demon's taint, and then Laeral would cleanse it from Qilué with Mystra's silver fire. To ensure the demon didn't gain control of her sister's body, Laeral would use a trick they'd once played on Elminster—a jest Qilué had made a cryptic reference to in her brief communication. Laeral would temporarily step outside of time, leaving Qilué frozen in the moment, ensuring that Laeral would get a chance to draw down the silver fire before the demon could try anything.

All good, in theory. But had this truly been her sister's idea—or the demon's? Qilué had admitted to being corrupted by Wendonai, but had assured Laeral that she was—at least, at the time of her most recent communication—fully in control of herself. But *had* she been? What if the demon was scheming to turn Mystra's boon against them? What if the silver fire consumed not Wendonai, but Qilué herself? Her body would remain—it could not be destroyed by mundane or magical means—but whose mind would it house?

If Laeral were a priestess, she might have asked for guidance from a greater power. But she was a mage, with only her own instincts to go by. And her instincts screamed caution.

A thread of moonlight through the bare branches above announced Qilué's imminent arrival. Laeral braced herself. An instant later, Qilué appeared. She landed in a crouch atop the block of weathered stone that had been the seat of the throne, the Crescent Blade held high above her head. Her robe was soaking wet, her ankle-length hair plastered against her black skin.

The sisters' eyes met: Qilué's, clear and determined; Laeral's, brimming with concern.

"Sister," Laeral whispered. "I . . ."

"May Eilistraee forgive me," Qilué said in a flat voice. Then, before Laeral could stop her, Qilué yanked the holy symbol from her neck and threw it down. The Crescent Blade swept up, and down in a deadly arc. Steel struck silver with a dull clank, slicing the holy symbol in two.

"It begins!" Qilué cried.

She chanted—words that twisted her lips and forced a spray of red through her teeth as she gritted them out. Her features changed. Her back hunched, her face erupted in boils, and her eyes clouded to a dull white. The fingers gripping the Crescent Blade elongated and grew thick, horny nails. A foul smell rose from her skin.

All this, in the blink of an eye.

Laeral reeled as she realized what her sister was doing. Qilué had cast aside Eilistraee's redemption, and was warping her very *soul* in order to invite the demon in. Laeral could feel the evil crackle past as it rushed at Qilué. It chilled, then burned. It whipped both sisters' hair into twisted knots, fouled Laeral's nightgown, and forced its soot into her lungs, making her cough. It shrilled past her ears with a mocking, high-pitched tittering.

No! Laeral thought. All the drow on Toril weren't worth *this!*

"Temfuto!" she screamed, halting time for all but her.

Silence. Sudden stillness. Her sister's transformation, halted. The very air, frozen. A falling leaf, checked in mid-descent. Laeral stepped past it—quickly, quickly, before her spell ended—and touched her hands to her sister's head. Qilué's scalp felt as hot as the Abyss beneath her ice white hair.

Silver fire wreathed Laeral's hands in a sparkling radiance. She readied herself to send it raging into Qilué the instant the time-halting spell ended, in order to burn the taint from her sister's body. But what then? Qilué had drawn some of the demon's taint inside her, but not all. Though Laeral's silver fire would burn much of it away, a portion would remain inside the Crescent Blade, which Qilué still held in her hands. If the sword had been lying on the ground, Laeral could have easily cast a disjunction to strip it of its magic, once Qilué herself had been cleansed. But with it locked tight in Qilué's grasp, the demon could slide back up the trickle of blood that connected steel and flesh. Qilué was an open vessel, bereft now of the blessings that had formerly protected her. The demon would slide into her as quickly as a sword into an oiled sheath. Faster, perhaps, than Laeral could react.

Laeral trembled with indecision. She had to decide. Now! Then it came to her.

A snap of her fingers transmuted the soot that grimed her sister into a dusting of crushed diamond, emerald, ruby, and sapphire. With her hands still on Qilué's hair, Laeral watched the leaf, waiting . . .

The leaf quivered. Time resumed its flow. Laeral cast her spell.

The leaf landed, and the rush of taint died away in an angry howl. Qilué remained motionless, the gem dust in her hair sparkling in the moonlight. She, alone, remained frozen in time, held fast by Laeral's transmutation.

Laeral hardly recognized the twisted thing Qilué had become.

"Oh, sister," she breathed. "What have you done?"

She didn't need to ask *why* Qilué had done it. She knew the answer. Qilué loved the drow with all her heart. She'd sought their salvation with every thought, with every word, with every deed. And this had nearly been her downfall.

Nearly.

Laeral, however, had just bought her sister a little time. Even if Laeral herself didn't know how to help Qilué, there was someone who did. Someone whose knowledge of demons—whose expertise in hunting them down, banishing them, permanently *destroying* both the demon and its lingering taint—far surpassed Laeral's own. The Darksong Knight, Cavatina. Laeral would take Qilué someplace safe, then fetch Cavatina.

Laeral touched her sister and spoke a conjuration, but something prevented her from teleporting away. It was as if Qilué were a lodestone, pulling in the opposite direction from the one Laeral wanted to go. Laeral wrapped her arms around her sister and tried to physically move her, but Qilué's feet refused to lift from the block of stone.

Suddenly, she remembered her vision and the ancient wizard's binding spell. The binding must have taken hold of Qilué, as soon as the demon's taint shifted inside her. Laeral knew a powerful abjuration that could break the binding, but casting it would also end the spell that was holding Qilué in stasis.

She stood, desperately thinking. A binding, she knew, could be undone not just by a spell, but also by repeating a phrase, a gesture, or by meeting other, very specific conditions set by the original spellcaster. She went over the vision in her mind, but it offered no clues. In time—and with a great deal of study—she might find that key.

She stared at her frozen sister. Time was certainly something Qilué had.

Unless someone came along in the meantime and cast a disjunction spell.

Laeral squared her shoulders. If Qilué couldn't be brought to the Darksong Knight, she decided, then Cavatina would just have to be brought here instead. That meant Laeral would have to leave her sister. In the meantime, she had to guarantee Qilué's safety. She hung her necklace around Qilué's neck to ensure that enemies couldn't scry her. Then she cloaked her sister in a glamer that would further conceal her.

"I'll be gone just a short time, sister," Laeral said, stroking the frozen hair, even though she knew Qilué couldn't hear or feel her. "I'll come back with Cavatina. She'll know what to do."

Her promise made, she teleported away.

The night deepened. The moon moved in the sky. Shadows lengthened.

So did a hair-thin strand of web.

A spider descended from a branch above, and landed on gem-dusted hair. It crawled down an ebon cheek and across parted lips.

It began to spin its web.

CHAPTER 10

Q'arlynd strode down the cobblestoned street, ignoring the stares. Alehouse patrons halted their conversations and gaped, a gnomish musician cranking a hurdybox faltered in mid-song, and pale-skinned elves gave him sidelong glances as they passed, their hands near their swords. Alarmed whispers swirled in Q'arlynd's wake—the word "drow" followed by low-voiced, hostile comments.

The air was uncomfortably hot, the sunlight blinding. The buildings on either side—tall, white-limed, and red-shuttered—were smooth and square, utterly unlike the fluted stalagmites and columns of Sshamath. Here and there, patches of welcome shade pooled under massive oaks whose branches held aloft the elaborate dwelling places of the surface elves. Yet these momentary respites were nothing compared to the cool, constant darkness of the Underdark. Q'arlynd's eyes lingered on the gnomish burrows down among the tree roots, and the heavy stone arches that led to the underhalls of the dwarves—not that those races would react with any less apprehension to a drow than the rest of Silverymoon's inhabitants.

Q'arlynd could easily have teleported to the precise spot in Silverymoon he needed to visit, but he wanted to take the measure of Flinderspeld's adopted city. Its inhabitants turned out to be a mix of surface elves, humans, and dwarves, leavened by the occasional surface gnome or halfling. All seemed hostile, despite the silver star that had been limned by the gate guards' magic on the back of his hand: his pass to move freely within the city.

He passed a white marble tower with star-shaped windows of "glass" made from thin-cut, sky blue jade. Clerics in blue robes and skullcaps—most of them surface elves or humans, and all bearing wands, staves, and a multitude of magical trinkets—passed in and out of its wide front doors. This was the Temple of Mystra, one of the goddesses Qilué honored. Q'arlynd wondered if the high priestess ever worshiped here. He nodded at Mystra's clerics as he passed, noted their raised eyebrows, and felt the tingle of detection spells washing over him. He lifted his hand slightly, drawing attention to the symbol.

Silverymoon was home to at least a dozen magical colleges: the World Above's equivalent of Sshamath. Schools devoted to the teaching of invocation, thaumaturgy, bardic song, and arcane crafting drew students from across Faerûn. Q'arlynd might have made his home here, were it not for the harsh sunlight, and the narrow-eyed stares of Silverymoon's citizens.

He shook his head, surprised at the path his thoughts were treading.

The surface was our home, the ancestors in his *kiira* whispered. The voice deepened to a male timbre: *Eilistraee willing, it will be, again.*

Sshamath is my home, Q'arlynd told them firmly.

His ancestors made no comment.

A bridge of frozen moonlight spanned the river. As Q'arlynd made his way across it, he glanced down at the boats passing below. The people of Silverymoon streamed across the bridge in either direction, walking on the near-invisible bridge as confidently as the drow of Ched Nasad had done across the calcified webs of their city.

Q'arlynd made his way to the market: a bustling hubbub of stalls, braying caravan beasts, and food vendors. Smells assaulted his nostrils: cooking meat, ground spice, ripe fruit, wafting incense, tanned leather, and cloth dye. Oddly, the smell of dung was missing and the cobblestones were clean. Though several shabbily dressed people of various races scurried here and there, it was hard to tell whom they belonged to; no one seemed to be directing them with lashes or clubs. Nor were there any obvious cripples, or shackled slaves—a stark contrast from the city where Q'arlynd had been raised.

His enquiries had confirmed that Flinderspeld was indeed working as a gem merchant, here in Silverymoon. Officially, Q'arlynd was in Silverymoon to purchase chardalyn, a rare black gemstone capable of absorbing spells. Silverymoon's wizards had perfected the use of it, casting a spell into a gem, and releasing the latent magic later by the simple expedient of shattering the stone. Flinderspeld was certain to stock it.

Q'arlynd hadn't told the svirfneblin he was coming. He wanted to see the expression on Flinderspeld's face when he first set eyes upon his former master. It would be an important clue to how Q'arlynd should word his request.

A hoodlike arch of brick marked the spot he was looking for: the stairs leading down to the cave where the svirfneblin trading caravans encamped. Q'arlynd hadn't seen any deep gnomes on his walk through the city. They kept below, it seemed.

He strode down the staircase into cool, damp darkness. By the time he reached the bottom of the stairs, his darkvision had reasserted itself.

The startled silence that fell upon the main cavern as he entered proved even more profound than the reaction his appearance had prompted in the streets above. The svirfneblin caravanners who'd been unpacking their lizards' saddlebags glared at Q'arlynd with open hostility. Many, Q'arlynd knew, were deep gnomes from Blingdenstone, the city Menzoberranzan had conquered and plundered. Q'arlynd trod warily, alert for the *twang* of a wristbow or the whispered hiss of a spell.

A gray-skinned svirfneblin, his bald scalp hidden by a leather cap, stepped in front of Q'arlynd, blocking his way. Bracers on his arms held a pair of matched daggers with pale yellow gems set in their pommels. "You're not welcome here, drow," he growled.

Q'arlynd observed the faint shimmer clinging to the deep gnome's body: an illusion. The real deep gnome would be standing nearby, probably blurred, with daggers in hand. Several other svirfneblin had blurred themselves. Those still visible drew swords or daggers and moved to encircle Q'arlynd. One or two thrust their hands into their pockets, and he hoped they weren't reaching for death-magic gems. He heard angry whispers. "Spider-kisser," they called him, and worse.

"I'm looking for someone," Q'arlynd told the illusionary svirfneblin in front of him—speaking in a loud, steady voice so the others could hear. "A friend of mine. His name's Flinderspeld. He's a gem merchant, originally from Blingdenstone."

The svirfneblin's eyes narrowed. "The drow are no friends of ours. Especially after Blingdenstone."

"This drow is," Q'arlynd said firmly. "After Blingdenstone fell, Flinderspeld became a slave. I purchased him—and set him free."

A female svirfneblin set down the pack she'd been unloading and moved closer. "What's your name?"

Q'arlynd bowed—just enough to acknowledge the waist-high female. "Q'arlynd Melarn, formerly of Ched Nasad."

"I thought I recognized you! You're the one who teleported

Flinderspeld here, four years ago. Flinderspeld often speaks of you."

Whispers spread like ripples on a pond. Q'arlynd waited until they ebbed, then looked at the niches that honeycombed the cavern—each of them, a merchant's stall. "Does Flinderspeld have a stall here? I'd like to speak to him."

The female chuckled and jerked her head at the ceiling. "He's upside."

Q'arlynd lifted an eyebrow.

"Upside," she repeated. "In the main marketplace. His customers are surface folk, mostly. They're less at ease down here."

"I see," Q'arlynd said. "Will you show me the way?"

The female nodded. "Follow me."

She led him back up the stairs, shielding her eyes from the sun with a hand as they wound through the maze of stalls. Flinderspeld's place of business turned out to be one of the shops that fringed the marketplace. Its elaborately carved door held a massive quartz-crystal knocker. A smaller door was set into the wall next to it: a gnome-sized entrance, fitted with its own handle and knocker. Next to that was a large clearstone window, scribed with a glyph of warding. Just inside the window stood a display counter. Precious stones of various colors glittered against black velvet cushions.

"Flinderspeld's done well for himself," Q'arlynd commented.

The svirfneblin nodded. She seemed to be waiting for something. Q'arlynd began to dismiss her before realizing what it was she wanted. He pulled a slim gold coin out of his pouch and handed it to her. She lifted it to her mouth as if to bite it, then stopped, as if thinking better of it.

Q'arlynd hid his smile. Poisoning a gold coin was such a time-worn trick that few drow bothered with it anymore.

She tucked the coin in her belt pouch and hurried away. Or rather, she pretended to. Out of the corner of his eye, Q'arlynd saw her blur, then duck behind a nearby stall.

He lifted the knocker on the larger door and let it fall. A moment later, he sensed he was being watched. Not by the people who thronged the marketplace; theirs was a steady stare of wary curiosity and harsh judgment. This scrutiny felt closer, more intense. Was it Seldszar, checking in on Q'arlynd's progress? The Master of Divination had given Q'arlynd a brooch to block scryings, but Q'arlynd suspected it contained a "window" that allowed Seldszar to scry Q'arlynd, in much the same fashion that Q'arlynd's master ring allowed him to peek in on his apprentices, and vice versa. Or perhaps the explanation was simpler. Perhaps the sensation of being watched was just Flinderspeld, peeking through some magical device to see who knocked on his door.

Q'arlynd ran a hand through his hair, smoothing it. He flicked dust from the hem of his silk *piwafwi*. He waited.

The door opened. A male svirfneblin wearing a leather apron smudged with polishing rouge stepped out into the sunlight and stared up at Q'arlynd. A gemcutter's loupe hung from a leather band around his forehead, the lens grossly magnifying his right eye. Gem dust glittered on his hands. He held a wooden stick with a half-polished gemstone affixed to its cup-shaped end by a blob of red wax.

A moonstone, Q'arlynd saw. Sacred to Eilistraee. He took it as a good omen. "Is your master in the shop?"

The svirfneblin had trouble speaking. "Q'arlynd?" he said at last.

Q'arlynd's eyebrows rose, despite himself. "Flinderspeld? You look . . . different."

That he did. Flinderspeld had gained weight since Q'arlynd had seen him last. The tight little lines at the corners of his eyes and mouth had smoothed out. He looked relaxed and solid, a far cry from the slave who had always been tensely poised to duck a swat or a kick.

Not that Q'arlynd had been that kind of master—and not that he'd let anyone else meddle with his property. Yet in Ched Nasad, a slave had never known when the lash would fall.

In days gone by, Q'arlynd would have crossed his arms and stared imperiously down his nose at the svirfneblin. But that had been another place, another time. Furthermore, it was important that things get off to a good start. He dropped down into a squat that brought his eyes level with Flinderspeld's, and smiled. He started to extend his hands in the arm-clasping gesture the surface elves so loved, but couldn't quite bring himself to complete it He was of a noble House, after all. He rested his hands on his knees instead. "Good to see you again, Flinderspeld."

Flinderspeld blinked behind the gemcutter's loupe. "What are you doing *here,* M—" He checked his tongue, and drew his shoulders a little straighter. He glanced at Q'arlynd's hands, which were bare. Q'arlynd had been careful to tuck into a pocket the master ring that connected him with his apprentices; he didn't want to remind Flinderspeld of his former servitude. Not yet. "What brings you to Silverymoon, Q'arlynd?"

"I'd hoped to purchase a chardalyn. Do you sell them?"

Disappointment flickered briefly across Flinderspeld's face. His attention slid to the crowd that was gathering, and his expression changed to one of understanding. "Of course." He stepped back and opened the larger door. "I stock them. Come in."

Flinderspeld closed the door, set down his stick, and folded his arms across his chest. "Now that Blinnet can't overhear us, tell me why you're really here."

Blinnet: that must be the name of the female who'd led Q'arlynd here. He waggled a finger at Flinderspeld. "You're entirely too smart, for a s—"

"For a what?" Flinderspeld interrupted, his nostrils flaring. "A slave? A svirfneblin?"

"For a shopkeeper," Q'arlynd said, affecting a hurt look.

"Oh."

"But then, I always knew you were an intelligent fellow." Q'arlynd nodded at the display of expensive gems. "Just look what you've built for yourself, in such a short time. This is quite the shop."

Flinderspeld glanced through the window at the knot of people gathered outside his shop. "What is it you want, Q'arlynd?"

"If I told you I came to see how you were faring, what would you say?"

"I wouldn't believe you. It's been four years."

There it was again: that flicker of disappointment.

Q'arlynd gestured at the frowning faces outside the window. "Visiting you might have caused you problems. I enquired after you instead, from time to time That's how I knew where to find you. I thank you for welcoming me into your shop, even though it will be bad for business."

Flinderspeld shrugged. "I was curious to see what you wanted." His eye settled on the tiny silver sword Q'arlynd had hung around his neck. "You wear Eilistraee's symbol, I see."

Q'arlynd hid his smile. "That I do." He plunged into his carefully rehearsed request. "It's temple business that brings me to Silverymoon. Together with some other wizards, I'm trying to learn the location of a surface elf temple that predates Eilistraee's banishment from Arvandor—a quest Eilistraee's high priestess has given her blessing to. The divinations we've tried so far haven't worked; you may have heard of the difficulties the augmented *Faerzress* is causing among the drow."

Flinderspeld nodded.

"We—*I*—need your help."

Flinderspeld turned to the counter. "What do you want? A scrying gem?"

"We've tried that already, and it didn't help. Nor, it turns out, did the gorgondy wine we purchased. I hoped to locate a more potent vintage."

Flinderspeld frowned. "Why come to me? I cut gems; I don't vint wine."

Q'arlynd spread his hands. "You're the only svirfneblin I know. And, more to the point, the only one who knows me. Years ago, you mentioned the Fountains of Memory. I need to look into their waters and use them to find the temple."

Flinderspeld gave Q'arlynd a guarded look. "What makes you think *I* know where they are?"

"I don't. But you must know someone who does—whoever told you about them. If not him, then a gorgondy wine vintner, or his supplier. Your business here in Silverymoon brings you into contact with scores of svirfneblin. Surely one of them will know where the Fountains of Memory can be found."

"They won't take you there."

"That's right. *You* will."

Flinderspeld's arms folded. "Or what?" He shook his head. "Are you going to threaten me?"

Q'arlynd spoke softly. "No."

"What then? Remind me that you set me free? I was your slave for *years* before you did that."

"I thought about trying that," Q'arlynd said. "Then I decided that it wouldn't work. You bear me too big a grudge; I can see that now. And offering to pay you for the information would only insult you. I'm forced, therefore, to resort to something a little more drastic."

He reached inside a pocket and pulled out two black rings.

Flinderspeld tensed and glanced around his shop, as if searching for a weapon.

Q'arlynd held out one of the rings. Flinderspeld's eyes widened as he saw which one Q'arlynd was offering him.

"If you can describe the Fountains of Memory, I can teleport us there," Q'arlynd explained. "You can ensure I bring you along by using the master ring to control my actions. Once I've glimpsed the temple in the pools, and we've used them to reach it, you can erase my memories of the Fountains of Memory, with a spell that's contained within this." He gestured at his forehead, and rendered the lorestone visible.

Flinderspeld's eyes widened. "A *selu'kiira!* And a powerful one, judging by the color. How—?"

"It's a long story," Q'arlynd said. "But the awarenesses inside it *can* do as I've described—something you can verify for yourself once you're wearing that ring. You'll be able to touch not only my thoughts, but theirs, as well."

Flinderspeld stared at the proffered ring. "Why would you let me do this?"

"Because I trust you."

Flinderspeld fell silent for several moments. Q'arlynd waited, trying not to betray the tension he felt. Svirfneblin were naturally mistrustful. Flinderspeld might reject the proposal out of hand, ring or no.

Flinderspeld thrust out a hand. "Give me the ring. And your trueseeing crystal."

Q'arlynd lifted the chain from his neck and handed over both gemstone and ring. He watched with a bemused smile as Flinderspeld studied the ring carefully through the gemstone, assuring himself that it was, indeed, the master ring—and not the slave ring, concealed by an illusion. His time among the drow had taught him to never be too trusting. He handed the gemstone back to Q'arlynd, and put on the master ring. "Your turn."

Reluctantly, Q'arlynd slipped the slave ring onto his own finger. He closed his eyes and braced himself as Flinderspeld thrust into his mind and rifled through his private thoughts. His jaw clenched. Then Flinderspeld delved deeper. Q'arlynd heard the svirfneblin's voice in conversation with the awarenesses inside the *kiira*. He couldn't make out the words.

One of his arms jerked up; Flinderspeld had taken control of it. Q'arlynd found himself walking jerkily forward. He spun when he reached the far wall, nearly toppled, and felt his arms jerk out to steady himself. He walked forward again and squatted, then jumped. He tried to glance at Flinderspeld as the svirfneblin walked him back across the room again, but his body wouldn't cooperate. Flinderspeld chuckled, and spun Q'arlynd around a second time.

Q'arlynd started to worry. Had he misjudged Flinderspeld? If so, he'd just condemned himself to a life of slavery. To a *svirfneblin*.

The insult had slipped into his mind before he could prevent it; Flinderspeld would certainly have heard it. Q'arlynd mentally shouted to the svirfneblin that he hadn't meant it, that he *didn't* think of the deep gnomes as a lesser race. But he knew this was a lie.

Thanks to the slave ring, so did Flinderspeld.

Q'arlynd's hand came up. His finger pointed—at his own forehead. He felt Flinderspeld yank an evocation from his mind. Sweat trickled down Q'arlynd's temples as he fought to form a word, but Flinderspeld held him stiffly in place. Strain as he might, all that came out was, "Nnnn—"

"Keep silent!" Flinderspeld shouted—a passable imitation of a drow master's command, an order Q'arlynd had used many times. A bolt of magical energy streaked out of Q'arlynd's fingertip and bored into his forehead, hot and painful. Q'arlynd's eyes watered. He groaned.

Suddenly, his body was his own again.

"We're even, now." Flinderspeld said. He tugged the master ring off and held it out to Q'arlynd. "And I don't want your ring. Controlling someone else's body was . . . interesting, but I didn't like the place it led me to. It felt . . ." He paused, searching for the word. "Wrong."

Q'arlynd yanked off the slave ring. "You won't help me, then."

Flinderspeld lifted an eyebrow. "I didn't say *that.*"

Q'arlynd squatted down to Flinderspeld's level, not quite believing what he had heard. "You'll lead me to the Fountains of Memory?" he asked eagerly.

"Not only that. I'll let you remember it afterward."

Q'arlynd's eyebrows rose.

Flinderspeld smiled. "Your ancestors have promised me they'll erase your memory of the pools, if you try to tell anyone where they are. I'm not sure if I believe them, but I'm willing to gamble that *you'll* keep your mouth shut, once the spell you hope to cast at the ruined temple is complete."

"My ancestors told you . . . what I'm planning?"

Flinderspeld's smile widened to a grin. "You'll have to trust *me* to keep quiet about that."

Q'arlynd nodded to himself. Flinderspeld was better at striking a bargain than he'd thought. No wonder he was prospering. "Well played."

"For anyone else, the answer would have been no. But you weren't all that bad, as drow go. You *did* set me free, regardless of what your motive was at the time. I owe you one, for that."

Q'arlynd smiled—a genuine smile of friendship, not the false one he'd practiced in the mirror before coming here. He clasped Flinderspeld's arms and said a word he never thought he'd utter, except in jest. "Friends?"

Flinderspeld returned the arm clasp and spoke in Low Drow. "Allies."

Q'arlynd's eyebrows lifted.

Flinderspeld burst into laugher. "Friends."

T'lar rolled a spike-spider back and forth between her palms, savoring the harsh pricks as its needles drove into her flesh. The metal throwing ball wasn't loaded, and its needles held no poison. She did it for the sensation alone. Each jab, each welling of blood was a penance for letting her target slip away. She'd learned that he'd departed for the World Above, but hadn't been able to find out where, or why.

In another moment, however, that little problem would be rectified.

She stood, together with the new high priestess, next to a black iron barrel hoop that hung from a chain by the ceiling. Inside the hoop, a spider descended on a thread of silk. The high priestess coaxed it in the direction she wanted with a morsel of raw meat, her free hand slowly guiding the hoop. The metal grated softly against the chain as it turned. She caught the spider and deftly moved it to the side, adhering the strand to the hoop. The final strand in place, she transferred the spider to her shoulder, and inspected its handiwork. Within the hoop was a five-pointed star, made entirely from web.

"We can begin."

T'lar nodded. She slipped the spike-spider into her belt pouch and wiped her bloody palms against the thighs of her skin-tight tunic. "Summon him."

The high priestess flicked the iron hoop, setting it spinning. Then she picked up a candle. She held it a moment near her face and invoked Lolth's name. As she did so, the flickering light illuminated her elaborately coiffed hair, obsidian blood-drop earrings, and silver crown. Only a short time ago, that crown had graced the head of Laele Zauviir, but the Spider Queen's temple in Sshamath had a new high priestess, now. *Streea'Valsharess* Zolond was much stronger than Zauviir had been—ready to grasp power in her own two hands, instead of licking up the crumbs the Conclave offered.

Streea'Valsharess Zolond touched the candle to the web inside the hoop. The strands of spider silk ignited. Sustained by magic, they continued to burn. "Lords of the Abyss, hear my command," she intoned. "In Lolth's name, send forth the demon Glizn."

A puff of yellow smoke erupted out of the center of the spinning hoop, filling the chamber with an acrid stench. Smoke drifted toward the spider carvings adorning the ceiling. A stationary figure appeared within the hoop, held by the burning web while the hoop spun around it: a tiny demon, barely twice the length of T'lar's hand, with batlike wings. It looked like a quasit, except that its skin was black and dry, instead of oily green. Instead of the usual horns, it had stiff white tufts of hair growing from its scalp. The demon's red eyes were too large for its face, and their expression was one T'lar was used to seeing on the faces of her targets. Fear. Deep inside those eyes, someone screamed.

The high priestess laughed. "What lovely irony! Whatever happened, quasit, to flip things inside out?"

T'lar glanced sideways at the high priestess.

Streea'Valshariss Zolond gestured at the demon, and chuckled. "Until recently, one of Q'arlynd Melarn's apprentices wore this demon."

"And now the quasit wears him?"

"So it would seem." She chuckled. "I'd been wondering why we hadn't heard from Glizn. I assumed it was because 'Piri' had been found out by his master, and slunk away."

The demon tugged, but failed to free its wings from the burning web. It shifted into centipede form, then into a squat toad, but still wasn't able to escape. At last it let out a thin squeak. "Why have you summoned me?"

"Where is Q'arlynd Melarn?" the high priestess said.

"I don't know!" the quasit squeaked. Fear oozed from it like a bad smell. "I haven't seen him since my lord called me back to the Abyss. So you might as well unbind me, and send me back, since I can't help you to—"

The demon's voice suddenly deepened. Words jerked from the tiny mouth. "I . . . can . . . find . . ."

The quasit snapped its jaw shut, biting its own tongue.

The high priestess studied the bound demon, her head cocked to one side. "Piri? Was that you who answered just now?"

The demon's face contorted from one emotion to the next: fear, anger, determination. A hiss escaped its lips. It might have been a yes.

"How can you find him?" T'lar demanded. "Tell me."

The demon's jaws creaked open. Shut. Open again. "Scry—" the deeper voice said. Then the mouth snapped shut. One hand jerked. A finger twitched.

The high priestess pointed at a tiny copper band on the quasit's finger. "How will you scry him? With that ring?"

The quasit's head jerked sharply: a nod.

The high priestess reached for it.

"No! Only . . . I . . . can . . ."

The high priestess scoffed. Her fingers closed around the ring.

T'lar caught her arm. "Leave it."

The high priestess glared at her.

T'lar pointed out the obvious. "If it *were* possible for either of us to use the ring, the apprentice wouldn't have told us about it." She stepped closer and pinched the demon's tiny chin. The quasit tried to bite her, but she held it fast. "Stop that!" she ordered. "Let Piri speak."

The demon winced.

T'lar curled her lip. Quasits were such pitiful excuses for demons. She drew her dagger—the one with the spider pommel that she'd taken as a trophy of Nafay's kill—and held it where the demon could see it. "What would you like in return for telling us, Piri? Release?"

Tears welled in the overlarge red eyes.

"Then fight the demon. Scry your master. Tell me where he is. If I believe what you tell me, I'll skin you free and send your soul to Lolth."

The demon's expression suddenly changed. The quasit spoke in its own shrill-pitched voice. "Oh no!" it squeaked. "That will *hurt!*"

The priestess laughed. "Only for a moment, demon. And think on this: if T'lar uses that pretty little dagger of hers properly, being parted from your skin will only temporarily kill you. As long as you die here, you'll re-manifest in the Abyss." She gestured at his body. "Free of that annoying wizard, I might add."

The quasit met the high priestess's eyes briefly, then let out a heavy, sulfurous sigh. "Fine," it said petulantly. "I'll let him do it." Its eyes slid sideways to T'lar. "But *she* has to swear by the Spider Queen, that she'll send me back clean. No skin."

T'lar smiled. "I swear it, by Lolth's dark webs."

The demon nodded. It tightened its ring hand into a fist, closed its eyes, and puckered its forehead into a frown of concentration.

The two drow waited. The silence stretched—long enough for the spider on the high priestess's shoulders to scuttle to the ground and spin a trap-web in one corner of the room. At last the quasit's eyes fluttered open. A high-pitched, tittering laugh burst from its lips.

"He saw him, he saw him, he saw him!" the quasit squeaked. "He was talking to a svirfneblin."

T'lar leaned closer. "Where was he?"

The quasit giggled. "Don't know."

Anger hissed from T'lar's lips.

"But he heard where he's *going!* The 'Fountains of Memory' he said."

T'lar glanced at the high priestess. *Streea'Valsharess* Zolond shrugged. It seemed she hadn't heard of the place either.

The quasit's head twisted so it could see T'lar. "You have what you wanted. Skin the wizard off me. Send me back to the Abyss."

"Not yet."

"But you swore—"

"Not until Q'arlynd Melarn is dead. Until then, you're staying right where you are."

"Noooo!" the quasit howled.

The hoop had almost slowed to a stop. T'lar reached out and gave it a nudge that sent it spinning again. "Yes."

Halisstra strode through the jungle, following the priestess. She'd slain the first priestess who had disturbed the penance ritual—the one who'd come bleating about the strange song the night twist tree was singing. The second priestess had been smarter. She'd taken the time to decipher the song, and reported it to her superior, rather than interrupting Halisstra. The superior, in turn, had waited until the ritual was over. Her eyes had widened in startled alarm when Halisstra sprang off the throne and caught her by the throat.

"Wendonai?" Halisstra shouted. "Here?"

Unfortunately, the priestess couldn't answer. Halisstra had crushed her throat. The other faithful had balked at that, but a soothing song had drawn them back into Halisstra's web, once more eager and grateful to serve her.

The priestess who had deciphered the song pointed ahead through the jungle at a black, leafless tree growing out of the remains of a tumbled building. A mournful sound poured out of it, the sound of weeping and pleading. The sound of weakness.

"Closer," Halisstra ordered.

The priestess didn't hesitate. Despite the danger the tree's song posed, she strode forward. After three steps, she crumpled to her knees, screaming. A moment later, the night twist's magical attack washed over Halisstra. A phantasm loomed in her mind: the image of Lolth in hybrid form, a spider with Danifae's face. *You will never escape me,* Lolth leered. *You are not a demigod, but a mortal—and you are mine.* The illusionary Lolth loomed over Halisstra, her bloated abdomen pulsing. Web oozed from her spinnerets. *I will bind and break you, just as I did before. Your weakness will betray y—*

Halisstra sang out a loud, clear note that shattered the illusion like glass. A second song stilled the priestess's screams. The smaller female scurried to Halisstra's side, trembling, as Halisstra listened to the night twist's song.

The priestess had been correct. The tree was singing Wendonai's name.

Halisstra looked around. Moonlight, as bright as a hundred torches, illuminated the jungle. Just beyond the night twist was a clearing littered with tumbled masonry. A glint caught Halisstra's eye—a faint light, like moonlight gleaming on metal. She walked toward it. Vines, animated by the night twist's mournful song, twined around her legs, but Halisstra was too strong for them. She continued to the clearing, tearing them like fragile spider webs.

The clearing looked empty. Yet the glint beckoned. Halisstra sang a melody that would reveal the invisible: nothing happened. She edged closer to the glint, alert for any sign of the demon. Wendonai could kill with the flick of a finger. Her memories of him crushing the life from her were still vivid. That time, Lolth's magic had restored her. But Halisstra was no longer the Spider Queen's pet plaything. If Wendonai broke her body a second time, Halisstra might die. Her soul would flutter back to Lolth, and the torment would begin anew.

No, she told herself sternly. That wouldn't happen. She was a *demigod* now. A mortal who had been raised to godhood by the worship of her faithful. Just like Sheverash, she'd been tempered by pain and suffering, and her soul had been hammered to the hardness of steel. She'd been reborn. She was free of Lolth, and the Spider Queen could no longer claim her.

Even so, she moved cautiously.

The glint hovered above a block of weathered stone. A faint odor wafted from it: the smell of diseased flesh. As Halisstra leaned closer, one of the spider legs protruding from her chest brushed against something. There *was* an invisible creature here!

She sprang back from the block of stone, her spider legs drumming nervously against her chest. Then she remembered her priestess was watching. She moved forward again, and patted the invisible creature with her hands. It was more or less drow-shaped, and unmoving—frozen in a crouch and covered in a gritty dust that transferred onto Halisstra's hands and sparkled in the moonlight. She patted the air above the invisible creature, where the gleam was, and hissed as something sharp sliced her hand. A more careful probing revealed a cool, flat surface: a curved sword blade, grooved with an inscription. Halfway down the blade, she felt a seam where the blade had been repaired.

Halisstra's lips parted in silent surprise. No! It couldn't be!

"Show me," she hissed. "I *command* it!"

She felt something twist, deep within her mind. By force of will, she clawed away the magical blinders that covered her eyes. The illusion of emptiness fell away, and the invisible creature was revealed. That *was* the Crescent Blade she'd felt—in the hands of a *demon,* no less!

Or . . . was it a demon?

The female had black skin and white hair long enough to reach the block of stone she squatted on. Her face, like Halisstra's, looked vaguely drow. Her body was as loathsome as Halisstra's own: hunchbacked, spotted with fungus-sized boils, and with grossly elongated limbs. The fingers gripping the Crescent Blade ended in clawlike nails, and her eyes were solid white. She was unmoving, utterly unresponsive to Halisstra's touch; When Halisstra tried scoring her flesh with a claw, nothing happened. She didn't flinch, didn't blink. Just kept staring at something silver that lay on the stone in front of her.

When she realized what it was, Halisstra gasped aloud. One of Eilistraee's holy symbols! The other half of the holy symbol lay on the ground, a pace or two away. The blade had snapped in two—in exactly the same spot as the Crescent Blade had broken, all those years ago, when Halisstra had repudiated Eilistraee.

A shiver coursed through her. She stared at the demonlike female. Was this another priestess who had renounced her faith? Another of those who had tried to return to Lolth's sticky embrace, only to be forced into an agonizing penance?

If so, what was she doing *here,* so close to Halisstra's temple? What did it *mean?* Had Lolth placed this fallen priestess here? Had Wendonai?

Halisstra snarled. There was no room in her temple for a *second* Lady Penitent. Halisstra wasn't going to share her fawning faithful with anyone. She wrapped her spider legs around the demon-drow and tried to yank her from the block of stone, but the female didn't budge. It was as if her feet were glued in place. No matter. Halisstra leaned in close and bit. Instead of sinking into yielding flesh, however, her fangs *scritched* away. The surface of the demon-drow's neck was hard and as slippery as ice. No matter how hard Halisstra bit down, she couldn't sink her teeth into that flesh. She sang a dispelling and tried again, but the ensorcelment proved too strong to break.

She sat back on her haunches, thinking. The female had to be under some sort of magical protection.

Lolth's?

Behind Halisstra, the night twist continued its mournful song. *Wendonai,* it wailed. A hot, salty wind coursed through its branches, twisting them against one another. Black bark creaked, and the song shifted. It wasn't the balor's name the night twist was singing, but something else entirely: a message, stabbing at Halisstra's heart.

We . . . don't . . . die . . .

"Yes, we do," Halisstra snarled. She understood, now, why the priestess had come here: to kill her. She must be a demon hunter, a Darksong Knight like Cavatina. Maybe this *was* Cavatina. Halisstra's laugh skittered at the edge of sanity. "You're not going to use the Crescent Blade on me!" She grabbed the female's hands and tried to unbend her fingers. She would have the Crescent Blade—she must! Yet the fingers didn't move. Nor could they be clawed away; Halisstra's nails skidded harmlessly off them. She placed a foot on the female's wrists, grabbed the sword's crossguard, and tried to lever the Crescent Blade out of the fallen priestess's hands. She strained until her muscles ached and sweat ran down her temples.

"Let . . . go . . . of . . . it!"

The priestess refused.

"Abyss take you!" Halisstra snarled as she let go.

A movement in the jungle caught her eye. She whirled, the spider jaws in her cheeks gnashing. The priestess who'd led her here! Halisstra had forgotten her. The spying, sneaking wretch had seen it all: Halisstra's humiliation, her anger . . . her fear.

Halisstra leaped to the spot where the priestess crouched, swept her up, and spun her around. Webs flew from Halisstra's hands.

The priestess didn't resist. "Queen of Spiders, I commend unto you my soul," she droned. "May I prove as worthy in death as I did in life."

"Have you learned nothing?" Halisstra screamed, outraged. "It isn't Lolth you serve, but the Lady Penitent!"

The priestess's voice grew muffled under the layers of web. "May I sing Lolth's praises through all eternity. May I dance upon her webs like a spider. May my soul return to her—"

"Stop it!" Halisstra shrieked. "Stop it, stop it, stop it!" She flipped the web-bound priestess and caught her by the feet. Then she swung her through the air like a club. Flesh met steel with a dull *thwack*. The priestess's head sailed away, parted from her body by the Crescent Blade.

There. *That* shut her up.

Halisstra hurled the body into the jungle. The night twist's vines eagerly caught it and drew it to the trunk. Halisstra sneered. Plenty more, where that priestess came from. "Return to Lolth," she taunted. "If you still can."

She turned back to the priestess who held the Crescent Blade—a little too quickly, still blinded by her rage. The female's body rocked slightly, then toppled to one side.

Halisstra started. She leaped on the fallen priestess and grabbed the Crescent Blade. But tug as she might, the priestess still clung to it.

No matter. Halisstra picked up the demonic looking priestess and tucked her under one arm. There were songs Halisstra could sing, later, that would remove the sword from those hands. And then she would use the sword to kill the interloper.

From there, who knew what might be possible? Perhaps Halisstra would finish what she'd started, so many years ago. Kill Lolth—and maybe Eilistraee too, while she was at it. Anything was within her grasp, now that the Crescent Blade had been returned to her.

Shrieking with laughter, she hurried back to her temple.

CHAPTER 11

Naxil struggled to rise. He wasn't held by ropes or chains—something he might have escaped—but by magic. The fanatics had bound him with words. "Follow," they'd said, and he had. "Kneel," they'd ordered, and he had. Now, "Drink."

He tried to wrench his head aside, but couldn't. Compelled by magic, he gulped down the licorice-flavored drug the green-robed fanatic tipped into his mouth. As the drug took hold, the world slanted dizzily this way and that. Though his body hadn't physically altered, it now felt like a puddle of molten wax, soft and compliant. A numbness settled on his mind, quieting the screaming voice within. He smiled. Drool trickled down his chin.

Part of him knew there was nothing to smile about—and everything to scream about. He'd only joined the Masked Lady's faith a year ago, but he'd lived in the Promenade long enough to appreciate the terrible stillness that had settled upon the Cavern of Song. The chorus of voices that had filled it with sacred music and moonlight since its founding had been extinguished, and it was no longer a holy place. Now it was blasphemed by oozes and slimes, and by the presence of Ghaunadaur's fanatics. One of them—a stunted male in purple robes whose tentacle rod clung to his body like a leech—stared at the captives from a hovering driftdisc. He smiled gleefully as he savored their humiliation.

Naxil would have choked the life from him, were it not for the magic that held him fast and the drug that sent the world spinning. He consoled himself with the knowledge he'd fought well, with dagger and spellsong. After shaking off the charm the green-eyed male had cast on him, he'd personally killed three of Ghaunadaur's cultists. He'd danced from shadow to shadow, attacking from behind, avoiding the oozes and targeting their masters. He'd kept fighting long after realizing the battle was already lost. He'd prayed, then, that death would find him—that he'd make his way to the Masked Lady's side and sit in her cool, calming shadow.

In the end, despite those fervent prayers, despite his valiant struggles, he'd been captured, not killed. He bowed his head and said a silent prayer. Eilistraee grant that whatever happened next, it happened quickly.

Dozens of other captives kneeled or lay nearby—most of them lay worshipers routed from the Hall of the Faithful after the bubbling ooze had bored through the songwalls. Naxil spotted Jub, the half-orc, and several others he knew by name. Those too badly wounded to walk had been left to die The remainder were forced, like Naxil, to drink. There was even a Protector in their ranks, her chain mail hanging in tatters and her singing sword gone. It wasn't Leliana—Naxil had searched anxiously for her among the captives, but failed to spot her. He prayed she'd gone to Eilistraee's grace via a quick death.

Oozes slithered back and forth across the Cavern of Song, reducing the bodies of the fallen to puddles of sizzling flesh. The fanatic on the driftdisc, meanwhile, ordered the captives to their feet. "Follow," he commanded.

Together with the others, Naxil shuffled after the driftdisc. A second fanatic walked beside the line of captives lashing out with his whiplike rod at those who lagged. The amber-colored tentacles struck the moon elf next to Naxil, and she screamed as her skin burst into flame. Naxil tried to catch her, but the drug he'd been forced to drink made him stagger, and the words to his healing spell tangled together in his mind. The moon elf fell to the ground, her pale skin charred black. The reek of cooking meat filled the air.

The fanatic raised his rod to lash Naxil. As his arm whipped forward, another fanatic caught it and said something to him. The first one's aim was thrown off and just one tentacle struck Naxil's shoulder. He gasped as its heat seared into his flesh. The intense pain gave him a moment of clarity, and he whispered a song. Flesh knitted together. His mind cleared fully as Eilistraee's healing grace pushed the drug from his body. Yet the magical compulsion remained. Obedient as a soldier, he marched behind the driftdisc. He passed the fallen statue of Qilué—its face now reduced to a rounded blob by the slithering oozes—and descended into the spiral staircase the statue had once hidden.

Together with the other captives, he wound his way downward. The narrow staircase forced them into single file. Naxil heard the driftdisc scraping against stone up ahead, but couldn't see it. Nor could he see the fanatic who brought up the rear. Now was his moment—while they weren't watching. He sang a prayer, rendering himself invisible.

They reached the bottom of the staircase and entered a cavern. Naxil knew of this place, but had never entered it: this was the cavern at the top of Eilistraee's Mound. There should have been a dancing statue here, sealing the Pit, but Naxil couldn't see it. A dozen fanatics formed a circle around the spot where it should have stood. A thick purple mist filled the cavern, blurring his view. Naxil smelled acid. His nostrils stung. He barely stifled a retch that might have given him away. The captives coughed weakly, their eyes tearing in the acid-tinged air.

The fanatic leading the captives ordered them to stand against the wall. Naxil complied—slowly and heavily. The mist held a magic that slowed movement to a snail's pace. He winced as fragments of stone crunched under his boots, and prayed the fanatics wouldn't notice the dents his invisible feet made. He tried desperately to think of a way to break free.

The fanatic on the driftdisc stepped off it and joined those who had circled around the spot where the statue should have been. His arms lifted, and the others drew breath. At his signal they chanted in an impossibly slow drone.

The chanting intensified. The mist roiled. It swirled above the Pit, coalescing into a knot that became an eye, as large as a serving platter. The eye blinked open, emitting a dull orange light that illuminated the fanatic leading the chant. Immediately, he prostrated himself on the rubble. Slowly, the eye rotated, its sickly light washing over the fanatics one by one. Each fell to his knees in turn, crying out the Ancient One's name.

"Ghaunadaur, Ghaunadaur, Ghaunadaur . . ."

Naxil stared, horrified. The puddle of orange-purple light didn't quite extend to the captives. He knew, instinctively, that Ghaunadaur considered them unworthy, beneath even its contempt. Naxil's stomach felt watery and weak, and his head swam even without the drug. Tears poured down his cheeks, soaking his mask. Beside him, the other captives wept softly.

He touched his mask to steady himself, and saw a hazy smudge: his hand, becoming visible. Hastily, he renewed his prayer, rendering himself invisible again.

The eye completed its rotation. Then it "spoke" in a voice that slithered into Naxil's mind like a damp, unwelcome slug.

Clear the Pit.

The fanatics closest to the Pit laid hands on the jumbled stone and chanted. The others touched their backs, and joined in the prayer. Chips of rock melted into mud. A stench like manure filled the cavern. The fanatics closest to the Pit made paddling motions with their hands. The mud churned. Foul-smelling steam boiled from it, rendering the air in the cavern hot and humid. The puddle of mud sagged, twisted like water down a drain, and revealed the top of a shaft with utterly smooth, glasslike walls.

The captive next to Naxil—Jub, the half-orc—fainted, either succumbing to his wounds, or to fear. Other captives tried to pray to Eilistraee, but only managed a slurred mutter, thanks to the drug.

The fanatics maintained their chant, and the mud continued to sink. With each passing moment, more fanatics descended the stairs and crowded into the cavern, lending their voices to the unholy chorus. Abruptly, the chant ended.

A second command hissed out of the floating eye. *Feed them to me,* it ordered. Then it disappeared.

Naxil tensed as the fanatic guarding the captives turned. "Forward," he commanded.

The fanatics parted, forming a corridor for the prisoners to walk through. "Ghaunadaur," they chanted. "Consume them. Consign them to oblivion. Devour them."

Compelled by the command, Naxil stumbled with the others to the Pit. A captive tripped and fell off the edge. Her scream wailed away into the distance. Another leaped into the Pit of his own accord, crying Ghaunadaur's name, causing Naxil's lip to curl at his cowardice. The other captives wavered at the edge. The magical compulsion wasn't quite strong enough to compel them to take their own lives.

Naxil stared down into a seemingly bottomless well. He'd heard the Pit was nearly half a league deep. Far, far below, he saw a bright silver glow. He wondered if it were the planar breach Cavatina had warned them about.

The fanatics closed in behind the captives. The push of a hand sent another of Eilistraee's faithful into the Pit. Others swiftly followed. Soon only Naxil, still hidden by his invisibility, stood at the edge.

Naxil listened to the captives' screams as they fell. Tears streamed down his cheeks and soaked his mask. He closed his eyes, unwilling to see more. He took a step back—and realized, to his amazement, that he was no longer under the magical compulsion.

Someone jostled him from behind: one of the fanatics, crowding forward. The fanatic started, glanced sideways at the spot where Naxil stood, and opened his mouth to shout. Naxil grabbed his robe and spun him off the edge. A flick of Naxil's fingers triggered a cantrip; his voice shifted to the falling cultist and followed him as he fell. "Ghaunadaur! Consume me!"

The other fanatics started. The face of the one who'd led the chanting purpled. He spun to face a green-robed cultist next to him. "Trucebreaker!" he howled. "What of your oath? Our Houses were to descend *together* to greet the Ancient One!"

The other fanatic whirled. "House Abbylan did not sanction this. He leaped of his own accord!"

As they argued, Naxil edged away from the Pit. Avoiding the fanatics was difficult, as the room was crowded. He wouldn't be able to climb the stairs—not with fanatics still descending. He'd have to make his way to the nearest wall, press his back against it, and hope his invisibility held out.

He decided to make his way to the spot where Jub lay, unconscious and forgotten. He twisted this way and that, slipping between the fanatics whenever an opportunity presented itself. Just as he reached the wall, a hand brushed against his shirt—and took hold of the fabric. He tried to wrench away, but the fanatic yanked him close.

"Ally?" the fanatic breathed. Then he coughed.

Naxil realized the "fanatic's" hand was lingering against his mouth—hiding it, as a mask would.

"Ally," Naxil hissed back.

The "fanatic" found Naxil's hand and pressed a gold ring into it. *Levitate,* his fingers flicked.

Naxil gave silent thanks to the Masked Lady for the boon as he shoved the ring onto his finger. He levitated just above the fanatics' heads, his back against the ceiling, trying to stifle the urge to cough as he breathed the acid-tinged air. He wiped his stinging eyes with the back of his sleeve, lest any tears fall on their heads and give him away.

Below him, the disguised Nightshadow eased into an indentation in the wall and cloaked himself in magical darkness. The fanatics, meanwhile, concluded their argument. They seemed to have come to some sort of agreement. The high priests called to their respective followers, and the fanatics lined up behind them, each with his hands on the shoulders of the one in front of him. Chanting Ghaunadaur's name, they shuffled forward, into the Pit.

At first, Naxil thought they were sacrificing themselves. The fanatics, however, didn't plummet. They sank gently into the Pit, their descent slowed by magic.

As the last of them disappeared into the Pit, a wind sucked the purple mist down after him, and the air cleared. The disguised Nightshadow stepped out of his darkness, crept to the Pit, and peered in. He cocked his head, as if listening to some distant sound. "The trap worked," he said at last with a smile. "They've been driven insane. All of them."

Naxil descended to the floor, the invisibility gone. He moved to where the other Nightshadow stood. Echoing up out of the Pit, from far below, came the sound of voices. It sounded as if all of the fanatics were screaming or crying out at once, in a frenzied cacophony.

Naxil began to tug the ring off his finger but the other Nightshadow gestured for him to keep it. Naxil nodded. "Thanks. . . ."

"Mazrol."

"I'm Naxil."

Mazrol glanced again at the Pit, and shuddered. "Let's get out of here."

They moved to the stairs. Naxil paused to check Jub. The half-orc was unconscious, with a nasty bump on the side of his head, but a prayer would rouse him.

Mazrol looked impatient. "Have you seen Valdar?"

"Who?"

Mazrol's expression turned wary. Naxil tensed. Something was wrong here. Instinct screamed at him that Mazrol had just become his enemy, yet that was ridiculous.

Naxil touched Jub's forehead and began his prayer. Out of the corner of his eye he saw motion near the Pit: the purple mist, rising again. A tendril of it swirled over the lip and crept across the floor, behind Mazrol. The other Nightshadow hadn't noticed yet. He frowned down at Jub. "What are you doing?"

Naxil didn't answer. It ought to be obvious. He kept singing.

Mazrol caught his arm. "Save your prayers." He nodded at the staircase. "If any oozes come slithering down here, we'll need them."

Naxil finished his prayer. "But Jub—"

"Leave him. He's not one of us."

Naxil rose—slowly—to his feet. "He's one of Eilistraee's."

Jub groaned, and rolled over. Naxil heard him cough weakly.

Mazrol stared at Naxil a moment, as if taking his measure. "Eilistraee is dead," he said, his eyes locked on Naxil's. "The Masked Lord killed her. Everything the priestesses taught you was a lie."

Naxil's jaw clenched. He'd heard there were males like this within the ranks of the faithful—Nightshadows who refused to let go of Vhaeraun. Naxil had never worshiped that god, having come to the Masked Lady's faith only after the goddess's transformation. It hadn't been Vhaeraun who had led Naxil out of the misery of Menzoberranzan, but the Masked Lady. Eilistraee.

Mazrol must have seen the flat disbelief in Naxil's eyes. He gestured at the Pit behind him. "Would Eilistraee have allowed this?" he cried. "Would she have *permitted* us to open a back door to her enemies? She's *dead*, Naxil. The Promenade is ours now—if we can hold it."

Behind Mazrol, two blood red eyestalks rose above the lip of the Pit. The eyes opened and stared at the two Nightshadows through the swirling purple mist. Naxil would have quaked in terror, had he not already been sent reeling by what Mazrol had just told him. The other Nightshadow had taken a hand in the Promenade's fall! So had others of the Masked Lady's supposed faithful, by the sound of it. "Us," Mazrol had said. The betrayal cut deeper than any dagger.

Naxil prayed silently. *Masked Lady, I am your sword, and your song. Temper me. Use my body as your instrument to lead this blasphemer to redemption.* Keeping his voice utterly steady, he spoke his accusation aloud. "Traitor."

Mazrol lunged forward to stab Naxil, but Naxil, filled with the Masked Lady's grace, twisted aside. Behind Mazrol, a barbed tentacle snaked up out of the pit, beside the eyestalks. It lashed out and slammed into Mazrol's back, knocking him down. The Nightshadow screamed as the tentacle dragged him to the Pit.

"The Masked Lady can save you!" Naxil cried, leaping forward in a futile attempt to grab Mazrol's hand. "Pray to—"

The tentacle yanked Mazrol out of sight.

Jub sat up. His eyes fell on the spotted, tentacled, sluglike creature rising out of the Pit, and his jaw dropped open. The creature was blood red and enormous.

"Run!" Naxil shouted. He grabbed Jub's arm and yanked him to his feet. Together, they raced up the winding stairs. The stocky little fellow was quick to recover; the Masked Lady's blessing and sheer terror likely had an equal hand in that. After a few steps, he shook off Naxil's arm and climbed without further assistance. "What," he puffed, *"was* that?"

"I fear the worst," Naxil gasped. "The slug . . . is one of . . . Ghaunadaur's forms."

"That's his *avatar?*"

"It did . . . come out of . . . the Pit."

Jub cursed.

Naxil heard a wet slithering behind them: the slug, squeezing up the staircase. Following them. He raced upward, Jub close on his heels. But when they finally reached the top of the stairs, a quivering gray ooze loomed. Naxil dodged to one side of it, Jub to the other.

"This way!" Naxil called. He sprinted across the Cavern of Song, struggling to keep upright on the slippery floor. He cast a frantic glance over his shoulder, but Jub was nowhere to be seen. Naxil cursed and started to double back to search for him, but oozes blocked his path.

Through a gap in their ranks he saw the slug squeezing its way out of the staircase. Six barbed tentacles waved in front of its face. Purple mist boiled around its slimy foot. The tentacles quested south, then north. Its decision made, it slithered toward Naxil. It squirted a stream of purple mist that swirled just short of him.

The oozes parted, leaving a clear path for the slug to follow. Were there fanatics somewhere in the cavern, controlling them? Naxil glanced around, but saw no sign of Ghaunadaur's cultists. The drow all seemed to have gone below, into the Pit.

Naxil suddenly remembered he still wore the ring Mazrol had given him. He could escape by levitating! Yet when he glanced up, he saw the ceiling was coated in green slime. A patch of it landed with a splat at his feet; he barely dodged it in time. Levitating in mid-air, he'd be unable to dodge aside if more of it fell.

"Masked Lady!" Naxil cried. "Guide me! How am I to escape?"

Everywhere he looked, oozes blocked the exits. They sat, quivering, in front of the corridors that led to the Stronghall, the Hall of the Priestesses, and the Hall of the Faithful. The only unguarded exit was the northernmost tunnel—but the oozes slithering toward it would block it soon enough. Naxil ran in that direction, certain that it was Ghaunadaur's avatar pursuing him. *That* was why the oozes and slimes were acting the way they did: they were obeying their master, letting the slug feed first. Naxil was keeping ahead of the avatar, but for how long? As he hurtled out of the cavern's only clear exit, he wildly debated which way to go. South, to the Hall of the Priestesses, or north, to the Hall of Empty Arches? He heard a wet, slapping sound to the south: another of Ghaunadaur's minions. That decided it. North.

As he drew near the Hall of Empty Arches he slipped and fell, wrenching an ankle. He lurched to his feet—and nearly screamed at the pain. He started a restorative prayer, but before he could complete it, an eyestalk poked around the corner. Ghaunadaur's avatar, closing in! A moment more, and it would catch him.

Suddenly, Naxil had an inspiration. The ring: it was gold! Maybe it would activate one of the ancient portals. He staggered into the Hall of Empty Arches, between the first two partition walls. He slapped his hand against the first arch: nothing. Stupid—that was the portal he and Leliana had returned through, the one that led *from* the mine tunnels to here. And the next portal was even less of an option. It led, he'd heard, to an infinite maze that would forever trap anyone foolish enough to use it.

Suddenly, he realized what he needed to do. He understood why the Masked Lady had helped him to escape being sacrificed in the Pit. She needed him—as bait. His frenzied run was the dance that would lead Ghaunadaur's avatar into a trap. Naxil would die, but his reward would be to dance at the side of his deity forevermore.

"Masked Lady!" he cried. "Lend me strength!"

He staggered to the arch and reached out to touch it. Yet even as his fingertips touched stone, a tentacle smacked into his back and coiled around his torso. Naxil grunted in pain as barbs drove into his chest and back. The avatar tried to draw him away from the arch, but the pull of the portal was stronger. It wrenched Naxil inside, tugging the tentacle in with him.

For the space of a heartbeat, Naxil thought this desperate ploy hadn't worked. He dangled above a stone floor at the crossroads of half a dozen corridors, the taut tentacle preventing him from falling. Then the rest of Ghaunadaur's sluglike body slid through the portal. The avatar landed on Naxil, flattening him under a rippling wave of slimy flesh.

Despite the crushing weight that drove the air from his lungs, Naxil felt an immense sense of pride. He'd done it: lured Ghaunadaur's avatar away from the Promenade.

Masked Lady, he silently sang. *I commend my soul to you. My dance is done.*

He died with his mask pressed against his face, hiding his smile, as the avatar slithered off into the endless maze.

Q'arlynd glanced around. He'd teleported to the place Flinderspeld had described: a wide ledge, high on the side of a mountain. Glancing down at the forest spread out below like a distant green carpet, he could see why this place was so little known. A faint trail led up the lower slopes of the mountain. Q'arlynd spotted two figures walking along it, far below. The trail, however, stopped well below the bluff. From that point, it would take a riding lizard or a levitation spell to reach this spot.

A breeze blew mist onto his skin, and he shivered. The sky was overcast, heavy with dark gray clouds. Thunder grumbled in the distance. He turned away from the view to observe the outermost of the "fountains." Just as Flinderspeld had described, a stream of water flowed *up* the mountainside, arcing over the lip of the bluff to land, splashing, in the pool.

From there, the water arced up and out of the pool, into a fissure in the bluff. From within the **V**-shaped cleft, Q'arlynd could hear the patter of the stream of water falling on the second pool. From there, Flinderspeld had said, the stream arced to the third pool, and then to the fourth and final of the Fountains of Memory: the one that looked deepest into the past.

Flinderspeld had originally wanted to accompany Q'arlynd here, but later decided against it. The temptation to use the pools himself, he'd explained, would be too strong. "Even the good memories will hurt," Flinderspeld had said.

Q'arlynd understood. Like Flinderspeld, he came from a city that now lay in ruin. Looking back in time to a Ched Nasad that was whole, to a life irretrievably gone would be . . . painful.

Yet for different reasons. Unlike Flinderspeld, Q'arlynd had no desire to return to the city of his childhood, even in reminiscence. Q'arlynd hadn't loved Ched Nasad; he'd loathed it. His memories of House Melarn's haughty, scheming matron mother—the female who'd birthed him—were brutal. Her capricious cruelty and callous disregard for her children had set the tone for Q'arlynd's siblings, a backstabbing brood of self-serving malcontents.

Within the *kiira,* Q'arlynd's ancestors stirred. *Was there no one in your family that you cared for?*

Q'arlynd laughed. "Tellik," he answered. And it was true. Q'arlynd had been close to his younger brother, for a time. As close as any two drow could be. Yet Q'arlynd had cast Tellik aside as quickly as a worn *piwafwi,* in order to avoid being killed alongside him after Matron Melarn learned that Tellik had taken up Vhaeraun's mask.

What about the others? his ancestors asked. *Was there no one who showed mercy, when you needed it?*

Q'arlynd started to answer no, then realized that wasn't quite right. "Halisstra," he answered at last. He touched the bump on his nose, remembering the time she'd secretly healed him. If not for that, he would have been dead decades ago.

Despite that act of kindness, Q'arlynd had continued to regard his sister as little more than a means of achieving his own goals. Only in recent years had he learned that people were more than mere playing pieces to be shoved about by those who were stronger and more cunning. Now he wondered what had become of Halisstra.

Four years ago, Cavatina had reported to Qilué that Halisstra had been left behind in the Demonweb Pits, after helping the Darksong Knight to slay Selvetarm. Had Halisstra died there? The questions T'lar had asked seemed to indicate that she had. T'lar had said Halisstra "angered" the Lady Penitent—Lolth, obviously—and had been killed for it. Strangely, the assassin didn't seem to understand why Lolth might have done this. T'lar obviously didn't know Halisstra's role in helping to slay the Spider Queen's champion.

Now Q'arlynd found himself pondering exactly how Halisstra had died. Guilt nibbled at him. He'd done nothing to aid in the search for Halisstra, just left it up to Qilué and her priestesses. He glanced down at the bracer he still wore on his wrist—at the symbol of House Melarn on his House insignia. The dancing stick figure also stood for Eilistraee. Would Q'arlynd meet his sister once more, in Eilistraee's domain, when he finally died? Or would Eilistraee fault him for abandoning Halisstra, just as he'd abandoned Tellik?

He shook his head to clear these distracting thoughts. He had important business here: locating Corellon's ancient temple. This was no time to be brooding about the past. Yet he might never have another chance to visit the Fountains of Memory. He glanced again at the first pool. Certainly one little peek to satisfy his curiosity wouldn't hurt. It might even be good practice. It would also help lay to rest the niggling doubt that Flinderspeld might have tricked him, and sent him to the wrong spot, despite all that had passed between them.

Mistrust was a habit that was hard to shake.

Q'arlynd kneeled beside the pool, his knees sinking into the moss that cushioned the stone. He did as Flinderspeld had instructed, picking one of the tiny blue flowers that speckled the ground and tossing it into the pool. "Show me," he said, concentrating on the rippling waters. "Show me how Halisstra was killed by L—" He paused, reconsidering. With divinations, it was best to get the language precisely right. What was the title T'lar had used? Ah yes. "Show me how Halisstra was killed by the Lady Penitent."

Though he could still hear the fountain tinkling, the surface of the pool stilled and became as flat as glass. An image appeared on its mirrorlike surface: Halisstra, dressed in armor, kneeling with two other females before a throne on which sat a massive black widow spider. Seven identical spiders crouched behind the throne, watching. The room's crazily slanting walls and floor were constructed of iron. Cobwebs filled the gloomy corners.

"Lolth's iron fortress," Q'arlynd whispered, his voice tight.

He recognized the female to Halisstra's left at once: the pout-lipped, scheming Danifae, battle-captive to Halisstra. The female on the other side of Halisstra also looked familiar. At first, Q'arlynd couldn't place her. Then he remembered who she was: Quenthel Baenre, the high priestess from Menzoberranzan. The presence of Danifae and Quenthel in the vision could mean just one thing: the pool was showing Q'arlynd something that had happened seven years ago, during Lolth's Silence.

"That's too early," he said aloud. He reached for another flower, intending to try again, but his hand halted as he saw what happened next. In the vision, Lolth lunged from her throne to bite Danifae. The battle-captive screamed as her head and shoulders disappeared into Lolth's mouth. Danifae's legs spasmed, then stilled as the goddess consumed her.

For a brief moment, no one moved. Then the other seven spiders crept forward menacingly. Q'arlynd expected them to attack Quenthel or Halisstra, but instead they surrounded the spider that had eaten Danifae. They grasped it—and began to tear the body apart. Yochlols hurried into view and hastened the process, ripping chunks from the spider's quivering body. All the while, Halisstra and Quenthel remained kneeling. Halisstra, Q'arlynd saw, had her eyes tightly shut. Her lips moved. Q'arlynd wondered if she were whispering Eilistraee's name. His sister held a sword in her hand—a straight-bladed sword. It should have been the Crescent Blade, according to what Leliana had told him. Halisstra, she'd said, had taken the Crescent Blade into the Demonweb Pits to kill Lolth, during the Silence.

Was that indeed the Crescent Blade, disguised by a glamer? If so, why hadn't Halisstra used it, instead of kneeling meekly before Lolth's throne? Had she lost her nerve, once in the goddess's presence? That was easy to understand. Even viewing the Spider Queen at a distance—and removed in time—sent a hollow chill through Q'arlynd.

The spiders and yochlols finished their grim task and stepped back. Within the remains of the spider they'd torn to pieces, a form stirred. Then it rose, revealing itself to be a spider with Danifae's face.

Was *this* the Lady Penitent? Was it Lolth, reborn?

The Danifae-headed spider turned to Quenthel and spoke to her, but the patter of the fountain obscured the words. Quenthel's face twisted with fury, but she bowed her head. Then she stood, turned, and departed.

That left only Halisstra. She looked up at the Danifae-headed spider, said something, and tossed her sword to one side. She threw herself face-first on the floor. The Danifae-headed spider leaned over her, smiled, and sank her teeth into Halisstra's neck.

"No!" Q'arlynd cried, despite himself. He watched, fists balled, as the seven lesser spiders lurched forward and sank their fangs into his sister. When each had left a bloody puncture, the Danifae-headed spider lifted Halisstra's limp body and twirled it round, spinning her into a cocoon. Q'arlynd, looking on, told himself that this couldn't be Halisstra's death he was watching. His sister had lived beyond the events he was viewing. She'd led Cavatina into the Demonweb Pits, three years after these events. She'd *survived* this.

Q'arlynd wondered if he would have been strong enough to do the same.

The Danifae-headed spider dropped the cocoon to the floor. For several long moments, nothing happened. Then something poked at the cocoon from within, and tore it open. Q'arlynd leaned forward, cheering his sister on as she defiantly tore at the sticky silken threads. "That's it, Halisstra," he urged. "Tear free. You can—"

The words died in a croak as he saw what emerged from the tattered remnants of the cocoon. It wasn't Halisstra in there, but a demonlike monster. The creature was twice the size Halisstra had been, with a hideously deformed face, spider jaws emerging from bulges on its cheeks, and eight spindly spider legs protruding from its chest.

Q'arlynd reeled back from the pool in alarm as the creature turned in his direction. He caught only a momentary glance of its face, but it was enough. The demon-thing that had emerged from the cocoon was indeed Halisstra, transformed.

"No," he whispered. Yet there was no denying it. The creature he saw in the pool was the "monster" he'd seen emerging from the Moondeep Sea, during the expedition to the Acropolis of the death goddess. That had been only two years ago—*after* his sister had helped Cavatina kill Selvetarm. Had the Darksong Knight seen what Halisstra had become? Why hadn't she told Q'arlynd this?

He shook his head. T'lar had gotten it wrong. Halisstra hadn't been killed by the Lady Penitent. She'd been transformed into something . . . demonic.

"Eilistraee," he whispered in a choked voice. "How could you have let this happen to one of your faithful?"

He backed away, unwilling to see more. He felt rough stone against his back and realized he was inside the cleft in the rock. A spray of water arced past his shoulder, into the second of the Fountains of Memory. Mist from the spray struck his face, and trickled down his cheeks like tears.

He wiped them away. His sister was lost, beyond redemption. There was nothing he could do for her now. He needed to focus on the future, not the past.

He turned away from the terrible vision, and entered the cleft in the rock.

T'lar swung gracefully up onto the ledge. She was exhausted from her long climb. Her arms and legs shook, but she didn't let that blunt her caution. She lifted the dark-lensed glasses that protected her eyes from the World Above's harsh light, and looked cautiously around. Half a cycle had passed since she'd spotted her target on this ledge—the sun had set, and the moon had risen since then—but Q'arlynd might still be here. She couldn't rely on invisibility alone to hide her. Not from a wizard.

Taking care not to give her presence away by knocking a loose stone, she moved to one side of the cleft in the bluff. She slid her spider-pommeled dagger out of its sheath. She wouldn't make the mistake of using the spike-spiders on Q'arlynd, this time; he was obviously immune to their poison. The same couldn't be said, however, of the svirfneblin wine merchant she'd left dead on the trail below.

She hummed the *bae'qeshel* tune that would ensure her invisibility was sustained, and eased into the cleft in the rock. Moments later, she cursed as she realized her target was no longer there. She'd been so close to catching him! Had he teleported away while she was climbing the bluff?

Thunder grumbled overhead. Rain pattered down. The drops blended with the sweat on T'lar's forehead and shaved scalp, and trickled down her body. She tasted salt on her lips. She squatted beside the innermost of the pools within the cleft. The stream that fed it was obviously magical; water didn't flow up a cliff and arc from one pool to the next of its own accord. She eyed it thirstily. Was the water's magic harmful or beneficial—or simply decorative? Would drinking from the pool kill her, or simply quench her thirst?

The innermost pool was about three paces wide and no more than a couple of handspans deep. She could easily make out the bottom of it. There didn't seem to be any fissures or gaps in the stone floor, yet the water flowed into the pool, but didn't go anywhere. It simply . . . disappeared.

Just a moment. Was that a flash of something, between the pattering raindrops? As she leaned closer, a palm-sized portion of the pool stilled. It was like looking through a tiny window: she caught a glimpse of a tree branch, then a mosaic made of oddly shaped pieces of green glass, then the back of a head with white hair and pointed ears. As the figure turned, T'lar recognized his face. Q'arlynd.

She smiled. So *that* was what this place was: a portal.

She curled her fingers into a spider and kissed them. "Lolth be praised," she said. The hunt hadn't ended; it had just changed direction.

She stepped into the pool and was teleported away.

CHAPTER 12

Laeral stared into her scrying mirror, her hands on either side of the gilded frame. "Where is Cavatina?" she asked anxiously. "Show me!"

She could see the Darksong Knight, but only dimly. Cavatina's body wavered within the mirror, indistinct and ghostly. Her hair was wild, her expression anguished. She wore armor, but carried no weapon, while the tunic beneath her chain mail was stained and torn. Blood from a scalp wound had dried on her forehead. She moved, apparently aimlessly, through an utterly featureless, solid-gray landscape.

Laeral's hands tightened on the frame. Was Cavatina dead? A spirit wandering the Fugue Plain? If so, why hadn't her goddess claimed her?

The landscape behind Cavatina suddenly shifted, as if she'd just stepped out of shadow into light. She walked along a street now, her legs embedded in solid stone from the knee down. The corner of a building loomed ahead of her. She passed through it and continued on. All around her, the indistinct blurs of people hurried through the street, as none noticed her. A wall-mounted brazier, filled with glowing worms, threw shadows but cast no light on Cavatina. Its light passed, unimpeded, through the Darksong Knight.

"She's ethereal," Laeral breathed. "But . . . Where?"

Cavatina startled, and looked wildly around. She glanced up at something that was outside the mirror's field of view. She "walked" upward, her body now parallel with the street below, to a metal cage that hung by a chain from a stout beam that spanned the street. A minotaur was inside the cage, gripping the iron bars. His face twisted with rage, and he repeatedly butted the inside of the cage with his massive horns.

Laeral recognized the landmark at once. Cavatina was in Skullport!

A short time later, Laeral stood outside the Deepfires Inn, wearing the disguise she habitually assumed while visiting Skullport: a plain, hooded cloak interwoven with protective dweomers and keep-watch magic. She'd teleported to Waterdeep, passed through the portal linking her former home with a cavern near Skullport, and hurried as quickly as she could through the Underdark city's streets.

She worried that she wouldn't make it in time—that Cavatina would already be gone. As she approached the Deepfires Inn, she pulled a pinch of grave dust from a pocket, tossed it ahead of her, and spoke a divination. It revealed a man in shabby clothes, lurking outside the inn's door. He started as he noticed Laeral looking at him, then slunk away through the foul-smelling muck that mired the street. Laeral swept her hand up, directing her spell at the minotaur's cage—and sighed in relief as Cavatina became visible. The Darksong Knight "stood" in mid-air beside the cage, peering into it intently and shouting at the minotaur, who shouted back at her. The words they hurled at each other were inaudible, as the spell revealed things to the eyes only.

Passersby craned their heads to look up at the spectacle. One nudged another with an elbow. Laeral picked out the words "Eilistraee" and "priestess" in his whispered comment. Ignoring them, Laeral spoke an incantation and made a twisting gesture. Cavatina's body visibly solidified, and her shouts became audible as she was wrenched, fully, into the material world. As she tumbled, . Laeral snapped out a word and pointed. Cavatina jerked to a halt a pace above the ground, and slowly drifted downward.

She landed, and began writhing violently. Her fists pounded the paving stones, and her body twisted this way and that, as if she were dodging blows from an unseen opponent. "The symbol of slime!" she shouted. "Sacrifice the dance to make the eye stop! It's looking at you! We can't allow it to come or it's lost the . . ."

Laeral started. Cavatina was raving like a madwoman.

Behind her, she heard a chuckle and a derisive comment. ". . . what they deserved. We won't have to worry about the Promenade no more. It's—"

She whirled and glared at the speaker: a drow who, judging by the heavy manacles he carried in one hand, was a slaver. "What did you just say? What's happened to the Promenade?"

The drow laughed. "Ask your friend." He mocked her with a bow and strode away.

Laeral was tempted to send a bolt from her wand sizzling through him, but there were more urgent matters to deal with. She rushed to Cavatina's side and tried to help the Darksong Knight to her feet, but Cavatina screamed and jerked away. Laeral pulled a pouch from her pocket, tipped out the preserved snake's tongue it held, and clenched it in her fist. She touched her hand to her lips. "I can help you," she told the Darksong Knight in a soothing voice. "Please follow me."

Calmed by magic, Cavatina followed Laeral through Skullport's garbage-strewn streets. She mumbled as she walked. The odd word was intelligible—"slime" and "gate" and "battle"—but Laeral could make no sense of what Cavatina was muttering. It was clear, however, that some calamity had overtaken the Promenade. When Cavatina suddenly shouted the name "Ghaunadaur!" Laeral knew what had happened: another attack by the Ancient One's fanatics. Of all the times Qilué might have chosen to draw Wendonai's taint into herself, this must surely be the worst.

Yet another indication that the time *hadn't* been of Qilué's choosing.

Laeral's destination was just ahead: the Sisters Three Waxworks. Kaitlyn and her sisters were friends of Laeral's, devotees of Chauntea who posed as simple candle makers. They kept a stock of healing potions on hand, and were adept at restorative spells. Whatever madness afflicted Cavatina, they'd be able to cure it. Laeral opened the door of the shop and coaxed the Darksong Knight inside. "Enter," she said, touching the fist that held the snake tongue to her lips as she spoke. "You'll find peace, here."

Cavatina stumbled into the candlelit shop. Laeral closed the door on the gaggle of Skullport residents who'd tagged along after them, mocking the Darksong Knight by imitating her frenzied, uncoordinated motions. "Kaitlyn," Laeral said to the woman behind the counter as she bolted the door shut. "My friend needs your help. She—"

Cavatina screamed and flattened herself against a wall, knocking over a display of scented candles. An instant later, her terror switched to rage. She hurled herself at a candle that guttered on the counter. "The ooze!" she screamed. Her fists pounded into the soft purple candle, splattering molten wax across the counter. "We have to stop the temple before the glow fills the river with the slime of the death and staunch the flow of blood!"

Kaitlyn had been arranging a display of candles on a shelf when Laeral and Cavatina entered. The brown-haired woman's mouth dropped open in surprise as Cavatina attacked her merchandise, but she sprang quickly into action. She whirled to grab a corked vial from a shelf behind her. "Hold spell!" she shouted. "While her mouth is open, if possible."

Laeral barked an enchantment that rendered Cavatina rigid, her mouth gaping in mid-shout. When the Darksong Knight toppled, Laeral caught her and eased her statue-stiff body to the ground. Kaitlyn uncorked the vial and poured the potion into Cavatina's mouth. "Quickly now," she said. "Dispel the hold, or she'll choke."

Laeral did. She took a quick pace back as Cavatina's body slackened, but the expected outburst didn't come. Instead of raving and flailing, Cavatina held her head in her hands. "I failed," she said in an anguished voice. "The Promenade is lost."

Laeral kneeled beside Cavatina and placed a hand on her shoulder. "What's happened? Tell me."

As Cavatina spoke, Laeral's heart sank. The Promenade, fallen to Ghaunadaur's fanatics? His avatar, released from the Pit? "Oh, Qilué," she said softly. "It's worse even than you thought, sister."

Cavatina wrenched around to stare at Laeral. "Where is she? Where's Qilué?"

"In trouble," Laeral said. "She needs your help." As concisely as she could, she told the Darksong Knight what Qilué had done to herself. Cavatina's face paled at the news, but as she continued listening, she climbed to her feet and took a deep breath.

"We're going to need Qilué to rally the priestesses and retake the Promenade," Cavatina said, her voice firmer now. She reached for her scabbard, realized it was empty, and looked around the shop. "Where am I? Is there a sword to be had?"

Laeral glanced at Kaitlyn. The shopkeeper started to shake her head, then shrugged. "There's my sword of mercy. Hardly a suitable weapon for slaying a demon. It's ensorcelled so that it will not kill."

Cavatina held out a hand. "I'll take it."

Laeral nodded to herself. With Qilué's body housing the demon, they needed something that could subdue, rather than kill. She pulled a gem from her belt pouch. "This should pay for the sword," she told Kaitlyn. She pressed the gem into the shopkeeper's hands.

Kaitlyn glanced down at it. "Too much," she said. Then she smiled. "But I'll keep it on deposit. Return the sword to me when you're done."

She pulled the weapon from behind the counter. To Laeral's surprise, the sword was made of wood. Judging by the way Cavatina hefted it, however, the weapon seemed to have the weight of a normal sword. Its magic shaped it exactly to the Darksong Knight's scabbard as she sheathed it.

Laeral caught Kaitlyn's eye. "Not a word of what you just heard. To anyone."

Kaitlyn touched one of the clumps of fragrant herbs that hung from the rafters. "I swear it, by the Mother."

Laeral glanced outside, through a slit in the window shutter. The crowd that had followed them to the shop lingered, talking with animated gestures. "We'll use the other exit, if you don't mind, Kaitlyn."

The shopkeeper moved aside the curtain that separated the front and rear of her shop. "This way."

She led them down a hidden staircase, through a short tunnel, and up a ladder that led to the back room of a nearby shop. Laeral and Cavatina exited, and hurried through the streets to the portal that would return them to Waterdeep. On the way, they conferred in hushed voices about what was to be done.

The first thing to do, they agreed, would be to force Wendonai back into the Crescent Blade. That would require an exorcism. "It will have to be a powerful one," Cavatina said. "We'll need as many priestesses as we can gather. We'll remove Qilué to hallowed ground—to the Dancing Dell in the Ardeep Forest. We'll channel the power of the Ladystone."

Laeral nodded. "But what of the binding? How can we remove Qilué from the throne?"

"Describe again what you saw in the vision."

Laeral did.

Cavatina shook her head. "I don't think Wendonai *was* bound. If he had been, he wouldn't have been able to break the octogram with his hoof."

"Then why did the demon submit?"

"Because Lolth ordered him to. She hoped he'd seed my ancestors with his taint. The coronal didn't summon him. Lolth *sent* him."

"But that would mean . . ." Laeral felt the blood drain from her cheeks.

Cavatina completed her thought. "That it wasn't a binding rooting Qilué to the throne, but something else: Lolth's invisible webs." She shuddered, and glanced at Laeral. "Which goddess do you honor?"

"Mystra."

"Pray to her," Cavatina said grimly. "Pray that it isn't too late—that Lolth hasn't already claimed Qilué."

Q'arlynd paced across the cavern where the teleportation circle was being drawn, fighting off the urge to clench his fists in frustration. "Qilué," he whispered. "Can you hear me? It's nearly time for the casting!"

Behind him, mages from the school of divination streamed into the cavern, carrying boxes filled with the enchanted items necessary to fuel the spells. The items were all from the vaults of Seldszar's College, as attempting to persuade the highly suspicious Urlryn and Masoj to contribute would have strained their already fragile alliance to the breaking point.

Eldrinn supervised the placement of these valuables, while Alexa scribed the teleportation circle that would convey Q'arlynd and the other three masters to the ancient temple. She'd been forced to draw it well away from the city, in this damp cavern, in order to be clear of the *Faerzress*. The cool, bare walls with their trickles of water would have been soothing, in other circumstances.

"Qilué!" Q'arlynd hissed again. "It's time! Where *are* you?"

"Is something wrong?" a voice behind him asked.

Q'arlynd spun. Seldszar sat cross-legged on a driftdisc, dark lenses shielding his eyes in preparation for his imminent journey to the World Above. Lying to him would serve no purpose. For all Q'arlynd knew, the Master of Divination was already reading his thoughts. "I can't reach Lady Qilué," Q'arlynd admitted. "She promised she'd participate—that she would come the instant she received my summons. But—"

"Does she realize the importance of what we're about to do?"

"Yes. Of course. It will be of enormous benefit to her faith. If the *Faerzress* no longer draws the drow below, her followers will have an easier time convincing them to come to the surface."

Out of the darkness, and into the moonlight.

Q'arlynd startled. Had he just said that aloud? He cleared his throat. "Could we put the casting off for a little while? Until we've located her?"

Seldszar shook his head. "Too much is at stake. By now, spies from the other Colleges will have noticed the shifting of so many magical items. They're bound to either make a grab for them or attack our Colleges while we're away. To delay would give them time to marshal their forces—and it might cost us the other masters' support." His head shifted slightly as he scrutinized one of the crystals orbiting his head. "Speaking of which, Masters Masoj and Urlryn will be here momentarily."

"I see. This cycle, then."

"Immediately—if not sooner." Seldszar glanced briefly at Q'arlynd. "Where is Lady Qilué mostly likely to be?"

"In the Promenade."

"Describe it. And describe her."

"If she's in the temple, you won't be able to scry her," Q'arlynd told him. "The Promenade is warded against . . ." His voice trailed off as he saw the look Seldszar was giving him over the top of those dark lenses.

He did as Seldszar asked. When he'd finished, Seldszar chanted a divination, and sat in silence for several moments. His lips parted, as if in surprise. Then a muscle in his jaw clenched.

"Were you able to see the Promenade?"

"I was. There were no priestesses there. Every cavern I scried was awash in oozes."

Q'arlynd felt a profound sorrow. To his surprise, hearing at arm's length that the Promenade had been lost struck even deeper than watching, first-hand, the violent demise of Ched Nasad, the city of his birth. "But surely it . . . Qilué . . ."

"Is neither within her temple, nor anywhere else I can divine. She's gone."

The certainty with which Seldszar said this worried Q'arlynd. He grasped at threads. "There's another shrine, in the Misty Forest. I know the priestess who presides there. I saved her life, once. Lady Rowaan may know what's become of Qilué. Even if she doesn't, she may be able to provide someone of equal stature."

"Go then. Don't waste time."

Q'arlynd bowed. He concentrated on the burl trees that housed the priestesses, spoke a word, and teleported. An instant later, he stood in a forest beside a massive tree. A thought sent him levitating to the nearest burl. As he rose, he saw its door was slightly open. Suddenly wary, he cast a protective spell. A flick of his fingers eased the door open from afar. He peered in and saw there was no one inside. The room within the hollowed-out burl looked as though it had recently been occupied, though: clothes hung from pegs, and the remains of a meal stood on the table, next to a half-full goblet. Wind blew through the branches above, making them creak and groan.

"Lady Rowaan?" he called. "Is *anyone* here?" He drifted upward, and knocked on the next door. It didn't open. He tried again at another door: again, no response. He descended and stood in thought a moment, before hurrying through the forest to the shrine itself.

The dozen sword-shaped columns of black obsidian were just as he remembered them. There was no blood on the circular platform of white stone, nor any other sign of struggle. Q'arlynd, however, couldn't shake the feeling that something was terribly wrong. He touched one of the sword-columns. The polished stone felt cool under his fingertips. Shouldn't there have been a priestess here, guarding the shrine?

He felt the *kiira* tickling his memories. *You took your sword oath here.*

"Yes." Q'arlynd didn't have time for reminiscences. He hurried on through the forest, hoping to hear the sound of singing above the sighing branches. It was night, and the moon was up. Perhaps the priestesses were dancing in the glade.

They weren't.

The mist that had given the forest its name swirled around his ankles like flowing water, reminding him there was one place yet to look. The sacred pool, he thought. There was always someone standing guard there. That priestess would know where Rowaan and the others had gone.

As he headed to the pool, the wind shifted. It carried a new smell to his nostrils: a stench like sour vomit. Cautiously, he approached the sacred pool. His eyes widened as he saw the tangle of toppled and rotting trees that surrounded it. The mist above the pool was a sickly greenish yellow. A bubble rose from the depths of the pool and ruptured, splattering the bushes next to Q'arlynd. Leaves sizzled, turned black, and dribbled away.

"By all that's unholy," he swore. He suddenly remembered that each of the sacred pools was connected, via portals, with the Promenade's Moonspring Portal. Had *all* of Eilistraee's shrines fallen?

A gurgling sound warned that the pool was about to erupt again. Q'arlynd backed hurriedly away.

What now, he agonized.

Are you the last?

"The last what?"

The last of Eilistraee's faithful.

"Impossible!" he told the *kiira*. "The priestesses must be around . . . somewhere." The emptiness of the forest, however, cried otherwise. Had Rowaan and her priestesses rushed to defend the Promenade, only to be consumed by oozes? For all he knew, the faithful at each of the shrines could have suffered the same fate: all plunging blindly into their sacred pools in an attempt to reach the Promenade, only to be consumed by the oozes that fouled them.

It must be you, then. You will be the one to call down the miracle.

"Me?" Q'arlynd laughed aloud. "I'm a wizard, not a cleric."

You belong to Eilistraee.

Q'arlynd didn't like the sound of that. It sounded too much like slavery.

We will guide you through the ritual.

"Why not take over my body and evoke the miracle yourselves?"

The prayer must be directed by the will of a living worshiper—a conduit to the goddess.

Q'arlynd nervously stroked his chin. He didn't want to think of what might follow, were he to let the other masters down. "What if I can't do it? What if it doesn't work?"

If your heart is filled with light and your cause is true, we shall not fail.

Q'arlynd frowned slightly. Those words sounded familiar—like the text of some half-forgotten spell. He glanced down at the dancing-figure glyph on his House insignia. *Was* he Eilistraee's? He'd spoken her sword oath for convenience's sake, but much had happened since then. He'd changed.

He glanced around the empty forest, wishing a priestess would materialize. Any priestess.

He started as a voice spoke to him. Seldszar's voice, clear and distinct, as if the Master of Divination were standing by his side. "The others are here. We're ready to teleport. Have you found a replacement?"

Q'arlynd squared his shoulders. "I have."

"Are you certain she's inside?" Laeral breathed.

Cavatina tensed She wished Qilué had taught her human "sister" the art of silent speech. "I'm not certain of anything," she whispered back. "But the trail of corruption led this way."

Laeral would have to take Cavatina's word for it. Skilled in woodland lore the mage might be, but she lacked the training to detect the subtle signs of a demon's passage: a wilted leaf, a strand of web twisting in the rot-scented breeze, the scuff of a claw on bark. Cavatina had followed the trail through the jungle to this spot. Just ahead, through a thick screen of trees and vines, she could see a blur of white—the tangle of spiderwebs that draped a hill in the jungle. It reminded Cavatina of a trap spider's lair. From somewhere within came a sound like a harp. The notes were jumbled and shrill, and the tempo kept changing, as if the player were uncertain of the melody, rushing through some parts and struggling with others.

"Keep watch," Cavatina whispered. "While I pray."

Laeral cast a spell, and Cavatina felt a protective screen of magical energy crackle to life around them. She touched the holy symbol at her throat and hummed. "Eilistraee," she implored in a voice no louder than a breath, "hear my prayer. Guide my footsteps through the dance that is to come, and answer my song. Is Lady Qilué within the ruin ahead?"

A voice, sweet enough to bring tears to Cavatina's eyes, sang into her mind. *Yes.*

"How can we get her out of there?"

Cavatina felt her goddess's hesitation. *You can't.*

Despair filled her. She heard Laeral's breath catch. The other female must have read the disappointment on her face.

"Is there no one who can save her?" Cavatina implored. "Not even you, Dark Maiden?"

A host of possible outcomes blurred through Cavatina's mind. She had a sense of pieces moving across a *sava* board too rapidly to follow, as some unseen force tested first this move, then that. At last they stilled. Eilistraee's reply came, in a voice tinged with a profound sorrow. *If Ao so wills, it shall be.*

Cavatina startled. What did Ao the Overgod have to do with this? As she pondered what Eilistraee's answer might mean, she felt the goddess slip from her mind, silent as a shadow.

Cavatina glanced up at the moon. Selûne wore her half-mask this night, and seemed to be staring down at Cavatina. Waiting. Her cold scrutiny tempered Cavatina's determination. "Go," she whispered to Laeral, "swiftly, to each of Eilistraee's shrines. Gather as many of the priestesses as you can. We must perform the exorcism here."

Laeral glanced around the gloomy forest. The air was thick with the stench of rot and mold, and in the distance, the night twist tree wailed its anguished refrain. "But isn't this the worst possible—"

"This is where it must be done," Cavatina said grimly. "Eilistraee has decreed it."

Laeral stood. "What will you do while I'm gone?"

Cavatina nodded at the web-shrouded mound. "I'm going inside."

"Shouldn't you wait until—"

"There may not be time," Cavatina said firmly. "Besides, I hunt better alone."

Laeral nodded. "Keep me alerted to everything you see. Speak my name, and I'll hear what follows."

Cavatina agreed.

Laeral spoke an incantation that whisked her away.

Cavatina rose to her feet. Her first impulse was to stride in boldly and challenge whatever foes might be within, but then she glanced at the wooden sword in her hand and nearly laughed. No, she decided, sheathing it. She'd take a page from the Masked Lady's new songbook, instead. Slip in quietly, and scout around. If need be, she would sing moonfire into existence, and burn the place clean.

She sang a protective hymn, then a glamer that would screen her from sight until she chose to strike a blow. Her third prayer would allow her to slip through the tangle of webs unimpeded. She crept closer to the mound and eased her way into the tangle of web. The sticky silk slid past her body as if her skin were oiled. Just ahead was a haphazardly spun cocoon. Looking around, Cavatina saw dozens more, each of them easily large enough to contain a drow. Several bulged and rocked, as whatever was trapped within struggled to get free.

"By all that dances," Cavatina breathed. "This looks like Halisstra's handiwork!"

Was Halisstra still alive? After betraying Cavatina to the demon Wendonai, she had reappeared briefly atop the Acropolis, then vanished without a trace. That had been two years ago. No one had been able to learn where she had disappeared to—not even Qilué.

A sound within the cocoon next to Cavatina drew her attention. Over the discordant music coming from within the mound, she made out a muffled female voice: a word or two of song, then a struggling gasp, then another faint note of song. She was debating whether to tear the cocoon open when another of the cocoons turned slightly, revealing a partially rotten hand protruding through a gap in its side. A spider-shaped ring adorned one of the death-stiffened fingers: Lolth's symbol.

Cavatina sang a divination. A dim purple glow leaked out of the cocoons that were still twitching: the aura of evil. Cavatina's eyes narrowed. Did each contain one of Lolth's faithful? Had Halisstra turned against the Spider Queen?

The answers, Cavatina was certain, would lie within the mound.

She spoke Laeral's name, and whispered what she'd just seen. As she did, she stared at the cocoons, debating what to do. Four years ago, she would have reveled in slaying an evil deity's helpless faithful, but now she found the thought repugnant. She said a prayer for those inside, praying they might survive long enough to be cut down and freed by the priestesses Laeral would soon bring. "May you find redemption," she whispered, her fingers touching the cocoon in front of her.

She crept on through the tangle of webs, closer to the hill they covered. A tree near the base of the hill had fallen, its roots tearing a hole in the earth, and inside this gap lay an adamantine door. More webs dangled, like a curtain, in the empty doorframe. She slipped into a chamber with a depression in its black marble floor and blasphemous murals showing masked spiders. Drying blood was splattered everywhere. The metallic smell of it overwhelmed the stench of the cocooned corpses outside. The far wall held a mural of a spider with a drow head and a lesser spider dangling from each arm; the abdomen was a dark hole in the masonry. The harp music came from inside it.

Beyond the hole was a second, stone-walled chamber. Cavatina spoke Laeral's name again and described what she saw. Nine corridors radiated from the second chamber. The harp music came from the one in the middle of the rear wall. More murals adorned the walls of this chamber, but they were obscured by webs and ruptured egg sacs. Movements on the floor caught her eye. Thousands of tiny red spiders, none of them bigger than a drop of blood, coursed back and forth, scurrying first in one direction, then another. They seemed to be moving in time with the music—scurrying, then stopping, then moving in another direction again as its tempo and melody changed.

Cavatina smiled grimly. She liked a challenge. She sprang through the hole and ran through the chamber, leaping gracefully from one clear patch of floor to the next in an improvised dance. The spiders thinned once she was inside the corridor, allowing her to slow her pace. After a short distance, the corridor opened onto a third chamber. Cavatina, still invisible, peered inside, battling the urge to pinch her nostrils shut against the sulfurous smell within: the stench of demon.

The room was larger than the first two, and circular. It was dominated by an enormous, black marble throne, carved in the shape of an upside-down spider. Halisstra sat atop it, her clawed fingers plucking hair-thin strands of steel that stretched, like harp strings, between the throne's curled spider arms. The harsh twang of the music trembled through Cavatina's body, leaving a sludge of fear in its wake. Instinctively, she reached for her singing sword to ward off the music's effect. Her hand closed around a wooden hilt, reminding her that the singing sword was gone.

Halisstra had her back to Cavatina. She stared intently at something on the far side of the throne. Cavatina cautiously circled the room, keeping near the wall. A crouching figure came into view. Half the size of the hulking Halisstra, the creature had dull white eyes and skin covered in boils. So misshapen was it that its gender was impossible to determine. At first, Cavatina's mind insisted that this *couldn't* be Qilué, that it was some blasphemous blend of drow and demon. But the "demon" held the Crescent Blade in its hands, and wore the amulet Laeral had described around its neck.

It *was* Qilué.

A lump rose in Cavatina's throat as she beheld what the high priestess had become. Cavatina had been raised within Eilistraee's faith. Her earliest memories were of her mother singing the high priestess's praises. Centuries ago, as a girl, Qilué had rekindled Eilistraee's faith from the ashes in which its spark had smoldered for millennia. She had conquered Ghaunadaur, established the Promenade over his Pit, and set up shrines across the length and breadth of Faerûn. But now the Promenade had fallen and Qilué had been reduced to. . . .

A tear trickled down Cavatina's cheek. She wiped it away. This wasn't the time for tears, but for action. It might not be her destiny to save Qilué, but she could take Halisstra down. Not permanently—unless Lolth had abandoned her, Halisstra wouldn't die—but at least long enough for Laeral and the others to whisk Qilué out of this foul chamber and attempt an exorcism. Cavatina would likely die in the battle she was about to undertake; her communion with Eilistraee had hinted of this. But that didn't matter. After the horrors she'd experienced during the fall of the Promenade, she was ready to dance at the goddess's side.

Halisstra seemed to have at last remembered whatever song she'd been attempting to play. Her clawed fingers settled into a rhythm, and the music became more melodic. Slowly, lest she make any noise, Cavatina drew the wooden sword. The fact that it didn't kill no longer mattered, since Halisstra couldn't die, anyway. It felt better to have a sword in her hand, even if it was only a wooden one. As the weapon cleared its sheath, Cavatina began the prayer that would send a bolt of twined moonlight and shadow through Halisstra's heart.

Halisstra ended her melody with a single, shrill note. The Crescent Blade suddenly shrank and transformed, becoming an assassin's strangle cord. Halisstra leaped down from her throne. As she reached for the transformed weapon, Cavatina unleashed her spell. Her moonbolt bored into Halisstra's broad back, sending her staggering.

Halisstra whirled, her face twisted with rage. Her eyes widened as she spotted the now-visible Cavatina. As Cavatina sang a second moonbolt into existence, Halisstra yanked the assassin's cord from Qilué's hands and flicked it upward. The weapon transformed back into a sword once more. She raised it above her head with a manic grin. "Yours," she said, her eyes wild, "will be the first soul reaped. Cast aside your feeble goddess, and pay homage to the Lady Penitent!"

Cavatina hurled her second moonbolt. It slammed into Halisstra's chest, sending her staggering. Cavatina leaped in close, thrusting with the wooden sword. Halisstra grunted as the point of it entered her body.

"Surrender," Cavatina told her, "and I'll show mercy."

"Never," Halisstra hissed. She leaped back, unwounded— the wooden sword penetrated flesh, but left no mark—and lashed out with the Crescent Blade. Cavatina instinctively parried—and suddenly was holding nothing but a wooden hilt. Furious, Cavatina dropped it and danced back, resolving to give her opponent no further chances. She sang a circle of blades into existence, and they whirred around her like a disturbed nest of steel-sharp bees. Qilué was directly in their path, but by the grace of Eilistraee she remained unharmed; the magical blades glanced harmlessly off her time-frozen body.

Halisstra seized upon Cavatina's momentary distraction and sang a harsh note. The magical blades that had been protecting Cavatina exploded into shards of light and vanished.

"Redemption is at hand!" Halisstra shrieked, the strings of her throne reverberating in time with her cry. Spittle flew from her lips, and the spider legs twitched madly against her chest. She menaced Cavatina with the Crescent Blade, springing—fast as a spider—to block the chamber's only exit. "Kneel before me, mortal!"

The words slammed into Cavatina's mind, forcing her to the ground.

Halisstra sprang back to her throne and raked its strings with her clawed fingers. Random notes jangled together. "Dance!" she screamed.

Cavatina shuffled forward on her knees across the flagstone floor. She tried to lift her hands to direct a prayer, but they rose above her head, twisting in a terrible parody of the sword dance. "Laeral," she cried. "Halisstra has—"

"Be silent!" Halisstra screeched.

Cavatina's throat tightened, preventing her from completing her warning. Where *was* Laeral? What was keeping her? She glanced at the room's only entrance, but it was empty. It was, however, faintly lighter, as if moonlight were filtering in from outside the mound. The spiders that had been in the outer chamber burst into this room in a wave, as if fleeing something. Cavatina heard a faint sound that might have been a song, drifting in their wake. The sound gave her hope.

Halisstra loomed over Cavatina, weaving the Crescent Blade back and forth, mockingly directing her "dance." The strings of her throne reverberated in a dismal, unending chord. Cavatina fought with all her will as she scraped across the floor on her knees, but to no avail. Halisstra had grown strong—more powerful than Cavatina had anticipated. Had Halisstra truly been elevated to the status of demigod, as she claimed?

"Who's the master now?" Halisstra asked mockingly. "I was your plaything once, but no more! Lolth's cast you aside. You're mine!"

Cavatina realized Halisstra wasn't talking to her, but to the Crescent Blade. Halisstra stood, caressing it, oblivious to the dribble of blood the blade had just opened in her palm. "You will serve me," she told it. She fingered the spot where the blade had been mended. "Or I will break you. Toss you away, like a piece of trash. Would you like to see how that feels?" She tilted her head, as if listening, then laughed. "Why should I believe you?"

She listened again, stared thoughtfully at the Crescent Blade, and smiled. "Yes. I can kill you, can't I? I can kill *anyone!*"

She strode over to Qilué, and touched the blade to her throat. The high priestess remained as still as stone. Cavatina, mute and shuffling on bloody knees, felt a rush of fear. Laeral had said that nothing could harm Qilué while she was frozen in time, but that was before Halisstra had found a way to tease the Crescent Blade from her hands. She watched, horrified, as Halisstra slowly drew the blade across Qilué's throat.

Eilistraee! she silently cried. *Your high priestess needs you! Save her!*

The chamber brightened slightly. Eilistraee, answering with moonlight?

Halisstra abruptly stopped cutting. She pulled the sword away and inspected Qilué's neck. The blade had left a hair-thin line of red, but no blood flowed from it.

Praise Eilistraee! Laeral's spell *had* saved Qilué! Cavatina wept with relief—but then the Crescent Blade began to glow with a ruddy light. An instant later, it burst into flame. Halisstra cocked her head again, laughed, and touched the sword's edge once more to Qilué's throat. The fire licked across the curved blade, and slid from it onto Qilué's neck, encircling it in flickering orange light. Then it disappeared into the cut on her neck.

Qilué's eyelids fluttered. Her head twitched. A creaking sound filled the air as wings burst from her shoulders and unfurled, and she rose. Her mouth opened, and a gurgling laugh came out. Low, deep, masculine.

Wendonai's voice. He was inside Qilué's body—dominating it!

The chamber seemed to spin around Cavatina. She felt ill, faint. *Not this, Eilistraee,* she prayed. *Anything but this!*

Wendonai held out a hand. Halisstra reached for it.

"No!" Cavatina shouted.

She didn't cry out alone. At the same moment that she spoke, moonlight filled the chamber. A voice sang out with a power that sent Halisstra reeling. Throne strings parted with a shrill *twang*. Spiders shriveled and died. The Crescent Blade vibrated in Halisstra's hand—so violently that she nearly dropped it.

A shaft of pure silver light coalesced at the center of the room: moonlight so intense Cavatina was forced to turn her head. It centered on Wendonai. Taint boiled from his body and fled across the floor in a wave of tarry black smoke, and the reek of brimstone filled the air. Much of the floor-hugging, sticky cloud was burned away by the silver moonlight, but a wisp of it lapped at Cavatina's bloody knees. She could feel it trying to force its way into her body through these wounds, but the strength of her faith forced it out. Then the last of it was gone, fled back to the Abyss, back to Wendonai's corpse, to revive it, But that was a trivial matter, compared to the events unfolding in this chamber.

The silver moonlight continued to burn down. Demonic flesh melted away like wax, revealing a drow female so beautiful Cavatina could barely breathe. She had Qilué's face, but framed with moon-white hair, streaked with shadow, that draped her naked body like a robe. A masked-shaped shadow screened much of her face. The eyes that stared out of it brimmed with silver tears as she stared at Halisstra, who cowered before her.

Cavatina's heart pounded so fiercely in her chest she thought it would burst.

Eilistraee's avatar!

No—something more. Qilué had become a vessel, and the goddess had filled it. Eilistraee had saved the high priestess, as promised. She'd stepped into Qilué's body and assumed mortal form—something that hadn't happened since the Time of Troubles.

It will end where it began, a female voice sang.

It will begin where it ends, a male voice harmonized.

Cavatina was no longer bound by Halisstra's foul magic. She rose, weeping and exulting, and cried out in praise. "Masked Lady," she sang joyfully, lifting her arms. "Lead me in your da—"

She remembered Halisstra too late.

The Crescent Blade flashed.

Cavatina felt cold steel meet her throat and heard the dull crunch of her spine being severed. The world spun crazily as her head tumbled to the floor. Then all went gray.

Q'arlynd glanced around. All was in readiness. A domed wall of force had been erected atop the glade where the ancient temple had once stood, to keep intruders out. Spheres of silver light circled its perimeter, ready to intercept and negate any hostile spells. The possibility of an enemy locating this spot, however, was remote. Anyone attempting to spy on the four masters would see only what Seldszar's glamer showed them: an empty glade, surrounded by forest and washed by moonlight.

In fact, the clearing was heaped with boxes—a veritable matron's ransom in magical items, arranged in three piles. Master Masoj sat on a moss-softened stone next to one stack of boxes, his diamond-dusted skin glittering like twinkling stars in the moonlight. The corpulent Urlyrn stood beside another, sipping wine from his goblet. Master Seldszar, his head moving back and forth as he tracked the gems orbiting him, sat cross-legged on his driftdisc, above the third pile. Dark lenses screened his eyes from the moonlight.

Q'arlynd stood with his four remaining apprentices, their minds linked by their rings. They would be adding their energies during his prayer. Eldrinn—clad, as usual, in pale gray clothes that made his skin appear darker— was rooting around in Q'arlynd's memories, satisfying his curiosity about what had become of Piri. Q'arlynd, heeding his promise to Flinderspeld, gave the boy a mental nudge when he strayed too near the portion of his mind that held memories of the magical pools.

Baltak had transformed his hair into the tawny mane of a lion and grown falcon wings in imitation of a sphinx. He kneaded the air, flexing his claws, reveling in the magical power that crackled through the night, proud to be a part of it. Zarifar, as always, was daydreaming. He stared up through the dome of force at the stars, drawing imaginary patterns between them.

Alexa watched the spot where the teleportation circle had deposited them. She nodded to herself as a section of ground turned muddy—a sign that the cavern had flooded as planned, preventing anyone else from coming through.

Seldszar cleared his throat. "Time to begin. Masters, please raise your fields."

Q'arlynd thought he saw a flicker of movement, out beyond the dome of force. He peered in that direction, then decided it must be some creature of the World Above. Whatever it was, the dome of force would keep it at bay. And if it was a person out there, well. . . .

He touched his braid. The hair clip was still there, providing a solid, comforting presence.

He returned his attention to the masters as Seldszar, Urlryn, and Masoj began their transmutations. Each pulled out a preserved eyeball dusted with powdered diamond, pricked his finger, and allowed three drops of blood to fall. The orbs on their palms spun, and three multicolored globes of magical energy sparkled into existence. As these fields spread, a hissing rose from each box they touched. The boxes rattled slightly, as if jiggled by a mild earth tremor. Ghostlike images danced above them like heat mirages, as enchanted rods, rings, potion vials, robes, and amulets were consumed. Q'arlynd glanced at Seldszar, wondering if the Master of Divination was wincing behind those dark lenses.

Seldszar raised his hand. At his signal, each of the mages cast his spell. Seldszar crossed his hands against his chest, and flung them apart, shouting the abjuration that would shatter enchantments. The magical field around him exploded, streaks of energy shooting out into the night. Urlryn dropped to one knee with surprising grace for a male of his girth and slapped a hand to the ground, shouting a curse-negating spell. The globe of energy surrounding him coalesced into thousands of drops of light that fell to the ground like rain. Masoj cast the third and most powerful abjuration, his fingers twining like knots. The globe of magical energy twisted into a tight, dizzying tangle—then shredded as he tore his hands apart.

Now it was Q'arlynd's turn. He took a deep breath—and felt each of his apprentices inhale as he did. He'd been nervous until this moment, but the touch of their minds steadied him. So did the cool presence of the *kiira* on his forehead. He sent his mind deep into it, and sought out the ancestor who had honored Eilistraee.

Are you ready? she asked.

Q'arlynd nodded.

Sing with me.

Words shimmered in the air in front of him—words that only he could see. It was like reading a spellbook. As his eyes fell on each word, its sound was conveyed to his mind, together with the note it sustained in the melody. He heard himself singing, and was amazed at the beauty of his voice. He'd never heard it so rich, so vibrant. His apprentices, their minds linked to his, provided the harmony: Baltak a bold bass, Eldrinn a higher tenor, Zarifar a soft falsetto that twined delicately around Alexa's alto. Directed by his ancestor, Q'arlynd touched thumb to thumb, forefinger to forefinger, forming Eilistraee's sacred moon. As he sang the final verse of the hymn, he raised his hands above his head to frame the moon in order to draw a miracle down from . . .

He gasped as he realized the moon wasn't there. Had he miscalculated the time it would set? He shook his head, certain he hadn't. The moon had been there, just a moment ago. High overhead and "half-masked" as the Nightshadows liked to say. And now it was gone.

It can't be gone! his ancestor insisted.

Baltak, Eldrinn and Alexa mentally echoed her alarm. Zarifar, however, shook his head. *He's right; the pattern's changed.*

Ridiculous! Q'arlynd thought. There must be some other answer. Sweat trickled down his sides, under his robe. He felt Seldszar, Urlryn, and Masoj staring at him. Waiting for the miracle. Q'arlynd's hands trembled above his head. "Negate the forcedome!" he shouted. "It's blocking the moon. I need to see it!"

Urlryn barked out a transmutation and pointed. A thin green beam shot from his fingertip and struck the forcedome, disintegrating it. All three masters looked up, apparently unperturbed by a sight that would have turned cold the blood of any surface elf. The moon had indeed vanished. A dark hole, bereft even of stars, punctured the sky where it had been. Only Selûne's Tears remained.

Eilistraee! his ancestor wailed.

"I . . . can't continue," Q'arlynd stammered. "Not with the moon gone."

"What trickery is this?" Masoj said, his voice tight with suspicion. He wheeled on Seldszar and shook a bony finger. "I will expect payment, Master Seldszar. I performed my part of the bargain."

"You shall have it," Seldszar promised.

Masoj folded his arms, thrust his chin in the air, and teleported away.

Urlryn glared at Q'arlynd, his face darkening. "You were supposed to call down a miracle, not bore a hole in the ceiling!"

"That's . . ." Q'arlynd bit his tongue against the urge to tell the ignorant Urlryn that it was sky above them, not stone. He heard his apprentices' mental laughter. He shoved them out of his mind. "The disappearance of the moon wasn't my . . ." He faltered as he caught sight of the adamantine oval that adorned his wristband.

The glyph was gone from his House insignia. Vanished, just like the moon.

Seldszar drifted closer and stared at him over his dark lenses. "I was led to believe we would succeed," he said softly. From anyone else, it would have been a threat.

"Your visions predicted success?" Q'arlynd asked. He wet his lips. "Then why didn't—"

It will. But you must be willing to make the sacrifice.

"I don't understand," Q'arlynd protested aloud.

Trust in me, sang a female he hadn't heard before. The voice was soft, distant, and echoing. *Take the next step in the dance. Leap!*

Q'arlynd could see it now. The future. The end to everything he'd ever known. One tiny step would take him there—take them all there.

He squeezed his eyes shut in terror. He felt the same way he had the first time he'd dared a free-fall from Ched Nasad's streets. His heart pounded with a mixture of anticipation and dread. Memories flooded back and were absorbed by the lorestone on his forehead. The step off the edge. The plunge through space, wind tearing at his *piwafwi.* The wild laugh that had burst from his mouth. The sudden, dizzying jerk as his House insignia halted him just in time, preventing him from dashing his brains out on the cavern floor that had, a few heartbeats previously, been so far, far below.

So far . . .

"And yet so near," he whispered.

He squared his shoulders. Opened his eyes. "I'll do it." He lifted his hands and completed the prayer.

Beside him, Seldszar smiled. Within the *kiira,* so did his ancestors.

"Something's happening," Baltak bellowed a moment later. He pointed. "There!"

"And there! And there, and there!" Zarifar cried.

Q'arlynd lowered his hands and looked around. A faint green glow that crackled and wavered like *Faerzress* formed a circle around the spot where they stood. The circle of light broke apart an instant later into several sections, each of which collapsed into a circle itself, then to a point. A sapling sprouted from the center of each, uncurled, and opened glowing green leaves.

Q'arlynd heard Zarifar counting. ". . . nine, ten, eleven."

"The miracle?" Q'arlynd breathed.

The miracle, his ancestors confirmed.

Q'arlynd felt something warm and wet strike his head. Drops pattered against the ground, and the dry earth drank them in. The others started as the raindrops struck them. Q'arlynd smiled to himself. They'd probably never felt rain before. Then a drop trickled down Q'arlynd's face, to his lips. He tasted blood.

Startled, he wrenched his head back—and saw that the rain was falling only on this spot. Falling, as if being poured, from that terrible wound where the moon had been. He suddenly shivered, worried he'd sung the prayer incorrectly. Done something wrong. Was this the Dark Disaster, all over again? The legends said the sky had wept blood. . . .

He heard a *pop* of inrushing air—Urlryn, teleporting away. Of the three masters, only Seldszar remained. He stared at Q'arlynd through those dark lenses. "Let him go. This no longer concerns him."

Q'arlynd nodded. He watched, fascinated, as the saplings grew tall as the Darkfire Pillars. The trees bent inward, their branches twining together to form a dome overhead.

"They're caging us in," Baltak growled.

"Should we teleport away?" Alexa asked.

Eldrinn turned to Seldszar. "Father?"

The Master of Divination patted the air. *Wait.*

Zarifar stared up at the sky. He raised a hand above his head, fingers and thumb curled to form half of the moon-symbol

Q'arlynd had just made. "The pattern's changed," he said. "Just like the moon."

Q'arlynd realized the blood rain had stopped. All that remained were drips, falling from the intertwined oak trees above. He looked up through their branches and saw that Zarifar was right. The moon had returned. It hung in the sky, a slim crescent of white, surrounded by a glittering halo that flickered from blue, to green, to lavender . . .

"Just like faerie fire," Eldrinn breathed.

The boy stood just to Q'arlynd's right, but Q'arlynd couldn't see him. He wondered why Eldrinn had cloaked himself in magical darkness, but realized the final transformation had at last come about. He could barely see any of his apprentices. Nor could he see Seldszar clearly, or the oak trees that had regrown in the shape of the temple, nor the forest beyond them. Everything was dim, and dark, and indistinct.

"What's happened?" Alexa's voice asked. "I can't see you—any of you!"

"Show yourselves!" Baltak roared.

Q'arlynd concentrated, and pointed at Baltak, but nothing happened. The faerie fire that should have outlined his apprentice failed to materialize. Instead he used an evocation. A flicker of fire danced above his outstretched palm.

He stared, wonderingly, at what the wavering light revealed. His skin was no longer black. It had turned brown. And his hair, when he flicked the braid forward over his shoulder, wasn't white any more. It had turned a glossy black.

He was no longer a drow.

Judging by the way his apprentices were fumbling about, they'd all been transformed as well. He laughed, realizing now what had drawn him to them, and to Seldszar: They shared a common ancestry.

"What's happened?" Baltak shouted. "Tell me!"

Seldszar's voice came from the darkness to Q'arlynd's left. It sounded cool and unruffled. "Our casting was successful. We've broken our link with the *Faerzress*. Just as the ancestors promised. We've undone the Descent. We're dark elves again."

The two shapes that were Eldrinn and Alexa gasped. The larger shape on Q'arlynd's left that was Baltak growled softly.

"Out of the darkness and into the light," Q'arlynd said. He felt triumph—they'd just reversed the magic of the Descent! Yet he also felt a looming dread. By transforming, they'd also condemned themselves.

Not condemned, but freed.

He caught a glimpse of moonlight glinting off glass: the dark lenses Seldszar was wearing. He smiled, realizing they hadn't been intended to shield his eyes from the light of the World Above. They were magical lenses, like those the surface elves needed in order to see when they ventured into the Underdark.

"You knew this would happen," Q'arlynd told the other master. "Didn't you? You saw what was to come, in one of your visions."

"Not quite," Seldszar said with a chuckle. He touched his forehead. "They told me."

"Why didn't you tell me?" Q'arlynd cried.

We did, his ancestors answered. *You agreed.*

"Ease yourself, Q'arlynd." Seldszar said. "All is as was foretold."

"But we're blind!" Eldrinn blurted. "Helpless as surface elves. How can we possibly survive back in Sshamath?"

"We won't be returning there," Seldszar said. "Preparations have been made. The College of Divination is already relocating as we speak; the necessity of fueling our casting with magical items provided an excellent screen for getting out much of our wealth. We're going to start afresh on the surface, in the City of Hope. The College of Ancient Arcana will do the same. We'll be welcome, there. The sharn have promised me that."

Q'arlynd had no idea who the sharn were—but he had the feeling he was about to find out.

"What about the others?" Alexa asked. "In Sshamath . . . and elsewhere? Have *all* of the drow changed?"

Not all, the ancestors told Q'arlynd. *Only those few without taint. Miyeritari, such as yourselves, and those who follow the dance. By Eilistraee's grace, they too will have transformed.*

Q'arlynd glanced at his House insignia, then up at the changed moon. "Are you certain about that?"

Before his ancestors could answer, he heard the whisper of a thrown dagger. He grunted as it slammed into the back of his neck.

CHAPTER 13

Halisstra lifted the blood-smeared Crescent Blade so Eilistraee could see it. "Wendonai said you would come. He said you couldn't bear to lose your high priestess." She smirked. "He was right."

"I came for another reason," the goddess replied. "To offer you redemption. Your heart aches for it." She held out a hand. "Reach for it!"

Swift as a hunting spider, Halisstra struck. The Crescent Blade flashed, and fingertips fell. They pattered to the floor beside the decapitated Darksong Knight.

Eilistraee's eyes blazed red. A bolt of braided light and shadow burst from her forehead and slammed into Halisstra's chest, rocking Halisstra back. The pain was intense, but it lasted only a heartbeat. Halisstra shook it off and menaced the other goddess with her weapon.

Eilistraee, however, didn't press her attack. She squeezed her hand shut and sang. A nimbus of moonlight played around her fist, and the blood flow halted as her wounds sealed shut. When she opened her hand again, however, the fingers were shorter than they had been.

Once again, the hand extended. "Come. Rejoin my dance."

Halisstra swayed forward—then angrily shook off the enchantment the other goddess had tried to ensnare her with. This time, she told herself, she would be stronger. She wouldn't kneel, wouldn't grovel. Not like she had before Lolth.

"I don't need your redemption," she snapped. "I'm stronger than you."

In one sense, it was true. Though Eilistraee glowed with an unearthly light, Halisstra wasn't blinded by it. She didn't wince and fumble about like a mortal drow. And though the high priestess's body had enlarged when the goddess stepped into it, Halisstra still stood head and shoulders taller. Eilistraee was the weak one, not her. Halisstra was stronger, swifter, and armed with the Crescent Blade. The other goddess was frightened of her. She didn't *dare* attack Halisstra.

"You can't kill me," Halisstra taunted. "If you could, you would have done it already."

"Are you certain of that?" A glint of blue danced in Eilistraee's moonstone eyes. She pointed at Halisstra's chest. "It looks as though Lolth is no longer healing you."

Halisstra glanced down. It was true. Black, tarry blood seeped from the wound Eilistraee's magic had bored—a wound that should have closed by now. That frightened her, more than she cared to admit. If she died, her soul would fly back to the Demonweb Pits. Back to Lolth's cruel embrace.

"I don't *need* Lolth!" Halisstra shouted. "I'm a demigod!"

"Then why do you pretend to be Lolth's champion?" Eilistraee whirled, her hair lifting like a skirt. When it settled again, tiny knots were in it. Inside each, a tiny figure writhed. "That's what these priestesses thought, wasn't it? They worshiped you as Lolth's champion, not as a goddess in your own right." She whirled again, and the knots disappeared. "And now they've gone to face Lolth's wrath."

"That's a lie!" Halisstra screamed. "They worshiped *me!* Through subservience to me, they'll be reborn."

Eilistraee's voice was soft and mocking. "If you're a demigod, then why do you need the Crescent Blade?"

"To kill you," Halisstra spat.

"Why haven't you used it? What's staying your hand?" Green-tinted eyes stared at her from behind the mask. "Could it be mercy?"

"Hardly that!" Halisstra laughed and brought the weapon to her lips. She licked Cavatina's blood from it, and smiled. "I like to savor my victories. I notice you weren't able to regenerate your fingers. I think I'll cut you apart, a little at a time. Make you *suffer*, just like I did."

Eilistraee didn't react to the jibe. "You're not Lolth's," she continued relentlessly. "You never were. You swore an oath to me. By song and sword. You bear my crescent on your knee."

"That was another me!" Halisstra snapped. "The mortal I once was."

Her knee, however, suddenly stung, as if freshly cut. She glanced down at the faded gray scar—the tiny nick Ryld's sword had made, when she danced around the blade to fool Eilistraee's priestesses. Ryld. The lover who had followed her into Eilistraee's faith, only to die. She shook her head. She hadn't thought of him in years.

"Do you remember my song?" Eilistraee asked.

Voices sang in Halisstra's memory. *Trust in your sisters; lend your voice to their song. By joining the circle, the weak are made strong.*

Had there been voices singing that outside her temple, just a moment ago?

Halisstra glared at Eilistraee. "Lolth did claim me for a time, but no more. I'm not hers—and I'm not yours. You abandoned me in the Demonweb Pits. You stood and watched as Lolth degraded me, consumed me. You watched and did *nothing!*" She was surprised at the vehemence that boiled out of her. She hadn't thought it would still sting. She gripped the Crescent Blade tightly, reminding herself that her mortal life was over. Done. She was Lolth's plaything no longer. She'd never have to look upon that gloating, Danifae-faced goddess again.

Until she killed her.

"Yes," Eilistraee said, softly as a sigh. "Kill Lolth. That's what the Crescent Blade was forged to do. That's what *you* were destined to do. You faltered, the first time. . . ."

Halisstra snarled. She didn't like to be reminded of that.

"But I'm giving you a second chance," Eilistraee continued. "A chance to redeem yourself. When Lolth transformed you, she bound you with webs of hatred and guilt. But any web can be broken, if only you are strong enough. Take your revenge on the Spider Queen. Use the disguise she has unwittingly given you. Lolth will never credit you with the strength you truly have."

"Strength?" Halisstra shrieked. She rubbed a throbbing temple with a callused hand.

"Yes, strength. Your penance has tempered you, made you strong as darkfire-forged adamantine. But now that penance is at an end."

"My . . . penance?" Halisstra echoed hollowly. Her thoughts felt thick, snarled in web. How could Eilistraee possibly "end" anything? Lolth had been the one to twist her body, to break her spirit, to name her the Lady Penitent.

"Your penance began before that," Eilistraee said softly. "The moment you broke my sacred sword, it began. But now it can end. Rejoin me."

Could it? Halisstra wavered. Would Eilistraee truly take her back, after all she had done? Halisstra could feel the power of the goddess who stood before her. It radiated from Eilistraee, filling the chamber. Cleansing it. Turning a place of darkness and death into a place of moonlight and song.

The tiny spark that had been flickering, near extinguished, deep inside Halisstra, longed to be fanned back to life. When that happened, her torment could end. She would be forgiven. Redeemed.

Eilistraee held out her hand. "Come," she sang. "Take my hand. Accept my mercy. Rejoin the dance."

Halisstra leaned close. She lowered the Crescent Blade. Extended her free hand . . .

She's lying.

The whisper was thin, metallic. It came to Halisstra's ears like the hum of a tuning fork, as the sword in her hand vibrated.

That's not Eilistraee.

Halisstra gasped. A trick! She saw it. The voice was right: that *wasn't* Eilistraee who stood before her. That wasn't a hand reaching for her, but a spider. Only one goddess could have bored a hole in her chest that would not heal: Lolth. The Spider Queen had tricked her!

Screaming her rage, she slashed with the Crescent Blade.

The eyes above the mask widened. "Halisstra!" Eilistraee cried. "N—"

Steel met flesh and bit deep. The goddess's neck parted. Her head tumbled from her shoulders and landed with a dull thump. Her body slowly twisted, then suddenly collapsed. Silver blood poured onto the floor from the severed stump of a neck. It covered the stone floor in a glittering silver wave, throwing dancing shadows across the walls, then faded to black.

Halisstra, panting, stared down at the headless corpse, her spider jaws twitching furiously. "I'm your Lady Penitent no more!" she screamed.

She felt a tickle on her chest. She glanced down, and saw that a spider had spun a web across the wound in her chest. It completed its web and yanked, drawing the edges shut. The ache that had resided there faded—as did the fainter sting in her knee. She turned her leg, inspecting it. The tiny, crescent-shaped scar was gone.

She heard a sharp crack The Crescent Blade suddenly felt lighter in her hand. Its blade struck the floor with a clang that echoed like the tolling of a bell. A wisp of black seeped from the broken hilt, then whispered away.

Realization at last shoved its way into Halisstra's web-shrouded mind. It wasn't Lolth she'd just killed, but Eilistraee. And now that the Crescent Blade was broken—she stared at the hilt in her hand—she never *would* kill Lolth.

This had been what the Spider Queen had wanted, all along.

Halisstra sank to the floor, too stricken to speak.

Laughter echoed through the chamber, light as the footsteps of a running spider.

Leliana urgently waved the newcomers forward. *Encircle the hill!* she signed with her free hand. *Join the song!*

The priestesses and Nightshadows Laeral had teleported here hurried to comply. They shoved through the jungle underbrush, joining the ring of faithful. Leliana wiped sweat from her brow, nodded at Qilué's human "sister," and sang fervently. The ring of moonlight the hymn had brought into being brightened with each added voice. Slowly, relentlessly, it spread inward, as the healing and hallowing energy they evoked grew stronger. The taint of evil boiled away in a heat-wave shimmer, the stench of rot and sulfur giving way to the clean tang of fresh water and growing leaves. In another moment, the mound itself would be hallowed ground, and the exorcism could begin.

Laeral hurried to Leliana's side. "Is your casting nearly complete?"

Leliana nodded without halting her song. She held up a hand and counted down with her fingers. Five . . . four . . .

The newly arrived priestesses and Nightshadows joined the chorus, strengthening the circle. The spider webs draping the mound burst into silver flame, and burned away. Corpses tumbled out of their cocoons, charred flesh sizzling. The smoke rising from them twisted in the currents of the hallowing, and became the sweet smell of incense.

Three . . . two . . .

With her singing sword in hand, Leliana watched the opening in the side of the hill. Three chambers, Laeral had said: head, cephalothorax, and abdomen. Qilué was in the third.

One . . .

The hymn culminated in a single, sustained note—and ended.

Leliana strode forward, beckoning the others to follow. They would lend their song to her exorcism. Qilué *would* be saved—and the traitorous Halisstra killed.

A branch creaked above. Leliana looked up just in time to see a massive figure hurtling down at her. Nearly twice the size of a drow, it had four arms and a body made of black obsidian. It landed with a thud that shook the ground, and its feet punched holes in the soft soil. A golem!

Leliana leaped back as the golem slammed its hands together, barely missing her. She turned the leap into a spinning attack, slashing with her sword. The golem dodged, but not quickly enough. Pealing a battle cry, the sword slammed into one of its arms. Stone shattered, and the sword vibrated so violently that Leliana nearly dropped it.

A shout came from behind Leliana: Qilué's sister, casting a spell. But whatever magic Laeral had just wrought had no visible effect on the golem. Avoiding Leliana's sword thrusts, it vomited out a stream of sticky white silk that knocked Leliana to the ground and entangled at least a dozen of the priestesses and Nightshadows behind her. Laeral was the only one unaffected. She levitated as the web slid past her body and failed to take hold.

Leliana heard thumps all around her: other four-armed golems, dropping from the branches above. Priestesses sang and shouted, swords clanged against stone, and drow cried out as obsidian fists pounded into flesh. The broken-armed golem lifted a foot to stomp Leliana, but she shifted just in time for it to miss her. A streak of raw magical energy whistled down from above—Laeral's silver fire—and struck the golem's head, exploding it. The headless body toppled like a fallen tree and bounced as it hit the ground, narrowly missing Leliana. She tried to rise, but the more she struggled, the more the strands of web adhered to her. "Eilistraee!" she cried, "grant me passage. Let me dance freely!"

The web slid away. Leliana leaped to her feet. She heard pounding footsteps and the snap of branches breaking: another golem, running at her.

"Go!" Laeral shouted from above as she yanked a wand out of its sheath. "Find Qilué!"

Leliana plunged into the mound. Eilistraee's moonlight filled it, scouring it clean. The stone walls were smooth and gleaming, the floor polished and clear. The only exit was a hole in the far wall—the perfect circle of the Dark Maiden's moon. Leliana leaped through it, landing in a rolling somersault in the chamber beyond, and sprang to her feet. She saw nine corridors, just as Laeral had described. Voices echoed from the one in the middle of the far wall. As Leliana ran for it, she made out words. One female voice, deep and bestial, insisting that she was a demigod. Another, like a chorus of voices braided into one, singing in reply, offering redemption.

The moonlight brightened as Leliana neared the chamber ahead. She halted just shy of its entrance, gaping. An enormous, demonic figure with spider legs protruding from its chest—Halisstra—stood next to a throne that looked like a spider with crumpled legs, holding the Crescent Blade in one misshapen hand. A headless body in priestess's chain mail and breastplate that had to be Cavatina lay on the floor at Halisstra's feet. Yet this wasn't what had made Leliana stop and stare. These two lesser figures were eclipsed by a third: a drow female who stood at the center of the room. The female had the features and build of Qilué, but was suffused with a power greater even than the high priestess's silver fire. Qilué, transformed, was radiant with moonlight, graceful as song, strong as the Weave itself. Her body, her voice, her every gesture had a beauty that made Leliana's breath catch in her throat.

"Eilistraee," Leliana breathed. She took a step forward, but a note sounded in her mind. *Wait,* it commanded.

Leliana halted. She listened as the goddess offered redemption to the fallen priestess. Leliana had glimpsed Halisstra once before, briefly, atop the Acropolis, but it was still hard to believe a priestess could have been brought so low. Halisstra was raving, clearly maddened by the tortures Lolth had inflicted. Yet she leaned ever so slightly toward Eilistraee, like a self-conscious dancer about to take a first, hesitant step. She ached for the redemption Eilistraee was offering with outstretched hands.

"Let her lead you," Leliana breathed. She lifted her own hand, yearning to touch that of the goddess. Tears of pure joy poured down her cheeks. "Dance. Sing. Take her hand."

Suddenly, Halisstra's posture changed. She cocked an ear, then howled in rage. The Crescent Blade flashed as it sliced through the moonlit air. It thudded into Eilistraee's neck—a sound that struck Leliana like a physical blow. In one terrible, frozen moment that would sear itself into her memory forever, Leliana saw the goddess' head tumble from her shoulders. The head landed with a thud, the goddess' body crumpled, and the moonlight went out.

Leliana fainted.

Laeral blasted apart the final golem with her wand and shouted to those priestesses and Nightshadows who still remained on their feet. "Hurry! Leliana needs our help!"

She spun to enter the mound—finally, the way was clear— but halted as she heard several of Eilistraee's faithful cry out at once. They stood, staring up at the sky, stricken expressions on their faces. One of them pointed with a shaking hand. "The moon!"

Laeral glanced up. The moon was gone. How? She shuddered, then pulled herself together. Qilué needed her. Too many precious moments had already been consumed by the battle with the golems.

She leaped over the fallen golem, into the mound. She spoke Qilué's truename under her breath. Perhaps, even in stasis, Qilué might hear it. "Ilindyl! I'm coming, sister!"

Too dark; she couldn't see. With a thought, she bathed her body in a sheen of silver light. As she passed through the second chamber, a demonic voice roared in triumph, up ahead. "I'm your Lady Penitent no more!"

Laeral plunged into the tunnel leading to the third corridor. Just ahead, she saw Leliana, crumpled on the floor. The priestess's magical sword lay on the ground beside her body. From the chamber beyond came the sharp clank of metal on stone: another blade, being dropped to the floor?

Laeral readied the components of a spell as she ran. "Stay strong, sister. I'm nearly there!"

A demonic figure leaped to its feet as Laeral burst into the room: Halisstra. Snarling, squinting against the glare of Laeral's silver fire, Halisstra hurled a broken sword hilt at Laeral, then leaped at her and spat out a deadly word. One clawed hand raked Laeral's hip, tearing it open. Laeral felt the power of the magic word bore through her. A less powerful wizard would have instantly withered and died, but she was sustained by Mystra's magic. The wound in her hip instantly healed. She slapped Halisstra with a hand, and shouted a transmutation. Halisstra ceased moving, her face frozen in an anguished snarl.

Laeral hurried past her. She fell to her knees beside two corpses, each missing its head. One was Cavatina, the other, Qilué, her body no longer demonic. The amulet Laeral had given Qilué lay in a puddle of blood, next to her head. Laeral touched her fallen sister's corpse. Already, the body was growing cool. "Oh, sister," she mourned. "What have I done?"

From behind her came a groan, and the scrape of metal on stone. Laeral whirled—but it was only Leliana, picking up her sword and staggering to her feet. The priestess walked with uncertain steps into the chamber. She shied around the time-frozen Halisstra, but never once looked in her direction. Her eyes, wide and horror-filled, were locked on Qilué's headless corpse.

"Eilistraee!" she keened.

"Pray for her," Laeral urged. "Bring her back."

"I can't!"

Anger made Laeral's silver fire flare brighter. "Pull yourself together, priestess, and *pray!*"

Leliana fumbled with the holy symbol hanging around her neck. She wrenched its chain over her head, and hurled the miniature sword down at Laeral's feet. "I can't!" she screamed.

The holy symbol was deeply tarnished, black and brittle looking. And Leliana herself had changed. Her skin was brown; her hair, black.

Laeral realized the priestess was crying. From the distance—somewhere outside the mound—she heard the sobs and wails of the other faithful.

Laeral rose. "One of the others will have a holy symbol. You can—"

"Don't you understand?" Leliana shouted. "Eilistraee's gone! She was inside Qilué when she was killed with the Crescent Blade. I saw Eilistraee *die!*"

A shiver of horror coursed through Laeral. She understood—suddenly, and with frightening clarity—the omen she'd witnessed outside. A missing moon, a vanished goddess. That was terrible enough. But there was something that stuck even closer to home. She half-turned to her fallen sister. "You . . . can't restore her to life."

"No."

Laeral clutched at straws. "Someone else then. A cleric of some other faith."

"No," Leliana croaked. "No one can revive her. The Crescent Blade killed her. Halisstra hacked out her soul—and Eilistraee's with it."

Laeral choked back a sob. Her beloved sister, gone. Laeral had always known that Qilué might die one day, but had been comforted by the knowledge that Qilué would dance at her goddess's side. But now that goddess was gone, and Qilué's soul destroyed.

All this while, Leliana had been staring at the frozen Halisstra. Now she spat out the name of the fallen priestess like a curse. Slowly, as if it weighed as much as a boulder, she lifted her singing sword. It was utterly silent, its song forever stilled. She touched the point to Halisstra's chest. "Your magic holds her?" she asked over her shoulder.

"Yes."

"Dispel it."

Eyes locked. Sorrow met grief. Laeral nodded, gestured, and spoke a word.

Halisstra blinked.

Leliana thrust her sword into Halisstra's chest. Blood, stinking of the Abyss, flowed hot over her hand. A faint tremble coursed through the blade: Halisstra's heart, beating one last time. The fallen priestess's spider jaws twitched, and her mouth opened.

"Eilistraee," she gasped. "Forgive . . ."

"She can't forgive you," Laeral said. "She's dead."

Halisstra's eyes clouded over, and she died.

T'lar drifted toward the spot where the mages stood arguing with one another, her body a breath of wind. Now was her moment. The wizards were agitated by their inexplicable transformation, and were intent upon their argument. By the sound of it, only the one seated on the driftdisc still had his darkvision. Careful to keep out of his line of sight, T'lar reformed her body behind one of the stacks of boxes. She'd waited here a long time for her target to show, and had been forced to delay further when he'd returned with his apprentices and three of Sshamath's masters. But T'lar was as patient as a spider in its web, and her target was at long last presenting an opportunity for her to strike.

Softly, she hummed the tune the Lady Penitent had taught her—the one that would allow her dagger to strike true. Then she readied herself. She hadn't bothered to merely poison her blade, this time. Instead, she'd had the weapon cursed. The next person it killed would remain dead, despite any resurrections a cleric might attempt.

T'lar adjusted her grip on the blade and focused on her breathing. A lesser assassin would have been forced to rise from her crouch to throw, but T'lar was one of the Velkyn Velve, and had *dro'zress* within her. She called upon it now, and felt it charge her body. In one smooth motion she stepped sideways through space and hurled her dagger. It whispered through the air, swift as an arrow, and buried itself in her target's neck, right next to his hairclip.

Her target collapsed. The other mages reacted with alarm. Even as they spun to search out the threat, T'lar sidestepped— only to find her target alive and well and standing directly in front of her—and holding her dagger in his hand.

"Looking for this?" he asked.

"How—?" T'lar grunted in pain. She looked down. The dagger was in her heart. She felt herself fall to the side, and heard the wizard's voice from the distance, through a thick gray fog.

"Contingency spell," he said. "In the hairclip. A combination of blink and illusion that . . ."

His voice faded. So did all sensation. Gray mist swirled around her. She stood on a table-flat plain that bore no landmarks, save for a walled city in the distance. She was dead, she realized. She had failed the Lady Penitent. Her torment would be eternal.

Some time later—a heartbeat? a year?—a form materialized next to her. Though she had no body, no life, T'lar sensed herself falling to her knees. "Lady Penitent," she said, contrition choking her mind-voice. "I failed you. Q'arlynd Melarn lives."

Wild laughter burst from the Lady Penitent's lips. "We're all dead!" she howled. She whirled to shake a fist at the mist. "Do you hear that, Cavatina? Your goddess is dead. I tried to redeem myself, but too late!" The Lady Penitent sank to her knees in the swirling mist, sobbing like a broken slave.

A shiver of fear lodged in T'lar's soul. She rose and backed slowly away, but the weeping figure lashed out with a hand, catching her wrist. "Your goddess is dead!" she screamed. "The Lady Penitent is *dead!*"

T'lar tore free of the Lady Penitent's grip. What madness was this? A strand of silk drifted down from the sky to brush T'lar's shoulder. She looked up, and saw a spider-headed female staring down at her. Lolth! Behind the goddess stood a balor demon, his bat wings wreathed in flame. Lolth's true champion. T'lar understood that, now.

Come, the goddess said. *The web waits.*

T'lar grasped the thread of silk. Power surged through it, into her hand. The mist-filled landscape faded. Tugged by the thread, she rose into Lolth's blackness. It surrounded her like a comforting black velvet shroud. At last she reached the eternal web that was the Demonweb Pits, leaving the piteous, false champion behind.

Cavatina stood on a featureless plain, surrounded by gray mist. Somewhere in the distance, a female voice raged. She recognized it as Halisstra's, but that didn't matter. Not any more.

She lifted her severed head to her shoulders, and felt the substance of her soul knit together again. She turned to the messengers who had come to convey her from the Fugue Plain. The two looked identical: elves, though she could not say what type. Beautiful, though she could not tell their gender. Each stood a little taller than she, and was clad in a shimmering white robe. Their names sprang, unbidden, into her mind: Lashrael and Felarathael.

"Daughter!" Lashrael cried in a voice bubbling with laughter. "Your life's journey has ended at last. Welcome home!" He clasped her arms and smiled.

"The Protector sends his greetings," Felarathael said in a slow, measured voice. The spirit half-turned, and gestured for her to follow. "Come."

"But . . ." Cavatina looked around. There should have been a beam of moonlight, piercing the mist. A song for her to follow. Or perhaps a pool of silent shadow for her to slip into. She pulled out of Lashrael's embrace. "But I am Eilistraee's."

"Alas!" Lashrael cried, his cheeks awash with tears. "Eilistraee is no more. She was slain—cut down, together with the high priestess, by the treacherous Lady Penitent."

Cavatina's soul trembled. "No!" she gasped.

"All part of the plan," Felarathael said calmly. "There is no further need for Eilistraee. The willing were saved, the unwilling cast down. It is time for the dark elves to return to Arvandor."

"So many!" Lashrael cried, arms thrown open wide. "So many souls to gather! Where will we ever begin?"

"With this one, Lashrael," Felarathael said in a patient voice. "And then, on to the realm where the remainder of Eilistraee's faithful dance."

Cavatina's mind spun. Dark elves? As if in answer, a mirror of silver moonlight framed in a circle of shadow materialized between Felarathael's hands. He held it up for her to see. She beheld herself as she might have been, had she survived. Brown skin, black hair, dark brown eyes. The mirror disappeared.

"Hundreds of you, across the length and breadth of Faerûn, were transformed," Felarathael explained. "Hundreds more, below ground. Even now, the mortals who serve our master are braving the Underdark, to guide their dark elf brethren back into the light."

"But what of Qilué?" she breathed.

"Gone!" Lashrael cried. The spirit sank to a kneel, his hands thrust high. "Dead! Forever dead!"

"Her soul was destroyed," Felarathael said solemnly. "But before she died, she saved many. She cleansed the taint from hundreds of drow who might otherwise have been condemned."

"But the rest!" Lashrael wailed. "Thousands! Hundreds of thousands! No hope of redemption for them, with Eilistraee gone. Condemned to darkness and despair, forevermore!"

"Another necessary sacrifice," Felarathael said without a trace of emotion. "Else the game would have been lost."

Lashrael rose and wiped away his tears. A smile replaced them—a smile as wide as the moon. "Now come, daughter. Felarathael and I have dallied here long enough. We've much work ahead, once we get you safely home."

"Home?" Cavatina asked.

Felarathael waved a hand. The mist parted, revealing a lush forest. A crescent moon hung above the oak trees, next to a golden sun. In the foreground, butterflies danced in a glade festooned with wildflowers. A warm breeze carried the scent of grass, blossoms, and clear-flowing streams.

"Arvandor," Felarathael announced.

"Arvandor," Cavatina breathed.

Each of the spirits held out a hand. She took them. Together they led her soul into the realm of the Seldarine.

CODA

Eilistraee startled. Lolth *hadn't* chosen the piece she'd expected. The Spider Queen instead was pointing to a slightly less powerful Priestess piece that stood next to the one with the curved sword.

Why?

Lolth pointed a web-sticky finger. "The sacrifice," she demanded. "Take that piece out, or forfeit the game."

"A moment, Mother," Eilistraee said. She tipped her head. "Do you hear that?"

The event she'd been waiting for had at last arrived. Her side of the *sava* board was a mess, her House riddled with holes Ghaunadaur had melted in the board. But the Priest pieces that had materialized with the Ancient One's arrival no longer had an air of menace and purpose about them. Instead they were babbling, uncontrolled, wandering across the board of their own accord.

A moment later, the ooze that had been melting Eilistraee's side of the board dribbled away down a hole one of Eilistraee's Priest pieces had just leaped into, abandoning its minions. The holes remained, but the rot's spread had at last been halted.

Lolth arched an eyebrow. "Well played, Daughter. You seem to have neutralized the threat. And without me even seeing your move. Your brother has taught you much in the art of sleight of hand—but it won't save your Priestess." She flicked a hand. "Do it. Sacrifice her."

Still puzzling over Lolth's choice, Eilistraee grasped the Priestess piece. As she removed it from the board, it spit into two parts with a crack like snapping bone. Sorrowfully, she let the head and body fall from her hand. They tumbled, then turned to mist.

Lolth immediately moved a demonic-looking Priestess piece into the vacant spot. She snapped her fingers, and her throne appeared. She lounged on it, staring across the *sava* board at Eilistraee. "Your move, daughter."

Eilistraee was thankful for her mask; it hid her smile. Lolth had just made an impetuous move, one that left the piece she'd shifted open to attack. Eilistraee reached for the Priestess piece that held the curved sword, then noted the slight tightening of her opponent's hands on the arms of her throne. The Spider Queen looked relaxed, but her fingers betrayed her tension. Why?

Eilistraee hesitated, her hand still on the piece, not yet moving it. She could see nothing amiss. The move looked secure. Yet something was bothering her . . .

There. That tickle at her wrist. Without being obvious, she shifted her focus slightly, looking at her hand, rather than the piece it held. Just above her palm, on the inside of her wrist, was a tiny red welt: the burn mark that had been left by the brief touch of Lolth's demonic Warrior piece, just before it had vanished. Eilistraee's Priestess piece—the one that held the curved blade—bore a corresponding mark: a tiny chip in its wrist.

A hole, bored deep—to its very soul.

Treachery! Yet that was only to be expected of the Spider Queen.

Eilistraee, however, also knew much of subterfuge, thanks to the mask she now wore. Another piece on the board bore a similar flaw: this one, in its knee. Eilistraee made the move Lolth was expecting, then feigned surprise and horror as the piece she'd just moved transformed into the Warrior piece and became Lolth's. The Spider Queen seized it and moved it triumphantly to the heart of Eilistraee's House, next to Eilistraee's Mother piece.

"Victory!" she cried. "Move whatever piece you like, Daughter. The game will be lost! Your Mother piece has no moves open. With my next move, I'll destroy it—and the drow will be mine!"

Eilistraee leaned forward, feigning a great sigh. She kept her eyes downcast, so Lolth wouldn't see the glint of gold in their depths. She lifted her Mother piece and squeezed hard, destroying it. The cut on her wrist opened, and her blood flowed. A drop of it fell on the Warrior piece, sizzled briefly in the hot flames that wreathed it, then vanished.

Eilistraee disappeared.

Lolth looked wildly around. Eilistraee was gone! She laughed a shrill, giddy peal of delight. "You concede?" she cried. "At last, the drow are . . . ?"

Just a moment. Something was wrong. Eilistraee's realm should have disappeared with her. Yet it remained, just on the other side of the board. Forest, moonstone fruits, stars . . . Everything was there, except for the moon. It had vanished from the sky, as if . . .

Yes, that was it. The moon wasn't gone; it was just eclipsed. Still up in that sky, somewhere. Just as Eilistraee herself was still here . . . somewhere.

Lolth's eye fell on the Warrior piece. A pass of her hand over it, palm down, confirmed her suspicions. She could feel the loathsome moonlight hidden within. The Warrior still looked as it had, but that was just a disguise. The piece was no longer hers.

Vhaeraun had, indeed, taught his sister well.

She could see now what Eilistraee's plan had been. The demonic Warrior piece stood on a line that led directly back to Lolth's Mother piece; one move would take the Mother out. But Lolth's bestial Priestess would soon put a halt to that.

Lolth picked up the bestial Priestess piece. It struggled in her hand, resisting her. For a moment, it nearly succeeded. Then Lolth snuffed out the last spark of will it contained. She moved it beside the Warrior piece, and attacked.

The disguise fell away. Eilistraee's Mother piece was revealed. It twisted wildly, like a madly pirouetting dancer, and let out a shrill cry that was almost a song. Then Lolth flicked a finger, tipping it over, and it stilled.

"Game," she announced.

On the other side of the board, Eilistraee's realm wavered. In another moment, it would disappear. Lolth touched her fingers together, then drew them slowly apart, spinning a web between her hands She leaned forward, poised to ensnare the pieces that buzzed in frantic panic, like flies, on the board below.

"Not so fast, Araushnee," a male voice said. The point of a long sword touched Lolth's chest.

Startled, she looked up.

Eilistraee's realm had not disappeared. Nor were her pieces forfeited. Her place had been taken by another deity who stared imperiously down at Lolth along the blade of the long sword: an androgynous elf with golden hair, wearing white robes, a sky blue cloak, and golden battle gauntlets. A crescent-moon amulet hung against his chest.

He flicked the long sword down. It sliced the web Lolth had been forming between her hands.

"How dare you!" the Spider Queen cried. "You've no business meddling here. You're god of the surface elves—and these are drow!"

"Look again."

She did. Rage swelled in her like a ripe egg sac as she saw what had happened. Eilistraee's pieces had changed. They were no longer black, but brown. Lolth tried to seize one, but it neatly sidestepped out of reach.

Corellon Larethian laughed. "My move, I believe."

DRAMATIS PERSONAE

Eilistraee's Faithful

Qilué Veladorn (KIE-loo-ay VEL-a-dorn), one of the Seven Sisters, chosen of Eilistraee and Mystra, drow high priestess of the Promenade

Cavatina Xarann (cav-a-TEEN-a zar-ANN), Darksong Knight, drow priestess of Eilistraee

Leliana Vrinn (lell-lee-AH-nuh VRIN), drow priestess of Eilistraee, Protector of the Promenade, mother of Rowaan

Rylla (REE-la), half-human, half-drow priestess of Eilistraee, Battle-mistress of the Promenade

Meryl (MAIR-ill), halfling cook, servant of Qilué

Jub (JUB), half-orc, half-drow lay worshiper of Eilistraee and resident of the Promenade

Horaldin (hore-ALL-din), moon elf druid, lay worshiper of Eilistraee and resident of the Promenade

Chizra (CHIZ-ruh), drow priestess of Eilistraee, Protector of the Promenade

Zindira (zin-DEE-ruh), drow priestess of Eilistraee, Protector of the Promenade

Brindell (BRIN-dell), halfling priestess of Eilistraee, Protector of the Promenade

Tash'kla (TASH-kluh), drow priestess of Eilistraee, Protector of the Promenade

Erelda (air-EL-duh), drow priestess of Eilistraee, Protector of the Promenade

Rowaan Vrinn (roe-WAHN VRIN), drow priestess of Eilistraee, head priestess of the Misty Forest shrine, daughter of Leliana

Nightshadows

Kâras (kah-RASS), drow rogue and Black Moon cleric of the Masked Lady, formerly of Maerimydra

Naxil (NAX-ill), drow priest of the Masked Lady, formerly a sorcerer's apprentice in Eryndlyn

Valdar Jaerle (VAL-dar JARE-lay), drow cleric of Vhaeraun, one of four who opened the portal between the domains of Eilistraee and Vhaeraun

Mazrol (MAZ-rawl), drow cleric of Vhaeraun

Lolth's Minions

Halisstra Melarn (HAL-is-truh mel-ARN), sister of Q'arlynd Melarn, formerly a drow priestess of Lolth in Ched Nasad, later a priestess of Eilistraee, now Lolth's "Lady Penitent"

Wendonai (WEN-doe-nie), balor demon, corruptor of the Illythiri dark elves

Nafay Mizz'rynturl (Nah-FAY MIZ-rin-turl), priestess of Lolth in the Temple of the Black Mother in Guallidurth

T'lar Mizz'rynturl (t-LAR MIZ-rin-turl), assassin (Lolth's Sting) of the Velkyn Velve, serving the Temple of the Black Mother in Guallidurth

Laele Zauviir (LAY-ell zow-VEER), *Streea'Valsharess* (High Priestess) of The Web of the Spider Queen, Lolth's temple in Sshamath, aunt of Guldor Zauviir

Jashnil Zolond (JASH-neel ZOE-lund), priestess of The Web of the Spider Queen, Lolth's temple in Sshamath

Ghaunadaur's Fanatics

Molvayas Philiom (moll-VAY-us FIL-ee-om), drow cleric of Ghaunadaur, Eater of Filth (High Priest) in Llurth Dreir for House Philiom

Shi'drin Philiom (SHEE-drin FIL-ee-om), drow cleric of Ghaunadaur in Llurth Dreir

Residents of Sshamath

Q'arlynd Melarn (KAR-lind mel-ARN), brother of Halisstra Melarn, battle wizard, formerly of Ched Nasad

Eldrinn Elpragh (EL-drin el-PRAG), drow wizard specializing in divination, son of Seldszar Elpragh

Piri (PEE-ree), drow wizard acolyte of the skin, apprentice of Q'arlynd Melarn, bonded with the quasit demon Glizn

Baltak (BALL-tak), drow wizard, transmogrifist, apprentice of Q'arlynd Melarn

Zarifar (ZAR-ee-far), drow wizard, geometer, apprentice of Q'arlynd Melarn

Alexa (al-ECKS-uh), drow wizard specializing in conjuration, apprentice of Q'arlynd Melarn

Seldszar Elpragh (SELDS-zar el-PRAG), drow wizard, Master of the College of Divination, member of Sshamath's ruling Conclave, father of Eldrinn Elpragh

Urlryn Khalazza (URL-rinn ka-LAZ-zuh), drow wizard,

Master of the College of Conjuration and Summoning, member of Sshamath's ruling Conclave

Guldor Zauviir (GUL-dore zow-VEER), drow wizard, Master of the College of Mages, member of Sshamath's ruling Conclave, nephew of Laele Zauviir

Antatlab of the Shaking Stones (AN-tat-lab), drow elementalist, Master of the College of Elemental Magic, member of Sshamath's ruling Conclave

Felyndiira T'orgh (fell-in-DEER-ah TORG), drow wizard, Master of the College of Illusion and Phantasm, member of Sshamath's ruling Conclave

Shurdriira Helviiryn (shur-DREE-ah hel-VEE-rin), drow wizard, Master of the College of Alteration, member of Sshamath's ruling Conclave

Tsabrak of the Blood (TSA-brack), drow vampire, Master of the College of Necromancy, member of Sshamath's ruling Conclave

Masoj Dhuunyl (mass-ODGE doo-NEEL), drow wizard, Master of the College of Abjuration, member of Sshamath's ruling Conclave

Malaggar Xarann (MAL-ag-gar zar-ANN), drow wizard, Master of the College of Enchantment and Charm, member of Sshamath's ruling Conclave

Krondorl Waeglossz (KRON-dorl way-gloz), drow wizard, Master of the College of Invocation and Evocation, member of Sshamath's ruling Conclave

Other Folk

Laeral Silverhand (LARE-all), one of the Seven Sisters, chosen of Eilistraee and Mystra

Flinderspeld (flin-der-SPELLED), svirfneblin gem merchant, formerly Q'arlynd Melarn's slave

Kaitlyn (KATE-lin), proprietor of the Sisters Three Waxworks in Skullport

RICHARD LEE BYERS

The author of *Dissolution* and The Year of Rogue Dragons sets his
sights on the realm of Thay in a new trilogy that no
FORGOTTEN REALMS® fan can afford to miss.

THE HAUNTED LANDS

BOOK I
UNCLEAN
Many powerful wizards hold Thay in their control, but when one of them
grows weary of being one of many, and goes to war, it will be at the head of
an army of undead.

BOOK II
UNDEAD
The dead walk in Thay, and as the rest of Faerûn looks on in stunned horror, the very
nature of this mysterious, dangerous realm begins to change.

March 2008

BOOK III
UNHOLY
Forces undreamed of even by Szass Tam have brought havoc and death to Thay, but
the lich's true intentions remain a mystery—a mystery that could spell doom for the
entire world.

Early 2009

Anthology
REALMS OF THE DEAD
A collection of new short stories by some of the Realms' most popular authors sheds
new light on the horrible nature of the undead of Faerûn. Prepare yourself for the
terror of the *Realms of the Dead*.

Early 2010

FORGOTTEN REALMS®

A Reader's Guide to

R.A. Salvatore's
The Legend of Drizzt™

THE LEGEND
When TSR published *The Crystal Shard* in 1988, a drow ranger
first drew his enchanted scimitars, and a legend was born.

THE LEGACY
Twenty years and twenty books later, readers have
brought his story to the world.

DRIZZT
Celebrate twenty years of the greatest fantasy hero
of a generation.

This fully illustrated, full color, encyclopedic book celebrates the
whole world of The Legend of Drizzt, from the dark elf's steadfast
companions, to his most dangerous enemies, from the gods and
monsters of a world rich in magic, to the exotic lands he's visited.

Mixing classic renditions of characters, locales, and monsters
from the last twenty years with artwork by Todd Lockwood and
other cutting-edge illustrators, this is a must-have
book for every Drizzt fan.